MALCOLM ISHIDA

Gastown

A Grimdark Epic Fantasy (Book 1 of 3)

Copyright © 2025 by Malcolm Ishida

All rights reserved. No part of this publication may be reproduced, stored or transmitted in any form or by any means, electronic, mechanical, photocopying, recording, scanning, or otherwise without written permission from the publisher. It is illegal to copy this book, post it to a website, or distribute it by any other means without permission.

This novel is entirely a work of fiction. The names, characters and incidents portrayed in it are the work of the author's imagination. Any resemblance to actual persons, living or dead, events or localities is entirely coincidental.

Check out www.gastowntimes.com for more information on characters and locations.

First edition

ISBN: 9798288510380

This book was professionally typeset on Reedsy. Find out more at reedsy.com

Contents

Chapter One	1
Chapter Two	13
Chapter Three	26
Chapter Four	38
Chapter Five	56
Chapter Six	72
Chapter Seven	82
Chapter Eight	98
Chapter Nine	113
Chapter Ten	131
Chapter Eleven	144
Chapter Twelve	162
Chapter Thirteen	180
Chapter Fourteen	197
Chapter Fifteen	209
Chapter Sixteen	222
Chapter Seventeen	235
Chapter Eighteen	248
Chapter Nineteen	260
Chapter Twenty	271
Chapter Twenty One	287
Chapter Twenty Two	298
Chapter Twenty Three	314
Chapter Twenty Four	329
Chapter Twenty Five	344
Chapter Twenty Six	354

Chapter Twenty Seven	369
Chapter Twenty Eight	382
Chapter Twenty Nine	400
Chapter Thirty	420
Chapter Thirty One	432
About the Author	448

Chapter One

Juan and Carlos Grimm

The chase was on. Over the ice topped walls, down the alleyways, across the canals, and scrambling up onto the frozen rooftops. The two boys moved quickly and silently, as only meat deprived trackers could. They did not want to give the pursuit away and alert others to join in the hunt. Scavengers like them who scurried in the gutters looking for anything to give them a nutritional edge. The quarry was too precious and the gild Mo Dickens would hand over would keep them in bludbrood for a full lunar. It might even spring for some worn out kamiks with enough tread left to keep their calloused feet dry in the Four Kith.

The billee was on to them from the start. It moved fast and furious and kept to the shadows, scurrying up and away from the persistent coursers. Mudlarks had tried before, but she was wise to their game and ran like the wind. She paused on an ancient beam, high up in the eaves of an old building, and peered down below at the two footers. They went past and she relaxed for a moment. Then they stopped and one of them looked up. He pointed a finger in her direction and they both started to climb up after her, hand over dexterous hand. They were denizens of the Slough and this was their world too. They moved through it with consummate ease. Killers to her and her kin. Consumers of billee flesh. If they could catch her.

Most kithfolk could not tell the boys apart, and they used it to their advantage. Pick a pocket and run. Pop up in another place and shout. Do it again from another corner and confuse the mark until he spun in a circle and chased his own tail into the ground. Always using the crowd and distraction to their advantage. Even Mo and JoJo got confused, and JoJo's best eye had the third sight.

"Come over 'ere, Carlos, an' give an ole girl a terrifik hug!" JoJo Dickens called. She sat in her large wooden chair carved out of a single piece of granite oak, her arms outstretched and her pendulous breasts swinging for effect. They were big enough to knock down walls, or crush a man's head between them. Jojo was a double hitter of tabak. A long clay pipe was clenched firmly between her blackened teeth, and she occasionally took a chew from a tabak plug. She spat brown tar into a large wooden bucket beside her feet, the one she also pissed in when she could not be bothered to clamber outside. Some of the tar juice never made it past her chin, and she wiped it away with the back of her hand. Years of spitting and wiping meant she had one ochre covered hand and one her more unnatural pallor.

"Iz not Carlos, yuz ole tart. Iz Juan. The gud lookin' one, remember?" Carlos said. He had a smart mouth for a boy who had only seen fifteen years.

Juan stepped out of the shadows and the two boys stood side by side. They were identical twins and the only distinguishing feature was they each wore one decrepit shoe they had picked off Stanford Stagg's barrow. Juan wore his on his left foot and Carlos on the right. Juan stepped back and left his shoe behind, and Carlos stepped into it. Then Carlos stepped back and Juan took over the footwear. Juan removed his left foot and moved to the side and Carlos slid in his own left foot. They stood side by side, arms over each other's shoulders and grinned at Jojo Dickens. They were thin and undersized, even by Four Kith standards. Their emaciated appearance enlarged the size of their eyes and made them look innocent and helpless. They were killers in the making.

"Eeny meeny mina moe," Jojo said, pointing at Carlos, or was it Juan? And then his twin. "Catch a Grimm boy by the toe. If 'e squeals…" Jojo

CHAPTER ONE

paused to spit another steam of hot tar juice into the bucket. She tapped the bowl of the pipe onto her head. "Iz forget 'ow the rest goes…"

"Let 'im go!" both boys shouted in unison.

Jojo flashed her blackened teeth and grinned. "Let yuz go? Why Iz just found the pair of yuz. I'll nev' let yuz go! Come over 'ere an' give a big fat lass a terrifik hug!"

She stretched out her arms wide again, and Juan and Carlos hurried over to be consumed by her tight embrace and mountains of rippling flesh.

"If yuz finished molestin' chillen, wez got work to do aroun' 'ere," Mo Dickens said from behind his butcher's block. He was a huge lumbering man with arms the size of tree stumps and a humongous belly that flopped over his thick belt like a snow slab on the verge of becoming an avalanche. His bald head had a large crater on the left hand side where the blunt end of a meat cleaver made contact with his skull. A metal plate inserted into the cavity kept his brain from exposure to the elements. However, in inclement weather he suffered from terrible headaches and took his anger out on the nearest apprentice.

Mo Dickens was Hetman of the Slagers and this was his domain, his fiefdom, his abattoir. He occupied a large cavernous stone room, built by the Old Ones, where he skillfully butchered his meat, conducted his business, ate his meals, and occasionally fornicated with his wife. He had one rule during the solar: no fire indoors. It had the potential for spoiling the meat. When the weather got extra cold, Jojo's arms and legs turned blue, but Mo Dickens never felt the effects of the icebox. He told his charges to move faster to keep warm. Once the solar's business was done, and the last carcass was carved and bagged, then the large roaring fire was lit in the vast fireplace, sending black smoke up the flue and crackling warmth to the room and Jojo's frigid bones. The old bag laughed then. She always laughed when she was warm, had tabak in her pipe, and a pot to piss in. She softened Mo Dickens's mood.

An apprentice loaded another carcass onto the butcher's block and Mo went to work with an oversized cleaver, demonstrating ruthless efficiency. He hacked the bushmeat into manageable chunks to be eagerly wrapped in a sackcloth by another apprentice, and tied up with hemp string. He was a purveyor of paranga, brought in from the Wildlands by the sanctioned trappers, though he also dealt with the poachers, the wild nomads, and the Four Kith folks who could catch anything left in the Slough. He drew the line at human flesh, and for that his reputation as a provider of clean meat was not tarnished.

"Why 'ave a man of twenty years when yuz can 'ave two boys of fifteen each!" Jojo cackled, demonstrating her arithmetical skills as she tumbled the twins against her bosom. They bounced around like two ships caught in a maelstrom.

"Let 'em go, you ole hag! I need them uns to load up the barrows," Mo said, though there was no hostility to his tone.

Jojo released her captives. "Alright. Back to work yuz go. Be off, before I smuther yuz in luv."

The Grimm twins ran off to the courtyard outside of the slagerhaus and set to work. Between the two of them, they loaded the sackcloth bundles onto the meat cart, ready for the barrowmen to come and sell Mo's finest paranga on the more civilized streets on the edges of the Four Kith, and even transported to the finer establishments in the Burghs. Never too far from the sanctuary of Mo's reach, and never in the territory of the rival purveyors of paranga. Mo might be the Hetman of the Slagers, but there were always others waiting in the wings.

Carlos once toyed with the idea of pushing one wrapped parcel under some burlap sacking, and selling it themselves. Luckily, Juan was on to him, cuffed his ears, and reminded him of the fate of apprentice Barnaby Billett who stole from Mo. Barnaby was sliced and diced on the butcher's block before you could say 'next please!' and dumped in the Basin to feed the fish. Or at least most of him ended up in the Basin. The Bassett family suddenly put on weight and gild never crossed the path of that twisted brood.

The Grimm boys considered themselves lucky. There were few openings for apprentices with Mo, the exit of Barnaby Billett being the exception and not the norm, and they were recently uplifted from the hardscrabble

CHAPTER ONE

streetlife thanks to a chance encounter with Jojo. Carlos had tried to lift her purse, and she caught him in the act. Rather than cut off his hand, which was her right, she took to the twins and persuaded Mo to let them occupy the lowest rung of the paranga ladder. They slept rough in the courtyard, but did not have to keep one eye open all night, and a daily slab of brood, dipped in the warm blud, and a mug of hot bier was more than their bellies could handle for now. It was also a significant upgrade from the slim pickings the Slough provided, and the lukewarm rotten vegetable stew dumped in the communal trough in the great hall of the Gut, the feeding house of the destitute. As they moved up in trades from carrier, to loader, to bushmeat wrapper, to barrow boy, and finally to butcher's apprentice, the quality and quantity of the cuisine would improve. There was also gild for those of an enterprising nature.

Mo Dickens took them to one side and whispered to them so the other boys could not hear. "Yuz boys look like the enterprisin' sort, an' ole Mo 'as a favor to ask. Are yuz up for it?"

The Grimm twins were already learned in the ways of Mo speak. *'Are yuz up for it?'* was an actual command rather than a request. Still, it did not stop Carlos stepping in it with one broken shoe and a calloused foot.

"What's in it for us two?" Carlos asked, defiantly as he jutted out his chin and stabbed a thumb in his own chest.

Mo moved fast for a large man, and his massive right hand cradled the back of Carlos's head and neck before the boy knew it was even there. As a prime butcher he was well versed in the anatomy of all things, and while a saw bones could put a man back together in relatively the same good order, Mo could take a man apart with ease. He gently changed the position of his ring finger which resulted in a torque in Carlos's neck. The least amount of additional pressure would induce a break and Carlos could feel his life was in imminent danger, without truly understanding what was going on.

Mo leaned in closer. Spittle flew from his mouth and peppered Carlos's face as he talked. "Why, yuz is a special one, ain't yuz? Juan is it?" His voice was calm, but there was an underlying menace to everything he said.

Carlos could not speak and Mo knew it. His finger pressure also prevented Carlos from vocalizing as every fiber of his body focused on not moving and self preservation.

"I'm Juan," Juan said. "This knucklehead mudlark is Carlos. It's always Carlos 'as the tarty mouth. An' yes. Wez up for it. Whatever up for it is. Wez your kithfolk for the task at 'and."

Mo released his hold on Carlos, and the boy immediately sagged and rubbed his neck. His lungs sucked in oxygen like never before. He was still alive and his body thanked him for it.

A big friendly giant grin broke across Mo's face. He leaned in closer and beckoned the boys to complete the circle. He towered over them, so lowered himself closer to the ground. "Come closer, boys. Come closer. Wez don't want t'other 'prentices 'earin' our ploy."

The Grimm boys joined the conspiratorial ring and smiled. Mo had not called them *'prentices* before. That was a serious step up in status. Carlos even forgot the man held his life in the balance only a few seconds ago.

"You know Jojo is still mad at ole Mo, on account of that flapper next door tryin' to catch me attention an all, with 'er wigglin' an' a jigglin'. She's a looker that one, an' ole Mo ... well, I 'as weaknesses for the flesh. But still, when I upset Jojo, things doesn't sit well. I can'ts abide when she gives me the cold shoulder. Me 'eart's not in me work, an' the paranga fights me on the block. Iz might be Hetman of the Slagers, but Jojo is Hetwoman of the Kogelbrekers. But wez can make it up to 'er, an' Iz need yuz 'elp. Are yuz up for it?"

This time both boys nodded vigorously.

"Well 'ere it is, then." Mo continued. "Jojo dearly luvs billee flesh, an' it's a true rarity in the Slough these solars."

"Ganga Flewman was sellin' one just the other..." Carlos started, before Juan could shut him down.

Mo reached out his hand again for the boy's head and neck, and stopped himself, fingers twitching. He forced a smile on his murderous face. "That was no billee, youn' Carlos. No billee indeed. 'Twas a potkan, if ever there was. A big potkan with the tail snipped off an' the snout removed, but no billee. We want a real billee for Jojo's table an' nothin' less. Are yuz up for

CHAPTER ONE

it?"

Mo stressed the last part which as good as said, *'get me a billee or don't bother coming back.'* Even Carlos, who was not as fast on the uptake as Juan got the message loud and clear. Get a billee and you were further up the food chain, fail and it was back to a life in the Slough at best, or one final wet trip into the Basin with weighted rocks for company.

So the hunt was on for Juan and Carlos Grimm and a tour of the other sections of Gastown in their search for the ever elusive billee. There was no use looking in the Slough, the shanty district within the Four Kith. Those bones had been picked clean many lunars ago, and any billee worth her salt had moved on to safer havens from this dark side of the river. The boys looked over the border, across the long bridge to the imposing citadel, to the land of the Gentry, and those who served them. As desperate as they were, they never thought for a moment of crossing into that forbidden realm. That left the Burghs, the Docklands, and the Mutton. Even on this side of the canals there were places they could venture only at night, and the risk of being caught loomed large. There were no trials for the kith denizens who trespassed into the Burghs, the domain of their betters, the carpenters, the merchants, the bookbinders, and the keepers of the tabernacles. Only death, hopefully quick and merciful, would be their just punishment. Still, Juan and Carlos ventured out, keeping to the shadows and moving like billees themselves. Five nights they searched, and their meager supply of brood from Jojo was long gone. They supped water from the gutters and tightened their belts.

They left the merchant burghs, vaulted over the moss covered walls, and crept back into the Slough, and across the bridge into the realm of the slagmaidens and their orange lanterns marking the entrance to their dens of vice, depravity, and anything goes mentality. An area collectively known as, *The Palace of Earthly Pleasures* by those marketing high end thrills, and as *The Mutton Market,* or simply *The Mutton,* by those hailing from the lower end of the social echelon.

The Grimm twins could move more freely in the Mutton, without the threat of getting murdered on sight. However, they had to be on constant guard and watch each other's backs. Young boys were fair game for any John or Sebastian looking for sport, and they were just as likely to be swept up by one of the Swell Daddy's out to expand his stable. They walked with purpose in the Mutton, like they belonged. Victims were easy to identify and generally fulfilled their own expectations. Juan and Carlos were also armed for the occasion. Nothing fancy, no Hallic steel knives or Bastic warhammers. Just two pieces of discarded metal from Mo Dickens's courtyard, sharpened on stone. Little stabbers to make a point and a quick escape.

The river fog was heavy in the Mutton. It hung over the collection of mottled inns, rustic taverns, and gaudy hauses of ill repute. Lights were always on in the Mutton, and fires burning. In the gloom, they gave off a strange eerie glow. A collection of red, yellow, and orange flames to attract visitors from the Onderworld itself, like depraved moths to the warped light. The fog also made everything damp, and the Grimm twins were soaking wet as they walked the streets in their billee search. It was another type of billee that called out to them.

"Take a butcher's at these two luvlies. Just what a girl ordered on a cold night when trades slower than a halfwit," a very fat woman said. She was standing next to a brazier with her dress hitched up warming her bare rear end. A sign hung above her doorway with an exaggerated painting of her with a big smile on her face and an even larger exposed derriere on display with a red bullseye drawn on it. The artwork was beginning to fade, and obviously represented her in a slightly less gargantuan time. Juan and Carlos could not read, not many in the Four Kith knew their letters, so they were unaware it marked the habitat of Big Bertha. She made JoJo Dickens look anorexic.

"Leave the youn' uns alone, you ole crone," another woman who went by the name of Long Peg called from an open bay window on the other side of the cobblestone street. She was sitting in a rocking chair with her obscenely carved wooden leg in full phallic display.

"Ere! If you're lookin' for work youn' uns, there's a Swell Daddy down

CHAPTER ONE

the corner name of Puzzle Pete who's addin' to his flock. There's many a perv who'd drop a purse of gild to shag a brace of twins," another hag who went by the handle Theresa Three Tit cackled.

"And don't forget to mention my finder's fee to Puzzle when you see him!" Long Peg called.

"Your finder's fee? Why I saw them first, didn't I, you long streak of misery," Big Bertha said, her hands on her fat hips and her face flushed. "I've a good mind to swing over and stick that bit o' driftwood you call a leg where the solar don't shine!"

"Don't do that, Bertha. She'd like it!" Theresa said, and all three women forgot their temporary animosity and broke up laughing.

Big Bertha turned her attention back towards Juan and Carlos. "Don't be mindin' us weyward sisters, boys. We're just havin' some fun at your expense. And we see greatness in you, don't we girls?"

"Greatness is the word, Bertha. Greatness. And Kingship," said Theresa.

"Oh, kingship is a grim word, girls. I see two boys, and only one king," chimed in Peg.

"And which one is it to be? Shall we pick for them?" Bertha asked.

"To be a king you have to kill a queen," Theresa said.

"Or become one," Bertha said.

"The choice is already made. Made long ago." Peg replied.

"What do we say about the kingdom of the blind?" Theresa asked.

"We don't care, as long as they have a pair!" Bertha and Peg replied in unison, and all three crones broke out laughing and cackling once again.

Carlos was fascinated by the prophetic freak show in front of him and gawked, until Juan pulled at his sleeve and pointed up to a nearby rooftop. Even in the fog, they could see a pair of eyes staring back at them. And just like that the chase was on.

"All hail King of the Four Kith! All hail the Lord of the Wildlands! All hail the Dux of Gastown!" the three weird sisters called, as their voices faded into the distance.

The Grimm boys were off and running, scampering and climbing, jumping and clambering, zigging and zagging through the alleyways and cobblestone streets of the Mutton. For a moment, they lost the billee, until Carlos looked back and saw it watching them. Curiosity got the better of it, and delayed the escape.

Juan and Carlos began their spidery climb, coming at the billee from different directions, trying to corner it so they could close in for the kill. But the billee was a survivor, an outlier of her kin, who escaped many a hunt by outsmarting two legs and cutting impossible angles between chasers and chancers.

Juan was the flusher, and drove the billee back towards Carlos the closer, and the inevitable trap. All was going to plan, until the billee suddenly changed direction and darted away, down and then up towards a high rooftop and safety. But Juan was prepared and his aim was true. He let fly with his best stone, the smooth one he kept for special occasions. The flight path was pure and the missile hit the billee behind the right ear with a thud. The billee dropped. If the strike did not kill her outright, the fall surely did. Down she went, her limp body bouncing off walls all the way down to the snow covered alley floor. The Grimm boys descended smoothly after her.

Carlos was about to drop down into the alleyway and pick up their prize, when Juan stopped him with an outstretched arm. Carlos angrily pushed it to one side, suspecting Juan wanted the trophy and the glory, for himself. Until Juan gestured towards some activity at the other end of the dimly lit alleyway.

There were two figures there. One was a slagmaiden, dressed in her seductive finery, and pressed up against the wall by a figure the Grimm boys did not see too often. A Dandy from the Gentry, in his finest white bearskin overcoat and white beaver hat, was wooing the lady in a way the boys had seen many times before in the Slough.

Carlos saw an opportunity while the grinding couple were preoccupied, and smiled at Juan as he slid down the wall, crouched down, and picked up the lifeless billee. He was about to start his climb back up when he froze. There was movement on the other side of the alleyway, but not the kind he anticipated. The slagmaiden let out a shout of surprise.

"Ere! What's this!"

CHAPTER ONE

As they watched, the Dandy moved with deceptive speed. He pivoted round to the side of the slagmaiden and then behind her. One gloved hand closed over her mouth and pulled her head back. Steel flashed in the other hand and a blade pulled across her throat. Blood spurted out, some even reaching as far as Carlos across the alley. He looked up and his eyes locked with the Gentry.

Carlos could not move. The shock of the sudden murder transfixed him to the ground, the still warm billee clasped in his hands. The Dandy was not disabled. He held the slagmaiden a moment longer, until the blood stopped pulsing out and gently lowered her to the ground, careful to avoid the blood still leaking from her sliced throat. He stared at her for a brief moment, and then delicately closed her eyes with two gloved fingers. He picked up his cane which was propped against the wall, and turned his attention towards Carlos. He took four steps forward and loomed over the boy.

"I'm afraid you've interrupted my sport, old chap," the swell said, though Carlos had no idea what the words meant. The Dandy was wearing a heavy scarf, which covered most of his face, and his language was of the conquerors and not the oppressed. The citadel folk conversed with the commoners through interpreters, and only a handful of specialists were ever permitted to learn the high language. Carlos knew none of this, and did not care. He did know his life hung in the balance.

There was a thud as a stone flew across the alleyway and made contact with the beaver hat. It was not strong enough to displace the headgear, but it was enough to make a solid dent, and gain the Dandy's full attention.

"Over 'ere," Juan said from the top of the wall on the other side. "I'm the one yuz want, not that sparrow!"

The Dandy turned around, which was all the time Carlos needed to scurry up his own wall and out of harm's way. "Over 'ere, beaver 'ead!" Carlos crowed from the security of his perch, the dead billee tucked safely inside his shirt.

The Dandy did not turn around. With amazing speed and dexterity for someone encased in a bear coat weighing all of fifty pounds, he bounded across the alleyway, pushed himself off and up the wall, and swept Juan's legs out from under him. Juan tumbled down onto the ground, rolled and came up on his feet. Before he could move again, the Dandy's cane was pressed firmly against his chest, pinning him to the wall.

"Well, what do we have here?" the Dandy asked, more to himself than to his latest prey.

"Let 'im go, or I'll do for you!" Carlos yelled, but it was all bark and definitely no bite. The Dandy ignored him.

"I'm afraid you've put a ding in the old beaver bucket. Shan't do. Can't ever wear the silly thing again after this, don't you know?"

Carlos kept barking.

"Does go on, that one. Quite a little yapper. I suspect the unwashed masses of Assaborg have a devilish time telling the two of you apart. I can rectify that, don't you know."

The Dandy twisted the silver wolf's head of his cane and pulled out a sword stick. He kept the sheath of the cane firmly pinning Juan against the wall. Juan looked at the point of the very thin blade, and then at the only visible part of the Dandy: the eyes. The right one was blue like most of the Gentry, but the left one was a cloudy green. That was the last thing he saw before a piercing pain stabbed through him. The Dandy pushed the tip of the sword into his right eye, rupturing it forever.

Juan dropped to the floor and covered his face with his hands. Blood and eye juice seeped through his fingers. He instantly went into shock.

The Dandy wiped the tip of his blade on the dress of the dead slagmaiden and placed it back inside the cane scabbard. He gently doffed his hat to the dearly departed, and left the alleyway whistling a tune to himself.

Chapter Two

Kasha : The Waheela Pack

She stopped her easy lope for a moment and took stock of the terrain. There was no cover in any direction, just neverending snow and ice. She raised her nose skyward and up from the trail and sniffed at the cold air. A gentle breeze from the north carried the sanguine smell to her flared nostrils and gave her all of the information she needed. The end was near. The blood scent said so. It was thicker now, richer in iron. Life was ebbing out of their prey as he sought to outrun them. That he could never do.

  Kasha gave a signal to her three sisters and they continued with the chase at a slightly faster pace. No reason to exhaust themselves, but they did need the meat. It was five solars since their last kill and their bodies pained them from lack of sustenance. The feisty one she had named Tuva took the lead for the last part of the hunt, as was her right. Tuva was the one who darted in and nipped the ankle of the giant poro and drew blood, and risked getting her head caved in with flying hooves. That allowed them to separate him from the rest of the herd and run him until his heart gave out and the death choke was applied. He would still be dangerous until the very end and they did have to show caution. More than one waheela had been gutted by the razor sharp antlers of the giant poro when the chase seemed over. But he could not escape them. They had his scent, and they hungered for his flesh and entrails. The distance between them shortened and they patiently stalked him down.

The change in terrain made movement more difficult as they left the hard packed snow and made their way up towards the mountain. The snowdrifts were deeper, and Tuva took the heaviest burden as she plowed a path for the others to follow. They went single file now until they could make the rock face up above. Kasha yelped at Tuva to slow down and conserve her energy for the kill, but she had the bloodlust upon her and she forged ahead, bounding up and down through the snow pockets.

Once they reached the base of the rocks, they stopped as a group and shook the snow from their shaggy fur. Tuva was exhausted and hung her head low as she panted. She was struggling to keep the lead position and was grateful when Kasha moved past her without reproach and led them forward. The blood trail was easy to follow and they knew the kill would happen soon. They were an efficient pack and worked well together. Sisters of the slaughter.

Kasha and her sisters had come across the giant poro herd not more than two solars previously. The herd were nestled in a valley, which protected them against the savage wind. They were grouped together for protection with the young in the middle, surrounded by the collective mothers, while the stags circled on the perimeter offering early warning and protection.

Waheela were large and aggressive, much bigger than their closest competitor, the direwolf. Some said they were the offspring of an ice bear and a direwolf, which might not have been too far from the truth. Their huge front shoulders were more bear-like than wolf, but their thick brown coat was more winter canine. The mismatch in the size of their front limbs to the smaller back limbs meant they did not move as elegantly as their cousins, but they made up for that with sheer power and perseverance. A waheela never gave up. Still, even a single waheela thought twice about taking on a giant male poro by itself. A pack of four determined females was a different question. Then they could engage from the front as a distraction, pin from the rear, and then lock in on the throat for the kill. Death did not come fast, and the feast on the innards started before the heart stopped beating.

CHAPTER TWO

This time, they were able to single out one of the younger males. He was overly aggressive in defending the herd, which was his mistake. While the older bucks stood their ground, they were more cautious and did not leave their flanks exposed. This male, either showing off for the does, or perhaps posturing for the other stags, came out too far from the sanctuary of numbers. While he charged at Kasha, Tuva slipped in behind and bit his back leg. It was a slight wound, but in the *Machala*, the open snow covered plains, it was everything. Now the sisters all had the scent and it was easy for them to single out the bleeding buck and drive him away from the herd. Then, his only chance was to run, which was not much of a chance at all.

They could see him now, his back against a sheer rock face, prepared to make his final stand. Steam rose from his overheated body, and he added to it by blowing loudly through his mouth and nostrils. The thick white mist surrounded him like an expanding fog. He raked his hooves in the snow, getting better traction on the hard ground underneath, and raised his head up and down as if practicing goring an opponent.

The waheela silently moved in. Each of them knew their position, and there was no need for barking signals. Tuva went to the front, though slightly over to the left, Kasha went to the right of her, and Liva over to the far left. Norn hung back for a moment, and then circled around trying to find a way to get behind the giant poro. If she could land on its back and break the spine their work would be easy.

As they moved in closer, Kasha looked at the eyes of the giant poro. They were red and inflamed. Fear registered, but also a willingness to fight to the bitter end. He knew he was going to die and he wanted to take at least one of the waheela with him. Many creatures gave up the fight at this point and accepted their painful fate. Not this one. There was going to be combat for his flesh and she or one of her sisters ran the risk of serious injury.

Tuva moved in at the point, and let out a low growl. It was more for distraction than anything else. She was the most impatient of the waheela, but even she played for time. With the giant poro watching her intently, Kasha moved in low. She got within a few feet of the stag, before he whipped his head around and struck out with his antlers in her direction. The heavy snow slowed down his movement, and Kasha was fast enough to evade the lethal strike.

As soon as the giant poro targeted Kasha, Liva moved in closer on the other side. Again, she got closer to the stag before he whipped his head back around and made her retreat too.

The waheela and giant poro game continued as the sisters sought an opening and the stag tried to strike with his antlers, or at least drive them back. The waheela could not risk an injury, and the giant poro had no such concerns. He was in a fight to the death and was prepared to take wounds before he departed. It also made him reckless. As Tuva bared her fangs and moved in one more time, he charged forward and pressed the attack, giving up his rear as he moved too far off the rock face.

As the battle with the three waheela continued, Norn circled to the rear and looked for some way to get behind the stag. With some difficulty, she managed to locate a ledge off to the right, and forty leg lengths or more off the ground. It was narrow, but the delay would be short, so she perched there and waited for her opportunity. It came when the giant poro charged out at Tuva and left enough room to leap behind him.

As soon as the opening presented itself, Norn dropped down into the vacated space, hit the ground on all fours, and immediately sprang up onto the stag's exposed back. Her front claws came out and sank deeply into the flanks of the giant poro, and she drove her fangs into the rear of the beast's huge neck.

The weight of the waheela on the giant poro's back caused him to buckle, but he resisted going down. He thrashed back and forth and tried to dislodge her, but Norn was locked in for the ride. He bellowed for help, but no one was coming to his aid. This was his final battle.

The other sisters moved fast with a three point attack. With the giant poro's head turned back towards Norn, Kasha lunged forward from the right and sank her teeth into the stag's neck. Tuva moved straight ahead and managed to get between the antler's on both sides and grabbed hold of the giant poro's snout and snapped her jaws shut. The stag bellowed in pain, but still did not go down. Only when Liva hit him hard from the left did the combined weight of the four waheela drive the buck to the ground. With the head pinned by Tuva's grip on the nose, the antlers were useless. All the stag could do was thrash with his hooves and hope to dislodge them.

Norn came over the top of the giant poro and sank her claws and fangs into the unprotected underbelly. The hide parted easily and the entrails seeped out. In fear of pending oblivion, the stag's bladder opened and his bowels released. Blood, urine, and feces mixed in with the churned up snow and dirt as the dance of death played out. Kasha tightened her grip on the throat and choked out any last breath. The giant poro went limp even as Norn tore at the exposed intestines, Tuva went for the tongue, and Liva worried at the testicles. There was one last spasm from the dying stag and it lashed out one hoof almost as a reflex action and it caught Tuva in the hind leg. She yelped and hobbled away from the fray and licked at her wound. The blow was strong enough for her to leave the promise of a bloody feast and see to her own well-being.

Kasha glanced over at her sister, but Liva and Norn were still caught up in the joy of the kill. They worried at the dead giant poro and pulled at the choicest pieces of the warm flesh and lapped at the congealing blood. Their gusto was short-lived.

The howl started low and rose to a high pitch and resonated through the mountains. They would have heard it from three leagues away, but it was close and familiar. The sound was unmistakable. It was his calling card, his way of marking his territory, his way of keeping control of his pack. Amarok.

The waheela were large, at least the height of the tallest man whose head barely reached their shoulders. Amarok was bigger still. He towered over the sisters and weighed twice as much. While their coats were a mixture of brown shades with some white patching, Amarok was all black. Some said his heart was too. His body was covered in battle scars from encounters with hunters from the Wildlands, direwolves, giant poro, and even the ice bears. Kasha had not named him. It was a name given to him by men. Some worshiped him as a god of sorts, all feared him.

The sisters cowered away from the kill and gave up ground to Amarok. He moved in towards the giant poro, baring his fangs and emitting a low growl to show this was his meat and he would eat first. The waheela did not dispute his right, all except Kasha. She had not been with the pack long enough to truly understand his authority and savagery. Her loyalty was to the sisterhood, and she truly believed Tuva should be honored for the pending feast, and not the late arrival who took none of the risks and all of the reward.

As the other three dropped lower to the ground in a sign of submission, Kasha remained in place. Her defiance was short lived and the lesson was painful. Before she knew what was happening, Amarok lashed out with his front paw, and sent Kasha tumbling over into the rock wall the giant poro had recently defended. For a moment she blacked out, and then shook her head to gather her senses. When she looked over, Amarok had already forgotten her. His back haunches were pointed towards her and he gorged on the flesh. The three waheela edged in closer behind him, but waited patiently for him to finish his meal before their turn came.

Not Kasha. Her belly still rumbled and the smell of blood and flesh tormented her. However, her pride was hurt and she slinked away and retreated up and around the mountain. There was one backward glance towards her sisters, and a pang of regret, but she needed to be alone. She needed to be away from the waheela for what she had to do next. She had forgotten herself of late, reveling in the joy of running with the pack and the thrill of the hunt.

The terrain changed as Kasha made her way around the other side of the mountain. At first there was more snow covered shrubbery and sparse trees. That changed quickly as she entered the outskirts of the great winter forest. Giant ironwood trees reached up high as if stretching upwards to the heavens to reach the little glimmer of light from the solar. The trees were massive, both in girth and height and there were thousands of them. Dark red, cold, and somnolent in the long winter freeze. Trees from another age, biding their time for the millennial thaw. Man's axe and fire did not reach this far to the northwest and the forest was safe for now.

CHAPTER TWO

However, there were other dangers and Kasha was on her guard for what she had to do next.

She found a clearing, and a nice nest at the base of a giant ironwood tree, which was already filled with a heavy carpet of pine needles, small branches, and thick leaves. Kasha sniffed at the ground to make sure no other creature had claimed the space for a home. Satisfied it was fresh, she crawled into the center of the foliage and lay down. She waited for the transformation to begin.

An excruciating pain coursed through her as all of her nerve ends came alive and burned with an intensity she had never felt before. It was as if every fiber of her body activated at the same time, moving, twisting, and changing. Kasha stifled a howl, and coiled up as a way of dealing with the agony. She closed her eyes and went inward before she remembered the right thing to do was to get outside of her own head and focus on something external. If she was an observer, the pain became more manageable. She could concentrate on what was happening, rather than simply responding to the torture of the physical change.

Her size changed first as she reduced from a large waheela down into the shape of a human girl. Her thick shoulders melted away, and with it the heavy light brown mane which covered her once powerful frame. Her front claws gave way to more delicate hands and her muscles danced under her skin as they shrank and changed shape. Kasha bit her lip and stared intently at an old ironwood tree to distract herself as the most painful part of the transformation occurred. There were loud cracks as her spine turned over and drew away from the shape of a waheela to the human form. Her hind legs pulled in at the same time and toes sprang from claws. It was a total rebirth and one she had neglected for too long. She had run the real danger of forgetting her human self and permanently locking into the waheela world: she knew there were worse things.

Kasha stood up on weakened legs. It would take a few steps before she was used to walking on them again and finding her balance on two of them and not four limbs. Her orientation was different too. Her eyes were further forward and she had trouble focusing, there was also more color than before. The world was brighter, sharper, and closer. Kasha immediately felt the cold. Her heavy fur coat was no more, and though there was a lot of hair on her body, it would drop off her human form in a short while. She could never understand why mankind had to wear the skins and coats of others to keep warm, though at this precise moment, she wished for one.

In her post transformational state, Kasha still felt some of the power she held as a waheela, though it would diminish in time, along with her keen sense of smell. As the latter receded, she neglected to pick up on his scent the way any self-respecting waheela would have done. She did hear him. His immense size made it difficult to move with any degree of stealth.

In any other circumstance a girl confronted by a giant ice bear would have been terrifying. He reared up on his hind legs and seemed almost as large as the ironwood trees which surrounded him. He was a colossus of nature, the alpha male of the north. The apex predator in a world of killers. He was also her father.

As Kasha watched, the ice bear slowly transformed before her. Either it was not as painful as her own recent struggle, or he had more experience in dealing with it. Most likely a combination of both. As an ice bear he towered as high as fifty arms. As a man he was still huge, but less than a third of the height. The bear shape seemed to stay with him even as he shifted, with massive powerful shoulders and a thick neck bulging with knotted muscles. They were not the pretty smooth muscles of a man in his youth, but the hard working muscles of an older male. His body was covered with thick hair which seemed to protect him from the cold, but did not hide his vast array of battle scars and black tattoos. His face bore evidence of conflict too. An old white scar ran down through his left eye and into his mouth.

"I watched your shift," he said, the words thick in his mouth as he wrestled with the shapes. "It was long and painful. How many lunars?"

"Too many," Kasha replied. Her words were also slurred as she struggled not only to speak but to focus on human thoughts.

"I warned you, Kasha. Do not get lost in the waheela world."

CHAPTER TWO

"How did you find me, Tornar?" Kasha asked. She was starting to feel the chill and sat down in the forest foliage to cover her nakedness and wrap herself in whatever warmth she could find.

"I'm your father. I always know where you are."

"And you'll come to me in my moment of need, is that it?"

"No. You make your own way in this cruel world. I can explain the consequences of your choices, but I cannot force the course you take, only suggest a different path."

"You're still mad at me for choosing the waheela, aren't you?"

Tornar shook his head. "No. I mean … yes. But you've made it, and there is no turning back. The dangers of running with the pack are real, and as a female, they bring their own set of challenges. An ice bear roams free and sets his own rules."

"I have my three sisters for company. Norn, Liva, and young Tuva…"

"You've named them?" Tornar said, incredulously.

"Of course!"

"They're not pets, Kasha! Waheela are cold blooded killers. They don't just take prey to eat, they get excited by the pain and the suffering they inflict. You'll take action as a waheela, which will spill over into your human world. If you needed to run with the pack you should have chosen a direwolf shape. At least there's a degree of noble savagery there."

"You don't understand them, Tornar. You never did, and you never will! I love my sisters. They'd do anything for me."

"And Amarok? What about him?"

Kasha stared at the ground. She picked up a small branch and threw it away. "Oh, he's not all that bad."

"Yes he is!"

"Alright, he is. But I've got it under control."

Tornar squatted down and placed his arms on his knees. His anger subsided and he spoke to her as a concerned father. "Kasha, you can't run with this pack anymore. That's what I came to tell you. You've already been locked into the waheela world for too long, and there's a real danger you'll forget your human existence if you continue. You'll never be able to shapeshift again. That's a lot to give up. And Amarok will mate with you when you come into heat. Do you want that?"

"I could persuade my sisters to turn on him. The four of us could drive him out. He doesn't do anything anyway. He just turns up when we've made the kill and takes the best parts for himself. If he wasn't a waheela, he'd be a pig!"

Tornar shook his head. "They won't give him up, Kasha. He has a role to play, and they need a pack leader. This is his territory and the other male waheela won't infringe on it. He also keeps the direwolves from overrunning your herds. No, Kasha. You have to leave before it's too late."

Kasha looked up at her father. She was still no more than a child of sixteen years, with childish notions. "You could make him leave. Amarok is no match for an ice bear. You could threaten him, drive him further north…"

"I can't do that, Kasha."

"You mean you won't!"

Tornar did not answer. He merely stared at his daughter, and hoped she would understand. If not now, then at least in time, however long that would take. He had brought many children into the world, but Kasha was the only girl. He had a special affection for her, but he could not show it. Not now. He had to show parental strength and resilience. Her life really did depend on it. There was a savagery about life in the Wildlands, but also a balance to it. It was not his part to upset it, or there would be consequences.

Kasha continued to pout. "I guess you're expecting me to give up the pack and return to a human way of doing things and settle down with one of the tribes."

Tornar nodded. "Just for a short time. Until you fully grasp the advantage of living in both worlds. You're a shapeshifter for a reason. There's no benefit in choosing one existence over the other."

"And where exactly do you want me to go?"

"Go southeast to Gastown."

Kasha's momentary resignation to her fate left her and she bristled at that one word. "Gastown?" She almost spat it out. "You can't seriously expect me to go all the way back to that hell hole…"

"I can and I do. Now listen carefully to what I have to say. I need you to collect something of value, an heirloom of sorts. One of your brothers will meet you there to provide extra protection for the trek back north. You have a long journey ahead of you Kasha, and the future of our kind depends on it."

After they had talked a while longer and Tornar had explained the mission in detail, Kasha was almost blue with the cold. Without the protective animal skins mankind wore, there was minimal protection from the harsh elements. Tornar changed first and slipped back into his ice bear form. He gave a final nod of his huge head to Kasha and left by the same path he came in. Kasha shapeshifted next, but it was not so easy. She struggled to get back to her waheela body, and the transformation was painful. Every sinew and nerve ending of her being ached as she finally dropped all vestige of human except her ability for higher thoughts.

Kasha needed to wait before she joined the pack one last time. The smell of two legged flesh would be on her for some time yet, and the odor would confuse her sisters and enrage Amarok. She stayed away for three full solars, alone in the wilderness with an empty stomach and a confused mind. Why did Tornar seek her out now, and why did she have to go to Gastown? she wondered. If a brother she had never met before was already heading there, why could he not complete the task on his own? Tornar explained the reason why, but she still pouted over the interruption to her waheela way of life.

Kasha's plan was to wait until the next kill before rejoining the pack one last time. Then she would head east alone until she reached the borders of so called civilization. She could move faster in waheela form, but once she was close, she could not risk being seen. Panic would spread amongst the settlers, and hunters would be on her trail for a prized pelt. An isolated homestead would provide her the opportunity to change back into human form. She would steal clothes and supplies if she had to, or kill as needs be.

Her mission permitted a ruthless approach and an emotional escape from any moral dilemma over slaying innocents.

Her path back to the pack to catch a parting glimpse of them was easy to follow and though the smell of the death scent of the giant poro was now faint, it was enough to point the way. She longed to see her sisters again, and snuggle up with them in the snow as they slept off the remnants of their meat eating orgy. Lost in her thoughts, her senses failed to perceive the presence of Amarok.

He landed on her with all of his weight and pinned her to the ground. His mighty mouth locked in on the back of her neck. Kasha immediately knew with a grip like that he could sever her spinal cord in one bite, so she remained still. She cursed herself for not being aware of the danger. It put everything Tornar had asked of her at risk.

Kasha tensed and Amarok increased the pressure of his bite, drawing blood and a whelp from Kasha. Her mind raced, she had to think of a way out of this. She immediately relaxed all of her body and went limp. Amarok took it as a sign of acquiescence and loosened his hold, and Kasha seized her chance and spun under the heavier male. Amarok's fangs ripped the flesh at the back of her neck and the pain caused her to cry out, but she was free of his hold. She immediately charged forward and took a large bite out of his shoulder, tearing the flesh out. Amarok pulled back and swatted Kasha with a heavy strike. His claws were out and seared through her chest muscles drawing deep bloody tracks. She pulled back, bared her fangs and growled.

Amarok was almost twice the size of Kasha and in a battle to the death she stood little chance of victory. She could see the look of a killer in his eyes. Kasha had dared to challenge him and for that he intended to rip out her heart and eat it as she lay in her death throes.

Amarok hunched forward and growled. Saliva and blood dripped from his fangs. Kasha should have been terrified, but she felt the thrill of the impending fight. Adrenaline coursed through her and she hunched forward too. She let out her own growl in answer to Amarok, letting him know this would not be an easy victory. She fully intended to inflict as much damage as she could before the end came. All thoughts of her sisters, her father, or her mission vanished. All she cared about in that moment was killing the beast in front of her. Many had entered battle with Amarok with the same thought. They all died.

Kasha did not wait for Amarok to take the lead. She charged forward into the attack, and Amarok met her fury with a charge of his own. The two waheela collided, and the impact was so violent, distressed birds took flight, and wildlife went to ground in fear. Fangs and claws lashed out, dealing savage blows. Blood and fur flew.

For all of Kasha's spirit she knew it was a lost cause, a final defiant act before she reunited with the Dreambringer, the Creator of this twisted world. Amarok was surprised by the initial assault, but he quickly gained the upper hand. He was a veteran of a thousand conflicts, and this was just one more trophy. A trophy he would devour while her blood was still warm. He pinned Kasha to the ground with his massive front limbs, and ignored the scratching with her back claws. He looked down at her for a moment and saw the recognition in her eyes. She knew she was about to die, but she was prepared. He opened his jaws wide to deliver the killing bite.

Chapter Three

Joe : The Assameister's Apprentice

Joe was late again, and as a penalty his father would make him stay in the steam room for the rest of the week with only the squeakers and the silent kolmen for company. He did not mind too much. The kolmen were no trouble as they fed the vast furnaces with the seemingly never-ending supply of black gold, their bodies slick with the dust and their sweat from working so close to the heat. They did not talk. They could not. Their reward for working in the heart of the citadel was to have their tongues ripped out so they would never divulge the secret few of them ever knew. Most of them died at a young age from the kol dust which lined their lungs and turned them black. However, they provided a good living for their families, and there was a steady stream from the younger generation to give up conversation, and pick up the shovel and pick. One life to feed many.
    The squeakers were no nuisance either. He had his favorites and fed them with hard brood and soft cheese, the best Andersen's hotshop provided. He always stopped at Andersen's each morning on his way to work, despite the complaints from their housekeeper Nell, that there was enough food in the pantry, and it shamed her to see anyone from the family eating victuals from a vendor. It was not just the food, though Mister Andersen made the best hot pies in the Burghs, and always supplied a supplementary treat. It

was entertainment too. Mister Andersen was a jovial fellow, with a smiling red face, which was always flushed, and jowls which seemed to hang to the floor. He was corpulent, a trait he had bequeathed to his brood of children, who popped out of Missus Andersen with alarming regularity. His special gift was flatulence, which he was unable, or unwilling to control. Each expulsion was followed by 'Oops, there goes another one,' which sent his giggling flock running in all directions as they pinched their nostrils closed. Joe loved the gaiety of it all, when his own abode was filled with gloom. There was the aroma too. Not from Mister Andersen's posterior, but the mixed smells of baked pastry and hot juicy meat.

The snow was coming down hard and covered Joe's hat and winter coat with a fine white outer layer. It did not lie on the hard ground or cobblestones for long. As soon as it touched down, it melted away into pools of water which washed away any debris and kept the streets and alleyways clean. It was always a strange sight to see the rooftops of all of the buildings, high and low, permanently covered with a winter blanket, and yet the ground below was free of frost. Occasionally, the contents of a roof slid from its perch and crashed down to the streets below. Unlucky souls were buried in the temporary avalanche, only to be discovered when the melt set in.

Joe glanced up at the large clock tower which dominated the central square of the Gastown marketplace. It was a smaller cousin of the much grander clock tower which stood upon the hill in the castle square. However, it was the one he used on a daily basis to mark his passage across the Bridge of Broken Souls from the Four Kith into the heart of the citadel . His journey from the merchant burghs to the tradesman's bridge ran through a sliver of the Four Kith. Even though it was patrolled by the Bully Boys, he still felt nervous under the watchful eyes of the beggars, vagabonds, thieves, and murderers, and he consciously avoided eye contact, and unconsciously quickened his pace until he reached the safety of the other side.

There was a commotion this crisp morning. A hue and cry ensued from the direction of the street vendors, who lined a path through the Four Kith towards the bridge. A young boy was running, something tucked under his right arm, and a baying crowd chomping at his heels. Fear spurred him on as he sped towards the bridge, but it was a fool's errand, and no sanctuary beckoned. A strong arm swooped down, and a Bully Boy scooped the child off his feet. He struggled for a moment, thrashing and kicking, and then went limp, but never releasing the tight grip on his precious cargo.

The crowd circled the Bully Boy, and an out of breath vendor was pushed forward. He pointed an accusing finger at the undernourished lad, dressed in rags a beggar would cast off. "He stole a loaf of brood!" he wheezed.

"I saw him with my own two eyes. Snatched it up he did," another concerned citizen said.

The Bully Boy prised the loaf from under the child's protective arm, and handed it to the merchant.

"That's it. I'd recognize it anywhere," the merchant said.

"Please sir. I was just tryin' to feed me sister," the child said in his defense. "She 'as a fever, an' is starvin.'"

"We have the Gut to feed the likes of you," the vendor said, as he wiped his precious loaf, before depositing it in an apron pocket.

"And a rope too!" someone offered, and the crowd cheered as a thick cord was passed forward.

Joe did not approve of stealing, but he strongly felt the punishment should fit the crime, and a life for a loaf did not balance the scales of justice. He blanched as the rope was thrown over the gallows post which blotted the picturesque view at the entry to the Bridge of Broken Souls.

The Bully Boy put the child back on his feet, and roughly tied his hands behind his back with a neckerchief. He was led over to the gallows and the rope placed tightly around his young neck. He cried hysterically, and peed himself.

Joe searched the faces of the crowd, looking for like-minded supporters who would be prepared to intervene on the boy's behalf. However, while the vigilantes in the pack bayed for blood and rough justice, the more fair-minded residents kept their eyes cast down and stayed silent. It would take more than the death of a child thief to stir them into action against

CHAPTER THREE

an obvious injustice. They would let the shame of it gnaw at them rather than get involved.

"He's just a child," Joe said, tears streaming down his own face.

"If you don't deal with a child thief, he grows up to be an adult thief," a hardened soul said.

"Hoist away lads," The Bully Boy said, and a group of vengeful citizens pulled on the rope and lifted the child into the air and on into the heavens.

Joe watched in horror as the child's face turned blue, and life was squeezed out of him. Then the clock struck the first quarter position marking the start of the working solar, and he cursed as the steam whistle sounded. It blew long, hard, and shrill. He knew he should be on the other side of the heavy eikwood door by now, and he was still at the edge of the bridge. One of the bridge guards in the gray overcoat and heavy bearskin hat smirked at him as he passed, wiping tears from his eyes, misconstruing the reason for the water works. His father was known as a hard taskmeister and his birchwood rod was always swishing in action, cutting through the air with a sound like a swarm of angry orange jackets. Joe put his head down and broke into a full out run, dodging the sullen night workers as they made their way home for their solar sleep. Joe glanced up at the bleak, dark gray citadel, the symbol of domination over all of Gastown. He just made the sanctuary of the door before it closed.

Once inside, Joe removed his heavy coat and hat and shook off the snow. He hung them on his private peg and ran the length of the long corridor to the top of the iron stairs. He had a trick for getting down fast and sat on the bannister and slid down to the next landing. He repeated this seven more times before he reached the basement floor and the heart of the boiler room. The temperature got progressively hotter as he made his way into the epicenter of the labyrinth. This was the engine which drove all of Gastown, and it was his domain. Or at least his father's.

The morning shift of kolmen were busy. Men, stripped to the waist, worked on emptying the barges which came though the underway canals. They used a system of pulleys, cantilevers, and large iron buckets to pluck out the kol from the barges. Other men transported it over to the vast stockpiles, which always seemed to be the same size, as more workers subtracted from the kol heap and fed the furnaces. They opened the massive metal doors, temporarily exposing the flames, fed the monster, and closed the doors again. On and on it went. Solar after solar. Lunar following lunar. Gastown depended on it.

Kol drove the furnaces, but kol did not drive Gastown. There was not enough of it to power the machinery or provide the necessary heat to keep the permawinter at bay. The town itself was built on top of a vast reservoir of liquid assa, and the heat from the furnaces converted it into a workable gas, which was combusted, and in turn melted the snow and generated the steam, which provided underground heating for everyone, and a regular temperature for the greenhauses.

Joe's father, Castor Willow, was the Assameister and on his frail shoulders rested the secret of the conversion process, and the maintenance of the mighty copper colored boilers which filled this vast cavern. He was not rich like the merchant burghers, or powerful like the Damm Warriors, but he alone carried the burden for the survival of Gastown. He alone defeated winter and allowed heat to triumph over cold. He was a mighty man in a feeble body. He was also dying.

Joe set about his checklist of tasks. He checked the temperature on the gauges to make sure they were constant, he polished the casings, and he examined the rivets for any breakage. There could be no leaks. Ever. He went about his job with clinical efficiency, and acted as if everything was as normal. As if his father had not noticed he was late again.

He heard the swoosh of the birchwood cane before he felt the sharp stinging pain across his shoulders. He winced, but did not stop his work for a moment. That would only bring another strike from the slender stick, and the slender arm which powered it.

"An apprentice will never be late. An apprentice will respect the craft. An apprentice will burnish and polish, spit and shine, knowing the boiler is a true friend of mine. Say it for me, Joe," Castor Willow said.

"An apprentice will never be late..." Joe said as he continued to work, even as the second strike of the rod made sharp contact with his back.

CHAPTER THREE

"An apprentice will respect the craft…" Another stinging blow landed and lacerated Joe's skin under his tunic.

"Very good! One does love it when the underlings are taught to respect their Meister."

Castor immediately stopped his punishment, turned and bowed. "Ma'am. I didn't hear you enter. My sincere apologies," he said, though he addressed himself to the Damm Warriors, and not the Dux directly.

Joe immediately stopped his faux polishing and dropped to one knee. His heart was in his mouth. Anything was possible with the Dux of the Citadel of Varstad and Gastown beyond the walls. A sudden whim led to death or a handsome reward. Uncertain actions led to fear while they endured, and euphoria when they were over. Provided one survived.

The Dux was a dumpy woman dressed all in black, with a laced black veil which partially covered her bloated face. Some said she took to wearing the color after the death of her Dandy husband more than ten years previous. Others claimed she always wore black in a vain attempt to mask the spread of chunk. She was roly-poly as a child, porcine as a young girl, and corpulent as a crone. 'Do I look fat in this dress?' was a phrase she often uttered and was never truthfully answered.

The Dux never traveled alone. She had her personal guard of four fierce Damm Warriors, in constant attendance outside of the bedchamber, and a troop of the best Red Shadows, all young fighting men pulled from the wealthiest families from the Burghs. Their service, and sequestration in the castle, ensured their families paid their tithe on time, and with only silent complaint. She was also surrounded by her pack of ugly little yappers, an undisciplined brood of four legged curs, who were so low to the ground they almost slid along on their bellies. They roamed the boiler room, ignoring the frantic attempts of the Curmeister to keep them under control, and shat copious amounts of green liquid all over the Assameister's spotlessly clean floor.

"Please continue with the lesson, Assameister," the Dux said in her high-pitched voice. It sounded pleasant enough, but it was most definitely a command.

Joe immediately got up from his kneeling position without a word from his father and turned to face the boiler. Castor Willow also turned to administer the punishment, as Joe polished.

"An apprentice will burnish and polish…"

Swish.

"Spit and shine…"

Swoosh.

"Knowing the boiler is a true friend of mine."

Swack. The Assameister put some mustard on the third blow as much to alleviate his own frustration with Joe as to make sure the Dux appreciated the lesson.

"Splendid!" said the Dux, clapping her pudgy hands, in a show of excitement. "The apprentice learns from the cruel hands of the meister. Now turn and tell me all about how the assa is doing. We want to keep our palace warm and scrumptious during this eternal winter. It just won't do if we run out and one's poor tootsies get the frightful chills … you there, that man!" The Dux stopped addressing the Assameister, and turned her attention to one of the Red Shadows.

The rest of the troop stood to attention and kept their eyes straight ahead, and a stoic look on their faces. Their hearts were beating fast under their steel shirts.

The Dux moved in front of the offending Red Shadow, lifted up her black veil and gave him the stink eye. "Just what exactly were you looking at while I was addressing the Assameister?" There was a decidedly malevolent tone to her voice.

"I-I … nothing your majesty," the sweating Red Shadow said. His legs were visibly shaking.

There was a loud collective intake of air from the four Damm Warriors. The rest of the Red Shadows remained as silent as they could and kept their eyes forward, trying hard to look at nothing in particular.

The Dux forgot the transgression which led to her singling out the Red Shadow. He had just committed a mortal sin in answering back to the Dux. Red Shadows were taught a smattering of the High Tongue when

CHAPTER THREE

they entered service, so they could follow commands, but they were not permitted to utter it. Only a select few, such as the Assameister, were allowed to converse in a limited capacity. To directly answer the Dux was not only folly, it was a death sentence. The Red Shadow knew it, and to make matters worse, his bladder did too, and emptied.

Two of the Damm Warriors immediately moved to either side of the piss-stained Red Shadow and divested him of his halberd and left buckler. They pinned his arms to just make sure he did not do anything stupid in his last minute of life.

The Dux paced back and forth in front of the trio, and scratched her hairy chin as if pondering a very difficult problem. "What's one to do with such an insolent soul? Talking back to the Dux, don't you know. Directly! Not so much as a by your leave, or a please Ma'am." She stopped walking as if she'd come up with an answer, and then sighed and continued with her pacing. She stopped again, and tapped the side of her nose. "I've got it, by Susan. I've got it!"

She pointed a pork sausage of a finger at the weeping Red Shadow. "Strip him!"

Without a word the other two Damm Warriors closed in on the hapless Red Shadow. They removed his steel helmet and unstrapped his cuirass. His thick gloves came off easily, but they used knives to cut off his heavy bear leather boots, his red tunic and pantaloons. In less than a minute he was completely naked, nicked by the razor sharp knife blades in a few places, and under the scrutiny of the Dux. His only hope was if she liked what she saw and granted a reprieve. She did not.

The Dux's eyeline was closer to the former Red Shadow's genitals than she was to his navel. Close enough to get a bird's eye view.

"I can't abide a man who doesn't wash his tinkle," she said with deep disdain. "Well, we don't have water to speak of but we do have something better to clean with. Assameister, if you please. Open one of your furnaces!"

The naked man knew what was coming and he struggled furiously against the firm grip of the two Damm Warriors. Another Damm Warrior gave a command to four of the Red Shadows and they immediately put down their halberds and bucklers on the ground and seized hold of their former comrade in arms. Two men relieved the Damm Warriors and twisted his arms cruelly up his back. The other two grabbed his legs and lifted him clean off the ground. The Assameister pulled on his protective gloves and walked calmly over to the nearest furnace. He opened the large furnace door with no little effort and exposed the heat and flames of Hel.

With another word of command from the Damm Warrior, the four Red Shadow carried their struggling burden over to the exposed incinerator, rocked his back and forth three times and launched him into the firestorm.

"Why me, why me!" he cried as he landed on the white hot kols and went silent. The Assameister immediately closed the heavy door.

"Who was he calling out to?" The Dux asked one of her Damm Warriors.

"Ma'am?"

"This Wyme fellow."

The Damm Warrior shrugged her large shoulders.

"No matter," the Dux said and turned her attention back to the Assameister, as if the momentary intrusion with the errant Red Shadow had never happened. "Well then?"

"Ma'am?" Castor replied in the high tongue, though once again he addressed the lead Damm Warrior, and not the Dux directly. A dew drop of sweat glistened on his forehead.

The Dux sighed. "I was asking about the assa? Doesn't anyone listen to me anymore? How is it doing, man. How is it doing?"

"Oh, the assa. We have an abundant supply, your majesty. More than enough for my lifetime, and many Assameisters after me." He gave a little cough and swallowed the blood which came into his mouth.

"I certainly hope so, Assameister. I certainly hope so. Who knows how long this dreadful winter will last. And we need our vegetable gardens to stay warm, don't you know."

Without another word the Dux spun on her heels and walked back to the steel cage which would take her all the way back up to her private chambers. The four Damm Warriors followed closely behind, and the Red Shadows at a more respectable distance, after they had picked up the

CHAPTER THREE

armaments, torn tunic, boots, and piss-soaked pantaloons of their former compatriot. One of them gave a backward glance at Joe before he departed.

The rest of the solar was uneventful for Joe. He continued with his daily chores and ensured the kol made it to the right furnaces, and the large assa boilers worked at peak efficiency. He stayed away from his father for most of the solar, and they would never talk about the hapless Red Shadow. Careless whispers led to torture. Open conversation meant certain death. No one ever questioned the Dux. Regal madness was a distinct reality for all of them.

Joe barely ate his lunch. He nibbled on the sour brood, but he hardly ate any cheese, and his Andersen pie was untouched. The squeakers appreciated that, since he had more to share with them today. The braver ones even took it directly from his hand.

There were a few more hours for the shift to finish, and Joe busied himself as much as he could. He wanted to forget about the hanging child, and the poor soldier who fed the furnace, but both images kept coming back to him. He longed for the steam whistle to sound so he could race across the Bridge of Broken Souls, away from the fear of the citadel, and back to the sanctuary of his father's modest haus. Before then, if he was lucky, smart, careful, and quick, he might catch a fleeting moment of happiness.

Time did not stand still. It always moved forward, no matter how slow it seemed for Joe. The steam whistle did blow, he did put down his cloth and gauge checkers, and today he did not have to wait and leave with his father. There was time to seek the thrill.

Joe was off before the last shrill note of the steam whistle ended. He walked at a fast pace across the vast assachamber. There was no running allowed in here, but a brisk walk was acceptable. Once Joe reached the foot of the staircase he could move as fast as he liked. Coming down was quick and easy, going up took considerably more effort. But Joe was young, slim, and lightning quick, and he bounded up all seven staircases in record time. He was out of breath at the top, and his legs were on fire, but he had gained some extra precious seconds.

People were streaming out of the castle as the solar shift ended, and Joe had to weave in and out of the crowd. It slowed him down, and he grew anxious as he lost the extra time just gained. He dodged past one knot of blackened kolmen, and made it to his final destination. There was an alcove they used for their rendezvous. Perhaps it was an old store room, or a place where the guards cached their weapons. It was not very big, but it served their purpose, and it was out of sight. Unless you were looking for it, you would not know it even existed.

The soldier was already waiting. His halberd and buckler were resting against the wall, and he took off his helmet as Joe entered the alcove.

Joe's logical mind knew the relationship was doomed from the start. Although they were both from the Burghs, they occupied decidedly different worlds, and if they were caught the punishment would be severe. Joe knew he was putting his father's life and reputation at risk too, and vowed he would end it soon. However, not on this solar. He needed a distraction from the two deaths, and to temporarily forget the secrets they nurtured in the Willow household.

He ran over to the soldier and they locked in an embrace. Their open mouths met and their tongues danced.

"You've been eating that green cheese again," the soldier said, when they finally came up for air. His name was Ori, but Joe referred to him as Passionfruit. At nineteen years, he was four years older than Joe, and considerably taller. Like all of the Red Shadows, he was selected for his physique. He towered over Joe, and his embrace was bearlike. Sometimes he squeezed too tight, and Joe could barely breathe. They met by accident in the great chamber, and snatched quick glances at each other. Their schedules barely overlapped, since the soldier moved between solar and night duty, and was occasionally called out on military maneuvers. The soldier did not know his letters, so Joe could not leave written notes in their secret alcove. Instead, he devised a coding system the two of them could share.

"It was horrible what happened today," Joe said with a shiver.

"Yes, I could barely restrain myself when your father put that birch rod to you," Ori said.

CHAPTER THREE

"Not that, silly. The burning. Was he a friend of yours?" Joe said with a shudder.

"Yes, of sorts. Devlin wasn't a bad sport. But there is a pot of gild at the end of this here rainbow. You see, Devlin saw us touching hands the other day in the great chamber. I warned you about taking risks like that. That's why he looked at you kind of funny in the assachamber and the Dux picked up on it, like. Well, the rest is herstory."

"Doesn't it bother you?"

"What?"

"That the Dux can give orders like that and everyone obeys the command without so much as a by your leave."

Ori grabbed hold of Joe's arms and tightened his grip. "Don't you ever say a word against the Dux, do you hear?" he growled.

"S-stop. You're hurting me," Joe whimpered.

Ori relaxed his grip. "These walls have ears. Don't even mention her name, do you hear? Never. What's done is done. We can't change it. Live and forget, I say. Now come here, and give us another kiss before the second whistle blows."

Chapter Four

Kasha : The Homestead

Kasha was prepared to die. Her futile battle with Amarok was over and she waited for his life-ending bite. She would miss her father, and her newfound sisters, and there were brothers she would never get to meet. She felt alive as a waheela, more so than her years as a human, but that time was now at an end. The moment to pass over was here. She had so much left to do, so much to see. Regret washed over her, and her resolve began to weaken.

Amarok stood above, pinning her to the ground with his front paws. She could not move beneath him, and all he had to do was sink his fangs into her neck and the battle, as short as it was, would be over. Victorious again, Amarok the Slayer, Amarok the Destroyer, Amarok the Killer: feared by all, worshiped by some. He opened his mouth wide, dripping saliva on Kasha, and looked down. There was something in the eyes of this waheela, which made him uneasy. They were almost *human*.

A heavy blow sent Amarok flying backward into the rock wall. The strike landed firmly across his open mouth and shattered his lower jaw. Before he could recover another thunderous blow came down on him and broke his rear right leg. Amarok howled in pain. The giant ice bear reached down with its left paw and scooped up Amarok like he was no more than a plaything. With one swing of his mighty limb he hurled the waheela over the side of the path and down into the snowdrift below. He lay there without moving. Caught off guard, it was not a fight, but a savage execution.

You were watching over me!

Tornar glanced over at his wounded daughter and nodded his head, as if he had heard her thoughts. He knew his intervention would have far reaching consequences, but he could not stand by and see his child torn to shreds. Amarok would leave a large gap in the waheela world, and others would now fight for supremacy. Dire wolves would be emboldened and ravage the herds. Wolves would multiply and run unchecked. Such was the way. Without another sound the giant ice bear turned around and lumbered off on all fours. Kasha watched as he faded away. All that was left behind was his huge prints in the snow.

As the battle rage and the strength it imparted retreated, Kasha started to feel the intensity of her wounds. The deep gashes across her chest stung sharply, and her blood dripped into the snow. They would heal in time. Other than a few cuts, bumps, and bruises she was intact from her conflict with Amarok. She moved over to the edge of the path and stared down at the once feared waheela below. Amarok lay broken, not moving from his landing spot in the snowdrift. Blood seeped from his shattered jaw and his rear leg was twisted at a grotesque angle. His blackness was in sharp contrast to the pure snow. For a moment, Kasha felt pity for her nemesis. Then she remembered his cruelty, and the fact she and her sisters were now free of him. A sense of elation took over. She felt immense joy with her sisters, and she longed to be with them, running across the snowy plains engaged in the thrill of the chase, the hunt, the kill.

Kasha turned her back on Amarok, and went down the trail to seek out Tuva, Liva, and Norn. All thoughts of returning to Gastown and fulfilling Tornar's request were pushed back to the far recesses of her human mind. Time for that later. For now, she needed the comfort of the sisterhood. To smell them, to nuzzle, and perhaps feast on the remains of the giant poro. She was ravenous.

Kasha saw Norn first, and then Tuva and Liva not far behind. She quickened her pace and made her way towards them, eager for their company. But something was different. Kasha could feel it immediately, and slowed down. As she came closer to Norn, her sister bared her fangs and growled. Tuva and Liva came up on either side of Norn and snarled. There was no welcome for Kasha. She took a tentative step forward, and submissively bowed her head, hoping Norn would relent. It was a futile wish. Norn lunged forward, and snapped at Kasha, who instinctively pulled back. Norn did not follow up, but stood her ground and continued to growl. Sisterhood was abandoned. The waheela could see her fresh wounds, and they could also smell Amarok's blood on her and acutely sense his loss. Kasha would never run with this female pack again. They were bonded to Amarok and Kasha was not. They had no choice but to reject Kasha and cast her out.

In her human form, Kasha would have shed tears. However, that emotional expression was denied to her as a waheela, and mournful howls would go unanswered from a pack who had spurned her. She was now a pariah to her three sisters, and would never again experience the joy of their companionship. She was on her own in an unforgiving world where the loner was at risk and constant danger was a way of life or death.

Kasha turned and ran. Not the steady lope of the waheela, but a full sprint to put distance between herself and her sisters. Only when her heart felt like it was bursting did she slow her pace, more out of necessity than desire. She could persevere in the *Machala* by herself, but it was not the waheela way. Alone, she could still track and hunt the herd animals, but without the cooperation of the pack, it would take longer and the risks were amplified. With the solitary lifestyle came loneliness. There was little chance of finding another waheela pack for now. Amarok's territory was vast, and until his absence was noticed, no waheela male would venture into it. Kasha knew Tornar was right: time for changing worlds.

Kasha stopped her aimless running and took her bearings. She sniffed the air for a sense of the right direction. The sour smell of Gastown, unwashed men packed together in tight communities, was not evident at the moment. However, she sensed the direction was to the east, and she took off at an even pace. She would need food soon. The chase after the giant poro had provided nothing for her, and she needed nourishment to sustain her on the long journey.

After the battle with the giant poro, taking a snow hare was relatively simple. The trail in the snow, the little hopping pawprints, were easy to follow and digging it out of the ground took seconds. The little beast did not even try to escape and simply hunkered down to accept its fate. There was a pitiful screech before Kasha scooped it up in her jaws, and crunched bone before swallowing it whole. It was enough to keep her going with another burst of energy.

Ten solars she ran on an empty stomach, barely stopping to take bites from the snow to slake her thirst. She moved at a steady lope, and covered as much distance as she could without thought for anything else, and entered the famine stage for the first time as a waheela. The nighttimes were harsh, as she curled up alone and dreamt wild dreams of hunting with her sisters.

Kasha was in dire need of food to continue with the snow trek, and she knew her best option was scavenging from others. Direwolves were out of the question. A pack of them, though smaller in size, were a match for a lone waheela. Wolves were something else. If she could find a wolfpack she could surprise them, and steal their kill. A wolf lunar helped to point the way.

Kasha heard the wolves long before she caught sight of them. The stupid beasts howled to the world and the lunar above about their kill, oblivious that something else might want to take it from them. Something bigger, stronger, and desperate. Her waheela night vision was acute, and she quickly picked out the pack, even with their white fur blending seamlessly with the snow. The alpha male, two subservient younger males, four females, and three cubs. It was not an oversized grouping and something she could deal with even in her weakened state, provided she showed a degree of caution. The alpha male was her main challenge, Silence him and the others would fall in line.

The alpha male was feeding first, tearing the flesh from an old male snow shoveler, an ancient who could not keep up with the herd, and was easy prey for the wolves to take down. The two juvenile males howled to the wolf lunar, and the females and cubs waited behind the alpha male, nudging closer to take their share of the kill they had helped to bring to ground. None of them were aware of the danger closing in on them.

Kasha did not want a fight, but was prepared for one if the alpha male stood firm. If sense prevailed, he would back down in front of a waheela more than four times his size. However, sense often escaped the male species when pride and an empty belly was at stake. This was all about show first, baring fangs, and a menacing appearance. If that did not work then wolf corpses would litter the frozen ground.

Kasha moved slowly out of the shadows and into the kill zone, straight towards the distracted alpha male. She could have pounced on him at that moment and crushed his spine, but a physical confrontation also risked injury. She wanted food, an easy meal, and a quick departure. She let out a menacing growl and locked eyes with the male wolf. Caught by surprise, he instinctively crouched down, a large piece of snow shoveler still in his mouth. The other wolves saw Kasha and began to collectively bark and growl, but none of them came closer. They all waited to see what the alpha male would do. If he engaged they would charge in, even if it meant certain death. If he backed off they would too.

Kasha could see the wolf was no fool. He was on the last leg on his journey as the leader of the pack, and he did not need his time shortened by a waheela. He had already taken his fair share of the snow shoveler, so it was his pack who would take the burden of losing their kill. He let out a low throated growl more for show than anything else, and slowly backed up, one step back for each step the waheela crept forward. The pack followed his lead and kept a distance. They all hunkered down and waited.

Kasha moved over the remains of the snow shoveler, but kept a wary eye on the alpha male. She would not give him any reason to react to a moment of distraction as she fed on the remains. The liver was already gone, but most of the heart was intact, so Kasha gorged on that first. She was hungry enough to devour the whole beast, but that would not serve her purpose. She needed to leave enough for the wolfpack for them to focus on their meal rather than trailing after her. After the heart, she chewed through some intestines, and then ripped free a large piece of meat. The rest she would leave for the wolves to consume.

The meal over, Kasha raised her bloody snout and let out a loud roar as a warning to the wolfpack to keep away, and slowly backed up. The wolves immediately moved forward. While the alpha male moved past the carcass and kept an eye on the retreating Kasha, the pack devoured the remains of the snow shoveler as fast as their jaws could grind and chew. They would leave nothing behind, consuming even the bones and hide. Kills on the winter wasteland were not an easy undertaking and they ate while they could.

Kasha backed off five more paces, pushed her muzzle in the snow to wipe off blood, and then turned and continued her journey in the general direction of Gastown and human society, leaving the wolfpack behind. She still had a long passage ahead of her, and who knew when an opportunity for another meal would present itself in the desolate winterland. Her stomach was full for now and she used the extra energy to quicken the pace.

For ten more solars Kasha pushed on. She rested when fatigue became overwhelming, but barely slackened her pace. She came close to a herd of snow shovelers, working their spoon shaped antlers and hooves to dig through the snow and get at the sleepy moss, lichens, and grass below. She thought about culling one of the older males, but the hunt would sap the strength she needed for the journey, and success was never guaranteed.

A large snow shoveler herd meant humans could be close, even this far north. In the flatlands outside of Gastown, herders and huntsmen roamed. Never in large numbers, but enough to pose a danger and raise the alarm if they sighted a waheela, who rarely came this close to civilization. Her pelt would be a special prize to lie on a floor or grace a bed in one of the wealthier merchant hauses, and the gild paid for it would keep a huntsman idle for a year.

Kasha's senses were on heightened alert as she drew closer to mankind. Her sense of smell, more than two hundred times stronger than in her human form, kicked in first. The dwelling was still some distance away but the strong scent of smoke from a heavy fire wafted through the air. There was a slight rise in the terrain, and as Kasha crossed over a small hill, she saw the compound in the far distance. Moving closer, but at a much slower pace, in case iron traps were set, Kasha was gratified to see it was not a large settlement, or a grouping of multiple families. Gastown was still many leagues away, so it was likely a single homesteader family eking out a living as best they could from the harsh terrain.

It was still early in the solar, but the family was already up and moving. Smoke billowed out of the makeshift chimney, so the wife was likely preparing the fast breaking meal. A man was in the foreground, chopping wood from a large stockpile, and his young son carried a bundle into the home. Trees were still plentiful in the boreal lands, though human habitation thinned out their numbers considerably. A small girl sat on a bench out front and wove a basket. A family at work with no time for idle play. A shout from the mother caused them all to pause what they were doing and head into the cabin. The morning meal was ready and so was Kasha.

Kasha stood naked in front of the frontier haus and raised a bucket of cold water over her head. She tipped the bucket and gasped as the icy shower cascaded over her body and washed away some of the homesteader blood. Not all of it, but enough for the first pass. She dipped the bucket into a large barrel the family used for their drinking supply and worked a cloth to scrub her body as best she could. She winced as the harsh rag brushed across her chest and glanced down at the claw marks, now a permanent reminder from Amarok. The wound still smarted, and scar tissue had not yet formed, but the healing process had already begun, so there was no need to seek out herbs and ointments for supplemental recovery.

The transformation back to her womanly form was not as painful as the last, but it came with other dangers as her human emotions and thought processes evolved. As a waheela, she knew to kill and eat to survive. There was no delineation between an adult and a child. Meat was meat, just sometimes in smaller, sweeter bundles. As a human she had to live with her waheela transgressions, and the butchery of an innocent family could cause deep and lasting psychological trauma.

She tried to reason innocence was in the eye of the beholder. The family lived by the fur and trapping trade, selling their wares in Gastown. They took many lives of their own. Only solars before she was prepared to massacre a wolf pack, including the cubs, over a fresh kill.

Was there any difference?

However, she took the family and consumed them by surprise in their home, without any means of defending themselves. She slaughtered them and fed on their flesh, a meal she needed for the remainder of the journey to Gastown. A waheela shows no mercy, she reasoned, but she still shuddered at what she had done. This was her first human kill. Tornar had raised her to be different, to understand the need, and to act with ruthless efficiency. He had also warned her it would not be easy.

Kasha struggled to come to terms with her upright physique as her waheela senses diminished. Her sight was constrained, and she could no longer see far distances, though there was the benefit of an additional spectrum of colors with a world of reds and greens. Her sense of smell changed as her ability to pick out a myriad of distinctive odors disappeared and she was left with a blunt instrument with limited range and function. Her hearing scope evaporated too, almost as if an invisible wall was placed around her to keep out the sounds of nature. Then there was the intense cold. The loss of her waheela coat meant no protection from the elements, and the fast flowing blood to her paws to keep them warm in the snow diminished to a slow moving stream to her human feet. The impact was immediate and Kasha knew she needed to get inside and bundle herself inside human garments if she wanted to survive.

The smell of blood and exposed guts, a major draw to a waheela, was sickening to most humans. There were some who craved it and lusted after the killing, whether cloaked in the glory of battle, or shrouded in murder, but not Kasha. The smell of recent death, scattered body parts, and crushed skulls greeted her as she stepped into the interior of the frontier haus. The fire still burned in the hearth, though not as strong as before. Kasha still had an instinctual fear of the flame, a useful and necessary tool for humans to keep predators at bay, but she knew she needed its warmth to take away the growing chill. There was a bundle of sticks and small logs beside the hearth, and she added them one by one to feed the ever hungry fire. The response was immediate and the flames grew and extended the heat range. The broken bodies cast large shadows as if they grew to threaten Kasha.

Another human trait, the ability for the mind to create unnecessary fear and imaginary threats.

Kasha needed clothes, and human food, and weapons, and a fire kit, and gild, if she was to last the journey to Gastown. A journey which would take four times as long as a human. She started with the clothes, rummaging through wooden boxes at the foot of the large, medium, and small bed. Kasha was exceptionally tall for her age and heavy boned, and the life of a waheela on the run had the benefit of adding to her human musculature and overall endurance. Her size meant the young girl's clothes were of no use, and her older brother's clothes barely fit. That left the women and even some of the man's garments as the optimal source. She scavenged as best she could, until she had most of what she needed, and some spare to carry on the road. Footwear, preferably kamiks, were still missing, and she knew the only way to get them was to remove them from one of the corpses.

Kasha glanced down at the twisted body of the boy across the table, and quickly looked away. She took a deep breath to steel herself, and then took hold of one of his legs, and placed her bare foot against the bottom of his.

Too small.

She moved over to the remains of the man, sprawled in the corner. He had tried to put up a fight when Kasha came crashing through the door, but with only a spoon in his hand for protection it was quick work. She went through the same motions, picking up a heavy leg and sizing her foot against the sole of his kamik.

CHAPTER FOUR

Too large.

The woman was next. She had not put up a fight, and sat frozen in her seat until Kasha tore out her throat. This time, when Kasha performed the foot check, the size was just right. Luckily, she was a small woman with very large feet. Kasha set to work pulling the kamiks free and examined them before she put them on. They were worn, and not in the best of shape, but they would do until she could buy or barter another pair in Gastown. She sat on the bench next to the table where the family ate their last meal, and put on her secondhand footwear.

The food was easy to find, and Kasha stuffed a knapsack with blackened brood, a jar of bear grease, wild honey, smoked meats, pickled cabbage, shriveled limes, and dehydrated cranberries. Her belly was full from the homesteader family feast, so there was no thought of food, but hunger would come soon enough and she needed enough supplies to last at least ten solars on the move. Then she would have to figure out another food source, Hunting along the way, or carrying too much from the outset would unduly slow her down.

The search for the firekit was next, and Kasha did not take long to find it. The small pouch containing the fire knife, the metal block, and dry tinder was buried deep in the man's jacket pocket. She also located a small bag of gild. No gold or silver coins, but a sad collection of clipped copper pennies, only enough to buy basic essentials. There would be more, and the accumulated family wealth was likely buried in the packed dirt of the earth, or hidden in an old jar. Kasha needed the gild for Gastown, and she proceeded to tear the homesteader haus apart to find it.

The search for the family's fortune took longer than expected, and Kasha grew increasingly frustrated. In her anger, she broke open jars, emptied out the chests and scattered the clothing, and sent kitchenware crashing to all four corners of the dwelling. She even took the spoon from the dead man's hand and used it to dig into the dirt floor in search of a hidden pot of gold. Kasha's fangs and claws had obliterated the homesteader family, and now her human rage desecrated their living space.

Kasha sat on the wooden bench, and clutched the small bag of coins in her hand. It was not enough. She needed more. She could take furs and sell them, she reasoned, but it would draw attention and she did not need that. It would also slow her down. She was about to give up, when something caught her eye above the doorway. It was no more than a thinly carved line in the woodwork, but as she looked more closely, there were other faint lines too.

Kasha moved closer and looked up at the carving. Perhaps it was just a protective sign some of the superstitious folk cut to ward off vengeful nightstalkers, but she could clearly see four lines in total, cut in the shape of a rectangle. She rubbed a thumb along the edges, and wiped away some of the dirt. Then she took the small knife out of the firekit pouch and traced along the lines. She jabbed the blade deeper into the groove, and leveraged with her hand to pry a piece of wood free. It fell to the floor, and behind it, Kasha saw a small box pushed into the hollowed out hiding hole.

The box was crudely made, but it served the purpose of storing the family gild. There was more coinage than Kasha had expected. Five full copper coins, two gold kruns, and thirty pieces of silver the like Kasha had never seen before. Kasha shuddered to think how long the family had worked to acquire this much wealth, and how much backbreaking work went into the accumulation. And now the fruits of their labor were in the hands of a killer and a thief.

Kasha emptied the contents of the box into a leather pouch she liberated from a chest at the foot of the homesteaders's bed. Her human instincts got the better of her and she removed four silver coins from the pouch and paced one on each of the bodies. It was payment for the boatman to take them safely into the Onderworld. It was not the custom of her father's people, but it was the lore of Gastown, and Kasha honored it.

Decked out in an ill-fitting assortment of the family's undergarments and furs, and with the knapsack on her back, Kasha looked around at the chaos and destruction she had caused. The death of the patriarch she could live with, but the wife and son brought her the burden of grief she needed to bury deep. Until now, she had avoided looking at the broken body of the young girl, but she forced herself to take it in. The girl's red

CHAPTER FOUR

hair, now matted in blood, reminded Kasha of her own, and another pang of guilt assailed her. She was the cause of the horrific murder and she would never escape that. Tornar told her shapeshifters lived by a different set of rules, but he also said all actions have consequences, and now she finally understood. She needed a keepsake, not as a grisly trophy, but something to remind her of the young girl's existence, so she would never be truly forgotten. There was a silver brooch depicting three entwined trees fastened to the girl's tunic, and Kasha took it, pinning it out of sight to her own undershirt.

Kasha could not leave the crime scene for hunters and trappers passing through to Gastown to find. They would talk about it in the taverns and billeehauses, and suspicious eyes would gaze at all strangers from the wilds. Even young women committed murder and townsfolk were quick to administer rough justice if the capital offense was revealed by a stolen purse. She also owed the family a funeral of sorts. The ground was rock hard and it would take too long to make a commitment to the earth. Fire was the answer, fire the purifier, fire the cleanser of broken bodies and souls. The homestead haus would make a perfect funeral pyre for a family on the final journey together.

Nothing special was needed to feed the flames. With her wanton destruction, Kasha had already laid the groundwork for the fire to spread. She pulled the heavy fur off the largest bed, and draped it over the body of the man and pulled one end closer to the fire. The other two bed furs wrapped the little girl and her brother. She covered the woman's body with a pile of untreated furs stacked in the corner, and then connected all of the bodies with an assortment of clothing. Only then did she take the fur corner and drop it into the embers. It took hold immediately, as if the fire exhaled a path out of the confines of the hearth and into the wider room. It would rage and burn, and consume the structure, free from the constraints as the servant of man, and then smolder and finally extinguish with nothing left to devour. Sleeping, waiting for the next human to bring it to life.

Kasha stood a small distance away from the homestead as the fire razed the building. Flames danced in angry shapes and smoke billowed into the sky, a beacon to the destruction of a family existing on the edge of civilization. And civilization, or what passed for it, was where Kasha was now headed. She pulled up the fur hood over her head, adjusted the snow goggles made from snow shoveler bone and sinew, tightened the straps of her backpack, and stamped her feet to ensure the bearpaws, the snowshoes woven from small branches, were tightly in place. She was armed for her journey too: a small axe on one side of her belt, a knife thrust in the middle, and a short sword attached on the other side. The heavy furs would keep her warm, but it would take some time to adjust to the smell of the accumulated sweat of others.

The pace was slow and the exertion required to push through the snow in an inferior human form was both frustrating and exhausting for Kasha. She longed to transform back to a waheela and effortlessly cover the remaining distance to Gastown. The restriction of being human sapped Kasha's energy, and she felt her other senses diminish too. She had a vague feeling of the right direction to Gastown, but she could not be sure. It would be easy to lose perspective in the tree covered landscape, known as the *Viorlanda* in the common tongue, and *Snacoilltean* in the language of her father, and wander in circles.

Kasha could no longer see the burning homestead haus behind her, but with little wind the smoke pushed up in a steady plume, both a warning and a magnet to those in the surrounding areas. Curious feline creatures would investigate, canines would keep away. Humans would do one or the other depending on their dominant animal nature. Kasha questioned her decision in making a funeral pyre and perhaps she should have simply buried the bodies in the snow, for the ice hogs to find and consume. She had made her choice, and again she needed to own the consequences.

As a waheela, Kasha could cover vast distances with only a mouthful of snow for sustenance. As a human, she needed to take breaks, eat on the trek, and ensure her pace did not result in too much sweating, which would sap her body heat and lead to freezing later. For the next few nights, she would sleep out in the open, with only a small fire for warmth and

CHAPTER FOUR

security, and the dangers the light exposure brought.

Kasha traveled as best she could through the snow and ice without any recognizable path. She followed some of the animal trails for easier passage when she could, always making sure to keep heading in a southerly direction. Based on her training, though there were no discernable landmarks to confirm it, she guessed she was somewhere between the disputed lands of the Nechtana and Fidacha, two of the seven tribes who made up the Cathulla people of the north. At present, there was an uneasy peace between the tribes, but hostilities over disputed hunting grounds were not unusual. The Nechtana suffered the most from the incursions of the homesteaders, who were always spreading north, though the massacre of settlers in retaliation was a thing of the past.

Kasha tried to ration herself with the supplies she had looted from the homestead family. However, she could not run on an empty belly the way she did as a waheela, and after ten more lunars of hard travel she was feeling the impact. She either had to pause for some time and lay out traps, or find another source of sustenance. The decision was made for her when she spotted a campfire in the distance.

She observed them closely and determined the numbers before she made up her mind to approach. It was always a risk in the Wildlands, and a group of men could be more savage than any beast. There were four of them in plain sight. One was tending something roasting over the fire, and the thought of fresh meat made Kasha salivate. Another was scraping a skin stretched between a frame clean of fat, while he chatted with a companion who was smoking meat. The final member of the group was collecting wood for the fire.

Kasha knew from the style of their clothing and the way they worked, they were not homesteaders, and for that she was grateful. She would have better luck with her own people, whose customs were more geared towards hospitality. The predominance of wolfskins indicated Nechtana, but she would not know for sure until she got closer.

Kasha knew she had to take a chance, and trust they were respecters of the old lore, men who still honored Tornar MacLorn and his forebears.

She stood up and advanced towards the camp, removing her snow goggles and head covering, and holding her sword and axe upside down by the handle indicating she came in peace.

The four men immediately stopped what they were doing and spread out in a half circle in front of Kasha. Three of them were armed with small hunting bows, and the one working the meat over the fire held a knife.

As Kasha got closer, she recognized the old man in the middle, and a smile broke across her face. It was Uradec from the Nechtana, who was out hunting with his sons and grandsons.

"Greetings, Uradec MacConnal. Permission to enter your camp," Kasha said.

The old man smiled when he recognized Kasha, and his eyes almost disappeared amongst the wrinkles of his ancient, tattooed face. He was still out hunting and teaching his offspring, when most men his age were either nursed by granddaughters, or buried within stone mounds.

"Greetings, Kasha NicTornar. You've grown since we last met. Enter!"

"You can tell your son Maelchron to come in too. He must be cold out there," Kasha said.

Uradec laughed, and waved to the fifth member of the party to abandon his guard position behind Kasha and join his family in the camp.

While most of the Nechtana gave Tornar a wide berth, Uradec was a believer in the old ways, and love for his true lord ran deep. The same could not be said for at least one of his sons. However, as long as the old man was head of the family, his word guided them. Uradec also had a mischievous nature.

"We have a fine snow fox on the spit, and a leg of it is yours, Kasha. But first, how about a wrestling match?"

Kasha knew she could not refuse, and a friendly bout for the amusement of the old man was a small price to pay.

"With you, Uradec? I suspect I'm no match for your tricks," Kasha said.

Uradec laughed. "Not I. My grandson Taran needs all the practice he can get."

As Kasha removed her bearclaws, put her pack on the ground, and stripped off her outer furs, Uradec's two sons used branches to make a circle in the snow to act as the wrestling ring.

Uradec's oldest grandson, Taran, stood across the ring from Kasha. He was significantly shorter than her, though roughly the same age, and did not display the same musculature. However, he was lithe and strong from a life in the Wildlands. The two combatants crouched down, and scooped up handfuls of snow, which they tossed behind them as an offering. Then Taran charged.

Kasha was waiting for him, and scooped him up and threw him out of the ring with more brute force than skill. As Taran landed on his back in a snow pile, Uradec slapped his knee and roared with laughter.

"Best of three," Uradec said.

Taran dusted off the snow, and faced off against Kasha once more. This time there was no reckless charge, but a locking up of arms and a test of strength. Kasha was surprised by how strong her adversary was, but after rocking back and forth for a few moments, she took advantage of her long arms, wrapped them around his back, and threw him to the ground.

Uradec was enjoying himself, and laughed at his grandson's discomfort.

"Did I say best of three? I meant best of five," Uradec said. "Last one, I promise. Let's see if you can keep your feet this time, Taran!"

Once again the two wrestlers squared off, and Taran employed the same tactics as before. He came in slowly and locked up. This time, when Kasha went to throw him, he grapevined his leg around hers, and prevented the throw. At that moment, his younger brother Garthnac decided it was a good idea to enter the ring, and charged into the battling duo to knock them both off their feet.

Uradec laughed so hard he almost choked, and one of his sons had to pound on his back so he could breathe,

"Enough! I've had too much fun for one solar. Time to eat," he said when he could finally talk.

Kasha tarried with the Nechtana for two solars, and ate more than her fair share of fresh meat at Uradec's insistence. Then, loaded down with a heavy store of dried meat, she thanked them for their hospitality, bade them farewell, and continued with the southward journey to Gastown.

Kasha traveled ten more solars, and covered a lot more distance in her solo trek. She had not spent as much time alone as a human, and she enjoyed putting the lessons she learned from Tornar into practice. She was more than capable of surviving by herself whether as a waheela or as a woman. However, she still had far to go, and there was always danger close by.

The solar was already close to setting and she needed to hunker down for the night. Just ahead there was a small hillock dominated by an old ironwood tree and a few subordinate seedlings, and Kasha decided this spot was as good as any for her base camp.

At the foot of the tree, Kasha removed her bearpaws, and used one of them to clear away the top snow until the bare hard earth beneath was exposed. She opened her backpack, took out a loose fur, and placed it on the ground. It would offer some comfort and protection against the frozen terrain. Next, she gathered fallen branches, though most were damp and would smoke before burning. However, with a little tinder and some luck she had enough to get a fire started.

Kasha sat with her back against the tree, and warmed her hands in front of the little fire. Her waheela fear of the flame had diminished and she felt the deep-seated human need for the heat it offered. She also craved warm food, a pot of bubbling broth, or a hunk of meat sizzling in a pan, hot stewed stone fruits, or even an assortment of boiled vegetables, rather than the raw meat, organs, bone, marrow, and hide she had consumed roaming free in the wildland. As a waheela, when night fell, the hunting began. Now, she bundled up as best she could, with feverish thoughts traversing across her brain. She was exhausted from the long trek, but sleep would not come.

The howls came. One or two in the distance, then more close by. They answered each other, passing signals swirling back and forth around the hillock, the ironwood tree, and Kasha. They knew she was there, crouched against the tree and behind her small fire. Her scent drifted miles and their eyesight was keen. One human all alone was worth the risk, both as a meal and retribution.

Kasha heard them moving through the snow, but she could not see them yet, and they had the advantage there too. From the barks and growls she knew they were wolves and not direwolves, which brought some sense of relief. At least she had a chance. She threw more wood on the fire to keep it burning bright, and picked up her axe and sword in each hand. She thought about removing her clothes and changing back into a waheela. It would certainly take the wolfpack by surprise, and it brought on a smile. However, she knew the time for that had passed. The transformation would take too long, and she would be completely helpless and at the mercy of the pack. She had no choice but to fight with axe and sword rather than fangs and claws. However, fight she would.

Kasha steeled herself for the conflict ahead, and she would let the wolves know who they challenged. As a shapeshifter she was also cursed with battle madness and the rage came with a rush of hot blood to her head, and bone and muscle and sinew readied for combat. Froth formed at the corners of her mouth and the white of her eyes streaked red. She inhaled deeply and let out a tremendous roar. She was ready for combat and death.

Chapter Five

The Slager Wedding

The transformation of Mo Dickens's meat emporium was almost complete. Although he had very little to do with the decorative touches, he had supervised the movement of his precious slager table, the massive woodblock put together from three mighty ironwood trees. The blud from a multitude of carcasses stained the wood like a sacrificial slab, and though he was very proud of his trade, and his status as Hetman within the slager community, he agreed to move it to one side and cover it over for this one, very special occasion. All to please Jojo and his very pregnant daughter.

JoJo Dickens moved with a steady purpose. She pushed, shoved, and cajoled her army of conscripted helpers to sweep up the old rushes, and put down fresh flooring, remove all the cobwebs from the eaves, scrub the walls clean of dried blud, and generally wash the place out from top to bottom. It was not just the huge chamber which received special attention, the large courtyard was spruced up too. Mo Dickens's apprentices grumbled at all of the work, but they knew a tremendous feast awaited them on the other end of all of the cleaning, so they muscled up and kept the complaints to a minimum, and outside of Jojo's aural range.

Juan Grimm stepped back and marveled at the decor with his one good eye. It had been two lunar cycles since the Dandy's stick sword reduced his sight by half and he was still getting used to the patch he wore, and the

CHAPTER FIVE

drastic change in his vision. The journey back to Mo's slagerhaus had been a tough one, and Carlos had in turn carried and dragged him back to their Four Kith sanctuary. Mo was nothing if not practical, and a ragged boy with a seeping eye socket, and a heavy touch of fever, was not an asset. He could easily have ended up in one of the canals, cast out and abandoned to his own fate. The saving grace was the billee flesh they brought back for Jojo. Despite the trials and tribulations of the return journey, Juan held onto it, stuffed inside his shirt and out of sight of the thieves and vagabonds who would kill for some meat to enrich their rotten vegetable and bean diet. They surrendered the carcass to Mo, Juan pulling it out of his shirt and holding it up triumphantly by the neck, before collapsing in a heap against his brother. Mo nodded his approval, proud of the sacrifice they had made for the sweet meat, an eye for a billee, and Jojo's motherly instincts kicked in as she tended to the wounded boy and nursed him back to health.

The decorations were a wonder to behold for the Grimm boys. It was like a FaderNord celebration with the mistletoe and goose feast of legend, the dab reckoning when newborns were plunged into the canal and life began, and the overgang when folks of status were returned to the earth fathers. Bundled together they made for one very special slager wedding. Fresh greenery was purchased from the tree traders, and skillfully wrapped from the beams to resemble living foliage. The best chalk artists were hired to decorate the walls with scenes of the old four seasons, before the winter chill permanently descended on their world. The Yule hunt dominated the wall where the great fireplace resided. Giant poro raced across the snow covered landscape, chased by mighty hunters in bearskins, and semi-tamed wolves as their companions. A gargantuan snow bear watched from a distance, high up on a mountain peak. No hunter ventured up there. A herd of wooly mamonts crashed through the snow trees, making their own clearing through the ancient purplewoods. Skovenmen, the wild watchers of the forest, observed them from their tree nests.

There were wonderful smells too. Jojo hired the best cooks in the Four Kith to man the kitchen and fire pits set up in the courtyard. Mo's best blud sausages, golden ducks, delicious stewed snow hares, slabs of poro ribs, spit roasted boars, and a mountain of savory meat pies, all added together to overwhelm the senses and tantalize the taste buds. There were pots of boiling potatoes, and enough steamed fresh carrots and cabbage to feed all of Gastown. The fare from the cold ocean waters were well represented too. Not the slimy bottom feeders once common to the canals, but deeper species: smoked lampreys, jellied silver eels, and cod pies. The chefs and their helpers, large women with meaty arms swinging cleavers, and slender men with dexterous knife skills, manned the stations, each working on their own version of deliciousness. A mountain of fresh baked brood and aged cheeses were delivered from the Burghs at a truly exorbitant price. Bottles of wine were there for the special guests, treacle grog for those in between, and barrel upon barrel of the finest black bier was on tap for the rest of the imbibers.

The denizens of the Four Kith came too. They were not allowed access to the courtyard, and Mo's hired guards ensured they did not block the entranceway. But smelling the banquet was free, and they huddled in small groups, driving themselves crazy with descriptions of the food, and how it would fill their meat deprived bellies. Drool filled every mouth. One man could not stand it. The aromas highlighted what he could never have, and he ran screaming to the nearest canal, jumped in, and disappeared from sight. No one gave him a second thought as the slager's feast held center stage.

It was a truly special day for Mo and Jojo Dickens. Their only daughter was about to leave the nest and they were seeing her off in style. Josie Dickens, soon to be Josie Heap, was a pleasant, comely girl in her own way. Being the offspring of Mo and Jojo, she was a big-boned lass with most of her teeth, but she still had some shape to her, at least before the ninth lunar swelling set in. Josie's main weakness was getting horizontal with her father's older apprentices, and one such excursion led to her current predicament. It was obvious to everyone, even Juan with his one eye, but no one said a word. A wedding was quickly arranged, but not with any of the lowly apprentices, that would not do for the Hetman of the Slagers' daughter. In the end, Mo found a suitable groom from one of the other slager families, and paid a small fortune for the dowry. Samwell Heap was a good match for Josie, more by accident than by design. He was a big man with strong arms, simple tastes, a heart of gold, and a forgiving nature. While Josie talked, Samwell listened. When asked for advice, he would simply tap the side of his nose and say 'Samwell thinks that be a grand idea,' followed by a knowing wink. There was not an original thought in his head, but he could swing a meat cleaver with singular purpose as well as any slager.

The Heap family arrived in fine style. Their slagerhaus was to the north end of the Four Kith, and too far to walk, which would have been Jobson Heap's choice. But their finery would have been compromised with a trek across canals and with mud under foot, and Mrs. Jobson Heap would hear none of it. She was a thin, wisp of a woman, but her voice preceded her by at least four blocks. Some said she spoke so loudly because Jobson Heap was stone deaf. Others said she made him that way. The old couple doted on one another, and their only son, though thick as a mason's stone, was a happy addition to the trio as they disembarked from the horse drawn carriage Mo Dickens so graciously provided as a means of luxurious transport. It was not every solar they rode in such grandeur, and Mrs. Heap positively beamed under her beak of a nose as she greeted Jojo Dickens.

"LOVELY PLACE, YOU 'AVE 'ERE, MRS. DICKENS. POSITIVELY LOVELY!" Mrs. Heap roared.

Jojo took a step back at the stentorian power of the little woman's voice, but quickly recovered her poise, and embraced her role as hostess.

"I'm glad you like it, Mrs. Heap. We do try to keep up appearances," Jojo said.

One of the apprentices, whose hair was slicked back with hog grease for the occasion, and was to act as page for the Heaps, snickered at how posh Jojo tried to sound as she forced the pronunciation of every syllable. A sharp elbow to the ribs from Jojo knocked the air out of him and reminded him apprentices should be seen and not heard.

"Welcome to our little slagerhaus and abattoir. Please do come this way,"

Jojo said with a little curtsy she had practiced all week, and followed by a delicate sweep of the arm and flick of the wrist indicating the direction.

Mrs. Heap appreciated the gesture and prepared to follow. The show was lost on her husband. Ever the professional slager, he was carefully studying the layout of the courtyard, checking out the sheds where the wagons were stored, and counted the number of apprentices Mo Dickens had on hand.

"Mr. Heap. Shall we?" Jojo asked, but Jobson Heap was oblivious, lost in his world of slager comparisons.

"JOBSON!" Mrs. Heap bellowed, and everyone stopped working, and turned to look at her.

Jobson turned and looked at his wife. "Did you say something, dear?"

"INSIDE. NOW!" Mrs. Heap screeched, causing Jojo to cover her ear closest to the thunderous voice.

"Ah, yes. Inside. Yes, we're interested in seein' inside," Jobson said. "Samwell, lead on ole chap."

Samwell scratched the side of his nose. "Samwell thinks that be a grand idea," he said, and winked at Jojo, who positively blushed.

The party of four, dressed in their finest garb, entered the inner courtyard, through a double line of spruced up apprentices, and on inside the main building. Jojo beamed as she took in the decor as if for the first time. There was a large fire burning in the oversized hearth, and it accentuated all of the wondrous decorations. This was one slager wedding people would be talking about for a generation, and she promised herself she would give Mo some special attention when it was all said and done for making it all possible.

Pews were lined up on either side facing the grand hearth at the front, and JoJo led her guests forward and over to the right hand side. The Heaps nodded to their family and friends who were already in attendance. Most of them had walked, and mud splattered the lower parts of their clothing. Samwell stopped more than once to greet a friend, and receive a hearty congratulatory slap on the back.

The army of apprentices filed into the slagerhaus and took their

CHAPTER FIVE

appointed seats on the opposite side of the Heap entourage. Juan and Carlos, like all of the apprentices, wore matching uniforms Jojo had created for the occasion, with Mo's haus symbol, two large cleavers crossed over a bloody boar's head, emblazoned on their left chest. None of them appreciated the cold water bath they were forced to take while the solar was still sleeping, but a hearty breakfast of brood, cheese and a blud sausage promised more fare to come.

A band of five musicians entertained the guests while they waited for the bride and her father, who were fashionably late. They played local favorites like, *The Slager's Breakfast*, *The Mudlark's Revenge*, *Molly Slopped a Dandy*, and *The Trollop Ate My Sausage*, and everyone looked forward to hearing, *The Slager's Wedding March* after the bride and groom completed their vows and Four Kith kissed to seal the deal.

The wedding crowd grew restless as they waited for Mo and Josie to appear. Jojo fretted something had gone wrong and chatted nervously with the Creation Mother who would perform the ceremony to unite the Dickens and Heaps in blessed matrimony.

The band saw them first—it helped to have a watcher in the courtyard signal to them—and immediately shifted to playing, *She's On Her Way At Last*, the traditional tune to indicate the future Mrs. Josie Heap was finally present, and the wedding was about to get under way. All chatter stopped and heads swiveled to observe father and daughter waltz down the aisle. Mo Dickens was overcome with joy, and smiled like a barking mad parent. The best outfitter the Burghs had to offer, tailored a fine suit out of an immense amount of cloth. Mo's Haus Dickens emblem was proudly on display too, and dominated the left side of his garment. He wore a heavy leather belt around his waist, which contained the tools of his trade, his mighty cleavers, which were positioned so he could cross draw them from their holsters. He also sported a heavy gold chain around his neck, and a gold cleaver at the end of it, signaling his authority as Hetman of the Slagers.

Josie, dressed from head to toe in the finest cream lace, waddled next to her father. Since she was so heavy with child, the journey to the blazing hearth took so long, and the band had to repeat, *She's On Her Way At Last*.

"OH, SHE'S POSITIVELY LOVELY!" Mrs. Heap said in a stage whisper, which they could hear all the way at the back of the abattoir.

Samwell Heap stood beside the hearth and ignored the blazing heat. He only had eyes for Josie, and the smile never left his simple face as she slowly closed the distance between them. Once father and daughter reached the front aisle, Mo took his place next to JoJo, and Josie stood facing Samwell. She was sweating a lot for a big lass, and the stains already appeared under her armpits. The heat from the fire did not help, and she took a glove and wiped away the perspiration from her brow.

The Creation Mother had a story to tell. The same story for all slager weddings. It centered on man and woman's need of meat for sustenance, and how the animals of this world were to be respected for giving up their flesh. It also extolled the skills of the first slager, and how he fashioned the original cleaver from flint. His skill at butchery was passed down through the ages, and now resided with the Hetman of the Slagers. It was a fine story, and one Mo Dickens never tired of hearing. He had a fine lineage, all the way back to creation.

"Touch hands, please," the Creation Mother said to Samwell and Josie.

The happy couple did just that. Samwell's hands were hard, scarred and warm. Josie's were flaccid and wet, though Samwell did not mind. He was in love and could ignore all of Josie's imperfections and indiscretions, large and small.

"Samwell Toppington Heap, slager by trade, name, and choice. Do you take Josie Prudence Dickens as the woman to bake your brood, cook your sausage, warm your bed, and raise your flock?"

There were a few snickers at the last remark, as the flock was already underway and the first sheep was a black one.

"Samwell thinks that be a grand idea," Samwell said, and winked at the Creation Mother.

"A simple yes will suffice," she replied with a scowl.

"Simple yes," Samwell said, which also drew some snickers. The Creation Mother let it pass and moved on.

CHAPTER FIVE

"Josie Prudence Dickens, Hetman's daughter. Do you take Samwell Toppington Heap as the man to slager your meat, mix your mustard, eat your brood, and raise your flock by hand?"

"Simple yes," Josie said, taking a leaf from her soon-to-be husband's uncomplicated book.

The Creation Mother groaned inside, before turning to face Mo Dickens. Mo Dickens. Hetman of the Slagers. Do you agree?"

"I do indeed," Mo said. He had practiced his lines all week, and was picture perfect.

The Creation Mother turned to face Jobson Heap. "Jobson Heap. Head of Haus Heap. Do you agree?"

Jobson looked confused. "Take a knee?" He turned to face his wife. "Why's she askin' me to take a knee?"

"AGREE, YOU DEAF OAF," Mrs. Heap said.

"Oh, agree. Yes, yes, of course I agree," Jobson Heap said.

The Creation Mother moved on, happy to get the ceremony completed before someone else said something stupid. There was only one final act left, and she hoped it went as smoothly as possible. More than one slager wedding had terminated because of a final mishap. She reached behind her, and took a small frying pan from the fire. It contained one blud sausage, handmade by Samwell Heap himself. She stabbed a fork into it, and nodded her head with satisfaction as a clear liquid oozed out over the three prongs.

"Step closer, please," she said to the bride and groom, and when they did so, she placed the hot blud sausage in both of their mouths. Josie was smart, and held it between her teeth, but Samwell wrapped his lips around it and burnt himself. To his credit, he did not let it drop from his mouth. That would have been a very bad omen.

"With this blud sausage, made by the hand of Samwell Toppington Heap himself, I call on all of you as witness to the sharing of the sacred meat. Let them meet in the middle and share as like does with like."

Josie was hungry with all of the waiting around, and she started noshing on the sausage before the Creation Mother had finished talking. The blud sausage was meant to be devoured equally, but Josie was never much of a one for sharing, and her greed got the better of her. She chewed her way through the meat, congealed blud, and barley like a boar with a truffle. Samwell did not mind. He slowly chewed from his end, and would reach Josie in the middle regardless of how long his end of the sausage actually was. And meet they did. With one final snap, Josie took the last bite, and their greasy lips locked to seal the union. The abattoir erupted with cheers as Haus Dickens and Haus Heap celebrated a successful merger.

There was only one last thing to do. Samwell and Josie Heap locked arms, Josie still chewing on her mouthful of sausage, and the two fathers formed up behind them, followed by the mothers. They took three steps forward in unison, and then one step back, which they continued down the aisle. As they passed each pew, the guests formed up behind them, as the whole congregation moved down the aisle and into the courtyard where food and refreshments waited. The band played, *The Slager Wedding March* as accompaniment, and the Creation Mother, happy her role was completed, drank heartily from a tankard of hot grog she had sequestered to the side of the great fireplace.

The slager wedding feast was everything Mo Dickens's apprentices hoped for and more. While the guests ate snacks of potted eels, skewered shrimp, and snow hare pies, and quaffed their way through copious barrels of ale, the apprentices picked up and stacked the pews to one side. They carried out long tables from one of Mo's abundant storehauses, placed them as Jojo had directed, and covered them with the blud red cloths. The table decorations followed next, thistle and vine, and flowers from the greenhaus, the like most folks had not seen in this lifetime. Silver plates and silver knives, forks, and spoons were carefully laid out and then it was time for the feast to begin in earnest.

The Master of Ceremonies, a tall skinny man with a pronounced stoop, a mostly bald head with long, loose strands smeared over the top, an eagle beaked nose, and a uniform with large red balls in place of buttons, bashed on a gong to let everyone know it was time to take their seats. The Happy Heaps went first to the head table, closely followed by their respective parents who sat on either side of them. The rest of the guests filed in and

CHAPTER FIVE

took their seats at the long tables running parallel to the head table. Once everyone was seated, the food arrived.

There were gasps from the wedding guests, and a lot of drooling from the apprentices as platter after hot platter was brought in and placed on the tables. The first dishes were devoured completely as folks could not believe their good fortune at the amount of meat on display. Once they realized the bounty was not slowing down, they started to pace themselves and actually chewed their food.

Juan and Carlos gorged themselves along with the other apprentices. They had promised each other to eat until they exploded, and were well into their third platter and showing no signs of slowing down. Carlos did not seem to mind what he ate as long as his mouth was full. Juan was a little more discerning and selected his food with a degree of care. His particular favorite was a large snow goose, roasted to perfection, and stuffed with a delicious sweet meat. It took five apprentices to take one down, and Juan marveled at the fact Mo Dickens had one for himself. The Hetman threw the mangled carcass to one side and moved on to a thick rack of poro ribs covered in a rich, hot red sauce.

Snow goose and poro ribs were followed by large blud sausages; whole fish the size of Josie Heap and baked inside a layer of salt; towers of snow hares which the guests plucked off with knives; and an open boar's head for every table, with the cooked brains available to scoop out. Rivers of wine and lakes of ale added to the general merriment and growing inebriation.

The Master of Ceremonies banged his gong again and brought a pause to the gastronomic extravaganza. All eyes went to the head table and Mo Dickens. It was time for the Hetman of the Slagers to speak. With knives and forks in hand, the guests banged the butts on the table in a steady rhythm with the rumble increasing until Mo held up his hands for silence. Everyone stopped but one.

There was a loud slow rhythmic clapping from the back of the room, one heavy hand making solid contact with the other. The sound echoed through the converted slaughterhaus and bounced off the rafters. All heads turned in the direction to see who had the audacity to interfere with Mo's pending speech.

Cotter Sullivan was a huge man. A tad shorter in height than Mo Dickens, but in terms of sheer bulk he was the equivalent of three ordinary men compressed together. His legs were thin and did not seem capable of supporting such a huge girth, but he was surprisingly nimble on his feet for such a gargantuan human being. Whereas Mo was old hard knotted muscle, Cotter was flab. He was a corpulent monstrosity with deviant tastes. He generally surrounded himself with a harem of small boys and some of them were with him today. They were in the front line, and behind them was a small army of Bully Boys. They were Cotter Sullivan's band of thugs, angry men with angry scars. Men who liked to inflict pain for the pleasure of it all. Men who sliced, diced, and killed when Cotter snapped his pudgy fingers.

Cotter could be charming when he wanted, but the smooth silky words came from a face which held little attraction. His tongue seemed to be a little too big for his mouth and he drooled when he talked. A large red scar running down his face did not help appearances, nor the fact he had one ear mostly missing as a result of a childhood fight with a rather ravenous opponent. His fat lips were rouged and he wore dark lining under eyes which rarely blinked and seemed to view the world as either his plaything, or something to destroy. He was malevolent, destructive, chaotic, and utterly ruthless. Like Mo Dickens he wore two slager blades at each hip. He had taken them from another slager, Dolan Macomber, in a relatively fair duel, at least according to the only witness who survived. Although it marked his entry into the slager world, most of the other butcher men did not recognize his right to be a part of the exalted fraternity of meat carvers. Few said it to his face, and Mo Dickens, although he had little regard for the man, was a stickler for the rules and regulations. He carried the blades, so he was an insider. However, it did not give him the right to gatecrash the slager wedding.

"What do you want 'ere, Cotter? You an' your kind aren't welcome, is all," Mo Dickens growled.

The sickly smile did not leave Cotter's face. He pulled a pink handkerchief soaked in lavender from his pocket and took a long sniff, before replacing it.

"I do luv a gud weddin'. Don't we luv a gud weddin' boys?" Cotter asked his crew. They all nodded their heads with enthusiasm. "But we didn't cum for the weddin'. No wez 'ave other things to attend to today." Drool ran from the corner of Cotter's mouth and he wiped it away with the back of his hand.

"What do you want, Cotter? Say your piece, an' leave," Mo said.

The smile finally left Cotter's face, and he pointed a finger directly at Mo. "I cum to challenge yuz, Mo Dickens. It be time the slagers 'ave a new Hetman, an' that man be me!" he shouted as he banged a hand on his own chest.

There was a loud gasp from Jojo. It was every slager's right to challenge Mo for the Hetman title. She knew the day would come and Mo had the opportunity to step aside or fight to the death to keep his position. She knew he would never step aside for the likes of Cotter Sullivan. Not in this world, or the next.

"It's a fight, yuz want, is it Cotter? Mo said.

"Yuz can always slink away into the night, if yuz want, like one of my boys after I've bent 'im over. But Cotter Sullivan would rather the blades did the talkin'."

"Then talkin' there shall be! Are yuz up for it, Cotter Sullivan?" Mo thundered, and stepped up on the wedding table. He reached down and pulled both slager cleavers from their sheaths. They were supremely polished and razor sharp, and they gleamed in the light from the fire. "Move back the tables boys. Give us room for this merry dance!"

Mo's apprentices went to work quickly, and ushered all of the guests to the sides of the great abattoir. They lifted the heavy tables and moved them back, creating an inner courtyard for the contestants. There was a buzz of excitement amongst the guests. They had not seen a death match for the Hetman of the Slagers in quite some time. Mo's transition was peaceful and expected. This one would leave one man dead and the other possibly mutilated for life.

Mo jumped down from the table and landed in the makeshift arena. Cotter stepped forward and unsheathed his own mighty cleavers. There was no fear in either man, and no onset of bloodrush madness. Cotter did drool, but it was not the froth at the mouth of a lunatic. Both men were calm, experienced killers. Mo did not necessarily enjoy it, but it was part of his trade and he went about it with ruthless efficiency. Cotter was equally efficient, but there was also a heavy association with pleasure. He enjoyed inflicting pain, and the power it gave him over others.

The men circled each other looking for an opening. There were a couple of feints, but no bites. They kept moving in this fashion, until Mo decided to change things up. He stopped moving on the outside and took a direct line at Cotter, both blades swinging. Cotter stepped up to the challenge and met Mo's onslaught with his own whirring blades. Sparks flew as metal made contact with metal. Two blades stuck together for a moment, biting into each other's metallic flesh, until the combatants pulled them apart. They stepped back and then in again, cleavers clashing. Mo's right blade made it through Cotter's defenses and took a slice out of Cotter's bicep. Blood flowed, but it did not slow Cotter down. Cotter's own right blade made it through next and caught Mo a glancing blow in the chest, enough to cut through his uniform and hack into the muscle below. Mo grunted, but it was the only outward sign he was hurt.

Both men were breathing hard now, but they continued to step in and swing at each other. Blows landed on both sides, blows strong enough to bring an ordinary man down, but not these two monstrous slagers. Blood flowed and mingled on the floor. The viscous liquid made holding the blades harder, as both men tightened their grips. Mo took another strike to the chest, deeper this time, and enough to temporarily lock Cotter's blade into muscle. Mo used the opportunity to swing his own blade in a wide arc and sink it into Cotter's upper arm. Flesh and fat came away, and Cotter lost his grip on his blade. Mo swung again, and this time he sliced Cotter's left thumb clean off. It lay on the flood in a pool of blood like a discarded drumstick.

Cotter stepped back, his left arm hanging useless at his side, and his

CHAPTER FIVE

hand bleeding profusely from the chasm of a wound where his thumb once resided. Mo used the temporary lull to put both his blades in his right hand and pulled Cotter's blade from his own chest with his left hand. There was a brief sucking noise as the blade came free, followed by a gush of blood. Mo did not hesitate, and with a swing of his mighty arm and flick of his wrist, he turned the slager blade into a projectile straight back at its previous owner. It was not clear if Cotter saw the blade coming his way, but he moved on instinct, and it sailed on past and into one of the wooden pillars where it stuck home with a tremendous thud.

Mo moved in for the kill. His adversary was badly wounded and it was only a matter of time before he caught up with him and delivered the death blow. He would not rush it, or take his time either, but two blades would triumph over one. Mo stepped in, slower this time, hampered by the wounds in his chest which were beginning to tighten up. There was less power behind his swings now, and Cotter could parry them away with his singular blade.

Cotter now relied on his movement, and guile. He would not challenge Mo's fight and die. That was not part of his plan.

"Bones, boys, bones! Bloody bones, greasy bones. Bones, bones, bones!" Cotter shrieked.

The wedding crowd thought Cotter had truly gone mad, and they waited expectantly for his demise. But Cotter's Bully Boys knew what their leader was shouting about, and they quickly went to work. They grabbed trays from the tables, and the boxes holding the discarded remnants from the feasting. They upended them on the floor, and pushed, threw and kicked them all across the arena. Cotter grinned and Mo frowned.

Cotter moved like a dancer. It was amazing to watch a blubbery giant perform with such grace. His left arm hung useless at his side, and he gushed blood with every step, but he glided in and out between the bones, never stepping on a single one. He twirled around Mo, taking delicate slices of flesh, or deeper cuts of meat with every turn. Mo grunted, and took his blows and strikes with stoic determination. He had only one single minded goal, the utter destruction of Cotter Sullivan. He would end his life forever, carve up his corpulent carcass and feed it to the bottom feeders in the Basin.

Mo was not light on his feet, he took heavy measured steps, and tried to ensure he had a firm connection to the ground before he moved on. It generally worked for him, but not this time. Cotter was just out of reach, and he had to chase him. He saw what he thought was an opening and he overcommitted. His next step landed firmly on top of a greasy snow goose carcass and his feet slid out from under him. He landed on his back with a heavy thud, and the back of his head cracked heavily against the stone floor. Blood oozed from his broken head, and in all likelihood, he was already dead. Cotter stepped forward to make sure. He swung his slager chopper in a vicious arc and embedded the blade deep into Mo's skull and into his brain. Life ended there for Mo Dickens, former Hetman of the Slagers.

Cotter reached down and took the blades from Mo Dickens's lifeless hands one at a time, and gingerly placed them in his own sheaths. He then removed his own blade from Mo's head, and proceeded to hack his way through the neck and sever the head of his opponent. He took the Hetman of the Slager's heavy gold chain, the symbol of his new authority, and placed it with some difficulty around his own neck, and then held up the head of Mo Dickens for all to see.

"Mo Dickens is no more! I'm the Hetman of the Slagers. Does anyone in this hall dispute that?" Cotter roared. He turned Mo's head to face him. "What do you have to say about that, Mo Dickens? Nothin'? Billee got ya tongue?"

Cotter spat a mouthful of blood into Mo's dead face, and then dropped the head and kicked it like a football across the room. It rolled to stop directly below Jojo's seat at the table. She stared down at it in disbelief, and then burst into tears. Mo's life was over, and her life was about to change and not for the better.

"As the victor, Iz claim my prize," Cotter said. "By rights, Iz can claim the Hetman's wife." He looked over at Jojo. "But no one would want to use that ole hag. It's the streets for 'er, and no one to lift a finger of 'elp, do yuz 'ear?"

He turned his attention to the heavily pregnant Josie Heap, who had collapsed against her husband's side. Samwell wrapped a protective arm around her and held her close as she cried a river.

"If not the wife, then 'ow about the daughter?"

Samwell glared at Cotter. There was no fear of the man. "Samwell thinks that not be a grand idea," Samwell said. There was no wink this time, or a knowing tap of the nostril. He was fully prepared to fight for his wife, and Cotter knew it.

Cotter shook his head. "No, not the daughter. She's a Heap now. I 'ave no quarrel with the Heaps, do yuz 'ear? So I'll take my prize elsewhere. Why, Iz think I know the very thing Iz want."

Cotter moved over to the side of the room and stood directly in front of Juan and Carlos. He looked down at both boys and smiled. A sweet sickly smile. A smile full of malice, and something else: desire. "I want that!" he said pointing at Carlos.

Carlos tried to bolt, but three of Cotter's Bully Boys were already on to him. They pinned his arms and held him firm. Juan tried to come to his twin's defense, but he was no match for the seasoned fighters who accompanied Cotter. Two of them beat him to the ground, kicked him a few times, and then dragged his unconscious body out of the hall and threw him into the courtyard.

"Now the rest of yuz, get out of my slagerhaus! My blud is up, and Iz 'ave some celebratin' to do."

Chapter Six

Chandra : The Children of the Prith

The garden was everything to Chandra and her family. Their very existence depended on it, and they toiled in it every solar, and many times into the early evening, before the light faded. Their world was a hot house, a covered environment safe from the inclement weather outside. They sweated in their garden, while the world froze all around them. If Chandra ever had the time she would stare through the glass dome and watch the snow falling. It never took hold, and instantly turned to water thanks to the steam pipes which surrounded the interior and provided the heat, and ran off into the vast tanks only to be cycled through the gardens to provide nourishment for the plants.

Chandra and her family worked this vast greenhouse with nine kindred families. Their color and code was Pacca, the base color of Mother Nature. They grew the leafy green vegetables; palakura, sweet when taken raw, sour when cooked; menthi, the bitter green leaves used to enhance the pulses; an assortment of vamuku, the sweet green sticks and a base for anything; as well as the thick pointed gourds and the long elephant tusk okra.

The other four clans consisted of the Erupu, who harnessed the power of the red vegetables. Fiery in nature, in taste, and excitement. The yellow and orange variants were the domain of the Narinja, who were light in nature, and gentle in spirit. The Banda grew the root vegetables with little color and heavy sustenance. They were doughty people, brown like the earth, and the base of the Andra existence. The Preena were the exalted ones, who took care of the herb gardens and provided the necessary spices and aromatics to make everything taste so good. They were the people of the floating world, always in the clouds and above the fray. Their color was a blend of all. The five clans melded together, each necessary for the existence of the other. A melting pot of flavor, harmony, and syncopation.

Little Sri worked beside his big sister. Ever attentive to how she cleaned the leaves of her charges, delicately plucked away the weeds, and fed nutrients to the life-giving soil, which sustained them all. He copied her moves, clumsily at first, but he was learning to cope with the garden too. It would be his life's work. Always in the garden from the solar he could crawl as a child to the end of solars when he would crawl as an old man, the cycle completed. Always in servitude to the garden. And the Dux and her Telupu, the pale people, who took the best of the produce for themselves.

It was not a bad life. There were no overseers, or punishments. They worked in the gardens under their own steam, and set their own hours. Long hours. Some of the women cooked for the Dux and her folk, but always the simplest of dishes, with few aromatic spices. What the Dux considered the worst of it, was consumed by the Andra themselves. The rest was churned up, and pushed down long pipes to the common folk within the township. A green, brown slop which nourished the body, but left the soul unsatisfied.

There was no mingling with the other races. The Andra married with their own, as long as they were not from the nine kindred families, in contrast to the leaders of the Telupu who married their first cousins and paid the genetic price. Generally, they remained strong in body, but over time, their minds became addled and their souls putrefied. They also drank their water from the metal barrels, which the Andra knew to avoid. Madness in its many forms came to all in time.

Chandra knew all this from her Amma, though her father always chastised his mother for saying such things. No good would come of it. Chandra listened anyway, fascinated by the stories. The Andra were the Chosen People. The givers of life, and the keepers of the gardens. They knew nothing else. They needed nothing else.

The long whistle from the clock tower signaled the end of another solar for Gastown, and for today, an end to the fieldwork for the Andra. Chandra stood up and straightened out her back. There was only mild stiffness from hours of toiling close to the earth. The older ones took longer to smooth out their spines. For some, like her Amma, they remained closer to the earth on a permanent basis. Amma said the soil and the vegetables pulled them nearer, and they had a deeper connection after years of communing together. When Chandra talked with her grandmother these days, unless she was sitting down, it was to the top of her gray head.

Chandra looked at Sri as he coaxed a particularly strong weed out of the ground. He pulled and tugged, and dexterously manipulated his baby-sized shears. His attention was focused on his one and only task. Chandra smiled and then lightly tapped her younger brother on the shoulder. He looked up and smiled. Words never came out of his mouth, and sound never entered his ears. However, brother and sister found a way to communicate through hand gestures, and facial cues. They made do, since they knew no other way.

Today was a special solar for Chandra and her family. The Andra were a communal people, and a wedding betrothal involved all of their extended nine families, and the nine families from the Erupu. Their vegetable charges were vibrant, rich, powerful, and heated. Eating them alone caused the spirit to burn, and tempers to flare. With all things, balance was essential. The Andra mixed their vegetable colors to balance the body and harmonize the soul. However, the Erupu pushed more towards the fire, and their natural tendencies were heated. Amma said Tana, Chandra's older sister, was more suited than anyone to join with the Erupu. She was always a spirited child with a sharp tongue, and prone to disruptive behavior. Now she would be with like minded folk, who argued when calm was required, and chattered like field mice when golden silence was the order of the solar.

CHAPTER SIX

Chandra took little Sri by the hand and followed the rest of the Pacca as they walked through the narrow pathways between their vegetable patches, careful not to step on any of the plants. They stopped at the water troughs and washed the sacred dirt from their hands and simple gardening tools before following the wonderful smells of the seasoned vegetables lovingly prepared by Chandra's mother and aunts. The feast was laid out on the woven mats and everyone took their allotted place. Some of the young men ate fast, and pulled out their musical instruments; the long stringed gourd; the pots covered in stretched cloth; the carved wooden stringed instrument Challa played with a bow; and the carved flutes of various shapes and sizes. Bhram started them off by vocalizing a complex rhythm which he easily translated to his heavy drum. The others picked it up and weaved in and out of the main line. It was beautiful heady music, which made Chandra want to dance. She started to get up, but her Amma pulled her back down to the ground.

"Eat first, child. Food for the body before food for the soul," Amma said.

Chandra did as she was told, and scooped up some palakura with a piece of her mother's wonderful bread, and popped it into her mouth. While she chewed she stared at her grandmother. She looked especially frail today, worn down by life in the gardens, and the dance of time. She was the oldest of the Andra, and yet even she had not experienced the voyage from the motherland. She knew the old tales, but they were handed down from her mother. She could recite the history of the Andra all the way back to Malaya and the *Great Flood*. Chandra loved the old stories and devoured them as quickly as she ate her evening meal. However, she especially loved the story of the *Great Journey*, and the time the Andra had given up their homeland and migrated to the gardens of Varstad and their present life.

"Why are you looking at me like that, child? I'm not ready for my ashes to mix with the River of Life just yet," Amma said as she spooned mashed vanga into her toothless mouth.

"Tell me about the *Great Journey* again, Amma," Chandra said.

"Oh, child. You must have heard it a hundred times already."

"Maybe a thousand," Chandra replied.

"How about the tale of the Fish God, instead?"

Chandra shook her head. *"The Great Journey*, Amma. Please?"

Chandra glanced across at her little brother, and for a moment she felt a pang of guilt. Here she was asking for stories Sri would never hear. Sri looked up at her and smiled, content in his own silent world.

"Don't worry about your brother, Chandra," Amma said, as if reading her thoughts. "He's a survivor, that one. He'll take care of you one solar."

"Blessed be that solar," Chandra said, bowing her head and putting the palms of her hands together in prayer.

Amma smiled and gently touched the top of Chandra's head. "A blessing on you, my child. The *Great Journey* it is."

A bright smile, radiating wonderment, innocence, and joy, all rolled up into one broke across Chandra's face. Amma smiled too, a toothless one, and basked in her granddaughter's beauty and youthful exuberance. Her luminous green eyes, the color she shared with her younger brother, her blossoming womanhood, and lustrous skin. Such radiance washed over her and pushed back the solar dial if only a few rays.

Chandra took hold of her Amma's wrinkled hand, and nuzzled closer. She took another guilty glance at her brother, but he was happily playing. She calmed her mind and focused on the Andra's migration tale.

We are the Chosen Ones, the Andra. Children of the Prith. The first gardeners, harvesters, and keepers of the seed. Our roots run strong, and deep. All life is sacred to us.

Our home was far far away from this cold world and the glasshouses we now occupy and nurture. It was a hot land, exposed to the elements, with long solars and short nights. The rain season was drawn out and harsh, and took many to feed the cycle, but we endured and accepted our place in the wheel.

They came from the north. Always the north. Men of violence and conquest. Men with horses, armor, and weaponry. Not life givers, but life takers. Their way was savagery and destruction. But we had one thing they craved. The thing they all crave. Our ability to grow crops and feed the people. Our work in the earthly gardens.

Like all savages, they ate the flesh of animals. But they also needed our vegetables, to feed themselves and their beasts of burden. So they needed us too. To continue with our ways, and to live for them, and to pay tribute. Tribute from the bounty of the land.

They were not the first, and not the last. We survive by the skills of our hands, and our commitment to the peaceful path. We are not a threat and we have much to offer. Such is the wheel.

We lived the cycle for many, many generations. Always adjusting with the solar, the deluge and the drought. The tribute to the north remained the same, so feast and famine were ingrained in us. Children of the Prith grow from seed, and return to feed the seed. The wheel continues.

All changed when the Black Ships arrived. We'd never seen such vessels before. They were much larger than the local craft which only ventured on the rivers, or the warships of the Northmen. They had sails, but they also moved swiftly through the waters even when the winds were calm.They bristled with weapons, and fired a salvo from their large cannons, which popped out of small doors on the side of the ship. This was both an announcement of their arrival, and a warning. The noise was deafening, and we covered our ears and instinctively cowered closer to the Prith.

The people of the Black Ships came to trade with the people of the north for cloth, porcelain, fine wares from the east, and precious metals. And then people. They were especially interested in us, but we didn't know the reason why. They observed us in the field, the tall Damm Warriors and their red soldiers, the workers who always scurried across the ships, loading goods, and scrubbing decks, and the short women, the Konna, who scratched everything down in their books. Only the Dandy remained indifferent as they lounged in the shade, drinking their intoxicating beverages, laughing, shouting, and crying. They lived a life of idleness as they do here.

They suffered under our solar, and many succumbed to the heat. But they didn't return the ashes to the Prith. Instead they took them back to their ships, wrapped in cloth, and preserved for a long journey. At least for the Damm Warriors, the Dandy, and the Konna. The lesser Telegu went over the side to feed the sea. The gods or the fish, we know not.

They sampled our produce, but not as we prepared them. Spices were not to their liking, They preferred their food simple, plain, and overcooked, with too much salt. They fed their bodies, but didn't nurture the soul, or the spirit. As a result their lives are shorter than ours. They grow tall and strong, and burn out like flaming candles.

We didn't know why they wanted us, why they came seeking. But the people were apprehensive. The elected leaders of the five clans gathered and there were heated discussions. But our ways were not of confrontation and violence, and our words were lost on the northerners. Five well spoken, and reasonable men were chosen to represent us, but they never returned. After that, we simply waited for our fate to present itself. The gardens remained, and our work continued.

We didn't have long to wait. One morning the harbor was clear, and the next the Black Ships were everywhere like beetles in the field. The men of the north were there too. Hundreds of them on their steeds, surrounding our villages. The people cried and sang songs of grief and despair.

The women with the ledgers, and the book slaves of the northern warriors worked together, walking through our villages and tallying the people. Then they separated out nine families from each of the four clans. They planned on leaving the Preena behind, but we wailed and cried, and they eventually relented. The women with the ledgers chose the young and vibrant. Older family members were left behind. Those selected gathered to one side and sang death songs through a veil of tears. Those who remained looked down at the Prith in guilt and relief.

We paid a price for leaving our elders behind. We had to recreate some of the Andra ways from memory, and rekindle stories from childhood. But the essence was the same, even if the path took detours.

The nine families of the Pacca were forced to gather only the belongings they could carry to the ships. We took bedding from our huts, spare clothes, our farm utensils, and seeds from storage. The women with the ledgers made sure to double check the earthen pots with the seeds. They were more concerned about their well-being than ours.

One man from the Erupu tried to evade his destiny. He was betrothed to marry a girl from another village and he couldn't bear the thought of leaving her behind. He didn't get very far. The Northmen speared him, and nailed his body with arms out wide to our sacred Banyan tree. His image became a symbol of our

CHAPTER SIX

exile, and the Erupu still wear the talisman around their necks.

The march from our village to the harbor was short, but took an eternity. We were leaving our homes, our families, and our way of life behind. We didn't know where we were going or why. We were loaded on the Black Ships, walking along the narrow planks two at a time. Herded on deck and stowed away in the cargo hold like animals. Only the eli snuck onboard to join us on the journey. They scurried below in the dark corners of the hold, We fed them what little we could, and ensured they stayed away from the seeds.

The Andra are people of the land, and the sea brought fear and trepidation. The constant rolling of the ships made us sick and the bad air polluted our lungs. The sea voyage was long and arduous. We had little to eat, only the food we brought with us. At least we did have the juices and fruit from the naaranga. That helped preserve our gums and teeth, and kept our blood flowing. The Telegu only permitted us on deck for short periods so we could bathe in the light of the solar. Many days there was no solar, and only stormy seas. We stayed below in the darkness, the wet, and the filth.

There were some exceptions. The short women selected a few women who were tasked with learning the common tongue of the Telupu. Not the high language of the Damm Warriors. They would be our interpreters, like your sister Tana is today, and also your chosen path. They labored long and hard, and mastered the barbaric tongue. They learned about the land of the Telupu, and the division of the people. Who to respect, fear, and dread. They did not learn why we embarked on this great sea crossing.

We lost many Andra on the Long Journey. We cried as the bodies were thrown to the sea. We had no fires to turn them to ashes and return them to the seed. They were lost to us forever, removed from the wheel.

Journeys do not come to an end, but the path changes. For many solar and lunars we were locked into the way of despair, self pity, and grief. But that is not the way of the Andra. We are a people of hope, happiness, forgiveness, and acceptance of the wheel.

We could feel the calmer waters before we saw the land. We could also feel the extreme cold. It was something we'd never experienced before. The Telegu called it ice, and snow, and the eternal winter. The intense whiteness of it froze our bodies and souls, but not our spirit. The Telegu gave us old, musky animal skins to wear against the cold. To our everlasting shame, we buried ourselves beneath them, and took what warmth we could.

The forward movement of the Black Ships stopped, and the rocking motion was different. More gentle and contained. We heard activity on the decks, heavy footsteps, cargo unloaded. Then the heavy grates above our heads were thrown open, and we were led above. A lost tribe in an unpromised land.

We'd never seen a city like it before, all stone, tarred timbers, the bustle of stores, and the putrid smell of the Telegu. Since we were locked up in the hold for too many solars, we were shadows of the Andra. But that would change in time too, as we rekindled our spirits.

The air was cold, and we could see snow on the rooftops, and ice on the water, but there was also a warmth beneath our feet. The red soldiers led us along the road from the docks up to the foreboding citadel on the hill. This was to be our home and the glass domes we occupy now. We would never see the town, the harbor, or the Black Ships again. We live our lives in gilded cages at the mercy of the Dux and the Damm Warriors.

We don't know who built the glass domes, or the people who occupied them before us. We only knew the gardens were barren, the soil was poor and void of life, and would grow little without our immediate care and attention. We had to nurture it first, before the seeds could take root.

We struggled in the beginning to make our way in this new world. But we now understood our mission. The Telegu were great warriors, and masters of trade and craft, but they were no gardeners. The menfolk of the town ate animal flesh when they could get it, but needed our vegetables and grains to sustain themselves. The womenfolk were more pure, and ate like us from the land. Spice did not appeal to them, so they consumed to survive and not to enjoy.

We knew our role, and understood our new path. The Telupu needed us to survive, and not be dependent on the food from others outside the citadel. Our long journey was one of hope and rebirth. We are the Andra. People of the Prith, and we are one with the wheel. We are gardeners, keepers of the seed, and we are blessed.

"We are blessed," Chandra said, bowing her head and putting the palms of her hands together in prayer.

Amma took a sip of water from the gourd. All of the talking parched her old throat. "Tell me, child. Why does the story of the *Long Journey* excite you so much? Most of the children shudder when they hear of it. It's a necessary tale in the existence of the Andra, but does it bring joy?"

It was not the first time her Amma asked Chandra this question, and she always struggled with a suitable answer.

"I can't really describe the feeling it invokes. I just know the story holds a special purpose for my life. I need to hear it again and again so the essence seeps into my heart, and I can bathe in the experience. I can relive the journey of our people and never forget."

Amma looked intently at her granddaughter, who blushed under her gaze.

"Why child? Wherever, did those words come from? Wisdom beyond years."

"I'm not sure I know what I said, Amma. It just came out in a rush."

"And now it's time to rush off and get ready for your sister's betrothal. Tana will need you by her side, as she makes her formal pledge to Manoj. It is never easy for a child to leave her family and join another. Especially one as fiery as the Erupu."

Chandra took her Amma's hand in her own, and pressed it to her forehead. She loved the old one with all of her heart. But as her worn hand made contact with her head, she had an ominous feeling their time together was limited. The wheel was about to turn again.

Chapter Seven

The Gut

"Do us a favor, youn' Juan and chew on this brood an' soften it up, sum. Me gums can't manage it no more," Jojo said, handing Juan an old crust she had bartered from an ancient woodcutter for a sloppy hand job.

Juan cast his one good eye at the moldy brood, shrugged his shoulders, and popped it into his mouth. It would take some softening before he could hand it back to Jojo in a form her worn gums and few remaining blackened teeth could handle.

Life had literally transformed in a heartbeat for Jojo and Juan. One glorious second they were enjoying the meats and fruits of the slager wedding and the riches afforded by close association with Mo Dickens. The next, Mo's heart stopped beating and his severed head slid across the slager floor. Lifeless eyes stared up at Jojo and everything changed. Gone was the luxury and warmth of the slager hall, with a full belly, hot toddy, and warm cuddles at the end of every solar. It was replaced by scavenging on the canal streets of the Slough, and visiting the Gut for an evening meal of lukewarm muddy slop.

The citizens of the Burghs never visited, and the denizens of the Four Kith rarely ventured into the Gut. It was the harbor of thieves, vagabonds, those down on their luck, and those who regular society no longer viewed as useful; the old and infirm who would end their solars on the street, or

CHAPTER SEVEN

tipped into the canal for the final journey to the Onderworld on Jorm the Ferryman's barge. Orphans and strays frequented the Gut. Easy pickings for the street merchants and the purveyors of flesh. Unless they bonded together and initiated their own gangs for safety sake.

JoJo Dickens gathered her own little brood of pickpockets, and Juan Grimm, being the oldest by a year or two at the ripe old age of sixteen or thereabouts, was her natural right hand. Three of the junior apprentices had joined them from Haus Dickens, ones who feared the unwanted clutches of Cotter Sullivan and his Bully Boys. Four others, including two young sisters, gravitated to them from the rank parts of the Four Kith, seeking out protection in larger numbers. JoJo, reverting to a street life before the protection of Mo Dickens, ran the little circle, directing their slender fingers to unsealed pockets, and teaching the art of cutting purse strings and lifting gold chains. It was a dangerous game with obvious risk and certain punishment. However, they shared what little coin they had, and JoJo fenced the jewelry to pawnbrokers on the lower end of the mercantile scale. Men who cared little for original ownership and bill of sale.

Jojo and Juan left the Dickens slagerhaus in haste. Juan was tossed out onto the icy cobblestones, unconscious from his Bully Boy beating, and Jojo was roughly escorted out with only her wedding clothes and nothing else. For her daughter's nuptials, she was pushed and pressed into the gown, like too much sausage filling for the casing. A few lunars on the street had changed that, and she was almost a fit. She had managed to purloin a musky old coat along the way, a patchwork of scrapings from paranga fur, which added little sartorial elegance to her street wardrobe, but it kept the cold at bay. Juan did not fare much better. His clothes were ripped and torn from his one-sided skirmish, and his bumps and bruises took some time to heal. Still, there was nothing broken, and apart from his missing eye, he was in relatively good shape for a stray, if a little on the wrong side of the starvation line. He did miss Carlos, and wondered how he was faring without a thinking twin to keep him on the straight and narrow. However, a journey back to the slagerhaus to find out risked both of their lives, and if nothing else, Carlos was a survivor.

The Heaps could not offer in-law familial assistance, forbidden to take JoJo in for fear of a full scale war with Haus Sullivan, and always respectful of the written Slager rules of engagement following a hetman change in leadership. Josie had the attention span of a fruit fly and mourned for a very short while. She soon turned her attention toward the newborn, developing a sharp tongue to point out Samwise's many unregistered faults, and maintaining her own health and wellbeing by consuming as much Haus Heap produce before it reached market. Samwise took it all in his stride. He doted on Josie and his cuckoo hatchling, and countered vitriolic suggestions on character change from Josie with "Samwise thinks that be a grand idea," and winked at his ever expanding spouse.

Life in the Gut was a serious adjustment from life in the slagerhaus. There was a degree of warmth running through the floors, but the surroundings were stark and bleak, the lighting was dim from the cheapest tallow candles, and the smell of rotten vegetable matter mingled with the stench of unwashed human flesh. Once you entered the Gut the bouquet attached to you, and marked you for what you were: a down and outer of the lower echelon; those with a dirty foot on the last rung of life's ladder.

No one really knew the origin of the name. Some said it was the bowels of the Four Kith, hence the Gut. Others said it was once a grand fish market, where the produce was fileted and the discarded innards were used for glue. The hall was vast enough to hold the fruits from the sea, but no seafood had graced the Gut in many a year, if at all. The Gut was strictly a vegetarian haus, courtesy of the Dux.

Like many functions in Gastown, there was a clockwork order to the proceedings. The slophunds of the Gut generally were not attuned to the dictates of a fourth dimension. However, they did understand the chimes at Gut time, and waited impatiently for the dinner bell to ring. They sat at simple wooden benches in front of immense wooden tables. A small wooden bowl and a wooden spoon carefully laid out in each slot.

The Slopmeister, or more officially the Etenmeister, stood at his self-designated place at the blackened steel door in the center of the west wall elevated over the unwashed patrons. The door was directly above a long chute, which started high on one side and ran down the length of the hall at a downward angle. The Slopmeister stood with his hand on a heavy lever on the door awaiting the allotted time. He was ramrod straight, with his chest puffed out, his other hand twirling an oversized waxed handlebar mustache. His chef's green toque hat was perched proudly on his head like a stuffed exotic bird, and his green apron was sharply pressed and immaculately clean. A large wooden spoon, bestowed on him by the Dux herself, stood proudly at attention from his breast pocket. It was a symbol of his culinary authority, though he never actually cooked. He fed the people by Dux largesse, an honor bestowed after years of service in the Red Shadows. Jaguar Drummel and no one else controlled the food source.

As the strong chime for etentime rang out, the slopmeister pulled on the lever to the sluice gate, and the earthy colored chunky liquid flowed down the chute to fill the trough to the brim. With a skill born from years of practice, Jaguar Drummel closed the lever at the exact moment to prevent any unnecessary overflow of the precious cargo.

"Line up you laggards, bowls in hand!" the Slopmiester bellowed, "One bowl, one scoop. No seconds on my watch!"

Only then did the ragged bodies stand up from their benches and line up along the length of the chute, all eyes on the Slopmeister for his next command. They moved as if ball and chain hindered their progression and the invisible fetters bound them together. No one pushed or shoved. The bowls held the same amount, and there was only one serving per diner. The Slopmeister's authority was unquestioned. A bark from him meant banishment from the hall, and he never forgot a face.

"Alright, my unwashed lovelies. Dip!"

At the Slopmeister's command, the front rank of the slophunds dipped their bowls in unison and filled each one to the brim with the mashed vegetables.

"Step aside, now," Jaguar Drummel barked. "Make room for the second rank. Dip!"

The Slopmeister's choreography was limited in steps but as efficient as any military maneuver. The first rank had already stepped aside and shuffled back to their benches, and the second rank moved forward and dipped their bowls on command. Before the third rank could follow suit, the Slopmeister held up a hand to pause the food line and opened the sluice gates once more to replenish the trough with more mush.

"There you go my lovelies, Only the best for you courtesy of the Dux, and don't you forget to show some appreciation. A kind word in prayer here and there never goes amiss. Now, dip!"

Jojo, Juan, and their little entourage were part of the second wave, so they took their seats on the sparse benches, grasped their spoons and prepared to tuck in. Before they began, Jojo gave Juan a sharp look, and tapped the side of her bowl. Juan played innocent for a moment, until JoJo tapped her bowl a second time with more authority. Juan leaned over and spat the softened brood crust into the vegetable stew. Jojo stirred it in, and then began to eat as if she was attending a banquet with the Dux, or was reminiscing about the slager wedding feast. She closed her eyes, took a spoonful, and smacked her lips with delight. Her charade, out of necessity or madness, made the meal more palatable.

No slophund ever claimed they enjoyed their free meal at the Gut. However, it was enough to keep them functional and sustain them for another solar of poverty and deprivation. Life in the Slough was one of survival, and a lukewarm meal kept some of the demons at bay. Without it, a champion of the downtrodden would emerge at the head of a ragtag army, and the delicate Gastown balance between the Merchant Burghs, the Four Kith, the Mutton, and the Gentry holdings on the seven hills beyond the bridge would tip into disorder and violence. A bowl of discarded vegetables was a small price to pay for an uneasy peace.

Jojo nudged Juan in the ribs with her elbow to get his attention. "Beez a duck, an' ask the kin' gentlemun for another bowl of 'is wunderful fare," she said, holding her empty bowl under Juan's nose.

"Not me, you ole tart. The last fella to try the bold act was extraplicated from the Gut, never to return, twisted in shame. *'Please sir, may I have more?'* More indeed. Ended up as eel bait in the Basin."

CHAPTER SEVEN

"How about you, Maisie?" Jojo asked, turning her attention to one of the waif sisters. "Your innocent ways will appeal to 'is better nature. Or get 'im stirrin' for things 'e shudn't 'ave."

Maisie's answer was to stick out her tongue, which set her sister off giggling.

"There be no respek anymore. No respek," Jojo said, hoisting herself up from the bench. "Come on then. If yuz all finished feastin, wez 'ave work upon us."

The nine companions made their way out of the colossal ironwood doors which sealed up the Gut once the evenfeast was over. No one was permitted to reside in the Gut overnight, not even the Etenmeister. Once his army of cleaners finished sluicing out the troughs; cleaned down the tables and benches; washed up the bowls and spoons and stacked them all away, and escorted out the lost souls who hovered between this world and the next, the heavy doors slammed shut. Only then did Jaguar Drummel insert his oversized key into the oversized lock and closed off the Gut for another solar.

The cutpurse coterie walked off into the cold night, Jojo a large lumbering bear-like figure in her worn fur coat, surrounded by skittish children with slop in their bellies and anxious fingers ready to go to work. It was the time for many in the Four Kith to find a warm floor for the night, and hunker down for the solar break. Jojo and her flock could have headed back to their slovenly nest on Tanner Bank and rested up. However, there was thieving to be done and pockets to pick. During the solar hours, when more marks were around, the group split up and toiled in smaller teams. At this time of night, when the pickings were slim, they labored as one. Jojo had coached them well, but did not join the hunt. Her role was to identify the target, and let Juan lead the troupe. Each child knew their assigned task, one played the begging innocent down on their luck, one darted in with shears, others acted as decoys and runners. All worked in unison in the grand play.

Jojo took her post on the corner of Grainger and Gray. It gave her a clear line of sight of any potential targets crossing the Bridge of Earthly

Pleasures, better known as Skank Bridge, over the Witten canal and on into the Mutton, and a view of her little army in their assigned positions. Her interaction with Juan was crucial, and they communicated with hand signs, flapping coats, and head gestures. Once the mark was identified, Juan would take over as captain and steer the good ship, *Purse Snatcher* to the port of misfortune for one and opportunity for others.

Juan always had a sinking feeling when they took up this post. He knew Jojo was right and the gateway to the Mutton meant marks had purses full of gild and were distracted about the pleasures to come. Still, his last real incursion into the Mutton had resulted in a lost eye and witnessing a murder. He would rather stake out the edge of the Burghs, but the protection there was higher and the retribution was swift. It was also the territory of Cotter Sullivan's Bully Boys, so better to avoid a confrontation in that direction.

Traffic from the Burghs to the Mutton was decidedly slower since the killings had started. Murders were not out of the ordinary in the less reputable parts of Gastown. However, they were usually singular crimes of passion, rage, or retribution. Three deaths in quick succession by the same deranged hand was a novelty, and the butchery was getting progressively worse. The victims were all notorious slagmaidens, and the Mutton was the hunting ground. It did not stop the women of the Burghs from sleeping with a lit candle at night, and insisting husbands stay indoors. Rumors abounded concerning the true identity of the slayer now known as, *The Terror*. Given the handiwork, some attributed the femicides to a demented slager, and the more fanciful claimed it was the ghost of Mo Dickens, though he had never stepped foot in the Mutton while he walked the earth. However, the majority opinion was a Dandy was the real culprit, and a watchful eye was cast on the few who descended from the citadel in search of lowly pleasures.

A heavy set man with mutton chop whiskers and his head buried in a cloud of self-produced smoke from his bulbous pipe, waddled towards Skank Bridge. There was a degree of affluence about him. His checkered waistcoat and unbuttoned overcoat were of fine manufacture, and carefully

CHAPTER SEVEN

matched his neatly pressed pantaloons. His polished high leather boots rounded out the outfit. The man walked with an air of confidence and distraction for one entering the Mutton. He blew a series of small smoke rings at regular intervals to puncture through the heady cloud, like musical notes coming to life in the frosty air. A blessed fool ripe for the picking thought Juan, who immediately identified him as a Tabakmeister, proudly displaying his wares. The rich woody smell of the tabak wafted through the air and tickled Juan's nostrils. He did not mind the odd chew, same as Jojo, and his teeth showed it, but smoking was not his preferred poison.

Juan looked at Jojo and nodded at the mark to get her approval to set the bear trap in motion. Jojo frowned and vigorously shook her head. She nodded her head in the direction behind the Tabakmeister, and Juan immediately understood his nonchalance. Five steps behind the Tabakmeister a man trailed him. He was a professional, obviously suitably armed beneath his heavy overcoat. For most of the Burghmeisters, protection was a necessity when venturing into the Four Kith, and the Tabakmeister was no exception, or fool. His man had a meanness about him, and strode with a fighter's gait. Juan blushed at his obvious mistake, and knew Jojo would rib him about it later, unless they found a better victim before the night was over. As Juan watched, the duo crossed over the hump of the bridge, the cloud of smoke hovering about them like a flock of birds and disappeared onto the Mutton side.

The long hour passed with no suitable quarry in sight, and the children were beginning to feel the cold with no activity. Maisie, and her sister named Flopsy, on account of her ability to swoon with the best of them, were particularly exposed as they discarded their outer garments to look more vulnerable. Their skin was already turning blue, and they huddled together for warmth.

Another potential target shuffled by. A tall man past his prime and stooping now from age, and a reliance on a walking stick. His overcoat was of good material, but was neatly patched in a few places. Not exactly on hard times, but no Burghmeister. The man was careful, and glanced from side to side, on the lookout for potential danger. There were no obvious signs of a heavy purse. Juan tagged him as an old soldier with little coin, a loner looking for occasional company, so better to avoid. No use losing one of the children in a squabble for minimum gain.

Time was running out and they had to make a move soon, or call it done for the night. Juan's fantasy about lifting a heavy bag of gild, and ending the solar with a hot toddy and a blud sausage, was quickly slipping away.

The next target was more promising. He had the look of the Wildlands about him, not a man raised in Gastown. His clothes were neat, but they appeared to be compiled from separate wardrobes, and thrown together for convenience and definitely not fashion. He was younger than Juan or Jojo liked, which meant a potential chase if they were not careful. Still, there was an obvious bulge in his right pantaloon pocket and the cord to his belt was visible and easy to slice. Juan's trained eye also spotted a silver necklace around his neck, which would break with a deliberate tug. This was their mark. He glanced over at Jojo, who hesitated for a second, and then perhaps influenced by the cold, nodded her approval.

The young man's name was Berric, and he was indeed fresh to the Four Kith, with the look and smell of an outlander. He was a head taller than most men of Gastown, and moved with a Wildlander's gait. He was on family business, which he hoped to conclude soon, so he could escape the filth of Gastown. His senses were attuned to the wilderness, and the city odors and noise polluted everything from his brain, to his sense of smell, hearing and sight, and clothes. He could not understand why people lived like this, confined together by choice.

Juan set the troupe into motion. Two of the younger apprentices were dawdling, so he snapped his fingers to get their attention. Maisie and Flopsy were the centerpieces. The outcome depended on them convincing the young man to stop for a moment so the others could move in for the sting. The young girls linked arms and slid sideways to get into the path of the country cousin. On cue, Flopsy flopped, and Maisie dropped to cradle her sister and put a raised palm to her forehead, leaned back, flicked her hair, and let out a forlorn cry.

Juan cringed. He had warned Maisie about being too dramatic. The trick

CHAPTER SEVEN

was to trap the mark, not put on a performance for a wider audience, since you could not afford to draw unwanted attention. However, the girl had artistic aspirations, and the drama got the better of her. Flopsy was not much better After the swoon, her role was to lie patiently at death's door. Instead, she started to flutter like a wounded dove. Not to be out done by her sister's theatrics, Maisie added plaintive sobs to the performance.

Berric's outlander origin was clearly on display because any self-respecting citizen of Gastown would have smelled a potkan and kept on walking. Berric stopped in his tracks. There was a look of real concern on his face.

"Please, kind youn' sir. Can yuz 'elp me sister? She 'as a terrible case of the floppin'. Did you see 'er go down?" Maisie said, in between sobs.

Berric leaned closer, which was all the time Juan and the gang needed. Gesmas Clay moved first. He was one of the bigger boys, almost the same size as Juan, and already skilled with the blade. He took up position slightly behind Berric's right pocket, and held his shears in his left hand at the ready. Topwell Jones stepped around Maisie and Flopsy on the other side and deliberately barged into Berric. At the exact moment, Gesmas's shears moved. He sliced the cord to the purse, and lifted it out of the pocket in one smooth motion. As Berric stood up, Maisie grabbed hold of the silver chain around his neck, and his backward motion was enough for it to break free. With his attention diverted towards Topwell. Berric failed to notice the loss of his precious necklace.

Now the handoffs kicked in and the trained sleight of hand Jojo made them practice came into play. Berric's defense mechanism automatically shifted his focus to Topwell, an obvious decoy who kept on walking. If Berric chased back and grabbed him, Topwell would profess his innocence, and of course he had nothing to show. Gesmas had the heavy purse, but not for long. He palmed it, and slid it across to Dismas walking towards the bridge. His task was to pass it again to Nico coming in the opposite direction with a final transfer to Juan. On the other side, Maisie slipped the silver chain to Shadduck, who took it in his stride, and glided off to the opposite side and made a meandering line towards Juan. He would only make the closing switch when he was sure the mark was not watching.

Unfortunately, not everything went according to the careful plan. Human nature, stage fright, and forgetting assignments all had a role to play. For whatever reason, Nico was too far away from Dismas for the purse exchange, and walked on past as if his role was the decoy. Dismas frowned, thought about turning back and walking towards Juan. Instead he kept on a course towards the bridge and over to the Mutton side.

Berric sensed something was wrong. His hand immediately went to his pocket, which was now missing a heavy purse. He pulled up the cord and saw the clean shear slice. He looked again at Topwell's back as he kept on walking. *No, it wasn't him. Wrong side for the purse cutting*, he thought. He glanced to the other side, and nothing caught his eye. He spun around to face towards the bridge, and noticed the two girls scurry off to either side. No point wasting time with them, they were decoys. As Berric scanned the people on the bridge, one boy turned and glanced back.

For all his faults, and thievery being chief amongst them, Dismas had an innocent streak. He looked back as if Jojo or Juan could give him some direction. Instead he caught the eye of the bumpkin mug. It was a dead giveaway. Rule number one from Jojo: *never look a mark in the eye if you're carrying the prize*. Decoys do that. Dismas was not the decoy today, and now he would be the hunted.

"Hey you! Stop!" Berric shouted.

The pursuit began. At Berric's shout, Dismas took off as if his life depended on it, which it did, and Berric gave chase.

"Stop that thief!" Berric cried.

Dismas weaved in and out of the sea of humanity surging across Skank Bridge. He was a seasoned mudlark and fast of foot. If he could make the other side of the bridge, then the alleys and side streets would offer some cover before he doubled back to the relative safety of the Slough.

Berric was no slouch. He took off after Dismas and his purse at a fast pace. Unfortunately, he could not weave in and out of the crowd with the same fluidity as the lighter boy. Moving at speed came with peril. As he dodged around one sturdy gentleman, he crashed into a rotund body

CHAPTER SEVEN

surrounded by a haze of smoke coming the other way, and sent him flying to the ground as his pipe went into the opposite direction. Berric stopped to help the man to his feet and offered his quick apologies, but as he did so a knife stabbed towards his chest, which he narrowly avoided.

"Thief!" the Tabakmeister's guardian growled.

"Wait, I'm no thief. I'm chasing a thief!" Berric said.

"Thief!" the bodyguard said again, slashing out at Berric with his knife. Luckily, his heavy overcoat slowed down his movement, and Berric easily slid back.

Berric knew an argument was futile, and the pickpocket and his purse were slipping away. He turned on his heels and ran across the bridge, the shouts of "Thief!" chasing after him, and he felt the shame of the false charge.

Dismas cleared Skank Bridge with ease and disappeared into one of the side alleys. He kept running, zigging and zagging his way through wider streets and narrow alleys, though avoiding the more crowded quarters of the Mutton. He kept running until the burning in his lungs forced him to slow down and suck in air to restore a sense of equilibrium.

Thinking was not Dismas's strongest asset. He had Jojo and Juan for that. He felt sure he had escaped from his pursuer, but now he had another problem. The Slough and the slightly more respectable areas of the Four Kith were known to him. He could navigate them with ease, since he had the knowledge. However, the Mutton was a different kettle of clams. Jojo's gang never ventured on this side by choice, as their marks were targeted on the other side. Only Juan had really crossed over to the Mutton, and lost an eye for the pleasure. It was a dangerous place for a boy with a fat purse, and a strong sense of guilt hovering over him.

Dismas rounded a corner from a side alley into a wider street and slinked along in the shadows. He glanced across the street, and saw three crones warming themselves in front of a brazier. The two tall ones faced the flames and held out their hands, the incredibly fat one had her dress hitched up and focused on toasting her tremendous rear. The colors of the Mutton cast strange shadows around the threesome as if they bathed in their own weird light show. Dismas hugged the walls and moved on past.

"He thinks we don't seez him, girls," Big Bertha said. "The shame-faced thief slips on by."

"No good comes from thievery," Theresa said.

"Except for us!" Peg said, and all three crones cackled.

"No time for penitence now, with someone howlin' at the moon," Theresa said.

"The Onderworld is callin'," Big Bertha said.

"I thought that were you passin' gas," Peg said, and they cackled again.

Berric punched a wall with both fists. He spun in a circle and bashed his hands against his own head. How could he have been so stupid to lose his purse. He needed the gild to complete his task in Gastown, and there was nothing else. He took a couple of deep breaths to calm himself down. There was nothing for it but to change. He would never find the thief in this maze unless he took drastic action. There was a huge risk involved, but he saw little alternative.

Once his mind was resolved, Berric moved fast. He stripped off all of his clothes and packed them into a small bundle and tied them together with his belt, which he tucked away out of sight in a dark corner. His hands moved to his neck and he noticed his necklace was missing. He frantically searched the ground around him, and ripped open his bundle and scattered his clothes as he searched in vain. It was gone.

The gild was one thing. He could lose it and still survive. The symbol of his clan was something else. His father had entrusted him with the family totem and he had misplaced the paternal confidence. Berric's future and the future of his kin depended on the completion of his mission, and he was off to a miserable start. He could already hear his father's scornful words in his head.

It was never a good idea to change when a rage was upon him. A calm mind led to calm action. His blood was up and nothing good would come of it. His mind felt the change first before it impacted his body. Human thoughts were pushed away as the blood rushed through his brain and the animal in him rose. The body transformation followed as his bones

CHAPTER SEVEN

extended, thickened, and twisted into a new shape. He dropped to all fours as his limbs took on their new form, no longer human, but the shape of a direwolf. The massive shoulders pushed out and up, the hind legs fleshed out as sinews hardened and tendons stretched. The hardest part to bear was the facial mutation as the lower jaw broke free and transformed forward, massive fangs punched through the gums, and the eyes switched to a yellowish hue. Berric's senses took on a dramatic change. The color sight of the human world was replaced with shades of blue, yellow, and gray. His night vision immediately sharpened. His sense of smell and hearing increased a hundredfold and was a rush to his system. The noise and aromas were overwhelming, until he settled into his new shape and adjusted to the world of a nocturnal predator.

Berric the human was still present although deep in the background as he gave rein to his direwolf self. There was prey to find: specific prey. A fearful boy running with a stolen purse. All his wulver faculties came into play, those similar to humans though enhanced vision in the dark, smell, and hearing. There were other heightened senses too, as he tuned into the boy's fear, and also his own belongings, the purse in possession of a thief. The overwhelming noise and the strange lights of the Mutton compromised his clarity to some degree, but he kept to the back alleys and the shadows. The boy was on the run and doing the same, which made Berric's job easier.

Berrric knew the thief was close, a few alleys over and a relatively short distance ahead. In his human form he would have no chance tracking the youth in this maze, but as a direwolf he was locked in.

Dismas stopped running. He did not want to get sucked too deep into the Mutton and take the risk of losing track of how to get back over Skank Bridge and into the safety of the Slough. His heart was still racing, but there was nothing he could do about that until he reached home. He wished Juan was with him, so he did not have to think for himself, but he was all alone. He felt a pang of guilt for the young man as he weighed the heavy purse in his hand. He consoled himself he was not the pickpocket, but he was the runner and the carrier, and he shared the burden. Thievery did not sit well with him, but there was little choice in the Slough. No one offered him a profession, there was no expectation of a rich benefactor emerging out of the fog. He stole to live, and he lived with the shame of it.

Dismas turned back, moved two alleys over, and headed back in the general direction of the bridge. There was no sign of life in the alleys and most people were over in the main thoroughfares of the Mutton, where gluttony and debauchery held sway. Some couples would peel off into the side streets on occasion, but most of the transactions were done in the relative safety of the billeehauses, or the upscale bordellos. Those in the streets ran the risk of a setup and ending their solars at the end of a sharp blade from a Swell Daddy's Crimper.

Dismas sensed the beast before he saw anything. There was an overpowering feeling of being watched. Something could see him, but he could not see it. The hairs on his arms stood up, and there was a pounding in his ears as his hearing sharpened. He tightly clutched the heavy purse in his right hand as the only weapon available. He saw the yellow eyes first. One second there was only darkness, then the eyes flashed and a heavy weight landed on him and a meaty paw pinned him to the ground. Dismas looked up at the wolfen head staring down at him, saliva dripped on his face. In a moment of inspiration, he threw the purse to one side.

"Fetch!" he said.

Juan waited at the entrance to Skank Bridge. It was over an hour since Jojo led her merry band back to the safety of the Tanner Bank nest. Dismas was not the smartest member of the gang, but even he had the sense to evade his pursuer in the side alleys and then doubleback to the safety of the Slough. Juan just needed to be patient and bide his time. He was also wrestling with his conscience. Before Jojo left, he handed over the silver chain to her, but he pocketed the rounded bone object with an embedded red stone, which dangled from it. Something told him to keep it safe. He did not know what or why. It seemed natural to hide it inside his empty eye socket, with his patch back in place, and out of sight of everyone including himself.

CHAPTER SEVEN

There was a trickle at first and then a flood. People streamed over Skank Bridge back to the Four Kith and many on to the Burghs. Some glanced over their shoulders as they moved, all embracing the safety of the crowd. Juan could hear murmurs among them. Drunken voices as they sailed on by to safe havens, with locks, and bolts, and heavy doors to protect them from *The Terror* in the Mutton.

"Another two claimed by *The Terror*. One with her throat ripped out, and the second … what beast destroys a person like that!"

"That's five he's sent down to the Onderworld."

"Six if you include the other one."

"That wasn't his doing, that's something else entirely."

"Besides, it was a boy."

Juan grabbed the stranger's arm. "Please sir, what did yuz mean by a boy/"

The man looked down in horror at Juan and brushed his hand away. "Unhand me, you rascal."

Juan looked sheepish. "Please, sir. I mean no 'arm. Yuz said a boy."

"Yes, a boy, or what's left of him. Torn to shreds he was. No blade did that business. Fangs and claws, I tell you. Fangs and claws!"

Without waiting to hear another word, Juan ran off to Tanner Bank.

Chapter Eight

Carlos : Fire in the Slough

Cotter lay on his back in the large ironwood bed specially commissioned by Mo Dickens, his heavily stitched left arm lay dormant by his side, with a bloody bandage covering the gaping wound his left thumb once occupied. His right hand was behind his head as a makeshift pillow. Blankets and furs covered his lower half, but his naked upper body was exposed to the elements. His chest and bulging belly displayed new stitchwork from his most recent combat with Mo, as well as a patchwork of old scars of previously torn flesh badly sewn together to keep the insides from spilling out. The battle lines traversed his body like the canals running through Gastown. Some were the result of duels to the death, the majority were a reminder of the power of numbers, and getting caught alone in the open by a gang of hot tempered roughnecks. One on one, Cotter was a match for any of his adversaries, but you always needed an army at your back. He had only made that mistake once in his younger solars, when bravado and pigheadedness almost cost him his life. Fighting and survival required a pack mentality, and Cotter was top dog.

"That was gud, youn' un. Scratched me itch, it did," Cotter said.

Carlos did not answer. He sat at the dresser previously owned by Jojo Dickens, and stared in the mirror at a reflection he barely recognized. The black mascara around his eyes was smudged, messed up by tears brought

CHAPTER EIGHT

on by fear, shame, and pain. Cotter's oppressive weight and smothering fat had sent weaker boys to the other side. Carlos breathed freely. He was alive for another solar.

"When yuz finished fixin' your face, get out there an' see them Bully Boys isn't stealin' me hearth an' 'ome from under me. Iz worked 'ard robbin' this place, an' no one's robbin; it from me!" Cotter said.

Carlos did not answer and none was warranted. The order was given and the expectation was clear. Cotter was not a man to offer second chances. Carlos fixed his makeup around his eyes and left the bedchamber for the main hall.

Cotter liked his fires. Fires to keep him warm and comforted and fires to burn and ruin others. Fire was his faithful companion, a reminder of toasty times in childhood, and the first time he put flame to flesh. He liked nothing better than to stare into the flames and dwell on the scorching of dead enemies, and relish the thought of a fiery end to those who still lived to cross him. The main hearth was ablaze now, and two boys were tasked with keeping it stacked and fed. It burned slowly during the night in a slumbering flame, but needed to be a roaring inferno by the time Cotter was out of his crib and barking orders at his Bully Boys, apprentices, and mites.

The slagerhaus was a shambles of the fine establishment run by Mo Dickens. Mo's neatness and order was replaced by slovenliness and imbalance. Cotter cared little about tidiness and cast bones on the floor with the best of them. He also used chaos as a way of keeping everyone on edge and under his control. Cotter still used the slagerhaus to butcher and carve paranga on the heavy meat slab. He was skilled with the cleaver, though now reduced to one good hand, and carved himself when the mood was on him. Not always paranga either. Broken men ended their solars on the butcher's block. Even Cotter drew the line at selling human flesh, but he disassembled bodies, and left them for pariahs to make the parts disappear.

These solars most of the real butchery was performed by Perfect Styles, a sinewy and sullen man with fast hands and a silent tongue. The moniker was not attached for his true cutting lines, but was bestowed by his parents on account of his ability as a newborn to never cry, and sleep through the night without the aid of mother's ruin rubbed on his tender gums. Perfect quietly grumbled about the constant blaze and the heat of the slagerhaus during the working solar. It spoiled the paranga, and he longed for the colder times under Mo Dickens's tutelage. He also bristled over the constant presence of the Bully Boys who ate more than their fair share of the butchered meat, though Cotter did have the sense to keep the finer cuts for sale. Perfect held his tongue around Cotter, and took it out on the apprentices. He was still a slager, and thankfully Cotter did not interfere with that trade too much. He had other business interests to satisfy his greed and quest for fearful recognition.

Cotter was immensely proud of his new title of Hetman of the Slagers. He wore the chain of authority around his neck at any opportunity. He did not care if the other Slagers viewed him with contempt and would celebrate a cleaver buried in his back. He knew none of the current batch would challenge him, and there was no up-and-coming slager he needed to cut down before he reached his prime. Destroying Haus Dickens brought two prizes; it solidified his position with the Burghmeisters as a Hetman in the Four Kith, and it offered the slagerhaus. This vast chamber was perfectly located for him to dominate the Four Kith, and spread his nefarious empire.

Selling paranga was one thing, and Cotter now took over all of Mo Dickens's contracts. However, it was only a part of his business dealings, and not the most profitable. There was more gild to be made offering Bully Boy protection to the Burgh folk crossing through the Four Kith and over the bridge to the land of the Dux. There was also the protection racket with the Four Kith merchants, who paid an unfair sum to ply their trade under Cotter's benevolent shield. Some took a little persuading and the mites needed to rob from them and smash and crash merchandise before they saw the errors of their ways and begged Cotter to intervene.

Cotter had one other peculiarity, besides his fondness for young boys. He could not abide pickpockets on account of his pocket having once been picked. Ten bewildered thieves paid the price for that transgression. Cut

CHAPTER EIGHT

purses, dippers, and sneak thieves were fearful enough to stay clear of the Cotter zone of the Four Kith. Only the Slough and the road to the Mutton were fair game for now. However, it was only a matter of time until he expanded his domain, and the robbers were on edge. There were even rumors he had his sights on the lucrative Mutton, though that offered a more violent proposition.

Gildlending and the numbers game rounded out his criminal portfolio. Merchants borrowed from Cotter without realizing it, quickly fell into debt due to the heavy juice owed the gildshark, and parted with their business and property. The poorer elements from the Four Kith lost their wives and children to gamble on three numbers picked by Cotter himself. Rumors were spread on the 'lucky' ones to choose that week, and Cotter made sure they usually were not selected. Occasionally they did come in to keep hopes alive and the seers and voyants in the common goodwill. Business was lucrative.

"Alright yuz mudlarks an' Bully Boys, Cotter wants yuz out an' about an' makin' gild," Carlos said with an air of authority he did not really have at the tender age of sixteen years.

The mites stirred and followed Carlos's command. He had already gravitated to the position as their leader on account he was Cotter's favorite, and had put one other mite out with a mighty cudgel blow to the head. The Bully Boys were something else. They were not about to take orders from Cotter's current bedwarmer.

"Look who's comin' on strong boys," Jonas Wheeler said. He was a leading figure amongst Cotter's Bully Boys, but not the designated number two. That distinction belonged to Patch Armstrong. Jonas's role was the self-appointed bellyacher, to voice the feelings of the other men, but always backing down before Patch, and never facing up towards Cotter. He was a sly little man, with never a kind word, twitchy fingers, and a sharp blade in his pocket which served him well.

"Didn't take 'im long to barkin' orders to 'is elders an' betters."

"Leave the boy be, Jonas. Cotter's orders is Cotter's orders, no matter the voice deliverin' 'em. Better be followin' em," Patch said, pushing his plate of chewed bones to one side. When other men liked the soft cuttings, Patch preferred to work for his meat. It kept his teeth active and his jaw strong. He was not an imposing figure of a man, more sinew than muscle, but he was Cotter's favorite killer. Overconfident men paid the price for underestimating Patch.

"Just havin' a little fun, is all, Patch. Didn't mean nothin' to it," Jonas said, the sneer still on his face. He spat on the floor in Carlos's direction, a transgression which would have cost him at least an ear if Mo Dickens was still in charge.

"Fun's over. You heard the boy, on your feet, Bully Boys, we have work to do," Patch said, standing up and stirring the gang to action. There were a few murmurs about leaving the warm fires, and heading out into the cold night air, but they stirred nonetheless. Not so much like a disturbed hornet's nest, but more like stunned bees from a smoked filled hive.

"Losin' your touch, Patch?" Cotter said. He stood in the doorway of his bedchamber, his right arm propped up on the doorframe, while his left hung by his side. His open dressing gown exposed his gargantuan belly. The hetman chain dangled from his neck.

At the sight of Cotter, the Bully Boys moved faster.

"They're movin' Cotter, they're movin'," Patch said.

"A quicker pace would be nice, Patch," Cotter replied.

Patch did not say another word. He moved into the crowd of Bully Boys and jostled and bumped them towards the door and another night's work of dishonest thievery and busted heads. Carlos and the mites were one step ahead of them. As soon as Cotter came through the bedchamber doorway, Carlos had them lined up and moving, as much to get away from Cotter as to get to the task at hand. There was a baker on the border of the Slough who needed some gentle persuading, and this one was personal.

Carlos remembered the baker and his establishment from his time roaming wild and ravenous in the Slough with Juan before Jojo Dickens took pity on them and temporarily plucked them free from the mean streets. The bakerhaus front was painted in enticing red and white candy striped colors, a magnet to the mudlarks of the Slough, who could not

CHAPTER EIGHT

afford the brood or the sweet confectioneries. They tormented themselves by standing in small gangs, sniffing off the doughy aroma of baked brood fresh out of the ovens. Occasionally, the younger of the two brothers who owned the bakerhaus threw a stale crust on the ground just in front of a gaggle of children, and laughed in savage amusement as they tore each other up to get the hardened brood.

The Geroni Bakerhaus had fallen on hard times. Four generations of master bakers with unsullied reputations meant nothing when the Haus was entrusted to a waster, a drunkard, a gambler, and a man of weak disposition all rolled into one unproven loaf. The two brothers jointly inherited the business from their late father. The elder was molded from the same baker's oven as his forebears, but his younger sibling was a man of cracked clay. While Guy Geroni was around the damage was mitigated. However, on Guy's untimely death, the result of an inopportune slip into the Basin, a bottle of grog in his pocket though he never drank, the business fell into the deepest shade of red. Joe Geroni was late to work, bought substandard base materials, took no pride in his baking, and lost generational customers as a result. He ate through family savings as fast as he consumed pastries, and reached out to the gildshark to cover his debts. His world had now collided with Cotter Sullivan, and there was a price to pay. Cotter did not need the bakerhaus, there was already a baker's dozen of them in the Slough, but he did desire the location. A property the size of the Geroni Bakerhaus could house ten families, and Cotter had aspirations of becoming a slum landlord too. All that was required was a little pyrotechnic magic to see Joe Geroni on his way, and the deeds turned over to Cotter in lieu of a portion of the debt owed. Not all arrears were forgiven. Cotter had a heart of stone, and a reputation to bolster.

Carlos looked at the front of the Geroni Bakerhaus. The red and white paint had peeled in many places and there was a rundown air about the establishment. Even the smell of brood was no longer appetizing, a more sour, rancid, cold smell than the enticing sweet warm aroma of a few years ago. His gaze shifted to the side alley and he shuddered as he remembered his encounter with Joe Geroni.

Juan and Carlos scouted out the Geroni Bakerhaus. They had no interest wrestling with the other mudlarks over a stale crust. They wanted a whole loaf of brood for themselves. Not a fresh loaf just out of the oven. That was asking too much. However, an apprentice, not much older than the twins, sold old brood from a doorway in the alley. Juan figured he could distract him long enough for Carlos to grab a loaf and make off in the opposite direction. Once out of the alleyway there was no chance they would be caught.

"*Oy!, how much for the brood?" Juan asked, approaching the apprentice.*

The apprentice was immediately on his guard. He knew a mudlark when he saw one, and he was sure there was no gild in this one's pocket.

"*Be off with you," the apprentice said. He wiped his flour dusted hands on his apron, and stood forward over the brood basket on the ground between his feet.*

"*That's no way to talk to a customer," Juan said, stepping forward and continuing with his bravado.*

"*I said be off with you. Now be off!" the apprentice said.*

"*An' who's gonna make me? Juan replied, stepping closer.*

The apprentice was bigger than Juan, but a baker not a fighter. "There's men inside who will see for you. All I have to do is sing out an' they come runnin.'"

"*Then sing canary, sing! If yuz can't stand on your own feet," Juan said, challenging his budding masculinity.*

The apprentice took the bait. He was scared enough to cry for help, but proud enough to stand his ground. He puffed himself up to look bigger. There was time enough to call out if needed.

While Juan engaged with the apprentice, Carlos slithered down the alley wall from the other direction. He moved fast and quietly, and with the apprentice focused firmly on Juan, he went unseen. Within five paces of the apprentice and his brood tray, Carlos went closer to the ground and once within striking distance, reached out to grab a loaf.

If Carlos had followed the plan and immediately grabbed the nearest one, Juan was sure they would have been a clear getaway. However, to his dismay, his twisted twin tested each of the loaves to find the freshest offering. Juan could not help himself. He glanced down at his brother now on all fours with a hand between the apprentice's legs engaged in the squeeze test, which tipped their hand

CHAPTER EIGHT

to the apprentice.

"Thief!" bellowed the apprentice, who closed his legs, and immediately toppled over Carlos. "Thief, thief!" he yelled.

A large pudgy hand from years of kneading dough reached out and grabbed Carlos by the scruff of the neck. Joe Geroni, a flabby man with flaccid morals, who despised his family calling, stepped out of the doorway. Unlike his apprentice, he did not shy away from violence, especially if his opponent was an underfed boy. Joe could have cuffed the boy just enough to teach him a lesson, but that was not his way. He held onto Carlos with one strong hand and proceeded to pummel him about the head with a closed fist. Blow after blow landed on Carlos until one vicious strike to the temple rendered him unconscious.

Juan was no coward and Carlos was all he had. Despite the size disadvantage, he sailed into Joe Geroni with both arms flailing. He made contact, but his strikes meant little to the oversized baker, who looked at him with bemusement.

"Here, hold this one," he said to the apprentice, releasing his custody of Carlos. "I have another thief who needs my attention."

Joe Geroni's punches were more measured this time, and delivered with force and accuracy. He did not just punch to the head, but saved some shots for the torso targeting the liver and spleen. Juan was soon reduced to a passive punching bag, and sagged with every blow.

"Joseph!" Guy Geroni shouted at his brother. "That's a boy!"

"This is a thief," Joe replied. But he stopped inflicting punishment on his unconscious victim.

Guy Geroni stepped forward. He was a small, thin man, who took pride in his work and appearance. He stared at the listless boy in his brother's grip, and at his doppelganger loosely propped up by the apprentice. The second boy was barely conscious himself, and unsteady on his feet, but there was still an air of defiance about him. He turned his attention to his brother.

"Joseph. We're bakers not savages. There's enough suffering in this world without inflicting more," Guy said. He rubbed his bald head and left a trail of flour handprints behind. "Enough, Joseph, enough."

Joe Geroni released his grip on Juan, who fell to the alley floor in a heap. "Have it your way, Guy. But I tell you, they'll steal the last crust from us if we let them,"

"If a crust is all it is, they're welcome to it," Guy said. "We don't need to be selling stale brood, Joseph. We make more than enough from the front of the store. Give it away to the poor."

Joe bristled. "The poor? Thieves and vagabonds, all of them. Better we end them quick than drag out a worthless existence," Joe said. He saw the world through a different lens than his older brother, one where pity and forgiveness had no home: a cold dark place for a cold dark soul. He pushed past Guy and went back to his hated station in the bakerhaus.

Guy looked at the twins again and shook his head. "Can you stand?" he asked Carlos.

Carlos pushed the apprentice away and swayed like a Mutton dweller on the grog. "Iz can stand well enough," he said.

Guy reached down and took a loaf from the brood tray. He gestured for the apprentice to pick up the rest and head back into the bakerhaus, which he was only too willing to do with only a fleeting backward glance.

"Then take this with the blessing from Geroni Bakerhaus," Guy said, holding out the brood to Carlos. "My brother isn't all bad. He's just headstrong," Guy said, though his words rang hollow and hung in the cold air like frozen lies.

Carlos thought about rejecting the loaf, but only for a second. If he did not need the brood, then Juan surely did. He picked up his brother first, who groaned, but slowly opened his eyes.

Carlos reached out and took the goodwill loaf from Guy's hand. "I won't forget", he said. And he would not, though not exactly as Guy intended.

Carlos and his gaggle of firestarters took up position on either flank of the property. The task at hand was simple, according to Cotter and Patch: just enough burning to gut the ground floor and nothing else. Then sound the fire warning to get the Slough volunteers moving and the blaze extinguished before too much damage was inflicted. The Slough had seen innumerable destructive conflagrations over the years, and flare-ups were generally bad for business. Carlos wished Juan were with him, but then shook his head vigorously to dislodge the unwanted thought. If Juan was around he would see his shame and try to do something about it. Cotter

CHAPTER EIGHT

would put a quick end to that. Better Juan lived his life free and hungry in the Slough. They would meet again some solar, he was sure of that.

Fleet Dawkins was the tinder mite for tonight's planned inferno. He was a head smaller and a year younger than Carlos, slight of size, and quick on his feet. The mark of his early work was etched in a sizable burn mark on the left side of his face, and up into his scalp line where the hair refused to grow. He looked like he could carry a fast flame and run through the streets setting everything alight in his path. Fleet could be trusted to keep his head, and keep his burn controlled enough to damage the Geroni Bakerhaus, but not put the building out of commission.

There were five other younger mites out on the mission with Carlos and Fleet. They were not involved in the actual arson, but would act as lookouts and raise the fire alarm once the early flames took hold. Two were by Carlos's side, and three others stood next to Fleet, eager to see him put his fire kit into action, and learn the tricks of the pyromaniac's trade.

With a nod from Carlos, Fleet got to work. He took a small bundle out from inside his shirt, and placed it on the ground. He unrolled the cloth slathered in bear fat on the inside, and wrapped it loosely around a makeshift torch. He placed a small pile of tinder, wood chips soaked in spirit and pulled lamb wool, onto a dry patch on the ground. Now the sorcery began, and the mites leaned forward to watch, always fascinated by the magic show. Fleet pulled out a small metal block, and a wicked sharp blade, which barely peeped out through his hand. With one, two, then three dexterous scapes, he fired sparks into the tinder trap. He breathed on it to bring his fire child to life. The result was immediate, and a baby combustion was born.

As Carlos watched from the other side of the Geroni Bakerhaus, the side next to the alleyway where he took his beating, he saw the small group of mites briefly illuminated by the sparks, and then the small blaze took hold. He saw Fleet dip his torch forward, and fire jumped towards it. Carlos was the backup pyro mite for this operation, and he gingerly fingered his own torch. His job was to enter from the side door in the alley, check Fleet's fire was burning, or spread it if needed.

Fleet looked over at Carlos, flaming brand in hand, and nodded. Carlos gave the greenlight and Fleet stepped forward to the front shutter. There was a gaping hole in the woodwork, a sign of the recent downward spiral of the Geroni Bakerhaus, and the entry point for Fleet's life changing Four Kith candle. He pushed his slender arm through the gap, looked through the hole for a suitable landing point, and launched his missile onto a stack of broken confectionery trays. Sparks flew as the fire stick landed, and immediately ignited the dry wood. The main blaze centered around the point of the torch, but smaller rivulets spread out as the bear fat splattered and the flames greedily followed.

Satisfied his work was done, and Carlos would not be needed to add to the bonfire, Fleet raised his right fist into the air as the backoff signal. No reason for Carlos to enter the building and risk possible injury. His blaze was enough to do the job, and all they had to do now was to wait a few moments and send the mites running to raise the fire alarm. As Fleet stared over at Carlos, he made no sign of moving. Carlos was transfixed by the flames, his two mites staring up at him, waiting for direction.

Carlos cast his gaze at the alleyway. In his mind he saw Joe Geroni holding onto Juan and beating him to a pulp. Blow after blow landed on his senseless brother. A river of blood flowed from every orifice. The contrast between Joe Geroni and Juan was stark, the large angry man all in white with flour dust flying with every meaty blow, and the helpless boy bathed in red of his own making. A blow landed, and blood spurted, another blow and Juan's vital fluid gushed out. Carlos saw himself, propped up by the apprentice, unable to move and come to his brother's aid. He was a helpless observer of the merciless thrashing. He could feel the rage inside himself, the burning desire to destroy, maim, and kill. He was paralyzed and the inaction ate him alive.

A flicker of fire inside the Geroni Bakerhaus came into Carlos' peripheral vision. It was enough to snap him back to the present and the task at hand. Without a word, he sprinted to the side door in the alley.

"What you doin', Carlos?" Fleet hissed. "No need to go in, you mudlark, the blaze 'as 'old!"

CHAPTER EIGHT

Carlos reached the door, and prepared to kick it in, but there was no need. The door was already slightly ajar. Security was obviously not top of mind for Joe Geroni and his failed business. Carlos did not hesitate, he pushed the door open and moved into the main shop area. The old display cases were empty, cake holders were tipped over, baking trays were irregularly stacked, and woven baskets, which once held the best of broods, were broken shells.

The fire had enough raw material to take hold, and a tidy blaze was already growing where Fleet had landed his torch. Carlos moved towards it and dipped his own into it and ignited the brand. He watched it for a moment, fascinated by the expanding flame. He felt the comforting warmth from the flare up and marveled at the spreading destruction as fire ate wood and wicker.

Carlos left the front of the shop and moved into the baking area at the rear of the building, where stale flour covered the machinery in a ghostly layer. Large ovens once manned by an army of apprentices supervised by master bakers, and turning out loaf after pristine loaf, now sat idle. Fire was a forced servant to them, twisting and turning, and burning fiercely within, shackled by the clay domes. No longer. Now fire would seek revenge and consume the ovens and turn them to ash. Fire would have vengeance sayeth the Lord of the Flame.

Something caught Carlos's eye. There was a tray on the back counter, and there were five loaves upon it. The only brood in the bakerhaus. The sight of them brought back memories in the Slough when a crust kept starvation at bay for another solar. He drooled without thinking. As the flames spread and consumed the bakery, Carlos walked over to the tray and tested the bread. One after the other, he squeezed.

"Stale brood," he said in disgust. They were rock hard.

Carlos scooped up one loaf and headed further back into the bowels of the building. He used his fire torch to illuminate the way until he came to the foot of the stairs. He went up at a steady pace, not knowing what he would find, but something told him he had a mission to compete, and it was more than just a spot of arson for Cotter Sullivan.

There were three doorways at the top of the stairwell, and Carlos pushed open the first one. The room was empty. The second room was piled with old papers and broken furniture, and Carlos put his firebrand to it to ignite the contents. Everything was bone dry, and the flames took immediate hold. On to the third room and Carlos found the prize he was seeking: Joe Geroni.

The large man was lying on top of his bed fully dressed and still wearing his worn boots. He held an empty goblet in his pudgy hand. He was snoring loudly, his belly rising up and down with each breath, oblivious to the fire consuming his business, or of Carlos's malignant presence. There was a large flagon on his bedside table. It lay on its side and a slow drip of grog fell to the floor and added to the stain on the floorboard.

Carlos glanced at the wall and saw his own large reflection loom over the sleeping Joe. Him and his shadow would end this tonight. Joe Geroni did not belong in the Four Kith, he did not belong anywhere in the world of men. Fire would take care of the grotesque flesh, but Carlos would take care of the man. He moved closer, and stared down at Joe. His face was puffy from too much demon drink, and his body bloated from gluttony. Without another thought, Carlos brought the hard stale loaf crashing down on Joe's temple, again, and again, and again. After the seventh blow, the bread began to shatter and Joe moaned. Carlos immediately dropped the brood, and picked up the heavy metal flagon. He crashed that down on Joe's head, until the man's skull broke, and blood and brains ran with the grog.

Carlos panted heavily, and the smoke rising from below did not help his breathing. His rage depleted, he dropped the flagon on the lifeless body, and put his torch to the bedclothes. The fire did not take immediately, so Carlos added a pile of clothes to the pyre and they ignited. He watched as the fat man began to melt.

Fleet had no clue what to do. His expertise was starting fires, not making decisions. Should he go in after Carlos, send the mites running for the alarm, or wait a little longer. He did not know what possessed Carlos to enter the building, but he was a strange bird. As he waited impatiently,

CHAPTER EIGHT

Carlos made the decision for him.

Carlos emerged from the alleyway and into the main street. He stood at the side of the Geroni Bakerhaus as flames consumed it. His face was covered in soot which highlighted his wild eyes, his hair was singed, and smoke seeped from his clothes. He was a fire imp in all his glory.

The Geroni Bakerhaus burned. The blaze punched through the front shutters, and as Fleet watched, smoke pushed through the roof and billowed out, followed by orange and yellow flames flickering in the night sky. The fire touched the thatched roof of the neighboring structure, and danced a drunken jig across the tightly packed water reeds.

Carlos walked over to Fleet and turned to face the death throes of the Geroni Bakerhaus. There would be no more stale brood sold from the alleyway, no more beatings at the hands of Joe the Baker. Death came to Haus Geroni.

"I didn't forget," Carlos muttered to himself, and for Joe, and Guy, and mostly for Juan.

"There'll be 'ell to pay with Cotter for this one. 'E asked for a smoker an' wez given 'im a bonfire!" Fleet hissed. "What to do now, Carlos? What to do?"

"Get the mites together an' back to the safety of the Hole. Stay away from Cotter an' Patch until Iz 'ad a chance to set things straight," Carlos said. The rage left him in the Geroni Bakerhaus and the killing of Joe Geroni, and an eerie calm was about him. He was fully in charge of himself and the situation. He had taken a fateful first step into criminal manhood.

What about the warnin'?" Fleet asked.

"None needed now," Carlos said. "Listen."

The sound of the fire bells rang out. First, one, then two, three and four. The Four Kith was awake and the citizens raced to stop the blaze before it spread through Gastown and destroyed them all.

Fleet did not wait around. He gathered the five mites and sprinted off to the safety of the Hole, away from the stirring citizens of the Four Kith, away from the spreading inferno, and hidden from Cotter and Patch until Carlos took his punishment.

Carlos watched as the fire spread to building after building in the street. There was a comfort and a cleansing in the savage conflagration. But the nemesis of fire was on the way: water was coming. Three fire carriages, each pulled by four horses trained to withstand the sight, smell, noise, and heat of the fire. Men, all volunteers from across the Four Kith, jumped down from the wagons. From two carriages, they extracted long hoses and ran them down to the canal. Two men on the back of each carriage hand cranked a pulley to extract water from the canal into a large barrel. Once they pulled the water and filled their barrels, two brave souls stood in front of the inferno, opened their spigots and let the water loose on the flames. The other wagon contained buckets, which the volunteer firefighters lined up from the canal to in front of the building. Each space behind the bucket was quickly filled by sleepy citizens, men, women, and children, who passed empty buckets down to the canal and full ones up towards the burning buildings. As they worked, another fire wagon laden with buckets pulled up, and another human daisy chain was set in motion. Fire pushed on to another house in the row. Water entered the fray to hold it back and quench the eternal flame.

Carlos had seen enough. He turned and walked away. Not in the direction of the Hole, or to the slagerhaus and the wrath of Cotter Sullivan. He went in search of his twin brother.

Chapter Nine

The Dux War Council

The solar started with tears. Like the one before it and the one before that. The Dux hated the morning as much as she hated the night. Bundled in heavy blankets within her oversized bed, and four Damm Warrior guards always in close proximity, sleep never came easy. She tried her best to lie still and let the darkness soothe her mind, but it never did. She blew air bubbles, and mentally counted the gild in her Treasury, but nothing worked. The night was overflowing with sinister shapes and shades, lost souls stalked and haunted her through the gloom. When dawn came and brought some respite from the night terrors, sleep was needed and sleep was denied.

"Come on my lovely, it's time to get up and face the world like the pretty young thing you are," Nan said cheerfully, as she pulled and cajoled her fat charge free from the blankets.

The Dux clung desperately to her cover and refused to be prised loose. "Shan't! Shan't do it, Nan. For once I want to lie in and sleep," the Dux pleaded.

Nan was having none of it, and she and the two ladies-in-waiting were well versed in dealing with the morning protestations and readying the Dux for the trials and tribulations ahead..

"Nighttime is for sleeping, dumpling, not the solar. You have duties to fulfill. Now come on, and embrace the world like the grand woman in charge that you are," Nan said.

Now in an upright position, the three ladies removed the Dux's nightgown, and used sponges dipped in warm water to wash away the night sweat. They brushed her hair and tied it back in a business-like bun, and applied white powdered makeup to her puffy face. In lieu of a bath, which the Dux detested, more white powder was liberally applied to her bloated torso. A bedpan was strategically placed between the Dux's legs and she peed standing up as always. Nan inspected the contents, gave it a quick sniff and nodded her head in approval. The bedpan passed off, she handed the Dux a leaden beaker full of a liquid not dissimilar in color from the most recent deposit.

"Drink this, poppy. It will make you feel better," Nan said.

The Dux took the drink without protest, pinched her nose and proceeded to drain the contents in one continuous swig. The task completed, she gave a cough and a shudder, before dropping the empty cup on her bed. The revival from the herbal concoction was instantaneous, and a light returned to her eyes and a sharpness to her tongue.

"I am the grand woman in charge, aren't I, Nan?" the Dux said.

"Yes, you are my sweetness. You are the Dux of the Var, Lady of Varstad, Mistress of Assaborg, and Dominatrix of Varlanda, and the world trembles before you," Nan said, with a deep curtsey.

No one had contemplated Agitha Freydasdottir rising to become Dux of the Var, or even surviving infanthood. She was always a sickly child, and though her regal mother was the epitome of what a Damm Warrior should be: tall, powerful, stern, and cruel, Agitha only inherited the latter attributes. In contrast to her statuesque younger half-sister, she had the body of a chubby bookkeeper, but she was the first born, and by the will of Frotha she was destined to rule.

"I think I'll wear the black gown today," the Dux said, and a lady-in-waiting hurried over to the closet. "The black one mind you," the Dux repeated.

Every gown in the closet was black. The Dux would wear black today,

CHAPTER NINE

like the solar before, and the solar before that. The Dux wore black every solar as a sign of mourning since the passing of her Dandy husband and her fourteen children. They did not take the long walk all at once, and some of the babies came into the world with their eyes already covered by pennies. They departed in a steady file, one by one into the dark abyss, grieved over by a mother who loved them in her own strange way, and ignored by a father who only cared for the company of Dandies and a steady flow of vin. Some say she rode her spouse into oblivion in a desperate attempt for a final female heir. When his flagpole drooped from constant consumption of vin, Nan's bitterroot concoction brought it back to attention, even when the body attached to it lay comatose beneath. Truth be told, the Dux Consort drowned in a vat of Riverside Red as he and a Dandy lover decided it was a good idea to dive in naked and drink the contents from the inside.

The Dux ate her breakfast alone sitting in an oversized chair in front of an oversized table. The simple meal consisted of a bowl of gruel, a handful of raw vegetables, and a cup of boiled water. Her constitution was not strong, and though she ate sparingly, she always managed to put on extra weight at the end of each lunar. She hated her body, and her body hated her back. There were few pleasures in her lonely existence and no one she could call a friend. Nan was still there, a permanent fixture in her life since birth. Nan to tuck her in at night, and rouse her from the nest in the morning. Nan who promised to place the pennies, and hold her hand when she took the final boat ride into the Onderworld to be judged by Hulda, her service of life tallied by Loti, and on to Frotha's hall. There were family members too, her half-sister somewhere out in the wilds, and her three nieces to assist with the running of the state, and squabble over the succession. However, duty was one thing, love something else entirely. Only her yappers brought true joy.

"Curmeister! Unleash my ferocious hounds!" the Dux bellowed.

A yapping and yelping rose from the far corner of the courtroom as the Curmeister released the portly pooches from their tethers and they rocked, rolled, and waddled their way across the mosaic floor to the Dux and an endless source of vegetable treats. The Curmeister's Assistant followed close behind with a mop and bucket to clean up any green deposits they left on the doggie trek.

"Come here, my lovelies, come here," the Dux said, scattering pieces of vegetables on the floor for her canine children. She reached down, and with no small effort picked up the chubbiest tail wagger and dropped it into her lap. They exchanged kisses, until the dog hopped onto the table and finished off the remainder of the Dux's breakfast. The other curs looked up in envy. One even tried a few hops in a desperate attempt to reach the tabletop, but soon gave up and tussled with its brothers and sisters for scraps amongst the geometric tile shapes on the floor.

For a brief moment, the Dux was just Agitha again. A carefree young girl who played with her puppies while her mother handled the affairs of state. Long before she was married off to a Dandy cousin and tasked with propagating the family line. Long before she learnt the cruelty of singular rule and spitting spiteful words at those who could not spit back. Long before she clicked her fingers and snuffed out life from those she barely knew, and immediately forgot. Now madness and sadness weighed her down in equal measure. She was the Dux of the Var and all feared her.

The Var were a warlike people who had come out of the west, driven by a frenzied quest for plunder and taking from others what they could not create themselves. Long ago, before the permawinter sealed the land and froze the rivers and lakes, they came in their longboats to *Varingr,* the mightiest of pirate raids, navigating the waterways, and portaging their craft across the connecting land. They were in search of the fabled city of gold, *Andalayim,* which lay at the end of the earth. It was an arduous journey, and many perished along the way, but those who remained grew stronger from the privations, and hardened for the task ahead. In those solars, the Dandies were warriors too, and fought alongside their womenfolk. Even the camp followers, servants and slaafs, were called into battle when needed. Together, they found the great citadel of Andalayim, and marveled at the high walls and the towering fortress beyond. It was a city of wonder, intricate artwork, scholars, and untold wealth. It was also a city in decline with a dwindling, aged population who could do little to ward off the

CHAPTER NINE

ferocious Var. They offered immense riches to be left in peace, but the Var wanted it all. Despite their stout defenses, there were too few inhabitants to defend the walls, and the Old Ones, as the Var now referred to them on account of their fabled longevity, were quickly dispatched. Only a handful of the most learned scholars were permitted to exist a little longer, until the most valued lore and secret knowledge contained in the great tomes were transcribed and translated into Varic runes. A class of Var scholars were created from the brightest and the enlightenment became their own. They used the knowledge they gained from the Old Ones to build their seagoing fleet, and now they built their wealth from oceanic trade.

At first, there were the same four seasons they were used to in the west. The winters were longer and colder, and the summers short and hot. The citadel was kept warm with the underground heating which ran below the floors. It was a science managed by a new class of Assameisters, a small group of raised low folk, who only answered to the Dux's Council. Then the airstone came crashing down from the heavens and landed in the far north, destroying vast forests, and blotting out the solar. The long winters came and obliterated the delicate seasonal balance. The winter frost meant the intricate heating system created by the Old Ones for their pleasure alone, was expanded into the town, and warmth underfoot was a permanent fixture. It was also a reminder of the power of the Dux, who could freeze them all on a whim. With the permawinter there was no danger, or even contact from the west, and their great Black Ships prevented incursions from the sea. Only the mighty Sul Empire to the south had the military resources to threaten Varstad, but they showed no interest in the frozen northland. A steady supply of furs as a way of tribute kept relations cordial.

Andalayim was renamed Varstad in their own language, and the citadel was populated by the Var women and their Dandies. Over time, the Dandies reduced themselves to concubines and kept men who reveled in play, while the women ruled and trained in the martial arts. The common folk, the traders, craftsmen, and seafarers, occupied the town of Assaborg, known to them in the common tongue as Gastown. They filled the space between the citadel of Varstad, and the great outer walls. Trade with other nations expanded their ranks, and some, driven by necessity or wishing to get away from the stench of the city and breathe the clean free air, took up homesteading beyond the safety of the fortress, though still under the jurisdiction of the Dux. The Dux ruled them all, and her word was law.

The Var pantheon changed too. Tiv was the supreme warrior, and his was the way of the sword and conquest. Frotha, his flame-haired sister, persuaded him to teach her martial attributes, and for a time they fought side by side as equals. No one, man or beast could stand before them. Frotha's throne was moved next to Tiv's and they ruled as one. Even gods succumb to temptation, and Tiv was no exception. He put down his sword, and sought comfort in intoxication and debauchery. He willingly gave up his throne next to Frotha, and took to lying on a couch at her feet. Frotha needed wise council, so raised up her two sisters to the level below hers; Loti the Learned, who loved books and study, and the art of counting; and Hulda the Boneless, who performed the thankless tasks no one wanted, and watched over the passage through the Onderworld.

A gentle cough interrupted the Dux's carefree moment, and her smile for her hounds was replaced by a stately scowl. She reached up and covered her face with a black lace veil.

"What is it, Bursa? Did you draw the black ball to come and fetch me to the Council Chamber?" the Dux said.

The Dux barely glanced at her Minister of External Affairs, a middle-aged woman who came before her dressed in sackcloth and with a strained look upon her thin face. She was a slight woman with constant bowel problems. No one knew if her ailment was the initial cause of her gaunt appearance, or if the pressure of her work was the cause of the pressure in her roiling gut. To facilitate a costive disposition, thin gruel was her boon companion and legumes were her nemesis. She appeared meek and self-deprecating, but her humbleness was reserved for the Dux and her council sisters. To her staff and servants she was a sharp-tongued malicious terror, and bombastic from both ends.

"The Council is gathered in the Great Chamber and awaits your pleasure,"

CHAPTER NINE

Bursa said, bowing as deep as her troubled stomach allowed. Seeping gas was a constant challenge.

"What is the excitement today?" the Dux asked. "Do you want to raise taxation and tithes for more merchant ships to breach the Forbidden Islands? Another false complaint from the Sul on the quality of our furs? Or is it another state visit from the odious meat eaters from Pashtak?"

"All noteworthy subjects, ma'am, and ones where your wisdom will clearly shine. But we have something more pressing," Bursa said, with a pinched smile.

"Which is?"

"War, ma'am. War," Bursa said with a pained expression.

The Dux sat up in her chair. "Finally, something of interest. Gather my army and prepare the Black Ships. I'll take us on a mighty Varingr raid as of old. Lead on, Bursa. My War Council awaits."

The Dux Council convened in the Great Chamber, a large cavernous room kept warm by an intricate airflow design. The chamber overlooked the towering walls of Varstad, Assaborg beyond, and the bustling harbor below. Shields, swords, axes, the war horn of the Var, and other military accouterments decorated the interior. They were superficial adornments over the rich mosaic patterns created by the Old Ones. Pride of place was reserved for the mighty Varbow of Stella the Great, the Damm Warrior who led the conquest of Andalayim. It was ruptured in the middle as Stella held it up to ward off a scimitar blow. It now served as a symbol of Var martial prowess, and how they could be tested as a people but never broken.

As the Dux and Bursa entered the soaring room, the three occupants rose from their high backed chairs and waited until the Dux stepped up on the dais and took her seat in her own, more magnificent sovereign throne perched loftily above the others. This was no round table. The majestic oblong block placed the Dux at the head, and the four council members, two on either side, with another empty chair just to the side of the Dux, reserved for her absent half-sister. They managed the affairs of the citadel with a degree of latitude, since the Dux had little patience or aptitude for the mundane, but the decisions and direction emanated from the little stout woman at the head of the table.

With a wave of her hand, the four Dux Council members took their seats. She motioned to an old woman in gray at the far end of the Great Chamber who was tasked with recording the proceedings. The scribe waited patiently, quill hovering over parchment ready to capture every word.

There were no men present. Strategic thinking was the domain of the women of the Var, and they were well represented. Aldith, who held the title of Domina, the Minister of War, and the Dux's own niece took the first seat on the left. She was a tall powerful woman just past thirty years, and the first of the Damm Warriors. She was not pretty in the conventional sense, and the bowl shaped haircut to cushion a war helmet and the dueling scar on her left cheek did little to soften her features, but neither was she plain to look at. She was born and built for fighting and her demeanor was one of action. She was prohibited from bearing arms in the Great Council Chamber, but outside a longsword was her constant companion, and like all of the Damm Warriors she was an expert with the varbow. As always, she wore a coat of chainmail under her white robe. The formal security of the Var, and the lands beyond the citadel walls belonged to her and her alone.

To Aldith's left sat her once loved and now hated half-sister, one year her junior, another niece of the Dux, as well as a rival for the Duxdom. Her mother had bestowed the name Bella on her the first solar she entered the Var world, but she was widely known as Rafyn, on account of her lank black hair and curved, thick nose. At first, it was an affectionate sobriquet, but the meaning changed over time as her constant presence when corpses were in the vicinity distorted the meaning. Rafyn bore little resemblance to her half-sister, or the rest of the Var sisterhood. While they were fair faced and light haired as a race, Rafyn, shared her coloring with the night. Some whispered her mother had congress with the darker men of the north as she traveled across the frozen wastelands, or consorted with the spirits of the Old Ones. Either way, Rafyn was considered the result of an unholy

CHAPTER NINE

union.

Rafyn was responsible for relations with the Burghmeisters, and maintained the spy network beyond the citadel walls, though her official title was Domestica, Minister of Domestic Trade. She was powerful enough in her youth to be a Damm Warrior, but chose the path of deceit, treachery, murder, and smooth talking. In short, she was a politician, and like the Dux her chosen color was black though not for the mourning of others, but to cast dread as she condemned innocents and sinners alike. Rafyn had no friends or companions, just lackeys, paid spies, and assassins who inhabited her macabre world.

Directly across from Rafyn was the humble Bursa, who meekly bowed her head and clutched at her churning belly. Next to Bursa sat Florenza, Exchequia, the Minister of the Exchequer, a small dumpy woman in frumpy brown with a jovial disposition, and always with a jingle in her pocket. Florenza was born to balance books, count beans, and hoard gild for the Dux. Her love of numbers stretched to infinity. If she asked for any gift it would be another set of fingers to count in double time.

"The council is now in session," the Dux announced, banging a little gavel on the heavy ironwood table, and the scribe duly recorded her words for posterity.

"What is the order of the solar? Bursa said we have war to discuss," the Dux said, tossing up her black veil and staring at her council members.

"Bursa got ahead of herself, my liege. First we must discuss more regular affairs of state, and address some commotion in the area the low born refer to as the Mutton," Rafyn said, glaring across the table at the hapless Bursa, who lowered her head still further, as if to beg forgiveness.

"Hrmph," said the Dux, dropping her veil back over her face. "Proceed."

Rafyn stood up. She was as tall as Aldith, but she no longer had the same warrior's frame. She stooped slightly, as if to conceal her true height. "Trade with the Burghs goes well. There were some grumblings when we increased the tithe to a second hand share, but none withheld payment and the collections proceeded as normal."

Florenza positively bounced in her chair at the news of more gild filling the Dux's already full coffers. Coin jingled in her pocket.

"There was a recent death in the Four Kith of note," Rafyn continued.

The Dux popped up from behind her veil. "Was it a murder? Is there a gruesome tale to share?"

"No, ma'am. Rather it was a fight to the death between two butchers for the role of Hetman. One Cotter Sullivan, a known villain, dispatched Mo Dickens with a cleaver strike to the head. Their vulgar rules permit death duels to settle leadership disputes. It doesn't disrupt the delicate balance in the Four Kith, and has no bearing on our trade within the Burghs. Just common folk getting on with common business."

"Hrmph," said the Dux and the veil flopped back down.

"Are you sure we don't need to dispatch a troop of Red Shadows to put them in place?" Aldith asked.

"No, sister. Everything is under control. No need for the iron gauntlet when the silk glove serves the same purpose," Rafyn sneered.

For the long Hour of the Horse before the mid sol, the Dux Council discussed more mundane matters. They including a possible change in the ranking of the Red Shadows; the selection process for girls entering the Treasury; the appropriate length of skirts for serving boys; a raising of the vin limit for Dandies; spice imports from the Murghar to the far south; and a loss of one merchant ship on the Gray Middens. To the utter dismay of the Dux, the Council even droned on about a new immigration quota for foreign merchants, traders, minstrels, vagabonds, and seafaring folk from distant lands seeking to set up shop and partake of the riches Assaborg had to offer.

The Dux slid further and further down in her chair. She blew on her veil to push it upwards and then let it sink back down over her face as a form of childish amusement.

"And now we have to discuss the murders in the area known as the Palace of Earthly Pleasures, or the Mutton, as previously mentioned," Rafyn said.

The Dux sat up straight on her throne and flipped up her veil. "Murders did you say?"

"Yes, ma'am. Horrible crimes. Bodies torn asunder, throats slashed, eyes

CHAPTER NINE

gouged, and innards exposed," Rafyn said pausing for effect.

The Dux waited less than three heartbeats. "Go on, go on, Rafyn. Spare no details." She was positively salivating.

"Six murders in total ma'am. One was a young thief who wandered into the Mutton from the Four Kith. He was torn apart like a wild animal was on the loose. Some say the markings of the direwolf were upon him, but that's highly unlikely. My spies tell me he probably lifted a purse from the wrong pocket and paid for it with his life. The signs of a wild beast attack were a ruse to cover human tracks. We can discount that one."

The Dux waved her hand in dismissal. "Yes, yes, Rafyn. Let's reject that one. And the other five?"

"Decidedly human, my liege, but with a twist. All five were ladies of the night. Women who sell their bodies to men for pleasure."

The Dux gasped. "You mean they pay men for the horizontal act?"

Rafyn shook her head. "No ma'am. The men pay the women for their own carnal desires. The low folk live by reverse rules to us."

"Why in Frotha's name would we allow such a thing?" the Dux said, horrified by the very thought.

"Taxes, ma'am. We permit the vile trade overseen by men known as Swell Daddies, as long as they keep the peace, and pay us for the privilege of existing," Rafyn explained.

"Taxes? Oh we like taxes, don't we, Florenza?" the Dux said, her mood lightening.

"Oh, yes, your Dux. We love all creative ways to fill the royal coffers," Florenza said, rubbing her greedy paws together.

Satisfied with the monetary justification for the flesh trade, the Dux returned to the subject of the slayings. "Rafyn, you were telling us about the murders. Is there more?"

"Yes ma'am. There is more, a great deal more. You see the gruesome nature of the killings gets steadily worse. The first girl simply had her throat cut. The second and third were gutted and slashed. The fourth one dispatched rather quickly. And the fifth one…"

"Yes, yes?" said the Dux, covering her mouth with her hands.

"The fifth one was a plaything for a monster with a knife. The body was torn asunder, organs and entrails scattered around, and the head completely severed. Some parts are still missing."

There was silence in the room as they all mused on who could do such a thing. Rafyn was well versed in the instruments of torture, the assassin's blade, and the administration of a poisonous dose, and Aldith had no hesitation in dispatching someone for the smallest slight. However, killing for pure pleasure was beyond this sisterhood.

"There's more ma'm," Rafyn said.

"More?"

"Yes, my liege. This is where it gets interesting. A Dandy has been seen in the Mutton and the common folk suspect him of the murders. They've named him, *The Terror.* They're stirring in their nests, and one more murder could set them off."

"*The Terror* you say. And a Dandy in the Mutton? We should cut his winkle off," the Dux offered.

"Unfortunately, more than one visit those dens of iniquity. They might be weak men, but they're our weak men, and people of the Var. And we need their winkles. We can't allow any of them to come to harm at the hands of the vulgar," Rafyn said.

"Then we would send in the Red Shadows," Aldith offered.

Rafyn bowed her head. "Yes, sister. On that we agree. But for now, no act of violence has befallen our menfolk. Rather than poke the hornet's nest, we will continue to observe. As an added precaution, we will prevent any Dandy incursions into the Mutton and see if things settle down."

"That's it then? We just wait?" the Dux asked.

"Respectfully," Rafyn replied with a deeper bow to the Dux.

"Hrmf," the Dux said. "Now can we get to the business of war?"

"Yes, my liege. I cede the floor to Bursa who will explain our dilemma."

As Rafyn took her seat, Bursa, the Minister of External Affairs, rather reluctantly got to her feet. Her stomach churned as she prepared to humbly make her case in front of the Dux. She bowed and scraped, and was loathed by her peers for it.

CHAPTER NINE

"As we all agreed, and graciously blessed by our noble Dux," Bursa started, looking around the table to ascertain the level of support. No one met her eye. "We established the colony of Agithawald in the far southern islands as a means of opening a warm weather port, gaining access to new timber supplies for shipbuilding, other articles of trade with our overseas partners, and of course, colonization of a new, and dare I say, warmer world. An outpouring of superior Var culture and traditions to rule over the native inhabitants."

"And how much has your little adventure cost us so far?" Rafyn sneered.

"*Our* little adventure, Lady Rafyn, and the initial cost will reap rich rewards," Bursa replied. Her tone was self-deprecating, and as humble as ever.

"How much?" Rafyn asked again.

Florenza, ever the efficient accountant, pulled a counting device from underneath her chair and placed it on the table. She moved a few beads back and forth on the rods, and gave a deep sigh. A capital outlay always gave her heartburn.

"Factoring in the recent supply ship and the cost and time of the mercantile crew away from other ventures, we're running at two hundred thousand gold krun," Florenza said.

Both Rafyn and Aldith gasped at such a large amount.

"But your own calculations showed we'll increase that amount tenfold in five years, Florenza," Bursa said meekly, rubbing her hands together.

"A projection sister. But until we see a return on our investment, we're running a deficit," Florenza replied.

The Dux had heard enough. Money talk and trade bored her, and she banged her gavel on the table to stop the chatter. "War! You promised me talk of war, and a true Varingr, which we haven't seen in lifetimes, and you're gibbering over krun and colonies! Will one of you kindly get to the point!"

"I believe you still have the floor, Bursa. Kindly explain matters to the Dux," Rafyn said.

"Thank you, Lady Rafyn. Your observance of protocol is always deeply appreciated." Bursa paused for a moment, while she contemplated how to deliver the news to the Dux.

"Well your Dux, it appears as if Agithawald has disappeared," Bursa said. Her armpits were now visibly damp, and her left leg was trembling. She desperately tightened her sphincter to prevent an untimely emission.

"Disappeared? Disappeared? How can my colony simply vanish? Are we sure we've looked in the right spot?" the Dux exploded.

"Not the buildings, my liege. Oh we found them, as fresh as the solar they were constructed. It's the people. Not a trace of them. It's as if the ground opened up and swallowed them all. Gone without a trace," Bursa explained, and wished the ground opened up beneath her at this very moment.

"Is that what happened then? They were swallowed? And do we go a Varingr against the ground?" the Dux asked.

"Not quite, your Grace. Allow me to explain," Rafyn said. "Bursa, if you don't mind, I'll take the floor." Rafyn stood, and Bursa, happy to take a seat, flopped into her chair.

"There were six score colonists in total. One score Damm Warriors under the capable leadership of Runa Herasdottir, your appointed Stewardess. An equal contingent of Red Shadows, a smattering of Dandies looking for adventure, and the rest tradespeople. The fortifications were strong, morale was high, and relations with the natives, though cool, were not overly hostile. And then something changed."

"Yes, yes. Go on," the Dux said, eager to hear more.

"We sent regular supplies to Agithawald, and ships to bring back the timber. Two trips ago, we got word, a new tribal leader from the north island was pushing south, and he objected to the taking of their sacred trees. There were a few skirmishes, but Runa felt she still had control of the situation. Then on the next trip, Agithawald was a ghost town. There was no sign of a struggle. No burnt buildings. It was as if our people were spirited away. Or as Bursa put it, the ground opened up and swallowed them."

The room fell silent and all pondered on the potential fate of the colonists. Darker minds considered the slaughter of innocents, unspeakable torture

CHAPTER NINE

and rude murder by wanton savages. More gentler spirits saw them taken away into captivity, safe for now, and ripe for rescue. The more fanciful considered the option of the colonists abandoning their settlement for a better location, and richer harvests. Whatever the musings, something had to be done. The Var were a vengeful people.

It was Aldith's turn to take the floor. She stood and Rafyn reluctantly slithered into her seat.

"It's time to send a military expedition," Aldith said.

"Yes, yes! A Varingr we shall go!," the Dux said excitedly. "Ready my Black Ships and my Damm Warriors, and I'll lead us to a glorious war! Bring me my chainmail, my longsword, and my helm of victory!"

There was a collective gasp from the room. "Not quite, my liege," Rafyn said. "Your place is here ruling the people. You're much too valuable to risk on a campaign. Besides, sea journeys upset your constitution."

"Then who will lead my fighting force, Rafyn? You?"

"Not I, my liege. My place is with you. Aldith is the chosen one to go a Varingr."

"And who will guard my Duxdom?"

"Lilith will hold down the citadel. Is our sister not capable, Aldith?"

Aldith nodded her head. "She is, though a little headstrong at times. I trust the Council will guide her on the right application of enforcement when required."

"Oh, we will, Aldith. You can be assured of that," Rafyn said.

The Dux flopped back in her chair. "Hrmph,' she said.

Aldith continued. "We'll need a thousand Damm Warriors and double that number in Red Shadows, plus our naval contingent, and a substantial number of Black Ships to successfully prosecute this Varingr. We don't know how many of the natives we're going against, and we don't know their war methods. We must crush them at the first opportunity."

"Oh, such a large number, Lady Aldith. I bow before your martial wisdom, but can we afford such a burden? Bursa modestly asked.

Florenza's hands whizzed across her counting machine. She stopped for a moment, tapped her nose, then quickly made a correction. The total surprised even her. "We're talking half of our available forces, and the supplies for the journey alone are astronomical. Then there's the loss of trade with so many Black Ships required for the best part of one year. If my numbers are correct, the grand sum, not accounting for any potential casualties, or offsetting gains from slave trading, comes to … eight hundred thousand gold krun. Why, I've never seen such an amount. It has the potential to cripple us, especially if the venture is not successful."

"What do you mean, not successful?" Aldith challenged. "We're the Var. We go a Varingr, or at least we used to. It's in our blood. We'll crush these people and take all of their lands! We'll kill the menfolk, and send the women and children into servitude. They'll soon forget who they were and where they came from. The Var are vengeful people!"

All eyes fell on the Dux for regal guidance. She remained silent, her chubby chin resting in her pudgy hands. She was lost in thought, and they did not know if she was contemplating the glories of battle and a victorious campaign, worrying over the exorbitant cost to her Duxdom and the possible end to her dynasty, or simply pondering over what she would eat for lunch. The wait for a royal pronouncement seemed to last an eternity, until the Dux suddenly roused herself.

"Pythoness! Petra the Stargazer, Keeper of the Tomes, and Oracle to the Dux. What do you have to say?" the Dux boomed.

The scribe stirred from her unobtrusive desk at the far corner of the Great Chamber. The old crone gently placed her quill down on her writing slab, and slid the scroll over to her assistant. With a nod of her head she instructed the young Pythoness-in-training to take over the record keeping, and she hobbled over to face her Dux. Petra would be called long in the tooth by those with a charitable disposition, but she no longer possessed any tusks of note. Even her wisdom teeth had judiciously moved on. Her most distinguishing feature, enhanced by the fact she tied her sleeves back, was the blue color of her forearms and hands, the result of working night and solar with rooter's ink, and the damn spots would not wash out. Her body was decrepit, weather worn like stone, and stooped from long hours of sitting and scribing and poring over ancient books. She was a little hard

CHAPTER NINE

of hearing, which meant the council records were often amiss, but her mind was still as sharp as a Hallic blade.

Petra shuffled closer to the great table and stood before the Dux. She curtsied with a degree of difficulty.

"Well?" the Dux asked.

"My Dux?" Petra replied.

"Do the signs portend to a successful campaign?" the Dux asked, slightly irritated.

Petra thought for a moment, and then stuck an inked covered finger in her ear and gave it a sharp wiggle as if to dislodge a worm, or an unwanted thought. "The journey will be long and arduous, and we'll lose ships and crew along the way. But in the end Lady Aldith will triumph. The native horde will be vanquished after a mighty battle and the Var will be victorious."

The four council members banged their fists on the great table gratified the omens were in their favor and success was all but guaranteed. Even the Dux playfully tapped her gavel in unison with the fist thumping. None of them noticed the quick glance exchanged between Rafyn and Petra.

Petra raised a hand. "However, there is one other important detail we must consider, my liege," Petra said, throwing an immediate dampener on the premature celebration.

The council members stayed their hands, and fists returned to open palms. All but Rafyn who glared at the Pythoness and tightened her grip.

"The stars are aligned and the Purge is almost upon us. With so many Damm Warriors and Red Shadows away overseas, we will have reduced military might to deal with a possible insurrection."

"Insurrection?" Aldith bellowed. "Why would there be an insurrection? The people know their place."

Petra shuffled from foot to foot, and seemed to shrivel in front of Aldith's wrath. "We haven't seen a Purge in our lifetime, Lady Aldith, but the records tell us they always bring unrest. The last one resulted in five hundred deaths based on the reports I read from Pythoness Havu in the reign of Bodil Astridsdottir."

"Five hundred? A trivial number," Aldith said.

"Are you saying we should postpone the Varingr until after the Purge? If we're being cautious, it does make sense," Rafyn purred.

"Absolutely not!" Aldith shouted. "This expedition goes ahead."

Rafyn turned towards Petra. Her eyes were piercing, but her words were soft and gentle. "Petra the Pythoness? Do we stay or do we go?" she asked.

Petra looked up from the ground, and glanced at each of the Council members one at a time. Florenza was on the fence, worried about the expenditure, but hopeful for the immense future profits. Bursa had a pained expression, which was difficult to read, but Petra knew she wanted nothing more than to make Agithawald a success, and remove the stain on her record. The blood was up with Aldith and she was impetuously settled on battle and conquest. And then there was Rafyn, always scheming.

Do we stay or do we go?

"We go," Petra said, and dropped her head again.

Chapter Ten

Justin : The Tower of Tomes

The door to the Tower of Tomes was not locked, and the library was unguarded. There was no need, as few in Varstad had any interest in poring over the vast collection of books, scrolls, and single leaf drawings, recorded on an assortment of plant fiber papers, parchment, and the more refined vellum. There were even some older works etched into clay tablets, but the language was lost to the ages, and none amongst the Konna, the learned women of letters, cared to take up the challenge of decipherment.

He had the great store of information all to himself, and his excitement was palpable as he unfurled a new scroll on the secrets of human dissection and the inner workings of the body, blew ancient dust from a beautifully inscribed weighty tome on mathematical principles and concepts, or pieced together parchment fragments to recreate a map of a wondrous world decorated with mythical creatures, unseen for a millenia.

The library never ceased to amaze him. The architecture, clearly illustrated and with precise specifications in many of the ancient works, evolved over time to reach a state of elegant grandeur. The tower itself spiraled up from the ground floor to the ceiling, and appeared delicate in its construction. However, strength lay in the design of the concentric circles. All the way up the mighty staircase, stone shelves and hidden alcoves were stacked with books. More than a polymath could read in ten lifetimes. At the top of the structure there was a retracting roof, which opened up for stargazing and the study of the heavens. The acoustics in the tower were also extraordinary. You could whisper on the ground floor, and every word and syllable was amplified crisp and clear up at the skyfacing observatory. It ran contrary to the silence generally required for study in the great libraries, but it allowed an astronomical watcher to monitor mundane events below, and the Pythoness used it to great effect to monitor her charges while perched above.

Only a small portion of the vast collection was translated into Varic runes, and these were sorted, and neatly ordered. The Konna used this reference material for medicinal means, potions to heal or kill, the study of astronomy and astrology, the construction of their great Black Ships, and the articles of war. Naturally, he consumed these first. However, his deep interest was in the hidden lore contained in the massive collection in the language of the Old Ones, or as he knew them, the Ma'din. He studied the dictionaries and grammar rules first compiled at the foundation of Varstad, and the overthrow of Andalayim, before the last of the Ma'din vanished. In its written form, it was a beautiful cursive style far removed from the brutal scratchings and harsh lines of runes. He borrowed the dictionaries, always returning them to their rightful place, and studied them until a degree of mastery evolved. He manufactured his own paper from plant pulp, and created his own ink and quills to copy and imitate in a flowing hand. He longed to speak the words out loud, but there was no one to emulate, other than the secret voice he heard in his dreams, and he was left with studying the dead language alone during the solar.

He knew from an early age he was not like the other Dandy boys. He refrained from the gymnastics practice they engaged in to keep their bodies toned and pretty. He had no interest in fashion, cosmetics, perfume, or jewelry, all staples of the Dandies' inconsequential existence. He avoided richly prepared foods, heavy with spices, and ate raw vegetables for sustenance only and not enjoyment. He preferred to dress in a simple black robe, with a rope belt around his waist, a male version of the garb favored by the Konna. He was mocked mercilessly by the Dandy boys for his fashion

CHAPTER TEN

sense, or lack of it, though they never resorted to physical punishment for his deviation. Violence was the remit of the Damm Warriors, and the Dandy boys relied on sharp tongues to do their cutting. *Justin the Jeweless*, they mocked him, more Konna than Dandy. He did not care. He never felt comfortable with their communal living, and he saw and hated what they grew up to be. Vain men who drank themselves into oblivion, or smoked the black tar until their brains melted, occasionally fornicating with the mighty Damm Warriors or the stout Konna when a new brood of children were required, or more likely cavorting with each other. It was considered unseemly to reach an old age, and Dandies were expected to flame out as their looks faded and their bodies turned to bloat. He wanted to live forever and read, and read, and read.

He did not know how long he had been engrossed in his studies in the upper chamber, lost in the world of poultice and liniment treatments for any number of human and animal ailments, from wounds, burns, inflammation, toothache, and the heavy consumption of rich foods. Footsteps and the sound of a cane tapping on the stone stairs pulled him away from his latest topic and back to reality. There were consequences for being somewhere he should not be, and it was better to safely hide away and read another solar. The disorderly array of books and scrolls meant he could disappear into any number of literary hideouts, but he settled on withdrawing behind a pillar of tomes on Ma'din mechanics and machine construction.

There were two voices, muffled at first, but clear as a bell as they entered the Tower of the Tomes. He recognized the sound of Petra the Pythoness, humble and deferential to the other, who dominated the conversation. The voices soared to the upper rafters.

"Are these your charts, Pythoness?" the woman asked. Her tone was harsh to Justin's ears. It was a voice used to commands and demanding servile acquiescence.

"Yes, Lady Rafyn. I drew them up after consulting the stars, and checked them thrice," Petra replied.

Justin thought about peeking out and checking what they were examining, but from this height, he would see nothing of note. He thought about swinging down the mighty stargazer Petra used, and peering through that, but it was too powerful for human observation. Perhaps, if he made a smaller replica it would be of some use. He stored that away for a future project.

"And you swear no one else knows of it?" the stern woman asked.

"I do swear, Lady Rafyn," Petra said. There was fear in her voice. "I came to you as soon as I deciphered the portent."

"Good. Now burn it."

"Lady Rafyn?"

"I said burn it."

"But it took over a lunar to construct. The calculations are complex."

"Here, this brazier will do. Let me help you, Pythoness."

Justin heard a rustling of papers hastily gathered up and then the crackling sound as fire licked at the edges, and quickly turned the contents to ashes.

"What if the Dux demands to see the omens?"

"Then create a false narrative. I need my sister's voyage to go ahead. Her preparations are almost complete and she sails with the fleet in three solars. I need her out of Varstad, and if a little ill luck should befall her along the way... do you understand?"

When he saw it, all interest in the conversation below evaporated. There it was before him, a book tantalizingly referenced by others, but hidden until this moment, It was a small volume nestled between two mighty tomes above and below. *A Treatise on the Aerodynamics of Man, and the Detailed Construction of Flying Machines* by Abbas Takurunna. He licked his lips at the thought of the diagrams and the calculations contained within. Comprehensive drawings of balloons filled with hot air, floating high above the ground with men below suspended in a basket, and man-made wings attached to a light wooden frame and maneuvered by hand pulleys. According to Mabannas, Abbas Takurunna tested his own contraption by strapping on his wings and jumping from the Tower of Flight. He sailed into the air and was never seen again.

CHAPTER TEN

He reached out to tug the treatise free, but the tome above pinned it in place. He pulled harder with both hands and the heavy volume on top tumbled too. He struggled to catch it and stumbled back into a pillar of mechanical books which crashed down all around him. It might have well been the Tower of Tomes itself for the noise it generated.

"What's that?" Rafyn asked.

"It's nothing. Books fall here all the time," Petra said. "Usually there's no one around to hear them."

"We should burn them all, Pythoness. I could use this tower for something more appropriate to the management of Varstad. Consider that while you contemplate portents."

Burn the books? Justin was horrified and held his breath as he clutched the treatise tightly to his chest, and sat surrounded by the fallen repository. Dust floated in a scholarly cloud around him, but he resisted the urge to sneeze.

"She's gone now. You can come down, Justin," Petra said.

Justin froze. Petra had caught him on prior occasions, and always sent him packing with jarring words, a tap from her cane, and threats of retribution if he ever entered the Tower of Tomes again. He always came back. The draw of learning was too powerful to resist, whatever the verbal or physical punishment.

"Justin! Come down!" Petra barked.

He had no choice. He extricated himself from the disorganized volumes and slowly walked down the spiral staircase still clutching the treatise to his chest, as if it would sprout wings and fly him free from the Pythoness's wrath.

He was tall for his age, though he already stooped slightly from habitually leaning over books and he was paper thin from a malnourished diet. He towered over the dumpy crone who rested both hands on her cane.

"Libraries are known for bookworms, and ours has a book rat. Tell me, Justin? What am I to do with you?"

"Let me work for you. I can sort the works of the Ma'din ... I mean the Old Ones, so they're easy to locate. There's a numbering system I've devised…"

"Justin, it won't do. You're a Dandy, not a Konna. Who ever heard of such a thing? Do you believe you were born into the wrong body? Is that it? I know of some Konna who dream of giving up the constant struggles of work and simply relaxing with a flagon of vin."

Justin shook his head. "I have no desire to be a Konna."

"But you dress like one. Look at you in your black cassock instead of a fine Dandy tunic."

"I dress like me. I think like me, and I am me. The Ma'din had male scholars, the *Habala'im*, men of letters. They studied the arts, science, astronomy, geography, anatomy, mechanics…"

"But it's not the way of the Var, Justin. We have strict divisions in the Gentry between the Damm Warriors, the Konna, and the Dandy. Each serves a function in our natural order. Why, to go outside of it would upset things. The Dux would never stand for it. She'd have your head off before you could say *bibliophile*."

Justin sat down on the mosaic floor, still clutching the treatise tightly to his chest. He hung his head, and let his long black hair cover his face, as if not seeing Petra meant he was safe.

There must be another way.

"I can translate," Justin said. He jumped to his feet. "I can translate the words of the Old Ones into Varic runes, so you can read all the material you want."

"You taught yourself their language? Why I can barely read it myself, and I studied for years under Embla the Wise. How could a mere boy learn so fast?" Petra asked incredulously.

"It's easy if you know how. There are only twenty-eight unique letters, and the grammatical structure is quite uniform. Of course that's for the written form. In the vernacular, I'm sure they break all of the rules as we do, though we have no idea how the words actually sounded. In my considered opinion, I think … " Justin stopped talking when he saw the scowl on Petra's face. He'd gone too far and he knew it.

"I mean, I could be your apprentice. Translate some of the works on say

CHAPTER TEN

potions, there's a fine little book by Plaxas called *The Elementals*. I could translate it and submit it for your review … and corrections, of course."

Justin waited eagerly for a response, but Petra just stared up at him in silence. He felt his life hang in the balance at that moment. Petra could banish him forever from the Tower of Tomes, and what would he do then? A life without books and learning was no life at all. Better to end it then and jump off the tower without the wings.

"Let me think on it," Petra said.

Justin jumped for joy and flapped his arms like a demented, clipped winged crow trying desperately to get airborne. He could have smothered the Pythoness in kisses of gratitude.

"Thank you, Pythoness! Thank you! You won't regret it."

"I only said I'd think about it. Now hand me that book and return to your chambers."

Justin reluctantly passed over the book, and watched as Petra ran a finger along the title, and first mouthed the words to herself.

"*A Treatise on the Ceramics of Man and the Detailed Construction of Frying Machines*? Why in the world do you want to waste your time with a cookery book?" Petra said, as she placed the unopened treatise down on a table.

Justin shrugged his shoulders. "Just some light reading, Pythoness. I'll pick a more suitable work next time." He turned to go, and then stopped and looked back at Petra.

"Pythoness? Did she really mean it about burning all of the books?"

"Better to forget the words of women, and the realm of politics, Justin. Stick to reading, and leave the rest to your betters."

Justin was in no hurry to return to the little chamber he sequestered for himself up above the Great Hall of the Dandies. The chambers were commonly used for visits from the Damm Warriors and Konna, seeking conjugal rights with assigned spouses and trysts with lovers. However, Justin made one his own and filled it with drawings, charts, drying paper blocks, homemade chalks and charcoal sticks, various colored inks he blended himself, and quills he carved from bird feathers. The materials were not easy to come by, but he bartered with the servants and tradespeople who worked in the citadel for portraits on paper fragments and handworked jewelry. Mostly, he was left alone. Occasionally, adjoining chambers were put to use, and he covered his ears to block out the grunts, groans, and muffled moans.

The chamber was his sanctuary away from the sound of frivolous laughter, constant chatter, and the occasional bouts of hysteria, which drifted up from the Great Hall below like disembodied spirits seeking attention. Alone, he worked on his studies from borrowed books, translating to Varic runes, and sketching the shapes of anatomical parts of the human body, birds in flight, animals in natural motion, and plant structures. Alone, he could not discuss alchemy, astronomy, astrology, cartography, philosophy, logic, or heaven forbid, the flowery language of poetry. There was no partner in crime, confidante, confederate or co-conspirator. There was no lover. Perhaps if he took a Konna wife, she would understand and nurture his desire for knowledge. However, he had no interest in the sexual act, and as the Pythoness reminded him, everything he desired went against the natural order of things in the world of the Var. Alone he remained.

Justin knew he was different from the Dandies in other ways too. While most of them were fair haired and fair skinned, his hair was black and his skin was a darker shade. That in itself separated him from his peers, and children were always quick to notice and point out the disparity. Most of the Dandy boys knew their fathers, though there was no special bond between them. Justin was fatherless from the beginning. He knew the Konna kept a meticulous family registry, more to protect the limited gene pool as best they could and prevent brother and sister unions, and the matrilineal line was the one of importance. Mothers generally severed ties with their male offspring after birth, and focused on nurturing the female progeny. The Damm Warriors, hardened by a military upbringing, had no interest in sons. However, some of the Konna gave in to motherly instincts and occasionally made contact with Dandy children, but their shallowness always led to bitter disappointment. Justin's love of knowledge led him to believe he came from Konna stock, but his height reflected Damm Warrior

CHAPTER TEN

descent. With no matriarch in his life it did not matter.

The dinner bell rang and Justin made his way down to the Great Hall for the evening meal. Mealtimes were the only occasion when all of the Dandies congregated, and Justin was expected to attend, even if he perched alone at the end of the table and nibbled in silence. They sat at the communal tables and dined heartily as servants filled trenchers with spiced grilled vegetables, an assortment of steaming breads with dipping sauces, and multicolored grains. The men quaffed flagon after flagon of vin from metallic cups, their faces turning red, and their senses dulled, as they laughed and shouted with full mouths, full bellies, and empty heads. It was worse than they knew. Justin suspected the metals leached into the liquid and poisoned the blood, rotted the brain, and destroyed the nervous system. For his part, he ate sparingly from a selection of raw carrots, beets, and kale, and drank only fresh water from a wooden beaker. He lingered longer than usual at the dinner table, lost in thought about working for Petra the Pythoness, and what wondrous codices and forgotten folios he would unveil for her. Finally, he stood up and headed back to his chamber, still distracted by scientific musings.

The shock hit him when he entered his room. He was meticulous in the ordering of his projects. He had devised a numbering system for cataloging his work, and he could find any notes, drawing, map, or translation, with ease. Even his quills, charcoal sticks, and colored chalks were neatly stacked based on the intended task. Chaos was something to study, but not a world he surrounded himself with. He needed to know where things were at all times. Order in the physical world allowed his mind to roam free, and now his papers were scattered, and his powers of reasoning stalled.

He picked up a drawing from the floor, and looked at the desecration. It was an anatomically correct rendition of a naked man with his arms outstretched. The normal sized male organ was overlaid with a crudely drawn giant phallus.

Giggling came from the doorway. Justin turned and saw three Dandy boys roughly his own age. They were all a head shorter than him, but their bodies were muscular and lithe from gymnastics practice. They wore richly embroidered tunics, their hairstyles displayed the latest curly fashion, and they were heavily scented with the in vogue perfume.

"Justin the Jeweless," one of them said, and his two companions snickered. "If you intended to draw me, I'm afraid a bigger member is needed, old boy."

The three of them convulsed in laughter, and one of them fell to the floor in an exaggerated fit before his companions picked him up.

Justin raged. All reason escaped him and a red mist swirled. He wanted to use his expansive vocabulary, to belittle them and reduce them to tears.

"You … you!" was all he could say.

This set them off again. "You … you!" they repeated and burst into laughter again.

Justin closed the distance between them, tightened his fist and punched the leader in the nose. The laughing stopped immediately, and they looked incredulously at Justin.

"You hit me!" the boy said, wiping his nostrils and examining his bloody hand.

"You hit him!" another boy said.

"Here's one for you too," Justin said and punched him squarely on the chin.

The third boy took a step back out of striking range.

"You'll pay for this, see if you don't!' The leader said, and the three of them retreated away in search of retribution of their own.

Justin knew he was in trouble. Fighting amongst Dandies was strictly prohibited, and the only violence they ever experienced was when a Damm Warrior got a little too aggressive in the bedchamber. At that moment, Justin did not care. A sense of exhilaration washed over him and he felt power course through his slender body as he looked at his clenched fist and the redness on his knuckles. It felt good to lash out and answer the taunts with strikes of his own. Just as quickly, the sense of excitement faded away, nausea hit him, he struggled to breathe, and there was an overwhelming desire to run away and hide. Instead, he stood in his chamber as his limbs shook uncontrollably.

CHAPTER TEN

I've done it now. Petra will never let me back into the Tower of Tomes.

Justin did not have long to wait. Two stern-faced Damm Warriors as tall as himself, descended on his chamber accompanied by four Red Shadows. Without a word, the two Damm Warriors seized him roughly by the arms and escorted him out of the chamber, while the Red Shadows, who were not permitted to lay hands on a Dandy, even a transgressor like Justin, set about gathering up all of his papers and paraphernalia.

"Pack them carefully," Justin called after them. "There's a system to it, don't mix them up!"

The Damm Warriors led him down the staircase and through the Great Hall as the Dandy men and boys watched in silence. It was a walk of shame for Justin, and his face reddened as he was frogmarched through the crowd. One by one, the Dandies turned their backs on him and declared him an outcast.

They took him out of the Great Hall and across a courtyard, trudging through the snow, and then into a castellated building Justin had never entered before. It was a grim looking monument with thick oak doors reinforced with metal, and no windows to speak of, just tiny slits in the stone work to let in slivers of light. Justin's heart sank as they led him inside and the weighty doors closed behind them with a heavy clang. There was little light inside and Justin could already feel the chill seeping into his bones. The warmth and comfort of the Dandy Great Hall was a thing of the past. Down they went, ever down, into the bowels of the building, the Damm Warriors's heavy footsteps beating out a steady tattoo on the stone steps of the spiral staircase. The cold beckoned them downward with icy fingers.

Justin quickly calculated the cell was less than half the space of his Dandy chamber, and the ceiling was so low he barely had room to stand up straight. The only furniture was a roughly constructed wooden bed in one corner, with a mangy bearskin as the only means of warmth. But what fascinated him the most was the source of light in the cell. Luminescent rocks embedded in the walls glowed.

"Daronite!" Justin exclaimed. "I've only read about them in Druca's *The*

Character and Origin of Rocks. Marvelous!"

They left him alone then, alone in the cell with only the bearskin and glowing rocks for company. Alone to contemplate what he had done in a moment of rage, and what he had given up as a result. He had longed to escape the Dandy Great Hall, and now he would give anything to be back in his chamber with his studies. Now he had nothing.

The rank smell of the old bearskin soon faded with familiarity, and Justin wrapped it about himself as a constant companion. With little to do for entertainment, he counted the daronite rocks, twenty-three in total, and named each of them. He sat cross legged on the bed and practiced the breathing techniques detailed in Sunaman's *Thirty Three Steps Towards Breath Mastery and Enlightenment* to help ward off the cold.

He slept then, and the unbidden dream came to him as it often did, though it felt more akin to a trance-like state. The setting was always the same, a shallow cave in the side of a snowy mountain, dominated by a large rock in the interior. The voice spoke to him as if it emanated from the rock itself, and always with new information. It guided him with instructions on what to study next, clarified his questions, and calmed his mind. The voice spoke to him in Ma'din and called him *Habala,* the seeker of the truth.

Food came once a solar in the form of a thin gruel, delivered by an old grizzled gaoler. Justin tried to engage him in conversation and asked for some raw vegetables, but he simply opened his mouth and pointed to an empty cavity with no teeth and no tongue. He was as silent as the daronite rocks.

He needed to write, draw, and engage his mind in creative activities. He needed to learn something new, expand his knowledge, or explode from the want of it. He started with the bed, and after a few unsuccessful attempts, managed to work free a long enough sliver of wood to act as a scriber, with a small stone sharpened on the floor, as a makeshift nib. As an ink replacement he thought about using his own blood, but that was too dramatic, and he did not relish the thought of a self-inflicted wound, and the risk of infection. Instead, he saved some of his gruel and utilized the thin liquid for writing. There was no paper or parchment, and scraping

CHAPTER TEN

the lining from the bearskin compromised comfort. He settled for the walls and floor of his cell as his canvas.

Justin dipped his scriber into the gruel ink and thought of a suitable phase to test his penmanship. He pondered for a moment and then wrote *Habala* in a flowing hand.

"*Habala*," a female voice said from the other side of the cell bars.

Justin was startled and dropped his pen. He had not heard her approach, and there was no flaming torch to give away the presence of another.

"You can read the language of the Ma'din?" he asked.

"That appears to be the case."

Justin stepped closer and it was like looking in a seer's mirror and seeing a version of himself, ten years older, but in a female form. They even dressed the same in black robes.

"You've gotten yourself into quite a pickle, haven't you? The Dandy with the mind of a Konna."

"Who are you?" he asked, though he recognized the voice from the Tower of Tomes, and it sent a chill through him.

"Let's just say we're related, Justin," Rafyn said. "And I think we can be of mutual benefit to each other."

Chapter Eleven

Joe : Willow Secrets

The steam whistle sounded for the end of another working solar, and Joe raced up the seven flights of stairs at a brisk pace. There was no meeting with Ori today, but he could not resist a quick glance at their secret alcove before he hurried on past with competing feelings of guilt and desire. There was a celebration of sorts at the Willow haus tonight, and he needed to get back and work with Nell on the preparations in the long hour before his father made it home after the last assa check for the evening.

The night air was particularly cold, and Joe pulled up his collar and thrust his hands deep in his pockets as he trudged through the sludge on the Bridge of Broken Souls along with all of the other workers from the Burghs cast out of the citadel for another bleak solar. Only a small group of nightwatchers crossed back in the other direction. Slow walking solemn men who gave up family life to earn a crust. He was gratified to see the body of the young thief was no longer swinging from the gibbet, and wondered if he was given a decent burial, or simply tossed into the canal for the bottom feeders to gnaw upon.

Caution was still the watch word as folks crossed through the narrow edge of the Four Kith. There was safety in numbers, but it also helped to have a small army of paid Bully Boys watching over the working crowd. Joe shuddered to think what would happen if the Bully Boys were ever

CHAPTER ELEVEN

given the order to turn on them. They were fierce men, who ordinarily picked fights for fun, and cared little for the sanctity of life. As long as the Burghmeisters continued to pay their masters, they were on their side for now. Without gild crossing dishonest palms, knives would slash and bully clubs would bludgeon.

Once in the security of the Burghs, there was a collective sigh of relief, Blue Jackets, the Burgh's own protection force, held sway here. They never ventured into the Four Kith, but they patrolled the Burghs in pairs in their heavy coats and their stovepipe top hats, one holding a lantern and the other a large staff. Their main duties revolved around escorting drunken lost souls back to their abode, guiding old women across the street, taking names of wayward children, rescuing billees from trees, and breaking up the odd fistfight over merchandise disagreements.

Workers dispersed to their own Burghs, designated by their respective trades. Stonemasons and sculptors; carpenters, sawyers, cabinetmakers, and woodcarvers; brightsmiths and blacksmiths; painters and jewelers; broodbakers and pastry makers; chandlers and quillers; cobblers and cordwainers; armorers and swordsmiths; bowyers and fletchers; gildsmiths, and whitesmiths. Even the kolmen, each carrying a small bucket of gratis kol to fuel their back to back hauses and warm the water to wash off the kol dust, had their own small district between the Four Kith and the Burghs proper. They were silent outcasts of sorts, not part of the burgh system, but necessary labor for Gastown to function, and so slightly elevated from the Four Kith. Only the Assameister was in the singular, and the Willow abode lay at the end of a lane behind the gild craftsmen.

Joe was always happy to return to their little two storied dwelling. It was a humble abode, with small rooms filled with modest furniture. Comfortable and clean best described it. Nell had candles blazing to light the way, and Joe knew the fire in the hearth would be roaring, and hot soup, warm brood, churned butter, and a side of homemade chutney would be waiting. Tonight there would be more on offer as Castor Willow planned to meet with a small gathering of his Burghmeister peers, and announce he was stepping down from the council after twenty years of loyal service. Time for a younger, more energetic man to pick up the chain of office.

The candles burned bright, but the flames flickered as Joe barged through the kitchen door and startled Nell, who almost dropped a tray of savory pies she had just pulled from the oven. Joe closed the door with a slam, grabbed a chunk of brood and raced up the stairs to his bedroom two at a time.

"Evening, Nell. Nice pies!" Joe said in passing.

"You wash your hands 'fore eating, mind you! Or you'll come down with a case of kolmen's belly," Nell shouted after him, and then went back to focusing on preparation for the feast.

Joe knew not much unsettled Nell Barley, but the thought of a room full of jolly Burghmeisters traipsing through the parlor, eating them out of hearth and home, and drinking more than their fair share of stout and grog had her flustered. She had given the always pristine cottage an extra scrub down in the morning, and had been baking and stewing, boiling and frying, ever since. Her best preserves and pickled vegetables were extracted from the cold cellar, and the cutlery and crockery reserved for special occasions, and each carefully stamped with the Willow crest, were brought down from the attic.

Joe paused before one room with a closed door, and gently placed his right palm on the polished wood. He bowed his head in silent prayer before going on to his own bedroom at the end of the corridor. He sat on the edge of the bed for a moment and finished eating the warm brood freshly liberated from Nell's kitchen table. Clothes for the evening were carefully laid out, and the wash basin, a jug of hot water, a bar of soap, and a warm towel waited to transform him into the Willow his father expected to see at the dinner table. Not the scruffy Assameister's Apprentice, but a shining example of the Willow lineage, the last in a long line of Assameisters, who could entertain the guests with dance and song, and poetry recitations. Joe would reluctantly play the part, always with a smile, but he preferred to be in the assachamber, or smooching with Ori in their love alcove.

As Joe came down the stairs and into the kitchen, Nell stopped what she was doing, wiped her hands on her apron, and brushed a loose strand of hair away from her eyes. A broad smile broke across her homely face, which was dominated by a nose slightly too large and crooked to the right to be handsome, and a burn mark on her left cheek from a hot poker, courtesy of an older brother with a predilection for hurting others. She had kind eyes and a comforting bosom always ready to offer warm hugs. Nell was a consummate homemaker without a home to call her own. She did the next best thing and entered the Willow haushold soon after the death of her own husband and the sad demise of Castor's young wife. She transformed the haus into a sanctuary of snugness and creature comforts.

"Come closer, and let me take a better look at you, Josephine," Nell said.

The young man in the Assameister Apprentice's leathers, hair tucked under a cap, and kol dust on chops was replaced by a young lady in a yellow silk gown, flowing locks, and delicately placed rouge on cheeks. Josephine Willow, the apple of her father's eye, his only surviving child would entertain for him tonight, and ensure his guests left the Willow abode with a favorable impression, and none the wiser for the Assameister's subterfuge.

Nell came closer and took Josephine's hands in her own. She could not help herself from inspecting the nails.

"Don't worry, I scrubbed them carefully to get all the raven oil out," Josephine said.

"A little polish to bring out the luster would be nice. Oh well, let's count our blessings for what we have, and give charitably for them that have not," Nell said, letting Josephine's hand go, and planting a peck of sorts on her cheek, being extra careful not to smudge the rouge.

"Your father will be home soon, and he'll expect everything to be in its proper place. Time to move sharpish," Nell said.

Nell shooed Josephine off to the main parlor, the formal room at the front of the haus they only used for guests and extraordinary functions. On a normal night, Josephine, Nell, and Castor sat in the sitting room or warmed themselves next to the kitchen fire, a makeshift family of sorts, though Nell was the housekeeper, and Castor's occasional bed warmer, and not the official matriarch. It was an arrangement which suited both parties with few complications, but it hung by a thread as Castor's health deteriorated while they managed the family secret.

Josephine knew about the relationship between her father and Nell. She had heard giggles and other related noises coming from his bedchamber as she lay awake at night. Although that was before her brother died and a somber mood settled on the haushold. They all grieved in their own way, Nell as much as the nuclear Willow family, but the impact took an extra toll on Castor's health, and he had limited time to resolve his affairs in a way to protect his daughter's future. It started with tonight, the transfer of power, the calling in of favors, and the preservation of confidential matters.

There was little for Josephine to do in the parlor, other than adjust a napkin, straighten out a spoon, or reposition a floral arrangement. Candles were already burning in their holders, illuminating a gay room and masking the facade. The two Willows would be bright and cheery as they entertained their guests, and sent them back to their burghs with fake smiles and hopeful promises of maintaining the status quo, and the delicate balance of power within the tradecrafts.

The kitchen door opened and slammed shut, and Josephine knew her father was home. She adjusted one more wayward piece of cutlery and hurried to the back of the haus to greet him. The Assameister stood in the doorway, covered head to foot in kol dust and dried raven oil. His face softened when he saw his daughter in all her finery, and the grim disciplinarian with a birchwood cane transformed into a doting father.

"Why, look at this one, Nell. Isn't she a pretty sight?" Castor said.

"That she is, Mr. Willow, and don't you be getting close to that dress 'fore you've washed off the kol and oil and dressed in your own finery. It's laid out for you on your bed, so shoo yourself off. We have guests coming," Nell said.

"You're a hard taskmeister, Nell. A right hard one. A man's just stepped into his kitchen, and you're pushing him out."

"My kitchen, if you please, Mr. Willow, and if it could talk, it would thank you for leaving your dirty boots at the door, and cleaning up like the rest of us."

CHAPTER ELEVEN

"On my way, Nell. Even an Assameister knows when he's not wanted," Castor said, removing his oil-soaked boots, and heading towards the stairs and up to his room. He stopped at the foot of the staircase and braced himself against the banister as a racking cough shuddered his fragile bones. Once the fit was over he took a handkerchief from his pocket and wiped his mouth.

Josephine instinctively went towards her father, but stopped a pace behind and refrained from offering a comforting arm. She knew his pride would get in the way, and he would shrug off any help. Better to let him be, for now. As he slowly climbed the stairs, Josephine wiped the oily handprint from the handrail.

The guests came one after the other. Six Burghmeister council members, duly selected by their peers, and all wearing their robes of authority and chains of office. They represented all of the tradesmen of the Burghs, and came from good families with a long history of service. Astley for the chandlers, Finch for the gildsmiths, Tumbly representing the stonemasons, Chipperton for the carpenters, Bap for the broodmakers, and good old Cartwright, ceremonial hammer in belt, for the blacksmiths. This was an informal council meeting, away from the town hall, but business was still on the agenda and spouses were not invited. All came through the front door, and were formally greeted by Castor and Josephine. For the most part, Nell remained in the kitchen, and ferried a steady stream of tray refills to the parlor.

It was a fine spread, as the Burghmeisters expected from Castor Willow. Savory pies quickly filled meaty paws; forks stabbed at jellied eels; pickled eggs were plucked from jars; spoons scooped up congealed blud; knives carved baked ham; and brood dipped into hot soup. There was pudding too; steamed spotted dick stuffed with grog soaked raisins and a rich white sauce; brood and butter pudding; light sponge cakes and cream; and spiced biscuits and appelflaps. A barrel of dark ale sat on the table and the tap was more often in the open position than closed while Josephine poured a rich grog from a flagon into eager glasses.

"Fine spread, Willow, fine spread," Bap the broodmaker said, popping another piece of cake and cream into his overindulgent mouth. "Almost as good as our bakerhaus offerings. I must get the recipe."

"Guarded secret, I'm guessing Bap. You'd need to marry Nell to get hold of it," Castor replied.

"Well, I'm in need of another wife, so I might look into that. Three's a charm they say. "

Josephine joined in the conversation, but steered it in another direction. "Tell me, Mr. Bap. What do you do with the fresh brood you don't sell?" She asked.

"Well, with a bake as good as ours, there's not much left over," Bap said proudly. "But if there is, we sell the next solar for half price, or throw it away."

"Couldn't you donate it to the poor in the Slough?"

Bap almost choked on his cake. "You mean, give it away for free? You can't be serious?"

"Why, yes sir. That's exactly what I mean. We have more than enough to go around, and I see no need why people should go hungry," Josephine said.

"My dear Josephine, wherever did you get ideas like that? It would upset the natural order of things. The Gentry rule, the Burghs produce and trade, and the poor … Well, the poor do what the destitute have always done. Each to their own world, I say."

Bap turned back to Castor Willow. "A spirited daughter, you have Willow, with a head full of strange notions."

"She was raised to speak her mind … at the appropriate time," Castor replied.

Josephine was about to comment on what she thought of Bap's view of the world, but a look from her father silenced her. Tonight was not the time to upset his guests.

By the way, Willow, isn't your son Joe attending?" Bap asked, changing the subject.

"Not tonight. We had a small emergency with one of the assa boilers and

CHAPTER ELEVEN

Joe stayed on to babysit through the night," Castor lied.

The Willow parlor was not overly spacious, and five of the seven Burghmeisters, as pillars of the community, displayed their prosperity as most well-heeled middle-aged men were wont to do. In short, they were fat. Some like Bap, grew into their present condition, and were positively bursting from their hose, jackets, tunics, and surcoats. Others like Cartwright, were gargantuan from birth. Apart from Castor Willow, only Astley the chandler was bone thin, and fat melted from his frame like burnt wax. He refrained from burning the flamestick from both ends and took small bites from a piece of plain brood and sipped sparingly from half a cup of ale. With the large table covered with the ample spread and the barrel of ale, there was no room to swing a billee. Josephine graciously danced through the throng of sweaty gentlemen with ease as she refilled cups, and Nell simply barged her way through to replenish the smorgasbord.

Although the men were acquaintances of many years, on council duty they referred to themselves by surname only. A tradition someone instituted long before the current members took office, and no one sought to challenge. Respecting tradition was in their blud, and the seven council members, always seven since there could be no abstentions and always a decision, served with equal measure of humility, bombasity, honor, and puffed up pride.

The council members chatted amongst themselves, and invariably some conversations touched on the recent killings in the Mutton, though no one confessed to ever visiting those nefarious quarters. Some wives had insisted on extra door bolts as long as *The Terror* was still at large, and husbands were called upon to put family protection before council business and stay home more frequently. This visit to the Willow haushold was a welcome escape for many of them.

In between refilling tankards and making polite small talk with the Willow guests, Josephine also took a turn with her lute, and sang *Waiting for Juno*, a wistful tale of a maiden who lingered too long for her lost lover to return and joined the Shadow People. This brought tears to Bap's eyes, and Cartwrtight blew loudly into his handkerchief. To lighten the mood, Josephine recited *Slap me Sideways, Slap me Silly,* a semi bawdy poem of a lusty wench from the Mutton who always managed to get the better of her cheating Swell Daddy. Even Astley let out a chuckle at this one before he could restrain himself. Finally, Josephine led the Burghmeister's in a rousing rendition of *The Jolly Molly,* a boatman's song they all knew since childhood, with a catchy chorus they sang in unison, and long verses they muddled through.

With glasses filled and bellies full, Castor Willow took a knife and rapped it smartly against his flagon to get everyone's attention. The small crowd stopped their chattering and gave their undivided attention to their host, who stood on a small stool so he could be seen above his stout guests. Castor coughed slightly, and for a moment Josephne worried another convulsion would overtake him at this inopportune moment. However, Castor steadied himself, swallowed the blud in his mouth and continued.

"Burghmeisters, thank you for coming to Willow haus today and on such short notice. I trust the food and beverages were to your liking?"

"Hear, hear," the Burghmeisters said in concert, raising their tankards in one hand, and meat pies and sundry pastries in the other.

"And the entertainment from my lovely daughter?"

"Never better," they cried.

"Splendid. Well, my dear Astley, Finch, Tumbly, Chipperton, Bap, and good old Cartwright, I have an announcement of sorts. I've worked with half of you half as long as I'd like, and the other half, half as long as you'd like. But there it is. Council work requires compromise, and we always got there in the end. Now I'm afraid this is the end. Goodbye to one and all."

"Goodbye? Whatever do you mean, Willow?" Bap said.

"Is he going on an unexpected journey?" Astley asked Finch.

"Assameisters don't journey, the Dux don't allow it," Finch replied sternly.

"Gentlemen, gentlemen. Settle down please," Castor said. "I'm not going anywhere in the physical sense, but it is time for this weary old man to leave council business for them who has the stamina, the desire, and the

CHAPTER ELEVEN

time. Mostly, the time, since I'm decidedly short of the latter."

"Never, there's always been an Assameister on the council," Tumbly said.

"Why both your father and grandfather served us well before you, and young Joe, when he comes of an age, will do the same," old Cartwright offered.

"Hear, hear," the Burghmeisters said.

"Gentlemen, therein lies our dilemma. I must step down, and young Joe is not of an age, and decidedly lacking in experience to take such a step. No, it's time for new blud on the Council, and I have a name to propose."

"It's highly irregular of you to propose council business in a non-council setting, Willow. Highly irregular," Chipperton said, who often took an opposite stance to Castor.

"I'm not proposing council business, Chipperton, just a name for your consideration, and one I think you in particular will like. We can take the vote of ratification at the next, and my last formal session," Castor said.

"And if Chipperton likes it, what about me?" Finch asked.

"I dare say you will find it favorable too, Finch. I'm proposing Tumblebrook takes my council seat," Castor said.

There was an audible gasp from Cartwright at the thought of a cobbler on the Burghmeister council, but there were nodding of heads from others who saw it as a good compromise. Tumblebrook, a young man of wise counsel, was, after all, the nephew of Finch and the son-in-law of Chipperton. Both men, often at loggerheads, saw the opportunity of swaying his vote in their favor. If there needed to be new blud, then Tumblebrook was indeed the man to step into the shoes, even if he made them himself. With Cartwright still pondering as he did with most decisions, and the rest of the Burghmeisters in agreement, the informal gathering broke up for the evening. All, with the exception of Astley, left with a bag neatly tucked under their arm. A farewell treat of pies, cakes, and biscuits, lovingly prepared by Nell as a midnight snack.

As the last guest left, Josephine quickly changed into her regular evening attire, and helped Nell clear out the parlor, sweep the floor free of pie crusts and trampled cake, and stack the mountain of dishes back in the kitchen. Between Nell and herself they made short work of the washing and drying, and returning the crockery and cutlery to the safety of the attic.

As the women worked, Castor gave in to his fatigue and flopped into his favorite chair in the kitchen beside the fire. He took his preferred pipe out of a box beside the chair, stuffed it with tabak, held a taper in the fire until it glowed, and put it to the top of the bowl. After one or two sucks, the flame took hold, and he exhaled a satisfying billow of smoke. It was quickly followed by a racking cough.

"I wish you wouldn't smoke that thing, Mr. Willow. Especially in your predicament," Nell chastised.

"Now, now, Nell. It's one of the last pleasures I have, and time is short," Castor said.

"And it won't be getting any longer if you keep puffing at that thing," Nell said, and dropped heavily into her own chair on the opposite side of the fire from Castor. She opened her own box, took out a piece of fabric, needle, and thread, and worked on an embroidery of the Willow family crest, which she never seemed to finish. It represented the Assameister's tradecraft, with a pair of copper boilers below, and two entwined firebirds, one white and the other red, rising above, and figuratively depicting the interaction of the assa and the flame.

Nell stopped in the middle of her backstitch. "I'm sorry, Mr. Willow. I shouldn't have been so sharpish. I'm just concerned about you ... and Josephine. Whatever is going to happen to her? And me too, when you're not around for us."

Josephine stood behind her father and placed a hand on his shoulder. "Don't worry about me, Nell. I'm fine. Father has me studying the craft. I'll have it down in no time."

"It's not a girl's place to work in the assachamber, and you know it. That was for your brother, not you. You were raised to be a fine young lady, and a catch for a Burghmeister's son," Nell said, pushing her needle through the tough fabric.

"Don't fret, Nell. Giving up council work means I have some time to

CHAPTER ELEVEN

solve our little problem," Castor said, taking another solid puff on his pipe. He sounded confident, but it was all for show. He had no idea how to come to a satisfactory resolution, and Josephine and Nell knew it.

"Little problem, Mr. Willow? Tosh, posh! I'd say it's a huge big hairy problem we have in front of us. It's more than a year since the fever took poor Joe, and his body can't stay in that room upstairs forever. He needs a proper burial. And Josephine? How much longer can she dress up in her brother's clothes and pass herself off as your apprentice?"

Poor Joe. He was always the weakest of the two siblings. He followed Josephine into the world nine lunars later, a frail little Gastown twin born of a frail little woman, who quickly slid off into the Onderworld, and now resided in the Willow Mausoleum with stern Willow in-laws she barely knew in life. A dove amongst crows. For Joe's part, he always tried his best to please his father and studied the assacraft as best he could. He was not quick with book learning, and the letters and numbers jumbled and tumbled together in unrecognizable shapes. Josephine stayed up with him at night to guide him through it as he learned by rote. He did better in the assachamber, and polished the boilers, and blended assa well, much to his father's silent pride. Castor remained strict at work, and loving at home. Then the fever came to Gastown and struck down many. Most recovered in time, but not poor Joe. His weak constitution was stretched paper thin by working with the assa and kol, and he breathed his last short shallow breath in his warm bed, which was now stone cold.

The death of poor Joe almost broke his father. Castor continued with his daily work, and trudged back and forth across the Bridge of Broken Souls with the rest of the Burghs' workforce. He consoled himself with feeding the boilers and ensuring Gastown stayed warm. But once he was back at the Willow haus, he dropped into his chair and wept. He forbade Nell and Josephine from calling the Death Collector, and transporting the body to the Willow Mausoleum where it rightfully belonged. Instead, Joe resided in his own private crypt, which was once his bedroom, covered in a shroud, while his father waited for him to miraculously rise once again. Castor convinced them he needed time to think this through, and Joe's passing had to remain their collective secret. Nell thought about reaching out to her estranged brother, who had a way of making bodies disappear, but she knew she could not put Castor and Josephine in his unholy debt. Instead, she wrapped poor Joe's corpse in a sheet, and took her embroidery kit, climbed over the emaciated body, and stitched him shut. She then locked the bedroom door, and placed the key in her apron pocket.

With one subterfuge in place another was quickly needed. Joe's absence from the assachamber would be noticed and a replacement was needed. Josephine took it upon herself to don her dead brother's work clothes and follow her father into the depths of the citadel. There was a strong family resemblance between brother and sister, though Josephine had a healthier glow about her, and none could tell the difference in her boyish disguise. Her assa lore was up to snuff after helping her sibling with his studies, but her lax work in the assachamber needed guidance from the Assameister and his cane, unless others doubted his authority. At work Castor remained stern with his son-daughter, and at home he was a loving doting father to his daughter-son.

Castor continued to puff on his pipe. "I need more time to think it through, Nell. The Dux has strange and cruel ways and doesn't allow females from the Burghs into Varstad. If she ever finds out, it will be the end of us all. Willows have always been the Assameisters for Gastown, and Josephine is the last of my line. She's learning the trade, picks it up fast, and can be Joe during the solar and Josephine at night. Only the three of us know about it, and it has to stay that way for now."

After the gathering with the Burghmeisters and helping Nell clean away all evidence of a party, Josephine took her nighttime candle, secretly hid a replacement under her gown, and retired to her room. It was already late, and she needed a good night's rest. However, she also needed to study the great books written in the High Tongue, and for tonight, understand the delicate art of blending resin, quicklime, black mountain stone, and assa condensates to make the volatile vitali blackfire, which was one of the secrets of the Gentry's maritime power. An Assameister's main function

CHAPTER ELEVEN

was to nurse the assa and keep Gastown warm through the long winter. But in time of war and conquest, and one was brewing, the Assameister also trained three distinct teams. The first group stored and nurtured the liquid in the great tanks in the bowels of the warship, the second group was responsible for the safe transport through the long pipes, and the third group, the siphon marines, opened the nozzle, expelled the black liquid past a small flame, and transported it over controlled distances into an inflammable inferno of death and destruction onto the surface of the water. No other vessel, or men aboard them, could stand before vitali blackfire. It was no use on land, and refused to ignite snow, but on the open waters it was an unholy terror. By the light of the candle, Josephine blended the ingredients in her head again and again, and her hands mixed and crushed the components together in an imaginary great granite pestel.

Josephine was late again for work. She had fallen asleep at her desk, with a book of murderous recipes for a pillow. It was still dark outside, but she knew her father was already at the assachamber and she needed to hurry to make it before the tower clock struck and the great doors closed. She splashed some cold water on her face, tied up her hair, donned Joe's unwashed and now familiar apprentice clothes, slipped into her brother's persona, and hurried downstairs. There was no need to visit Andersen's hotshop today as there was plenty of vittles leftover from the Burghmeister gathering, so she placed a savory pie, a chunk of brood, and a hunk of cheese to share with the squeakers, onto a meal cloth and tied the corners together, and dropped it into her lunch pail. There was another hard solar's work ahead of her in the assachamber, but she did not mind. It was preferable to meeting with Ori and the message she had promised herself to deliver.

Josephine weaved her way through the crowd crossing the Bridge of Broken Souls into the citadel and made it through the large ironwood doors with time to spare before the great clock rang out and the guards closed off the outside world for another solar. Seven slides down and she was in the familiar smell and heat of the assachamber, and quickly went to work polishing boilers, checking gauges, and watching over kolmen as they opened up furnace doors and fed the inferno.

After a short and hurried lunch, and little chance to feed the disappointed squeakers, Josephine was summoned to one of the great chambers, which was ordinarily under lock and key. As Josephine entered the cavernous room for the first time, she was surprised to see three groups of twenty men each, all dressed up in their finest livery, and the attire signaling their specific roles. Josephine almost did a happy dance as she recognized from her studies the night before that these were the crews who managed the vitali blackfire on the great Black Ships. They were here for a master class from the Assameister in the finer arts of vitali management.

Josephine's father took her to one side before the training got underway. "Listen carefully, Joe. You're not to say a word, do you hear? You're an apprentice, so remember your place. Follow my every instruction, and assist when I need you. That's all," Castor said.

"Yes, father, I mean Assameister," Josephine replied.

"Then let's get to it. There's a war brewing, and the Dux wants these navy bluejackets trained up at a quicker pace."

The men were not new to their tasks as other crews ensured they knew more than the basics. However, this was their first introduction to the Assameister, and he pushed and cajoled them through their paces. The storemen were first, and they gathered around a large tank containing the volatile liquid, which they then transported to a smaller tank resembling the one in the bowels of the Black Ships. It had to be maintained at a constant temperature, which meant repeatedly checking gauges, and the liquid was in a perpetual state of motion to prevent congealment and the free flow through the pipes. The men were all sweating by the end of their training, and it was not all down to the heat. Still, they absorbed the finer details from the Assameister, which emboldened them all. Next up were the pipers, small rubbery men, who had the most dexterous role. A cutaway of the belly of a great ship was their training ground, and they crawled through the narrow wooden tunnels, following the pipes from the vitali blackfire tank all the way up to the siphons. They checked for potential leaks, and how to plug and seal them. They ensured no potkans,

CHAPTER ELEVEN

which always managed to find their way onto sea-going vessels, built nests in the crawl spaces, and nibbled on pipes. It was the least glorious of roles, but essential nonetheless. Last up were the siphon marines, who stood at the prow of the ship and channeled the vitali blackfire from the great tanks, through the pipes, and past the nozzles of their siphons onto the seawater. One by one, they took the front position, exposed to the elements, and the ever present danger of seaspray carrying the inferno back to them and the risk of a human bonfire. For this reason, the siphon marines worked in pairs. If the first marine accidentally ignited himself, the second quickly ejected him over the side.

The final act of all the training was a demonstration of the lethality of vitali blackfire. A great tank of sea water sloshed back and forth with man-induced waves, and one by one, the siphon marines practiced opening up their nozzles and firing the black liquid at selected targets at various ranges. As soon as the vitali blackfire hit the seawater, flames erupted, and burned with an intensity which was both horrifying and glorious to witness.

Josephine stood with her mouth open as she watched what her mind's eye had conjured up the previous night become a monstrous reality. The heat was intense as the vitali blackfire and the seawater combined to give birth to a firestorm no one could survive. Josephine marveled at what man's ingenuity had brought into life, but shuddered at the thought of burning in such a Hel flame nothing could extinguish.

The great chamber was locked up until other training crews descended into the assachamber, and Josephine, after finishing her final tasks for the night, walked slowly up the stairs for what she had decided would be a final rendezvous with Ori. The death of Devlin, the hapless Red Shadow, was warning enough, and her father's deteriorating health meant she did not need the perilous distraction. Besides, Ori wanted Joe and not Josephine, and any childish thoughts of conversion were cast out.

Josephine took the time to wash off the kol and oil from her face, but she refrained from taking a swig of water to rinse out the taste of strong cheese from her mouth. Better to leave the sour taste in case Ori asked for a parting kiss.

Joseph reached the alcove first but did not have long to wait before Ori appeared. He put his halberd down and came towards Josephine, expecting a flurry of kisses. Instead, she reached out an arm to stop him in his tracks.

"We have to talk, Ori," Josephine said.

"There's no time for talking. Come here," Ori said, searching for Josephine's lips.

She pushed him away. "No Ori. We can't do this anymore. That's what I came to tell you."

There was a look in his eye which scared Josephine. A look which said his manhood was on the rise and any form of higher reasoning was buried deep.

Ori grabbed hold of Josephine by the arms and spun her around, pressing her roughly against the alcove wall. "Break up? We've just got started," he said, kissing her neck and ear.

"No Ori. Let me go!"

"Time to take this up a notch, Joe," Ori said, breathing hard. He placed a firm hand in front between Josephine's legs and squeezed. He froze for a moment, and then stepped back. "What's this then? A eunuch? I've never been with a eunuch before."

Josephine turned around to face him. Her blood was up after the rough treatment. "How did I ever let myself get involved with the likes of you! They say a burgh boy leaves his brains behind when he joins the Red Shadows, and you're living proof. I'm a girl, you blockhead. I'm not Joe. I'm Josephine!"

A look of horror came over Ori's face. "A-a girl? You mean to tell me I kissed a girl?" He took another step back and spat on the ground. There was a rage in his eyes as he looked at the Assameister's Apprentice in a different light for the first time. His mouth twisted into a snarl, and he lashed out with his hand and hit Josephine with a backhanded blow to the face.

Josephine crashed back into the wall and her head made sharp contact with the stone. She fell to the ground in a heap and had no way of protecting

CHAPTER ELEVEN

herself as Ori kicked her again and again in the stomach.

Chapter Twelve

Carlos : First Blud

Carlos kept to the shadows as he moved from one end of the Slough to the other. The work of a pyromaniac was evident. His hair was singed, soot and ashes covered his face and clothes, his black mascara was smeared around bloodshot eyes, and he stank of smoke like a denizen of an ancient tabak shop. He was fully prepared to face Cotter Sullivan and his sneering Bully Boys and accept his fate for the fiery transgression, but first he needed to confess and ask for forgiveness from the only person who could understand him. He needed Juan.

Carlos thought of his twin brother every solar since their forced separation. They had been constant companions since they entered this unforgiving world together. They had no collective memory of their parents, just two forgotten faces in the sea of unwashed humanity who inhabited the Slough. Maybe they were still alive, maybe they were dead and were dumped in the Basin long ago. Carlos did not know or care. They had provided seed and incubation and nothing else. All he had was Juan, and Juan was cast out into the night while he was fattened, warmed, and pawed in the slagerhaus. He grieved for his twin, and lamented over his harsh existence in the belly of the Slough, unwashed, underfed, and always cold. He was brotherless in a living Onderworld, a castoff amongst thieves, pickpockets, and vagabonds. Alone in this black den, he had little

CHAPTER TWELVE

chance of survival.

Carlos knew he could not return to the Slough with his brother and fight the world together again. Cotter would seek them out and kill them both. Leaving Juan alone and forgotten meant he lived free for the pair of them, if only for a short time. It was a heavy price to pay, but Juan would understand, if only he could find him and talk it through. Juan was always the reasonable one, the counterpoint to his rashness and wild ways. Juan would calm him down and ease his troubled mind.

Carlos did not know why, but something compelled him to make his way to Skank Bridge, the connecting point between the Four Kith and the Mutton. He still kept to the shadows and slithered from pillar to post. He did not risk stepping out onto the bridge itself, but found a watcher's spot in the broken doorway of a derelict building with only scurrying potkans for company. One brave rodent crept closer, and nibbled at something on Carlo's shoe, until he tired of the attention and kicked it away.

The wait was relatively short, but chilling. Carlos entered the outskirts of the Slough with a fire in mind and was not dressed for a night-time vigil. He stamped his feet and blew on his hands for warmth, but he shivered nonetheless. He was on the point of giving up on his binary seeking mission, and returning to the warmth of the slagerhaus and his fateful meeting with Cotter, when he caught sight of his lost twin. Juan's back was to him, but he knew his brother as well as he knew himself. When the figure turned and Carlos saw a gaunt expression of his own face with an eyepatch over the right eye, he knew for certain. Juan was there on the bridge, but he was not alone. A part of Carlos wanted to find his brother isolated and lonely, weak from hunger, and needing his twin to survive. However, in Carlos's distorted view, Juan thrived and was content in the company of others. Carlos had grieved for his brother every solar and Juan had seemingly moved on in an instant.

There were other mudlarks with Juan, boys and girls alike. They seemed happy and carefree, prospering in the putrid Slough. And JoJo Dickens. She had an arm around Juan's shoulders and they were laughing.

Come over 'ere, Carlos, an' give an ole girl a terrifik hug!

Except there were no more hugs for Carlos Grimm. His fragile mind, pushed to the limits by the unwanted attention of Cotter Sullivan, and burdened still further by the murder he had just committed in retribution for a past grievance, refused to break. Instead, he embraced darker ruminations and fully committed to survival by any means. The thoughts of better times shared with his twin, which had helped him hold on to his sanity, were jettisoned.

Carlos viewed Juan and his companions though a warped lens and reality offered a more balanced insight. They played and joked not to be carefree, but to forget their constant plight with living rough in the Slough. The happy faces Carlos saw were actually gaunt, their clothes barely kept out the biting cold, and their meager diet banished fat from their malnourished frames. Juan continually thought of his twin brother, and if Carlos had stepped out of the shadows he would have greeted him with open arms and a mended heart.

What little grip Carlos had on reality to get through each solar and deviant night evaporated. At that moment Carlos loathed JoJo Dickens for the love she bestowed on a singular twin. For the first time in his short existence, he also felt hatred for his brother. There would be no redemption. He had killed Joe Geroni for the both of them, but the crime and the burden was all his. No forgiveness. No warm embrace and a *thank you, Carlos.* He felt the separation as if a surgeon had taken a knife and severed their connecting lifeline. Twins no more.

Carlos despised what he had become. A plaything for Cotter, an arsonist, and a murderer. He felt unclean and alone. It was not Juan who had suffered after the demise of Mo Dickens, it was him. He paid the price for the rise of Cotter Sullivan, and Juan had forgotten him. He knew at that moment, he could not talk with his brother. There was no absolution for him tonight, or any night. His path was set and all he could do was walk it without fear, at his own solitary pace, and on his own terms. He wondered how he could have been so stupid to expect redemption and kind words from his twin to set his troubled boat back on an even keel. Juan was the thinker for both of them, and he was the one who acted first.

CHAPTER TWELVE

Not any more. He could be as smart as Juan. If his brother was dead to him now, he could at least think like him to solve his predicament.

He took another look at Juan, who was playing a game with his new friends. One of them acted as the mark, while one of the girl's flopped in front of him. Another lifted an imaginary purse and yet another passed it off to Juan, who flipped it to Jojo.

Enjoy your new family, Juan. Yuz an' me is finished. Iz 'ave no use for yuz an' your kind.

Carlos turned and began the fateful journey back to the slagerhaus and Cotter's wrath. Along the way he pondered on how his imaginary twin, the Juan of old and not the one frolicking on Skank Bridge, would approach this predicament. He freely shared his cracked mind with the make-believe double, and together they formulated a bold plan which would play on Cotter's greed. He knew the man well enough to know he would forgive the destruction of the bakerhaus and the death of Joe Geroni as long as there was a pot of gold at the end of the row of burned out hauses.

The distance between Skank Bridge and the Sullivan slagerhaus was relatively short, but Carlos took a meandering path to what was likely his final destination on Cotter's butcher's block. He no longer crept in the shadows, hiding himself from mankind, but walked openly in the streets and across canals for all to see. Passersby gave the strange ash covered boy with the burnt hair a wide berth. There was something about his demeanor and especially his eyes which screamed stay away.

The yard of the slagerhaus was deserted, but there was activity in the main hall. Carlos could see the candles burning and feel the heat of the main fire even from a distance. He could also hear the murmuring of many voices, rather than the usual raucous Bully Boy noise that emanated from Cotter's establishment. Carlos paid it no mind; he knew what he had to do, but first he needed to clean up before facing his likely executioners. He took a small branch from a pile of kindling and used it to beat on his clothes to loosen the fire dust. It came away in a cloud and gradually faded into the night air. Next, he used the butt end of the branch and broke the thin ice covering the water in the washing barrel. He scooped out handfuls and washed down his face and hair, and scrubbed the grit and grime from his hands. He was ready.

"Iz wouldn't go in there," a voice hissed.

Carlos turned to see Fleet Dawkins, standing behind him. The boy was scared.

"What yuz doin' 'ere!" Carlos hissed. "Iz told yuz to make for the Hole with the mites."

"We did, Carlos. But Patch sent Jonas and a gaggle of Bully Boys to fetch uz back," Fleet explained. "Rough 'anded they woz too."

"So they know about the Hole, doz they? I wonder who gave that secret away. No matter."

"They're waitin' in there for yuz, Carlos, 'nd it ain't a pretty sight. Run while yuz still 'as a chance."

Carlos laughed. "Run where, Fleet? Likes it or not, this is my slagerhaus. Time to pay the slager bill."

Carlos turned from his fire mite, and calmly walked into the main chamber of the slagerhaus, which was set up like a courtroom with row upon row of tables and chairs on either side of the central aisle, furniture last seen at Josie's wedding. The boisterous Bully Boys filled the chairs, while the cowering mites, some battered and bruised, skulked in the shadows against the walls. In the center of the room, Cotter sat in a regal chair on a raised dais. His shirt was open, displaying his colossal belly, and above it, the Hetman of the Slagers chain he wore with pride.

Cotter was flanked by Patch Amstrong and his bookkeeper, Black Jack Cuttle, a muscular brute with the face of a killer, but who got his jollies from twisting numbers rather than necks. A large roaring fire, fed by two mites blazed behind them. It was strong enough to bubble the varnish on the back of the stolen chairs. The Bully Boys saw Carlos enter, stopped their chattering, and turned to look at him. Carlos caught Jonas Wheeler's eye and the man sneered at him, before drawing his thumb as a mock blade across his throat. Off to the side, Perfect Styles stood over his bloody butcher's block and worked on sharpening a mighty cleaver while his apprentices busied themselves in cleaning up and scrubbing down. Perfect looked at Carlos, but his face gave nothing away.

Carlos walked down the path between the tables and stopped in front of Cotter, a condemned boy awaiting his sentence before first enduring the mock trial.

"Well, look what the billee dragged in," Cotter said, and his Bully Boys laughed on cue.

"What do yuz 'ave to say for yourself, youn' Carlos? Iz sent yuz out on a little job, an' yuz decided to fire up the Slough. There's a price to be paid for dereliction of duties in this 'ere establishment," Cotter said as he drooled.

"I did yuz a favor, I did," Carlos said, as he stood defiantly before the three men who would be his judges, jury, and executioners.

"Well, would yuz look at the balls on this one, Patch. Right big ones, he's got, wouldn't yuz say?" Cotter asked.

"Big ones for sure, Cotter," Patch said, nodding his head.

"An' what shall we do with them big ones?" Cotter asked.

"Cut 'em off!" Jonas shouted from the crowd, and a few of his closest Bully Boys cheered and banged their fists on the table.

"Enough!" Cotter growled. "There'll be no interruptions from the gallery unless Iz order it!"

When the crowd settled down, Cotter turned to Black Jack. "Mister Cuttle, please be so kind as to read the charges brought up against this imp."

Black Jack unrolled a scroll, on which the ink was barely dry, squinted at his own handwriting, and proceeded to outline the indictment.

"Carlos Grimm, most recently a privileged resident of the Sullivan slagerhaus, you were charged with the simple task of igniting a small fire on the ground floor of the Geroni Bakerhaus, said property of one Joe Geroni. Do you agree?" Black Jack paused and looked at Carlos for confirmation.

"I do," Carlos replied.

"Instead, you willfully carried the flames to the entirety of the building, resulting in an inferno which consumed the whole block, and which is still smoldering as we speak. In addition, one Joe Geroni met a toasty end, no loss there I might add, drawing unwanted and uncalled for attention. Our plan, which you brazenly ignored, was to pressure one Joe Geroni to sign over the building to one Cotter Aloysius Sullivan, currently present…"

"That I am," Cotter said.

"And said Mister Sullivan planned to nobly turn the property over to needy families to provide a roof over their impoverished heads."

"Nobly," Cotter repeated and puffed out his chest.

"He planned to squeeze twenty families in there like potkans in a barrel, an' charge 'em a pretty penny for the pleasure, " Jonas said to the amusement of his friends.

"Quiet Mister Wheeler, if you please, I have the floor," Black Jack chastised.

"An' yuz floorin' uz with this highfalutin talk!" Jonas barked.

Cotter growled and Jonas and his cronies fell silent. "If you please, Mister Cuttle, pray proceed."

"Carlos Grimm, you've heard the charges placed before you. How do you plead?" Black Jack asked.

"Guilty," Carlos replied.

"Out of the mouth of babes," Patch said, and the Bully Boys began to murmur amongst themselves.

"And are you well aware of what a guilty verdict means, Master Grimm?" Black Jack asked, staring at the boy in the imaginary dock.

Carlos nodded his head. "Most likely Iz'll end up on Perfect's butcher block, an' me parts will feed the bottom dwellers in the Basin."

"Then on your own admission you leave us little choice," Black Jack proclaimed. He put down his scroll, fumbled in his pocket, and produced a black rag, which he used to wipe his sweaty pate, before delicately balancing it on top of his bald head. "Carlos Grimm…"

Carlos held up his hand. "Wait one moment before yuz bring down the cleaver. I 'as what's called mitigatin' circumstances."

"What's a *mitigatin'*?" Jonas asked. "Is that when the madness comes

CHAPTER TWELVE

upon you?"

"He wants to take the edge off of 'is crime," one of Jonas's cronies offered.

Black Jack turned to Cotter. "What say you, Mister Sullivan? Do you care to hear the reason for the flagrant disobedience of your direct command?"

"Well, we cud use a gud laf, couldn't we boys?" Cotter asked the crowd, and they shouted to hear more.

"Well, Master Grimm. In non-legal terms, and in the vernacular even Jonas can understand, give it your best shot," Black Jack said.

Carlos had the floor and the undivided attention of the audience. Everyone wanted to know why he disobeyed Cotter at the certainty of his own demise. Was he bravely fulfilling a family feud, or was he simply a weak minded pyromaniac, who could not control his fiery urges, they wondered.

"Why take one when yuz can 'ave 'em all," Carlos offered as his opening gambit.

"You're not making sense, Master Grimm. Kindly explain yourself," Black Jack asked.

"The task at 'and woz to burn out Joe Geroni, an' Joe alone. One haus among many on offer. One haus to fill with poor folks. Where's the profit in that?" Carlos sneered.

"Careful with 'em remarks, youn' Carlos. I'm not a man to be trifled with," Cotter growled.

"No triflin' Cotter, just speakin' the truth," Carlos replied. "Iz burnt down the block for a reason. There's a profit to be 'ad. A tidy sum an' more to come. Yuz see, the Geroni family wot's left of 'em, 'ave no choice but to give yuz the land as payment for Joe Geroni's debts. Or they 'az to take it all on themselves, an' they can't even spring for the vig. The other kithfolks who lost 'em hauses, can't build back. An' if they tried, we'd stop 'em. Scare off the carpenters and whatnot, burn out the frames. Now they 'as to sell to yuz for bottom price. Now comes the best part," Carlos said with bravado, trying to sound older and more experienced than his sixteen years.

"Go on," Black Jack said, leaning closer. Carlos's ploy had him intrigued.

"Why do folks 'ave to cross Skank Bridge into the Mutton for their pleasures? Who set 'em rules, yuz?" Carlos said, pointing a finger at Cotter.

"Not I," Cotter replied. "It's just the way things are done."

"Then it's time to break 'em rules," Carlos said. "Build back them hauses into fine flesh parlors, billeehauses if you will, and stock 'em with girls, boys, fat ladies, contortionists, an' imps. If it fills an urge for the burghfolk an' 'em that can afford it from the Four Kith."

"The Swell Daddies won't like it," Patch offered.

Carlos spat. "That's what Iz think of the Swell Daddies. A tosh on 'em an' all their kind. We 'as enough Bully Boys to see 'em off, and I 'ave my mites to spread more fires an' burn an' build."

"Your mites?" Cotter asked.

"Yes! My mites," Carlos replied, puffing out his chest and standing his ground. "Come out of the shadows, yuz lot. No more skulkin' in fear of the likes of Jonas Wheeler," Carlos said.

They were reluctant to move, but Fleet Dawkins was first to come forward and the others followed in dribs and drabs. They were a ragged group of misfits, and their rough handling from the Bully Boys showed on a few faces. They gathered behind Carlos, and meekly stood before Cotter and his two captains. They did not know what was coming next, but at that moment, they trusted in Carlos Grimm.

"This little army is goin' to make yuz a very rich an' powerful man, Cotter Sullivan," Carlos said.

"I'm already a rich an' powerful man," Cotter said, carelessly fingering his hetman's chain. "I'm Hetman of the Slagers, an' top dog in the Four Kith! No one messes with Cotter Sullivan, 'ain't that right, Patch?"

"Never a truer word," Patch replied.

"Them Swell Daddies don't bend down before yuz, an' the Burghmeisters works with yuz out of necessity an' not fear. Now if yuz build up the meat parlor game, yuz cut off the trade of the Swell Daddies, an' yuz get to know all of the twisted secrets an' perverted pleasures the Burghmeisters keep 'idden from family an' neighbors. Them secrets is as gud as coin in the pocket. Now they fear yuz, Cotter Sullivan!" Carlos said.

CHAPTER TWELVE

The room stirred. The Bully Boys with half a brain could see the sense in Carlos's plan. They were already spending the riches brought in and cavorting with the boys and girls from the brightly lit bordellos. They were Cotter's men and would reap the rewards. Others were less thrilled with going up against the Swell Daddies and their own army of hired thugs, the Crimpers. It would not be an easy battle and casualties would be high on both sides. There was already a profit to be had and no one challenged them within the Four Kith. Sleeping dogs lay best in their own kennel.

"You thought this all up by yourself, Master Grimm?" Black Jack asked.

"No one else 'ad an 'and in it," Carlos replied. "It's mine alone, an' if yuz don't like it, I'm prepared to take my punishment like a man."

"A man yuz 'aint!" Jonas Wheeler said, getting to his feet. "Just a snot nosed boy who likes playin' with fire."

There were less Bully Boys eager to support Jonas this time. All of Carlos's talk about riches and pleasures had wormed into their heads and tunneled deep inside. They waited on Cotter and his council to make their decision.

Cotter looked at Black Jack Cuttle, who nodded his head. He glanced over at Patch Armstrong, who shrugged his shoulders. Cotter even looked over at Perfect Styles, who went on sharpening his cleaver, and still gave nothing away.

"Alright, youn' Carlos, we like your way of thinkin'," Cotter said. "Don't we, Mister Cuttle?"

"That we do, Mister Sullivan, that we do. This boy has a fine head on his shoulders and we think it should remain there for the time being," Black Jack said.

"Then do us a favor, Jack. And remove that black rag from your 'ead! There's no passin' of sentence today, and mitigatin' circumstances is accepted!" Cotter said.

Black Jack reached up and took the rag from his head, wiped his face and returned it to his pocket. "Carlos Grimm, the court finds you 'Not Guilty', and declares this session closed," Jack said, and proceeded to roll up his scroll as an act of finality.

Not everyone in the slagerhaus was onboard with the verdict or the plan. Jonas Wheeler was still smoldering and he was not about to let things go without some kind of punishment for Carlos. Even at the risk of Cotter's wrath he would have his say and mete out his own form of primitive justice.

"First Blud!" Jonas shouted out. "Despite 'is fine plans, he disobeyed a direct order. I demand First Blud!" Jonas banged his fist on the table, and moved to stir the crowd. Even those swayed by Carlos's argument felt some disciplinary action was in order, and joined the chorus for retribution. If nothing else, it provided further entertainment.

"He's just a boy, Jonas. You said so yourself," Black Jack said.

"'E's already killed a man, Jack. That makes 'im qualified. Besides, I'm only goin' to nick, 'im. Maybe carve off an ear as a trophy," Jonas replied, pulling a blade from his pocket, and testing the sharpness against his calloused thumb.

Cotter sensed the mood of the crowd, and after a shared look with Patch Armstrong reluctantly agreed with the match.

"Alright, Jonas. First Blud it be. But no more than that, yuz 'ear me?"

"Iz always 'ear yuz, Cotter. But maybe 'e won't after this little dance," Jonas said with a smirk.

With a command from Patch, the Bully Boys removed the heavy tables and chairs to the side walls of the slagerhaus chamber, and formed a wider circle around Carlos. Jonas pushed his way through the crowd, and stood menacingly across from Carlos with a fighting blade in his right hand. He was already stripped to the waist, his lithe body a patchwork of knife scars.

Carlos turned to Fleet Dawkins, who stood with the rest of the mites directly behind him. "No worries. 'E'll likely cut me quick, and it's over with," Carlos said.

"Not exactly. It's Bully Boy rules, not a Slough knife fight. They normally don't let outsiders watch, but Iz snuck in. Them little cuts don't count. One deep one is called for. Don't worry, it's no death match. But be careful, Jonas is a terror with a blade, an' 'e 'as a mean streak for yuz," Fleet explained.

"Then it's not First Blud is it?"

CHAPTER TWELVE

"Well, if yuz put it like that, not exactly. 'E'll likely play with yuz first, Iz seen 'im do it before. Do yuz 'ave a decent blade of your own?" Fleet asked. "Iz can fetch one from Perfect if needed."

Carlos pulled out a small blade. "I 'as me pig sticker, which will do just fine for the likes of Jonas Wheeler," Carlos said. He showed a brave face for the mites, who offered him words of encouragement, but his insides were churning. All he wanted to do was go hide in a corner and curl up in a ball away from the baying crowd. However, he had to face up to the fierce knife fighter, despite the odds stacked against him. One deep cut would not be so bad, and then it was over with. He would figure out a way of dealing with Jonas later.

Patch Amstrong stepped forward between Jonas and Carlos, and beckoned man and boy to come forward. Jonas moved in with an easy confidence, swishing his blade back and forth in a figure eight pattern to intimidate his opponent. Carlos moved in a couple of steps closer on shaky legs. He gripped his blade tightly, but kept it by his side. There was a marked difference between the two combatants, not just with their level of confidence. Jonas was not tall for a man, but he was still a head above Carlos. He was not a savage pugilist like some of the Bully Boys, or a dab hand with a blackjack or billy club. His particular poison was a dexterity with bladed instruments, and it was his method of choice for dispatching victims and carving malcontents. Carlos carried a blade as a necessary tool for life in the Four Kith, but it cut rope, tabak, and hard brood, not men.

"Off with the shirt then youn' Carlos. We have to see the cuts and determine the deep one," Patch said.

Carlos put his blade on the floor for a moment, and pulled his shirt over his head. Life in the slagerhaus meant he was not as scrawny as his twin now was, and a steady supply of paranga meant he was filling out. His muscles were not defined like Jonas's, but he was quick on his feet, and speed and distance would be his friend. He stooped down to pick up his blade, and then shook out his arms to release the build up of tension.

"This is First Blud, and there are rules to observe, do you hear me Jonas?" Patch said.

Jonas grinned and nodded his head.

"A deep cut ends the fight, scratches don't count. No bitin', kickin', hair pullin', punchin', or use of foreign objects. And definitely no stabbin'," Patch continued. "Keep it clean, and may the best man … or boy, win."

Patch opened his hand and stretched out a long piece of thin red cloth and offered one end to Carlos.

"What's this for?" Carlos asked.

"Put it in your mouth, son. The two of you need to stay close. No takin' to your heels and runnin'," Patch said.

Carlos groaned, but did what he was told, and put the end of the cloth in his mouth. Jonas took the other end when Patch passed it to him and bit down on it. With the red cloth taut between them, the distance was just outside of striking range. Once the cloth went slack, they were close enough to slash flesh.

The Bully Boys were raucous at the anticipation of spilt blood. They cheered, stamped their feet, and punched the air. Most of them were for Jonas, but a handful silently wished for his failure, even though there was slim chance Carlos would get the better of a seasoned bladesman. The mites were caught up in the excitement too. With the exception of Fleet, they had not seen a true First Blud contest before, and they firmly supported their juvenile leader.

Man and boy circled, with the red cloth held tight between them. Jonas kept his blade back closer to his right rib cage, and his left hand in front as a guard hand. Carlos did the opposite, and held his blade forward in his left hand, more to ward off Jonas than as a real threat.

Jonas moved first, and with a tug of his head and a quick release, Carlos was pulled off balance and the cloth went limp as Jonas stepped within striking range. Jonas's left hand parried Carlos's pigsticker, and his own knife slashed forward. Carlos felt the sharp sting across his blade arm, and could not help but glance at the thin red line, which began to ooze blood. He shot a quizzical look at Patch, who shook his head to indicate it was considered a scratch.

Carlos pulled his head back to tighten the red cloth and increase the distance between him and his adversary. He switched stances to match Jonas with his own blade hand now back and his right guard hand out in front. They parried fingers as they continued to circle until Jonas made a chopping motion against Carlos's right wrist, and shot his fingers forward to make contact with Carlos's right eye. Carlos winced in pain and as a defensive motion slashed his knife forward. Jonas easily passed it and slashed his blade arm once again, this time on the inner bicep.

"Foul," cried Fleet, and the mites booed.

"No dirty blows, Jonas. This here's a knife fight. Keep it so," Patch admonished. "Just another scratch, youn' Carlos. No First Blud as yet."

Carlos was now breathing heavily and holding the cloth in his mouth did not help. His left arm was tingling with the two cuts, and he watched his own blood drip onto the floor. The vision from his right eye was blurry and his right wrist burned where Jonas had chopped out at it. He pulled the red cloth taut once again and continued to circle.

Jonas was not done with his games. He wanted one more slice to humiliate Carlos and teach him a lesson about respecting his betters before moving in for a deeper First Blud cut to end the one-sided fight and leave a permanent impression on the boy's body. He circled again, testing Carlos's balance with the pulls and releases of the red cloth. The boy learnt fast, Jonas gave him that. He had quickly figured out the use of the cloth as a tool and matched Jonas's head and body maneuvers. But there were feints too. Jonas lunged forward, seemingly overcommitted, and Carlos moved to counterattack with a slash of his own. It was a ruse. Jonas stopped his forward momentum in an instant, and as Carlos's blade sliced through air, Jonas stepped in and traced a thin line from belly to shoulder. Carlos winced in pain, and spat the end of the red cloth from his mouth and jumped backwards, his body involuntarily curling inwards.

"Foul!" cried the Bully Boys.

Patch picked up the end of the red cloth from the floor and took the opportunity to examine Carlos's latest wound. He shook his head.

"Just another thin slice, youn' 'un. It's a bleeder, but not enough to call First Blud," Patch said. He offered the cloth to Carlos, who gamely put it back in his mouth. Patch smiled and nodded his head in recognition of Carlos's bravery. He turned to face Jonas with a scowl on his face. "Finish this, Jonas. No more games."

Jonas nodded his head. He had messed with the boy long enough. It was time to make a deeper cut, one which would leave a lasting disfigurement on Carlos. He desperately wanted to stab the little shit and end his miserable life, but that would bring retribution from Cotter, so he would settle for a deep slash under his left armpit and sever the tendons and ligaments. Carlos's dominant arm would be useless and even holding a blade would be difficult. Cotter's unnatural interest in the boy would pass soon enough, and then he would settle for Carlos Grimm and dump his remains in the Basin.

Carlos knew he was no match for Jonas, and without some kind of intervention, outright miracle, or a lucky accident, he was done for. Adrenaline kept the deeper pain at bay, but he could still feel the sting of the three cuts, especially the one across his torso, and his blood was spilling all over the floor. He looked over at Jonas, and their eyes locked. There was murder in that stare. Maybe not now, and he would have to settle for a deep carving, but murder was coming.

Man and boy circled again. This time Carlos worked on position, and a feint of his own. He stopped his movements, and pulled the cloth tight. He positioned Jonas over the spot where he had just been standing, and where his spilt blood was the thickest. It was now or never. He tensed his body and committed to spring forward. Jonas saw it, changed the angle of his knife to reach up and under Carlos's left armpit and make the boy a cripple. At that moment, Jonas's lead foot slipped in the blood, and his strike sailed past the intended target. Carlos's lunge continued, and his own blade bit deep into Jonas's chest, and cut a long gash.

The two separated, and the cloth dropped from both of their mouths. Jonas's left hand immediately went to his wound, as if to hold it closed, or to hide it from Patch's inspection. His right hand fell to his side. Blood poured from the gash. His mouth hung open in disbelief. The match was over and he knew it.

CHAPTER TWELVE

"First Blud!" Patch shouted, and the mites, the slager apprentices, and a handful of Bully Boys cheered. The rest of the encircling crowd stood in stunned silence. Jonas was their knife champion, and he had lost to a mere boy who barely knew how to carry a blade in combat.

"That's an end to it, then," Cotter said from his vantage point in the regal chair high on the dais. "Well done, youn' Carlos. First Blud is yours!"

The fight was over, but Jonas could not accept defeat from a boy. In that moment, he knew his life was as good as over. He could not run with the Bully Boys anymore. There was no respecting a man who lost First Blud to the likes of Carlos Grimm. He would be an outcast, laughed at behind his back, by mites, apprentices, and especially his former friends. He had to do the boy in, and face his punishment. At least he would go out like a man.

Jonas raised his blade and moved towards Carlos. His purpose was to kill, and kill quickly before Cotter could stop him. No more games, no more cutting. No more feints, or skilled maneuvering. It was a kill shot he was after, and he changed his grip to a hammer fist to puncture Carlos's torso repeatedly with the boy's heart as his main target.

The crowd saw Jonas's intent and fell silent. No one made a move to intervene, not even Patch. The killing lust was heavy on Jonas and it would be a grave mistake to get in front of his blade. Punishment would come later from Cotter for breaching the rules, but only after Carlos was stiff and cold.

"Stay that 'and, Jonas!" Cotter bellowed. But even his command fell on Jonas's deaf ears.

Carlos saw the look in Jonas's eyes and knew he was dead in a matter of moments. A thought of Juan flashed before his eyes, but he was laughing and cavorting with JoJo Dickens and his pickpockets, and not worrying about him or his plight. He came into the world with another, but he was going out alone. He gritted his teeth and held up his bloody blade.

Jonas did not rush the attack. He hunched his shoulders and seemed to thicken out his torso. In that moment, he was more beast than man. A beast with a blood lust and a death wish. He moved forward on Carlos with his blade held at chest level, ready to strike repeated blows.

Carlos's will to face Jonas head on broke. He was just a child before a killing man, and his body screamed run away. He took two steps backward as Jonas pressed home the attack, and slipped heavily in his own blood. As Jonas stabbed forward, Carlos fell to the floor beneath him, and as a reflex action shot out his own blade. The pigsticker buried itself deep into Jonas's inner thigh just below the groin. Jonas howled in pain and stepped past. Carlos pulled out his knife and rolled away. Jonas's femoral artery was severed and his life blood gushed out. He dropped to the floor, and the deep red arterial blood spurted ten feet into the air like a crimson fountain.

Patch Armstrong rushed forward. If he could apply pressure to the wound with his knee, and then tie off a tourniquet, they could still save Jonas. It was a long shot, but he had seen it done before, and Perfect Styles could stitch anything closed.

"Let 'im be, Patch," Cotter commanded. "'E made his choice. Let 'im lie in it!"

Patch had sense enough to obey his leader. He stopped short of Jonas, and watched the man bleed out. His face had already gone pale with the loss of blood, and he was going into shock. His body convulsed with every diminishing spurt of liquid as he faded away. The hot blood cooled and congealed as it spread around his dying body.

"At least he held onto his knife. He'll need it in the Onderworld. Lots of enemies waitin' for that one," Patch muttered

Patch moved over to Carlos, and picked the boy up from the ground. "You alright, youn' 'un? Neat trick."

"Iz slipped," Carlos said.

"Sometimes a slip is all it takes. Well done. You survived First Blud and a Death Match at the same time," Patch said, holding up his arm as the victor.

The crowd parted as Patch led Carlos forward to stand before Cotter and Black Jack Cuttle still sitting in their high chairs upon the dais. Cotter fidgeted with his Hetman of the Slagers chain around his neck.

"Well done, youn' Carlos. No small feat takin' out Jonas Wheeler. He was a weasel of a man, who 'ad trouble followin' orders, but a dab 'and

CHAPTER TWELVE

with a blade," Cotter said. He looked over at Perfect Styles. "Perfect, send over sum of your 'prentices to clean up that mess, an' pitch wot's left of Jonas into the Basin."

Perfect gestured to four boys with his cleaver, and they ran over with buckets and mops to clean up the blood lake and lift the lifeless body of Jonas Wheeler onto a cart for the unceremonious transportation and dumping into the icy black waters of the Basin.

"Mind yuz weight 'im down first," Cotter said. "We don't want 'im bobbin' back up. An' make sure to give 'im a coin for the Ferryman too. A copper one will do for the likes of Jonas Wheeler."

Cotter turned his attention back to Carlos. "Well, youn' Carlos, it woz a grand fight for the ages, but it's done with now. With all this bludlust, I 'as an itch needs scratchin', an' yuz is just the boy to scratch it."

"Iz a man now, Cotter. Get sum other mudlark for ya pleasure," Carlos said defiantly. He was still clutching his blade tightly in his left hand. It did not go unnoticed from Cotter or Patch.

"Yuz a man, when Iz say yuz a man!" Cotter bellowed. "Now get Perfect to attend to 'em scratches first, put your eye paint back on, an' get yourself to the bedchamber!"

"Fightin's over, boy. Put the knife away," Patch said gently.

Chapter Thirteen

Kasha : The Queen of the Snow Travelers

Kasha waited for the wolfpack to show itself, short sword and axe in hand. They had the advantage of numbers and nocturnal vision, but a fully armed and alert human with fire as a companion was not as easy as chasing down an ancient snow shoveler on the run. They circled the hill and came on slowly, hesitant to be the first to press the attack and risk a life threatening wound. With a bark from the alpha male, two of the younger more aggressive males edged closer to the warrior. They were bold enough to take her on.

    Kasha's senses were heightened as the battle madness took full hold. Her hearing sharpened, her vision expanded, and strength surged through every sinew and muscle. She felt invincible in that moment, and a sense of joy at the impending fight. She let out a full throated roar as a challenge to her canine opponents. She frothed at the mouth, stamped her feet, and banged sword and axe together to let the sparks fly. She was Kasha NicTornar, and she was prepared to die.

    The two snow white wolves edged closer and into Kasha's line of sight. She could see the red of their eyes reflected in the fire light, and hear the low growls as they prepared themselves for combat. Kasha knew they were the advanced guard, and there were likely many more in the background, watching and waiting. A determined and hungry pack would take her down eventually, but not before a fight. These two would go first.

The two wolves stopped in their tracks and slowly backed away, until they blended into the nightscape. The howls and barks stopped, and Kasha could no longer feel the ominous presence of the pack. The sudden retreat confused her. She was prepared for combat, longed for it, and now the fight was taken from her. The battle madness began to fade, and the fog of war lifted. She wiped the back of a gloved hand across her mouth to remove the excess spittle, and spat blood from a bitten lip into the snow.

Kasha saw the line of torches coming down from the north and closing the distance towards her like a fire dragon worming its way through the snow. She understood why the pack had fled. A caravan out in the Wildlands was winding through the frozen lower *Snacoilltean* of her people, the forested snowlands known as the *Viorlanda* to the Var. They were likely on a well known path to Gastown, though there were no tracks to mark its passing. She gaped at the length of the convoy, and wondered about the cargo they transported. She soon got her answer as the lead sledges passed by at the base of her hillock. She marveled at the size of the mighty transporters, the ships of the snow, as they moved steadily along on their massive steel runners, each pulled by a team of twenty or more semi-tamed snow shovelers, who were partially obscured by the expiration cloud from their breath caused by the frigid air.

The cargo was a rich harvest of what the north had to offer. Mighty timbers carved from the old growth forests, where man rarely ventured. Ironwood, eikwood, oak, and larch. Trees older than Gastown itself. Wood to fabricate hauses, construct harbors, and build the imposing Black Ships and the remnants for the smaller fishing vessels. Furs filled other transporters, piled on high. Furs from poro, wooly mamont, bear, snowcat, and giant beaver. The latter much prized for the hats and coats of the Dandys. There was too much meat to consume, and the carcasses were mostly abandoned to freeze where they lay, or picked upon by the predators who followed the northern herds. It was the devastation of the *Faratha*, the far northern uplands Tornar told her about in a revered tone.

The caravan did not stop for Kasha, but continued on the slow, arduous journey to Gastown, where they would sell their wares and indulge in the pleasures city life had on offer, before continuing with their destructive cycle of plundering from the north. One or two of the drivers, hard men with hard bodies and harder faces, fashioned by the inclement conditions, glanced over out of mild curiosity. Most could care less why a girl was all alone out in the Wildlands.

A sleigh, much smaller than the lumbering transporters, and pulled by four giant poro, left the line, and slid over to the base of the hillock in front of Kasha. The driver in front was a huge bear of a man with only holes where ears should have been, and a face reddened and weather scarred by the harsh elements. He reminded Kasha of her father for his sheer size, though there was no family resemblance. The driver managed the poro with ease, by pulling four separate reins through his fingers. There was one passenger in the sleigh, and Kasha could see there was an air of authority about her. She was wrapped from head to foot in lavish, light gray furs, though Kasha did not recognize the species. She had a box on her lap, which she flipped open, selected a delicacy, and casually popped it into her mouth.

The driver pulled the sleigh to a halt, and gently assisted the woman down to the ground. Kasha was shocked to see the woman towered over the driver, and though he was immensely broad, he was squat with it, as if some playful god had pressed him down, and only allowed outward expansion. Sitting down in the sleigh his height was merely an illusion. The woman was as tall as Kasha. She removed her fur hat, tossed it back into the sleigh, and smiled.

Kasha did not smile back. She was not used to being around city folk, and social etiquette would still take some adjustment. She was grateful for the intervention with the wolves, but she did not want to convey weakness.

"I'm not your enemy, child. Kindly lower your weapons," the woman said.

It was only then Kasha realized she was standing at the ready with sword and axe in hand. She glanced over at the driver who had a hand on his own axe, and a scowl on his face. She sheathed both weapons, but did not relax

CHAPTER THIRTEEN

her stance. She remained alert and on edge.

"Wolves," Kasha said.

The woman smiled again. Up closer, Kasha could see she was an older woman with long silver hair, but a strong body lay beneath the heavy furs. There was beauty in her face, despite the red scars beneath both eyes.

"I believe introductions are in order? I'm Beira Freydasdottir, though flatterers call me, *The Queen of the Snow Travelers.* Others use less flattering appellations such as, *The White Witch of the North*," Beira said. "And you are?"

"Kasha NicTornar, or Tornarsdottir, in your language," Kasha said, though the words did not come easy. Even listening to the common tongue of Gastown was a challenge after so long.

"Tornar of the North?" Beira asked.

"Some know him as that," Kasha replied.

Beira bowed slightly, though Kasha could not tell if it was genuine respect for her lineage, or a form of mockery. Many people held Tornar in high regard, but many others loathed or feared him, and still others wished him dead. She wondered to which group this woman belonged.

"You're trusting to share your true name with me. Many in the Wildlands, and even in Varstad, would pay dearly to know Tornar has a daughter, and a potential weakness."

Kasha bristled. "I don't hide my name from anyone, and I'm far from weak, as your stubby man will find out if he doesn't take his hand off his weapon."

Beira gestured to her driver to take a step back. "Don't mind Drest. He's fiercely protective of me." She changed the subject to soften the moment. "You have beautiful red hair, my child. A rarity in these parts. You're a Chosen One, and great things are expected of you before you leave this world."

A Chosen One? Kasha had not heard the term before. Then her thoughts wandered to the young redheaded girl she had recently torn apart. Her path of destiny came to an abrupt end. She fulfilled nothing and the only trace of her time in this world was a silver tree brooch pinned to an undergarment of her killer's breast. Kasha knew she should feel normal human remorse, but shapeshifters walked a different path to survive in the cruel world. Tornar had taught her well.

"And tell me Kasha Tornarsdottir, what are you doing out in the Wildlands all alone?"

The question caught Kasha by surprise. She realized she did not have a plausible story. She had not planned to meet any travelers on her journey to Gastown, but had hoped to reach her destination with little fanfare, and slip into the township unannounced, find her brother as Tornar had instructed, complete her mission, and slip out again. Although how the two of them planned to get to the *Faratha* in the far north she had not yet considered. Perhaps her sibling had the route already mapped out.

"I was traveling with traders to see the Nechtana tribe, but got separated," Kasha offered. It was the best she could come up with at that moment.

"And why were you out in the frozen wilderness in the first place?" Beira inquired.

Kasha hesitated. She was not used to being grilled with questions. Before she could come up with a false answer, Beira softened.

"No mind, child. You're here now, and safe from the wolves. Though who knows if they'll come back. Persistent creatures, wolves. I suggest you travel with us to Varstad. It will be far safer, and your journey will be halved," Beira said.

"I can pay my way," Kasha said, pulling a stolen silver coin from her purse, and handing it over to Beira.

Beira took the coin, examined one side, turned it over and inspected the other. She gave Kasha a quizzical look. "A coin from the founding of Varstad. Fine craftsmanship. I wouldn't be showing the likes of this in Gastown if I were you."

Beira turned around and walked back towards her sleigh. She stopped and turned to face Kasha. "Come, child. We still have a long ride ahead of us, and the caravan waits for no one."

"Wait, my things," Kasha said, and ran up the hillock to recover her backpack and bearclaws. She extinguished the remains of the fire by

CHAPTER THIRTEEN

kicking snow onto the smoldering wood, and stamping on the pile with her worn kamiks for good measure.

Drest reached out a hand, and helped Beira up into the back of the sleigh. He offered the same calloused hand to Kasha, but she ignored it and jumped up beside the Snow Queen. Kasha noticed Drest was sitting on a raised seat, which led to the deception of false height. She stashed her belongings underneath her own fur lined bench, and sat back. Beira covered both of their laps with a heavy snowcat pelt, and Kasha settled in, thankful for the warmth.

"May I offer you a little treat?" Beira said, opening the lid of her wooden box, and displaying an array of confectionery. "Pashtak Pleasures. Deliciously sweet, and they simply melt in your mouth. Flavored with rosehip, orange, and lemon."

Kasha shook her head. She was still distrustful, and wary of eating food from strangers, which could be poisoned. Perhaps it was all a ruse to drug her and sell her off in the slaaf market, or the flesh parlors of the Mutton.

"No? Do you think I'd use candy to bend you to my will? There are other, more subtle ways to do that, my child."

Kasha still refused the offering.

"Suit yourself," Beira said, before popping a delicately powdered orange sweet into her mouth.

Kasha sat back in her seat, and before realizing it, fell into a deep sleep. She dreamed of running free over the *Faratha* away from civilization and the malice of mankind as the sleigh pulled her closer and closer to Gastown. She loped north with a direwolf by her side, moving easily through the snowdrifts and ice sheets. Always north, guided by a giant ice bear who stayed just out of reach.

Kasha woke up with a start, unsure of where she was, or why she was moving. She instinctively reached for the knife at her belt, before a strong hand pinned her arm.

"Easy, Kasha. There is no threat here," Beira said, though she would not release Kasha's arms until she was sure the danger had passed.

Kasha let go of her knife, and only then did Beira soften her grip.

Beira reached down and picked up a flask. "Hot soup for breakfast. We won't stop until mid-solar to rest up the snow shovelers. Only vegetables, I'm afraid. I don't allow meat in my presence. Even Drest up there eats plant food. Though I'm sure he sneaks off at times for a plate of ribs."

Kasha was ravenous, and this time she did not refuse as Beira poured her a cup of warm broth. Kasha rarely ate vegetables even in human form, and she was surprised by the complex flavors and the delicate seasoning. Outside of a fresh raw poro liver, it was the most delicious thing she had ever eaten.

"How far?" Kasha asked, as she took another sip of her soup.

"A full lunar to Gastown. I had been hoping you'd stay up a while longer and help me pass the time through the night. No matter, you were exhausted and needed sleep. We'll have plenty of time to talk along the way," Beira said.

The rest of the journey to Gastown was uneventful, though Kasha was less belligerent as she softened her attitude towards her gracious host. As they got closer, she noticed more and more homestead settlements. People who preferred to live on the outskirts of the town, but close enough for protection from the dangers of the Wildlands. They stopped occasionally to rest and feed the beasts of burden. The men barely raised camp fires, and ate dried meat on the move, and out of sight of Beira. They never washed, as Kasha's nose could testify. All were eager to get back to Gastown after a long hard trek to the north and back. Six lunars was a long time to live on the road away from loved ones and creature comforts. But there were rich rewards, provided you survived the hardships, which came in many forms. Death from felled trees, death from a hunt gone wrong, death from predators, both beast, human and demi-human, death from accident and disease, without a sawbones or herb witch to ease the passage.

Along the way, Beira did most of the talking. She explained to Kasha about the life of a snow traveler, and the arduous treks through the *Viorlanda* to the edges of the *Opplanda* and back again. She described the exhilarating feeling of starting off fresh on the expedition with a caravan as long as a winding river weighed down with supplies and trinkets for the

CHAPTER THIRTEEN

scattered northern tribes. How there were thrilling adventures at every turn, and the intoxication of a life free from the constraints and rules of the city. And the homebound journey laden with the northern harvest to sell for vast profits in Gastown. Finally, enjoying the fruits of their labor, until the call of the wild pulled them from a warm bed and wrapped in furs they followed the stars to the virgin lands further and further north. Always north.

Kasha listened and nodded her head at the appropriate places. She broke brood and ate vegetable broth with Beira, but her thoughts were on Gastown and the meeting with her brother. She gave little away about herself, and remained guarded, and always on edge. Occasionally, Beira asked her about Tornar, and what he was like as a father, and what he was doing now. Her interest seemed somewhat personal. Kasha deflected as best she could and steered the conversation back to snow traveling.

The sight of Varstad was overwhelming. She had left Gastown as a young child, spirited away by Tornar from her foster parents when the first signs of shapeshifting came upon her. She lived an isolated life for some time with her father, getting to know him, and learning from him how to be self-sufficient and independent. Learning to understand what she was, and how to control the switch between worlds, and what it meant to be a waheela. What it meant to be a human she was still figuring out. Tonar left her then, to go on her own journey of discovery, while he headed to the far reaches of the *Faratha*. However, he was always in her thoughts.

The walls of Vastad were truly majestic, and towered above the flat landscape. They surrounded the entire city, with only one huge gateway as the entry point through Gastown itself, though the gates had not been closed in over a hundred years. Ice and snow covered the walls, but huge blocks of stone lay beneath. Stones moved by giants, the kithfolk said, since they were bigger, and heavier, and constructed in a way the current occupants could not replicate. New construction was crude, and relied on mortar to hold the baked brick and chiseled stone together. But they were merely superficial facades on the ancient and vastly superior foundations. Above the outer walls and Gastown behind them, rose the mighty citadel of Varstad itself. A citadel built on seven hills, and dominating the town and the valley beyond.

Beira noticed Kasha was no longer listening to her story of how they took down a wooly mamont herd by driving them off a ravine. The girl was mesmerized by the sight of the city.

"Impressive, no?" Beira asked. "My people didn't build it, but we've occupied it for over a thousand years. The Var are mighty warriors, if a little insular. I'm afraid inbreeding will be the death of us."

Kasha was not listening. She only had eyes for Varstad and what lay beyond the vast city walls. She hoped the topography of the streets, canals, and bridges would come back to her as clearly as her childhood memories, and finding her brother would come easy.

The snow traveler caravan trundled though the huge gateway and between the two vast towers on either side of it. Stone warriors in ancient garb manned the walls, though no living soldier was on guard duty patrolling the heights. Times of peace lessened fear of attack and resulted in lax defenses. Varstad was no exception. The Dux and her Damm Warriors still ruled with an iron fist, but trade was king.

It was still early in the solar, but the merchants were already stirring, preparing their wares for the market. Some were setting up stalls, others carting goods to their shops. Craftsmen carrying the tools of their trade hurried on to their next assignment, some stopping for a breakfast along the way. All heads turned and kithfolk moved to one side, as the huge sledges on their iron rails and pulled by the mighty snow shovelers moved steadily through the Four Kith, and on to the vast warehouses near the docks.

Drest guided the sleigh to the front of one doorway and pulled up to a stop. He got out and offered the customary hand to Beira, who graciously accepted it and stepped down. There was no hand for Kasha, and taking her belongings, she jumped down to the ground. Beira reminded her weapons were not permitted in Gastown besides a knife for common use, and a small axe for chopping tinder, and she convinced Kasha to leave her backpack, sword, and bearclaws behind for safekeeping.

CHAPTER THIRTEEN

"You're more than welcome to stay with me a while longer, Kasha Tornarsdottir. I thank you for listening to my stories on the last leg of the journey. It was a pleasure to have company other than Drest," Beira said.

Kasha shook her head. "I have to go and find my brother, Berric."

"As you wish. But remember what I said. Guard those silver coins."

Kasha bowed slightly and turned to go.

"Kasha?" I feel we have unfinished business. After you find your brother, seek me out. I could use a girl like you on our next great journey north. And your brother. A son of Tornar must be familiar with the Wildlands. He's welcome too."

Kasha nodded her head and left before Beira could say another word.

Once she was out of sight of the warehouse, Kasha sought one of the street stalls offering food. There were a number of them already set up and selling their varied cuisine to the workers on the move. The general mix of aromas was enticing: hot stews, pork belly strips, mulled drinks with an assortment of herbs, even baked vegetables. Kasha settled for a vendor carving from an oblong lump of charred meat circling over a low flame, and serving it with fried onions wrapped in a brood blanket. Fat dripped from it and congealed on the floor. After a lunar on a vegetable diet, it was a mouth watering treat.

"Is the meat fresh?" Kasha asked.

"It was when alive," the pot bellied vendor replied, spitting tabak juice into the flames and watching it sizzle.

"What kind of meat is it?"

"Paranga," he said, which meant it was really all the scraps and cuttings from the slager's block all mixed together.

Kasha handed over a full copper coin, and expected some clippings as change. However, the vendor simply put meat and onions into the brood, rolled it, and handed it over. Kasha took a hearty bite, and savored the rich flavor. Her stomach might regret it later, but for now it was pure perfection.

"Do you know where I can find, *The Copper Coin?*" Kasha asked between bites.

"There's a nice one in my pocket, you just handed over," the vendor said, chuckling at his own weak joke.

"The inn. I'm looking for *The Copper Coin*, the public haus," Kasha asked.

The vendor scratched his head with the point of his meat cleaver. "Why, I believe that's over in the Mutton, though I don't go there myself. Dangerous part of the world, the Mutton is." He looked more closely at Kasha. "Not a place for youn' girls, unless you're lookin' for work. The unsavory kind. There's a killer on the loose too. Folks call him T*he Terror*. Best stay out of the Mutton, if I was you."

"I'm meeting my brother, and I can take care of myself."

"Then fool he is for pickin' a robber's paradise. Anyways, it's over there," he said pointing with his cleaver. "Three canals over and across the bridge. You'll need to ask again on 'tother side for Sot's Square."

Kasha thanked him, and then stepped back as other patrons picked up their breakfast, and hurried off to work. Most were making their way to the docks, where they waited in groups for a foreman to select them for a hard solar's work for a half solar's pay. Others worked in construction, or destruction, which was in perpetual motion in Gastown.

The mass of people increased and Kasha felt claustrophobic amongst the motley crowd as they twisted and turned through the streets, trudging through the sludge beneath their feet. She pressed herself against a wall and took a deep breath to steady her nerves. She glanced down at her worn kamiks, which were not improved by the Gastown mire. The noise was already overwhelming, and Kasha jumped when the steam whistles whooshed, signaling the start of the working solar in the citadel.

She took another deep breath and pushed off from the wall and into the crowd, following the scant directions given to her by the meat vendor. Passage was more difficult as she swam against the tide. Whilst her destination was towards the Mutton, everyone else was going in the opposite direction. By the time she reached the second canal crossing, the numbers had thinned out considerably. At the final bridge, she was all alone. The Mutton was a nighttime destination for Burghmeisters and kithfolk, and the solar was for the crew who called it home. Most slept

CHAPTER THIRTEEN

during the solar hours, and those who kept the taverns open for scant business were generally in a foul mood.

Kasha had a dilemma as she crossed the bridge, and entered the Mutton. There was no one in sight to ask directions. The streets were deserted and the first line of bawdy hauses were locked up, and the purple windows where the slagmaidens displayed their painted flesh were closed for business. They were geared towards nightfall traffic, and the gaudy signs and garish paintings were dim and dingy in the solar light. She kept moving from street to sleazy street until she came to an open area surrounded by buildings, which had to be Sot's Square. There were bordellos here too, but also an assortment of alehauses. Kasha could not read runes, but she could make out some of the names by the associated signs they all displayed. *The Drunken Duck, The Strong Arm, The Blind Beggar, The Running Maid,* and *The Green Man.* At the end of the line she saw the sign she was hoping for, *The Copper Coin.* There was no mistaking it, the image of a copper coin with a regal Dux head emblazoned on it. Kasha had seen the same image on one of her own copper coins. It was the depiction of an early ruler of the Var, although she did not know or care which one.

The oak door to the alehaus was closed, but it opened easily enough when Kasha pushed on it. There was little light in the interior, just two candles on the counter, and a dying fire in the hearth. There was one drunken patron sprawled across a table and snoring loudly like a pig and a frog in conversation. A sullen barkeep was behind the counter casually emptying slop from dirty flagons back into a barrel.

Kasha walked up to the counter and placed both hands on it. She tried to appear confident in front of the innkeeper and not let her nerves show. Projected strength was everything and weakness was preyed upon. The rules in the Mutton were the same as the rules in the Wildlands.

"I'm looking for a man called Berric," Kasha said.

The barkeep, a roly poly fellow, was a head shorter than Kasha, and he looked up at the strange girl dressed in furs for life in the *Viorlanda.* "Never 'eard of him."

"He'll be a large man, taller than me. Likely dressed in furs."

The barkeep shook his head. "Haven't seen his kind during the solar. The strange ones come out at night."

"Then I'll wait. Black bier," Kasha said.

"Bit young to be drinkin' even in the Mutton," the barkeep said, making no move to get Kasha's drink.

Kasha slammed down a copper coin on the counter. "And not from your slop barrel either."

The barkeep shrugged and poured Kasha's bier into a clean flagon and handed it to her. She took it, and found a seat in a dimly lit corner where she could observe anyone entering the premises, and keep her back safely against a wall, and her knife loose in the sheath.

It was a long wait. *The Copper Coin* remained empty for most of the solar. Only when the lunar raised her lazy head did patrons emerge from their dens and frequent the alehaus. With business picking up, the solar time barkeep was replaced by a heavyset man, who looked more capable of dealing with trouble, and a woman with a mountainous bosom and cleavage on overflowing display helped to keep the flagons of ale moving, and the customers amused. A young pot lad brought the fire back to life, and collected flagons from the tables. He stole quick swigs when he could, and swayed wildly like a soused sailor, mugs in hand, by the time *The Copper Coin* was half full.

At first, Kasha checked out the customers as they came through the heavy oak door. However, it became more difficult as the night wore on and the tavern filled up, and her clear line of sight to the doorway was impaired. Heavy clouds of tabak smoke decreased visibility even further and stung Kasha's eyes. The vapor from an assortment of clay, briar, and the occasional fancy calabash pipe, billowed up to the rafters, and then settled back down on the inebriated throng like an aromatic fog bank.

Kasha could not keep a bench occupied unless she was a paying customer. She ordered two more black biers, a hunk of equally black brood and a tangy blue cheese which smelt like old kamiks left out in the rain. The barmaid brought it to her, which meant she kept her seat, and remained mostly out of sight in the corner.

CHAPTER THIRTEEN

She did not see the man or feel his presence until he was sitting down in front of her. She was startled he had managed to get so close without her senses kicking in, but there he was.

"Berric?" she asked, but she knew as soon as she uttered the name it was not her brother. He was an older, slim man with a pockmarked face, well groomed black beard and mustache, and slicked back hair. He wore a fancy fur jacket over a red tunic, and his heavy cloak was pinned by a silver brooch of a man and woman fornicating. His black eyes were piercing and shiny. He smelled of lavender and danger.

"I can be Berric if you like, but most folks know me as Puzzle Pete," he said. "I keep an eye out for fresh newcomers. If you're looking for work, I'm your man. A redhead would bring a fine bonus," Pete said.

"I'm looking for my brother," Kasha replied.

"Ah, the Berric you mentioned."

"Do you know him?"

Pete opened up a small silver case and took out a pinch of snuftabak, which he placed on the back of his hand, and sniffed up his nose. His mouth opened and his eyes closed, and he sneezed into his sleeve. He offered the open case to Kasha, who declined.

"I know lots of Erics, and Derrics, but unfortunately I don't know any Berrics. It seems to me you've been waiting a long time, and he's not coming."

"He'll be here," Kasha said firmly.

"The Mutton is a dangerous place, especially for a girl all alone. I can help you there. Come with me, and you'll never be alone again." He reached out to touch Kasha's hand and she immediately pulled it away, and reached for the knife at her side.

"I think you'd better go," Kasha said.

Pete made no move to leave. "Why, I just got here," he said. "Can't we just be friends?"

"You heard my sister. Move on," a man said.

Kasha looked up and saw a younger version of her father looming over the table. He was not as tall as Tornar, very few men were, but he was powerfully built, and had the look of a fighter. He dressed in Wildland clothes, similar in style to Kasha, and lacked the veneer of a Gastown native.

Puzzle Pete should have been scared, or at least on guard, but he continued with his nonchalant behavior without a care in the world.

"Ah, Berric, I believe. You look like a fine strapping fellow from the country based on your rustic dress sense. I can always use another strongarm in my line of work," Pete said.

"We don't deal with the likes of you. Now move on before I make you," Berric snarled.

"And if that doesn't get your attention, maybe this does," Kasha said, sliding her knife from the sheath and holding it for Pete to see.

"Well, well. A couple of wild ones we have here," Pete said, still showing no signs of fear. "I know when I'm not welcome. So I'll bid you a goodnight … for now. As a parting gift, I'd caution you both on making unnecessary enemies when an offer of friendship was there for the taking, and callously rebuffed."

Pete pushed back his chair and stood up. He glanced up at Berric, who towered over him, and touched a finger to the side of his head as a salute. He turned to face Kasha. "And a word of warning, my redheaded beauty. Never pull a knife unless you intend to use it. A blade thirsts for blud."

Berric watched him go, and then sat down in the empty chair facing Kasha. They stared at each other for a moment, each looking for the family resemblance as a means of verification. Kasha saw her own eyes staring back at her, and the nose had the same shape. Their coloring was different, and Berric's hair was black like Tornar's in his youth.

"How do I know you're really Berric?" Kasha asked. "Father said you would have a talisman to identify yourself."

"Nechtan's Eye," Berric said.

"Carved from a knuckle bone taken from Cathul's right hand," Kasha added.

Berric looked down at the table in embarrassment. "I lost it."

"You lost it?"

CHAPTER THIRTEEN

"A thief stole it."

"And you're supposed to help me get to the *Faratha*?"

"That's what father asked me to do," Berric said sheepishly.

There was an awkward silence as neither sibling spoke, then Kasha broke the ice. "If you don't have a talisman, what else identifies you as Berric MacTornar?"

Berric rolled up his left sleeve. "I have this," he said, showing Kasha a simple tattoo of an ice bear. "It's the first of many father put on me. All of his flock are marked with this."

Kasha smiled, and rolled up her own left sleeve and revealed the same marking. "I guess we're related after all. And the right arm? What's there?"

Berric rolled up his right sleeve and displayed the tattoo of a direwolf. "And yours?"

Kasha showed her own tattoo, and watched as Berric stared in horror.

"A waheela? Whatever possessed you?" Berric said.

Kasha immediately covered up her arm and sat back in her chair. "You're just like father," she grumbled.

There was another delicate silence then Kasha spoke again. "How did you know it was me," she asked.

"Well, there were two obvious signs. You're the only redhead in Gastown, and you're dressed like you stole your clothes from an assortment of people after coming out of a shapeshift," Berric said. He signaled to the tavern wench for ale.

Kasha blushed, as she recollected stripping the clothes from the homestead family. "So I do have a brother," Kasha said, changing the subject.

"Seven in total, but you're the only girl child Tornar has, and I didn't believe it at first. Shapeshifters are menfolk."

Kasha bristled. "This one isn't, and I can shift as well as the best of you!"

Berric held up his hands in mock self defense. "I didn't mean to cause offense. It's just you're rare. A real Chosen One."

"You're the second person to call me that," Kasha said.

"There will be more, I'm sure of it."

Berric was silent as the busty barmaid placed his bier in front of him with a jiggle of her breasts, and took payment as another copper coin changed hands. He clinked flagons with Kasha. "Here's to Tornar MacLorn, King of the Cathulla!"

"And to a family reunited," Kasha said.

"A highborn family," Berric replied, and took a deep pull of black bier. He wiped the back of his hand across his mouth to remove the froth. "Let's get out of this smoke trap. I have lodgings not far from here. It's not much, but it's clean, and we have catching up to do."

Kasha felt lightheaded as she stepped outside of the tavern and a combination of the crisp night air and the effects of the black bier hit home. She chatted casually with her brother as they weaved through the side alleys towards Berric's lodgings. There was more life in the streets now, and scantily clad women, seemingly oblivious to the cold, cavorted with customers, or quarreled with each other over slights, real or imagined. Someone sneezed behind them, and the sound caused Kasha to stop in her tracks. She had heard its twin in *The Copper Coin*.

Kasha turned and saw the little man standing next to two lumbering heavies. Berric tapped her on the shoulder, and as she looked forward, she saw three more thugs blocking their path.

"Hello, my lovelies," Puzzle Pete said. "I trust you have a coin left in your purse to pay the Ferryman. I did warn you about biting the hand of friendship."

Chapter Fourteen

Lilith : The Terror

The cavern beneath the great citadel of Varstad was Lilith's sanctuary. She found it as a child, when her love of exploring the depths of old Andalayim bore fruit. No one else ventured down this far, scared by the old crone's tales of hidden menace and certain death from the specters of the Old Ones, and the monstrous worms of the earth. Even Aldith, her older sister, the bravest of the Damm Warriors, stayed firmly above ground. But Lilith dared, and Lilith triumphed. This was her world, and she could breathe down here, free from the constraints of her military duties and her madness.

The walls were studded with lilac and lavender stones, which provided a soft warm glow and dim light for the chamber. Lilith augmented this with her own fire torches, which were necessary at first to find her way down the deep dark descent. Now she knew the way with her eyes closed, but she kept the torches to help illuminate the beauty of her den, and to assist with her other work.

There was a natural hot spring as the main focal point of the chamber, and Lilith wondered if the Old Ones had used it for healing purposes, or for sacrificial ones. She sat naked in the smaller pool to the side, and poured the red liquid, a mixture of blood and spring water, over her head and body. It was old and lackluster, and she knew the healing powers she craved from it had dissipated.

Lilith stepped out of the blood pool and imagined herself as the First Born, the giver and taker of lives. She paused for a moment, watching the diluted blood run down her legs as if the lunar time was upon her. She immersed herself into the hot spring and washed herself with mineral water to cleanse the sins she never felt.

She was as tall as Aldith, and just as capable with the longsword and Varbow. Her constant training meant she maintained a Damm Warrior's muscular physique, and the strength and subtleness to go along with it. Like all Damm Warriors, her hair was cropped short as a natural cushion for her helmet. Unlike most, she bore no dueling scars on her face. No one in her warrior class was good enough to inflict them upon her, and excess vanity aided her reflexes. Her face was pretty enough, but there was a constant coldness about it. Her distinguishing feature was her eyes, one blue and the other a cloudy green, which never saw a solar. It made her unique and easily identifiable.

Lilith climbed out of the pool, shook off the excess water, and quickly dried herself with a towel. She did not dress herself back into her Damm Warrior garb, with linen undergarments, chainmail, white cloak, and sword buckled at her waist. Instead, she tightly bound a cloth around her breasts to keep them pressed in, and donned the trappings of a Dandy. The finest silk undergarments covered by a rich tunic, trousers, waistcoat, and jacket, heavy leather boots polished to a fine sheen, and a scarf wrapped around the face to only expose the eyes. The final accouterments to the wardrobe were the heavy bearskin overcoat, the beaver tophat, and a Hallic steel knife tucked into her belt. It was time to go hunting.

She picked up her cane, twisted the silver wolf's head handle to pull the thin sword free, and then closed it again with a satisfying click. She took down a fire torch from the cave wall and headed down the high tunnel towards the Mutton. Worms made these tunnels, she thought. No human hand could bore so smooth. Worms of the earth, who she imagined still burrowed their way through the rock and soil beneath her feet. If she closed her eyes she could feel their vibrations as they inched along, boring

CHAPTER FOURTEEN

through rock, always moving, never still for a moment.

Lilith hummed a Dandy tune to herself as she traversed the tunnel. *The Thrill of the Kill,* it was called. An apt little ditty composed by a drunken minstrel who only raised a knife to stab at innocent vegetables. Her blade would slice and dice human flesh, carve through tissue, hack into fat and bone. She ended worthless slagmaiden lives, but got no pleasure from it. And she craved the rapture. The first one was a simple cut throat on the night she was interrupted by the two boys, a test to see if it brought any excitement. However, there was no emotional stimulation as blood flowed and life ebbed away. The second and third involved more dissection, similar to how she had toyed with small animals as a child, but still no elation. The fourth was pure butchery. The nightwalker took her back to her own quarters rather than conduct business out in the streets, which gave Lilith much more time. She opened up the slagmaiden like a pig on the butcher's block, scattering entrails and severed body parts, and draining blood. She felt nothing as she decorated the room in gore. There was another killing that night the kithfolk attributed to the serial killer, but it was not Lilith's work. An impostor simply used the cover to slit a slagmaiden's throat.

The murders had the Mutton on edge for over four lunars. They suspected a Dandy, and according to Rafyn's spies they had even dubbed him, *The Terror.* That made Lilith chuckle, but it also meant she had to be vigilant. No one in the Mutton would dare touch a Dandy, on punishment of death, but they would shun them, close off business, and refuse their silver coins. Swell Daddies would protect their fornicating flocks, and only the lowest of the low of slagmaidens would venture into the mating game with a potential Dandy killer. Lilith was not unduly concerned. The murders had served their purpose, and although she vainly hoped for arousal of some sort, they masked the real reason of distraction. With a killer on the loose, no one would pay attention to the odd disappearance, and she needed to harvest the blood of young girls to rejuvenate and remain sane.

Getting into the Mutton was effortless. Lilith's worm tunnel ended under an old warehouse, and a stone disc easily rolled to one side to allow access into the basement. The timbers were rotten, but Lilith moved fluidly through the frail structure, despite the hindrance of the heavy bear coat. She paused at the entranceway to make sure no one was watching, and then slipped into the shadows.

Children in the employ of the Swell Daddies were on the lookout now, but they stayed on the main streets and did not venture into the dark alleyways. The Mutton was still a dangerous place for them, and there were other killers and sexual deviants besides *The Terror*. They whistled back and forth to each other when they picked out a potential perpetrator, and runners were sent to the heavies who provided protection.

Lilith took it all in and analyzed their patterns. Snow began to fall, which meant they stayed closer to the doorways and not out in the open. When she was sure it was safe to move, she glided down the alleyways. Like all expert predators she had the patience to wait.

She knew the Mutton well by now, all of the alleyways, side streets, and the alehauses in the main square. She had frequented them, and picked up two hapless victims enticed by silver coins, from within their tabak stained walls. They were off limits now, and would go silent if a Dandy so much as entered. She also avoided the flesh parlors, which were watched over by the Swell Daddies and their army of thugs. The game there was not just to sell coital pleasures, but to spy on the clientele and garner secrets. Young, relatively fresh girls were always on sale in the Mutton, and she knew a Swell Daddy would part with them for the right price, no questions asked. Blackmail would come later, it always did from men driven by greed and no imagination. Besides, she preferred to pick out her own gifts for ritual slaughter. They were easy to find. Lost souls wandering the Mutton, before they were scooped up by a cordial Swell Daddy, who promised love and protection, but delivered a life of misery and shame.

Trade was slow tonight, and the snowfall did not help. Human foot traffic faded away, and there were no visible tracks as the snow covered the ground in a soft white blanket. Lilith knew there would be no slagmaiden to desecrate tonight, but she held on to a glimmer of hope she could find a

CHAPTER FOURTEEN

young girl to give up her life blood. She needed it. Her mind was beginning to race in different directions, thoughts overlapping and colliding, voices competing for attention. The sacrificial blood would calm her down and make her whole again.

She heard voices and a commotion, two alleys over. Ordinarily, a fight in the Mutton meant an opportunity in the other direction. However, Lilith sensed something different tonight and she was drawn to the disturbance like a cat to a cradle. She moved cautiously, still wary of anyone tracking her. More than one hunter had become prey to another due to negligence.

It was an unfair fight, four against two, and two others waiting in the shadows. However, Lilith gave the odds in favor of the young couple, who both fought with animal savagery. The bloodlust was on them as they battled for their lives. The young man moved fast, and had some skill with a knife and short sword. It required dexterity to wield two weapons simultaneously, especially when fighting dual opponents. He gutted one attacker who immediately went down holding in his innards, and closed with his other assailant. The girl was not as skilled, but she fought ferociously with a small axe and knife, forcing her two opponents to take backward steps. She would make a fine Damm Warrior, Lilith thought.

The fight was not going the way the thugs intended. As Lilith observed, a small man put his fingers to his mouth and let out two shrill whistles. The call was immediately answered in kind from two directions, and more ruffians ran up to join the fray. As the young man dispatched his final opponent, four others took his place, and pressed the attack. The man let out a wolflike howl, and charged into them.

The girl took down one foe with a crushing blow from his small axe, However, he was quickly replaced by four more. She made an overreaching strike with the axe, and slipped off balance, and had to lunge with her knife to keep an adversary from closing in. The men were wary of pressing the attack on the girl, and appeared content to separate her from her male companion. The distance between them widened. Divide and conquer.

As one opponent lunged in with his knife for a stab to the heart, the young man slid to one side, and slammed his sword into the man's jaw, sending teeth flying. The man staggered back, holding his wounded face, and then something flew in from the shadows. There was a thud as a blackjack made contact with the back of the young man's head, and he went down on both knees. The thugs moved in with boots inflicting damage. A large man who had been holding back, slid behind the young man, pinned both of his arms to shake the weapons loose, and pulled him roughly to his feet. The other man from the shadows, slimmer and smaller than the rest, stepped forward. A butcher's knife flashed in his hand and penetrated the young man's liver up to the hilt. The girl screamed, as he tumbled to the snow, and clenched at his right side. Blood seeped from his deadly wound and through his fingers.

The girl was fighting five of them now, and despite her determination to continue the fight, she stood little chance. A fist caught her on the jaw, and she went down. Kicks to the ribs knocked the air and some of the fight out of her, but not all. She had dropped the axe, but gamely tried to slash at her opponents with her knife. A thug stepped on her knife hand pinning it to the ground, and another tough savagely kicked the side of her head.

The small man knelt beside the stunned girl, and lifted a pouch from her pocket, while two others ransacked the young man's clothes and lifted his purse. He opened up the girl's pouch, and poured coins into his hand and inspected them.

Just thieves. They were after their gild.

To Lilith's surprise, the man put the coins back in the pouch, pulled the cord straight, and put it back in the girl's pocket. He gestured to his men to leave them, and with their brutal work done, they followed their diminutive leader out of the alley, carrying their wounded comrades. As they left, the girl gained consciousness, and clawed her way across the ground, and cradled the young man's head in her lap.

Lilith saw her chance. No one else came to investigate, not in the Mutton, and she stealthily moved in on the bleeding duo in the snow. She had no interest in the young man, and he was dying anyway. Her focus was on the girl, and what she would provide. She was a fresh one, and a fighter. Her

CHAPTER FOURTEEN

blood would provide sustenance for two lunars at least, perhaps longer. She took the rag from her pocket, a rag doctored with a sleeping liquid stolen from Petra the Pythoness's cabinet, and moved in from behind.

The girl had very little energy left, and her strength waned. Lilith wondered what sort of fight she would have put up if she were not injured. In her present condition she was no match for a seasoned Damm Warrior, and Lilith held her tight with the rag around her mouth as the drug went to work. Within moments the girl went limp and slipped into unconsciousness.

A part of Damm Warrior training meant carrying a partner two leagues in the hard packed snow over your shoulders. Lilith excelled at the exercise, and heaving the girl up and over was relatively easy. The entrance to the worm tunnel was only three blocks away, and the distance back to the cavern was exactly one league. She relished the exercise, especially with the bloody bounty on the other end of the journey.

The girl was heavier boned than Lilith anticipated, but she would not hamper the trek back to the cavern. Cane in hand and the girl evenly balanced over her shoulders, she made her way back to the abandoned warehouse. She paused again at the entrance to make sure no spies were watching, and then made the precarious way down to the basement. As she stepped on the final rung of the ladder, the rotten wood snapped and Lilith landed heavily, twisting her right ankle. She winced as the pain hit home, and she took a few deep breaths to steady herself. Walking back through the tunnel on a compromised leg would pose an additional challenge, but she had the cane for support. With another deep breath to steady herself, Lilith began the long limp home.

By the time she reached the sanctuary of the hot spring cavern, Lilith was breathing harder than she thought possible, and she was sweating under the heavy bearskin coat. It did not help her human cargo stank under her assortment of motley furs, and some of the stench, along with blood and drool had transferred to her overcoat. She knew it was ruined, and she would have to burn it and find another. Her ankle was on fire. Each step through the worm tunnel was an exercise in controlling pain and pushing on.

Lilith lay the unconscious girl on a stone slab, and felt immediate relief as the burden was removed from her shoulders. She stripped off her heavy bearskin coat, and threw it along with the beaver hat, away into a corner. She sniffed her own armpit and wrinkled her nose at the musky smell. She needed a refreshing hot bath, but not before she attended to her new charge.

She needed more light, and the slow burning torches were down to a faint glimmer after the time spent in the Mutton. She replaced them and fully illuminated the cavern once again. Next, she went to the shelf where she kept the sleeping potion she liberated from Petra's cabinet, dowsed another rag, and held it over the girl's mouth and nose, long enough to ensure she stayed under and submissive until called to her final rest.

Lilith stripped the girl of her furs and undergarments until she lay naked and vulnerable on the stone slab. She opened the purse and poured the silver coins out on the open space next to her. There was something different about this girl Lilith could not quite understand, something animalistic. There was an underlying strength to her, and her limbs were dense, sturdy, and springy, even compared to Damm Warriors of the same age. And she had seen conflict before, as the wound across her chest attested. Her face was a bloody mess where the Mutton thugs had left their mark, her right hand was swollen, and there was a heavy bruise forming over her rib cage. Lilith examined her red hair, and traced a finger over the many tattoos, which inked her body. The girl was certainly different from the ones she had previously abducted from the Mutton.

She removed her own soiled garments, unraveled the cloth constricting her breasts, and threw them into the same pile as the bearskin coat. She scooped up the girl, hobbled over to the hot spring bath and submerged them both. The heat was relaxing, and she soaked in it for a moment, before she began to gently wash down the girl. The minerals in the spring water would do their job and draw out the grease from her hair and the dirt deep in the pores of her skin. Next, she took a comb and gently untangled and groomed the girl's long red hair. Loose strands floated and swirled in

CHAPTER FOURTEEN

the gentle current of the hot spring.

Lilith placed the girl beside her, and put a gentle arm over her shoulders. She leaned over and kissed her on the cheek. She knew this girl was the one who could help restore her broken mind. Her life blood would still the wandering wicked thoughts, and allow peace at last. She closed her eyes, and settled back to enjoy her bath for a few moments longer. Soon she would carry the girl over to the smaller blood pool. A sharp blade would open both of her wrists and her vital fluid would gush out. They would delight in this last bath together, as the girl slowly and quietly slipped away, and Lilith was reborn.

"Not this one, my sweet," a woman said.

Lilith opened her eyes. There was no fear. She had known the voice since her time in the womb. "Mama. How did you find me?"

"I always know where you are, daughter," Beira said. She moved into the chamber and sat down on the stone slab where the girl had lain before. The heavy furs were gone and were replaced by a simple gray gown. Her long silver hair cascaded over her shoulders. She wore no jewelry other than a gold chain of office as an elder stateswoman of the Var and advisor to the Dux.

"But my secret chamber?" Lilith asked.

"You're not the only one to venture under the citadel, Lilith. Curious minds before you were intrigued by the tales of the hidden chambers the Old Ones carved out of the rock and the worm tunnels beneath the earth. Those who were not afraid of the folk tales ventured down. I've known about this cave and the hot springs since I was an adolescent."

Lilith reverted to a child before her mother, and her disappointment at her secret being discovered showed on her face. There was a sense of desecration, and even betrayal.

"Does Aldith know about it?" Lilith pouted.

Beira shook her head. "No, Lilith. Aldith is only interested in being the best of the Damm Warriors and in the affairs of state. She has no time for dark games. The chamber is all yours now. No one else alive other than the two of us knows it exists. You're free to use it as you wish, but not with this girl."

Lilith stood up, naked before her mother, and folded her arms in front of her. It was the pose she always struck when she wanted to defy her authority. As she did so, and with no one propping her up, Kasha slid down into the water, and her head submerged.

"She's mine. I found her. I'll keep her," Lilith said angrily.

They were words Beira had heard before. When Lilith took the cur puppy still suckling from her mother, and held it too close until she smothered it to death. When Lilith took the Andra baby girl who crawled out of the gardens and she tried to make her fly. *"She's mine. I found her. I'll keep her,"* Lilith had said as her mother gently prised the lifeless bodies from her grasp.

"Her name is Kasha Tornarsdottir, and she's the Chosen One," Beira said calmly. "And kindly pull her up from the pool before she drowns and is no use to either of us."

Lilith glanced over at Kasha who had sunk to the bottom of the pool. She was angry at her mother for wanting her human toy, and any gentleness shown towards Kasha evaporated like the steam from the hot spring. She reached down and roughly pulled Kasha up by the hair, and pushed her over the edge of the pool. Mineral water oozed from Kasha's mouth and nose.

"That's better," Beira said calmly. "Now tell me, how did you come across her, and why did you injure her?"

"It's not my work," Lilith said indignantly. "I rescued her from villainous men in the Mutton. Bad men with knives and clubs. I saved her and brought her here."

"To kill her?"

Lilith sat back down in the pool and hugged herself closely. "Not kill, mama. No, not kill. Kill is a harsh word. To sit with her in the pool. Just let her go to sleep in the nice warm water. And maybe take a little blood?"

"I need this girl, Lilith, and she needs all of her blood. I'll send Drest out to find you others to replace her."

"I can find my own sparrows," Lilith spat out. "Why this girl? What's so

CHAPTER FOURTEEN

special about her?" Lilith angrily splashed water over Kasha's unconscious body.

Beira reached down and picked up Kasha's soiled tunic and a handful of silver coins. "Because of these," she said, showing Lilith the silver tree brooch pinned to the cloth. "I gave this brooch to a young redheaded child I purchased in the southlands, and left with a homestead family for thirty pieces of old Varic silver. They were to keep her safe until her time came and I could take her to the Opplanda to meet with *The Sisters*. She's gone. But I have Kasha in her place, and Kasha is ready now."

Lilith listened, but she did not fully comprehend. "The Sisters want her?" she asked.

"The Sisters need her."

"Then The Sisters shall have her, mama, and I'll find another."

Beira smiled at her twisted, sweet, murderous daughter. "That's a good girl. I can always count on you. Now come out of the water before your skin gets too wrinkled and help me dress Kasha back into her clothes. There's another worm tunnel which leads down to the docks. I need to take her to my quarters there."

Lilith stepped out of the hot spring and helped her mother lay Kasha out on the stone slab once again. She quickly dressed back into her Damm Warrior clothes and then aided her mother to redress the comatose girl.

Lilith wrinkled her nose. "These furs are stinky."

"They'll serve her well on the journey to the far north. Tell me, my sweet, was Kasha all alone when you found her?"

"Not found, mama. Rescued, remember?"

"Yes, of course. Rescued," Beira said as she pulled on one of Kasha's worn kamiks. "She was looking for her brother. Berric is his name, I believe."

"Dead … or dying," Lilith said, pulling on the other boot. "A little bad man stuck him with a knife. He's lying in the snow three blocks from Sot's Square. Do you know it?"

Beira shook her head. "I'll send Drest to fetch him. I have a use for Berric too, dead or alive. One other thing, Lilith."

"Yes, mama?"

"No more killings in the Mutton. With Aldith sailing to the Southern Islands, I need you to focus on protecting Varstad. Do you promise?"

"I promise ... until Aldith returns."

Once dressed, mother and daughter propped up Kasha between them. Lilith limped on her bad ankle, and used her wolf's head cane for support, as they carried Kasha down the long tunnel to the lower docks. Lilith hummed *The Thrill of The Kill* as they made the slow hidden walk into Gastown.

Chapter Fifteen

Tana : The Andra Wedding

An Andra wedding was something to behold. It was the only time the Var allowed all of the five clans, the Pacca, Erupu, Narinja, Banda, and Preena to unite in celebration, and so the Andra rejoiced in the occasion. Fifty betrothed couples joined together, and the women began their new lives by taking their final color. For the ceremony, and as a sign of respect, the groom wore the color of his future in-laws. It was a small token of appreciation since no gifts were exchanged. There was no concept of a dowry. The bounty was the bride joining, sharing, and contributing to her new family.

 Tana marveled at how beautiful she looked in her new red Erupu dress, a gift from her future mother-in-law. Her own mother worked tirelessly all morning applying the kajal, the scented oils, and clarified butter to soften her skin. She combed her hair until every strand was free, and glistened perfectly in place. Tana did not complain like she normally did, even as her mother tugged and pulled. The result meant even amongst the other attractive brides, she was radiant. Today was a special solar and so she remained silent. Her sharp tongue cut indiscriminately, but the deepest lacerations were aimed at her younger sister, Chandra. For some reason, she wounded those closest to her. Not on this solar. She was in high spirits and all was forgiven. A wedding washed away all transgressions. The wheel turned.

Manoj was a lucky man to get her for a bride. He was still rough around the edges, spoiled by an indulgent father and doted on by a soft mother. He was handsome, though a little too sure of himself. Tana would change all of that in short order, she was sure. An obedient husband was required, and in time, obedient children.

The dome of the Preena clan, the exalted ones, who floated above the fray, was always the chosen place for the wedding festivals. Snow fell outside of the dome, and quickly melted away due to the generated heat from the steam pipes. Rivulets of water ran down to be collected in troughs and recycled into the gardens. Inside, there were rainbow colors, and the heady smell of the fresh herbs and the vibrant spices provided an intoxicating bouquet. Families gathered in their respective colors of green, red, yellow and orange, earth brown, and the rainbow combination. Excitement ran through the crowd, from the youngest child to the oldest amma. A communal wedding was more than a union of couples. It was a sacred commitment to the Prith, the Mother Earth they all revered.

Tana's stomach growled as she impatiently watched the other couples line up. Her mother begged her to eat the usual breakfast of pulses, insisting she needed all her strength for the ceremony. Tana adamantly refused. She wanted to look her best in the wedding dress, and each mouthful meant extra weight. She would gorge herself later when the wedding feast broke her fast. And what a feast! All of the families contributed, and there was every vegetable, pulse herb, and spice imaginable. The aroma as they simmered in pots and blended together, as the Andra themselves were united, overwhelmed her senses.

There was music too, quietly playing in the background for now, but soon to rise and whirl around the dome as the marriage ceremony concluded, and the dancing began. The best musicians gathered for weeks in advance to select and practice the familial songs. Her cousins Challa and Bhram were there, and they beamed with pride as they bowed their instruments along with the syncopated rhythms from the assortment of drums and flutes. Each complicated musical part weaved in and out and intertwined

CHAPTER FIFTEEN

with its neighbor. Always working together and never competing.

Tana looked over at her happy family as they sat in their place of honor along with the other immediate relatives of the brides and grooms. Her mother and father, who never said a mean word to each other. Her Amma, the only person who would not put up with her bad behavior, and rapped her knuckles when she misbehaved as a child. Chandra, not quite as beautiful as her, but made in her mother's image in looks, spirit, and temperament. She was still too young for a preliminary betrothal, but Amma said her father would make arrangements with one of the families from the Preena. The rainbow color would suit Chandra, and her love of herbs and spices made the selection a fitting one. And little Sri. She did not understand her brother, and refused to try. She left that to Chandra. She wondered how he would manage without Chandra in his own silent world when she finally left to join the Preena. For now, he happily sat at Chandra's feet, snipping at a herb patch with his miniature garden shears.

She stood directly in front of Manoj, who had a beaming smile on his face, love in his eyes, and desire in his heart. All the other couples were lined up too, and women from each of the five clans moved between them and offered up a jar. When it was their turn, and the Erupu woman stood between them, Tana and Manoj dipped their thumbs in the red paste. Tana went first and placed a red thumbprint directly between Manoj's eyes. Now it was Manoj's turn.

"Don't smudge it," Tana chastised.

Manoj smiled and delicately placed his loving seal on Tana.

By tradition, the fathers made the betrothal selections, and compared notes with each other for compatible matches. Two fiery tempers burned too brightly, silent couples meant no harmony, and lack of passion led to weak offspring. The children were not excluded from the arrangements, and Tana was very vocal in her own selection. She rejected the first two potential suitors, before she landed on Manoj. She admired him for his good looks, his dancing skills, singing prowess, and most of all, his willingness to please her. There were supervised visits, once work was done for the solar, and they had time to get to know each other before the wedding night and their first union. Tana told Manoj exactly what she wanted, and he nodded his head in agreement. The smile never left his face.

The fifty couples held hands, each bound by a unifying bracelet of flowering herbs, and collectively recited the wedding vows of the Andra in song. As the last note sailed high into the upper reaches of the Preena dome, the couples broke off one after the other, and twirled into dance. It was a sign for the musicians to pick up the tempo and the volume. The Andra clapped and cheered as their children grew before their very eyes and would labor diligently for families of their own. The wheel turned.

The wedding song never really ended. Like all Andra melodies, it morphed into something else. First, a drum section changed the rhythm, and the other instruments blended in, until a new arrangement took shape in complex patterns, cadence, and syncopation. It was dance music, the harmonic sound of the Prith. The rest of the community joined in and let themselves freely express their inner flow without the restriction of prearranged choreography. The men in particular whirled and twisted, and leapt high into the air.

There was no formal arrangement for the wedding feast. Families came up to the banquet tables as they saw fit, and helped themselves to the rich assortment of food. They took plates and bowls, and sat on the ground on blankets to consume with bread and with their hands. Some went back to the dance, others for a second helping. Tana broke her fast with a shared plate of mixed vegetables with Manoj, and the sweet, creamy laddu which he popped into her mouth, like he was feeding a baby chick.

Tana watched as Chandra gorged herself on a sambar stew, and mopped up the liquid with dosa, until she seemed to remember her musician cousins needed feeding too. Chandra hurried back to the food tables, and prepared two plates which she carried over to Challa and Bhram and placed down before them. Little Sri followed, carrying the breads while he chewed on a vada. The cousins nodded their appreciation, but did not drop a beat. Other musicians had already stopped playing as they ate, and Challa and Bhram would eat when they returned to the ensemble.

CHAPTER FIFTEEN

Tana wished the solar would never end. Her stomach was full, and her ears overflowed with music. She wanted to dance, but she worried she would look foolish next to Manoj and his fancy steps. Her mother and father had no inhibitions, and they danced like Tana had never seen before. She was leaving their nest, but there was no sadness for them. Tana frowned. She wondered if they rejoiced because they were happy for her in starting a new life, or if they were simply glad to see her go.

The music did not stop at once. Some of the musicians saw them first, and put down their instruments. The sound died out until only one drummer with his eyes closed and lost in his own rhythms thumped out a solo beat. A friend tapped him on the arm, and his pitter-patter ceased.

Tana's mouth dropped open and she stared in disbelief as the tall soldiers they called the Red Shadows flooded into the Preena dome and formed up on either side of the wedding party. They had halberds in their hands with heavy blades on top, and they held them up at an angle over the Andra. At a moment's notice they could move them down and assume a fighting stance. Once the Red Shadows were in position, the Damm Warriors entered the dome. There were ten of them, each dressed in chainmail, conical helmets with a nose bar protecting the center of the face, and a white cape stamped with three intertwined silver trees at the right breast. They were armed with longbows, each with an arrow nocked, and a heavy quiver filled with replacements. In the center of the ten stood the leader. She carried no bow, and her sword was sheathed. She wore the same garb as her kinswomen. Next to her was a small woman in a brown cowl, who stood in marked contrast to the statuesque Damm Warriors. Tana immediately recognized Katla, her teacher of the common tongue: kind, patient Katla, who gently corrected her mistakes and never chastised.

The leader of the Damm Warriors strode forward with her diminutive companion by her side. She removed her helmet, and Tana saw hard eyes in a hard face. There was a red scar under her right eye which made her seem all the more fierce. In contrast to all of the Andra, who wore their black hair long, her blonde hair was cropped close.

There was silence in the dome. When the music stopped playing, all of the chatter and happiness evaporated. The Andra waited in hushed silence for the Damm Warrior to speak. They dreaded the words, but they knew the custom of the Var. Most years the weddings were festive occasions with no interference from their Overlady. However, the longsword of the Damm Warriors always dangled overhead. It fell tonight and the wheel stopped turning.

The Damm Warrior's voice boomed through the dome for all to hear. She spoke in the high tongue and the Andra did not understand a word. Katla stepped forward and translated.

"My Lady Aldith, Domina of the Var, and First of the Damm Warriors brings a blessing to your wedding solar. Who amongst you speaks for the Andra?" Katla asked in the common tongue of Gastown and the intermediary language for communication.

Most of the Andra lived in their own garden world, and they only left for the final journey as the funeral pyre burned and leftover ashes floated into the Andra canal. The language of the Andra was all they knew or needed. A few gifted souls were selected to communicate between the Var and the Andra, and Tana was one.

Katla sought out her most gifted student, and beckoned her over. "Step forward, child. I need you to speak to your people," Katla said. "Don't be afraid."

Tana was afraid. She was afraid of the Red Shadows and their menacing spears; she was afraid of the fierce Damm Warriors and their longbows. She was afraid of speaking in front of all of the Andra, and she was afraid of making a mistake and looking foolish.

"Hurry child! Step forward! It doesn't do to keep Lady Aldith waiting," Katla said.

Tana did step forward, but her legs were shaking. "I…I don't know what you want me to say," Tana said hesitantly in the common tongue.

Katla smiled. "Just take the words I give you and repeat them in your own language. That's simple enough isn't it?"

Tana glanced over at the tall Damm Warrior, and saw the hard eyes staring at her. She immediately looked away in fear. She focused on Katla's friendly face, and some of the fear dissipated.

"Do you understand, child?" Katla asked, and Tana nodded her head. "Good."

Katla turned and said something to Aldith in the high tongue. The words were harsh to Tana's ears, a deep guttural language with dissonance and metallic sounds. It was far removed from the sweet, lilting tones of the Andra language. Even the common tongue with its barbarous syllables which made Tana's throat burn was less severe. Tana did not know if the language determined the nature of the people or the other way around. She just knew the combination frightened her.

Aldith's voice boomed again, and Katla converted to the common tongue.

"Lady Aldith commands all of the wedding couples to assemble in front of her for inspection," Katla said.

Tana took a deep breath and spoke the words in the Andra tongue. Her voice was weak and did not carry to the crowd. Katla put a reassuring hand on her arm.

"Again, my child. Louder this time."

Tana nodded and spoke again. This time her words reached the Andra, and the wedding couples slowly moved forward, the fifty grooms in the front, and the brides behind.

"Tell them to hurry," Katla said.

Tana repeated the command, and the couples shifted into place. She looked at Manoj standing alone. They exchanged glances, and she saw fear in his eyes. He smiled bravely trying not to let it show. She took her place behind her new husband.

Aldith moved up and down the line slowly inspecting the fifty couples. Some of the brides held tightly to their husband's hand. Others cried in fear, knowing what was to come. All hoped they would be passed over for another and were shamed by their thoughts. Aldith stopped in front of Manoj, and Tana's heart skipped a beat. The Damm Warrior reached out a gloved hand and lifted up the necklace around his neck. She spoke to Katla.

"What is this symbol?" Katla asked.

"It's the Hanging Man, the symbol of the Erupu men. Before *The Long Journey*, and our voyage to the land of the Var, a man was separated from his bride to be. He did not accept that fate, and was nailed to a banyan tree for all to see. It symbolizes our pain and suffering," Tana explained.

Katla translated, and Aldith smiled as she let go of the necklace. "It's a fitting symbol," Aldith said in the high tongue. "There is no need to translate that," she said, as Katla opened her mouth to convey the words into the common tongue.

Aldith stood in front of the fifty couples. She towered above them, and appeared even more menacing as she placed her helmet back on her head, the nasal bar obscuring part of her face again. She drew her sword, and there was no sound as it cleared the leather scabbard: the indomitable warrior.

The rest of the Andra remained silent, waiting for the formal proclamation. Some glanced back at the Red Shadows behind them, waiting to either raise up their spears, or drop them to herd the Andra. Whatever the result, there was no going back to the wedding celebration. The joyous solar was over, and the Andra would go back to their gardens, grow vegetables, and serve the Var.

Aldith's voice boomed once again.

"This is a truly special solar for the Andra, when the Lady of the Damm Warriors chooses to grace your wedding ceremony. It is a right we seldom act upon, but we do so now. Our Lady comes for *Fyrst Nott!*" Katla explained.

Tana could not look up. She was terrified to translate the words, but she knew she had no choice. Katla had selected her amongst the Andra women to speak the words, and she was duty bound to let her people know. She found strength from somewhere and raised her voice.

It was fifty years since a Damm Warrior Lady graced an Andra wedding, but the people still talked about it, especially old Binod, who regaled those who cared to listen, and even those who did not, about his special night. Andra men were known for their great flexibility. Working in the gardens required remedial treatment and they twisted and uncoiled their oiled

CHAPTER FIFTEEN

bodies with a series of pliable exercises. It aided in the bedroom too, as they spiraled and undulated for their partner's pleasure. According to Binod, the Damm Warrior was fierce, strong, and relentless. She bent him like a jalebi, and pleasured herself on his contorted form many times until the solar finally came up. A smile was permanently fixed to his face all the way to his final funeral pyre.

Aldith pointed her sword in Manoj's direction.

"My lady chooses you!" Katla said.

Manoj fell to his knees before Tana translated from the common tongue. He kissed his Hanging Man amulet and then kissed Mother Earth, the Prith. He turned to face Tana. "I promise I won't enjoy it. I'll endure for one night, and then … when I've recovered, we'll start our life anew. I won't smile like Binod. I won't tell anyone about my ordeal, I promise!"

Tana did not believe him for a moment. Her fear was replaced by anger, She stood with her hands on her hips and glared at Aldith. The sword was pointing at her.

"Not him, my child. The Lady Aldith chooses you!" Katla said.

"What do you mean, me?" Tana asked. "An Andra man is chosen for Fyrst Nott."

Katla shook her head. "There is no written law on that. The Lady Aldith walks her own path, and for tonight, you will join her on that journey."

"What's happening, Tana?" Manoj asked, still on the ground. "She's not changing her mind, is she?"

"Quiet, Manoj!" Tana barked. "I'm talking here." Her blood was up and she addressed Aldith as she spoke to Katla. "I'm not some plaything for this woman in armor. Let her take Manoj with my blessing and be done with it."

The time for talking was over. Aldith barked a command and four Damm Warriors slung their bows over their shoulders and advanced on Tana. Two of them grabbed her roughly by the arms and pulled her past Manoj, while the other two bowled over some musicians and took the carpet they sat upon. They laid it out on the ground before Aldith's feet.

The Andra stirred, and the Red Shadows lowered their halberds. The remaining six Damm Warriors pulled back on their mighty varbows and aimed at the crowd.

Manoj jumped up. "No, let her go! Not my Tana!" he screamed. He advanced on Aldith and certain death, before four grooms with the sense to calm things down seized hold of him and held him fast.

Aldith pointed her sword at Manoj and placed the tip on his forehead where Tana's red thumbprint lay. She nicked him and a trickle of blood ran down between his eyes. "Don't become a Hanging Man," she said.

Manoj did not understand the words, but he knew the meaning. Tears rolled down his face as he hung his head in shame and sobbed.

Tana had time for one last glare at Aldith before she was unceremoniously lifted from her feet and placed on the carpet while the two other Damm Warriors rolled her up. The four of them hoisted carpet and Tana up on their shoulders and carried her off.

The Andra were the chosen ones, the children of the Prith and their roots ran strong. Their way was the peaceful path. This solar, some like Manoj let anger and rage seep through them. They clenched their fists and teeth, but did nothing. Violence was not their way. And most of all, they were subdued.

Aldith and Katla left first, followed by the remaining Damm Warriors. When they were safely out of the glass dome, the Red Shadows returned their halberds up to the guard position and filed out. The Andra drifted out too, Tana's father leading his weeping wife away, the musicians rolling up the remaining carpets, and packing up instruments, brides and grooms retreating for their first tentative night together. Only Manoj remained behind. He sat on the Prith and held the Hanging Man in his hand, waiting silently for Tana to return.

Tana could barely breathe and saw nothing tightly wrapped up in the carpet. Her arms were pinned by her side, and she longed to get a hand free to scratch her itchy nose. She was sweating with the heat, and worried about ruining her beautiful red wedding dress. She was also disgusted to think only moments ago the carpet was occupied by the smelly bottoms and stinky feet of Adarsh and Matanda, two drummer boys from the Banda.

CHAPTER FIFTEEN

The carpet, a simple representation of the five colors of the Andra clans, was the result of poor weaving from their mother, Saanvi. At least she deserved a better carpet to be carried away in dishonor.

What exactly did the Damm Warrior want with her? she wondered. Her mother had explained how to please Manoj on their wedding night, but this was altogether different and shameful. Andra women did not engage in such things. She felt helpless, not just because she was wrapped up inside a carpet, but because this Lady Aldith could do exactly as she pleased without any recourse.

Since she could not see, Tana focused on listening, but all she could hear was the steady thump of the footsteps of the strong women who carried her. They were not gentle, and Tana wanted to shout out to them to be more careful when they took a sharp turn and almost bent her in half. There seemed to be a steady climb at first, but then a long descent, and a great deal of left and right turns. The journey lasted an eternity, but like all journeys it came to an end. This one with a bump as the Damm Warriors dumped her on the ground.

Tana heard the footsteps fade away, and then nothing. She was still trapped inside the carpet, and could not wriggle free. She could feel a steady undulation beneath her as the floor rocked back and forth. Fear hit her then. Fear of the unknown. Fear of being violated. Fear of the shame and what her people would think.

Why did she choose me and not Manoj? How will I face the embarrassment when I'm returned tomorrow? Will Manoj want me back? Will I smile incessantly like old Binod?

There was a heavy push, and she was rolling and rolling, until she flew out of the end of the carpet, and landed in a heap. Her head was spinning, but as she moved wayward hair from her eyes, she saw a tall figure standing before her.

Aldith stared down at the beautiful girl with the long flowing black hair, green eyes accentuated by the delicately shaped eyebrows and eyelashes, and the rouged lips. She was a little worse for wear after her carpet ride, but as bewitching as the solar she first saw her taking language lessons with Katla in the Courtyard of Tongues.

"Welcome to *Matilda*," Aldith said.

Tana jumped up. The ground was rocking slightly beneath her, but she kept her balance. She stood with both hands on her hips. Her fear dissipated now she had a target for her tongue in front of her. "You speak the common tongue? Then why did you use Katla to say your words?"

"The high tongue commands authority, even if the people hearing it don't understand," Aldith said, as she undid her belt buckle and removed her sheathed sword. She placed it on a nearby table next to her helmet.

"Help me out of this chainmail shirt," Aldith said. "I've been wearing it all solar and it's beginning to chafe." She undid a clasp behind her neck and held out her arms towards Tana.

"You put it on, you take it off," Tana said defiantly.

Aldith shrugged. "As you wish." She leaned forward, and with some effort shrugged out of the heavy chainmail, which fell to the floor with a thunk. She sighed with the liberation from the weight, and rolled her neck and shoulders to release the tension. She scooped up the chainmail, the rings clinking together as she folded it and placed it beside her helmet and sword.

Tana stared at the Damm Warrior who towered above her. She was menacing in her armor, but equally formidable out of it. Standing there in her linen undershirt and leggings, she exuded power. Her body was ripped from wearing armor all solar and the result of constant military training. Her arms and legs were bigger and stronger than any Andra man. She made Manoj seem like a weak boy.

"Why do you wear that all solar? The armor?" Tana asked, struggling for the correct word.

"Why do you wear your clothes when you dig in your gardens?" Aldith responded. "It's what I do. It's who I am."

Tana surveyed the room for the first time. It was alien to her. Unlike most of the Andra, she spent limited time out of the glass domes and away from the gardens, to study in the Courtyard of Tongues with Katla. She saw some of the life and ways of the Gentry, but in brief glimpses before

CHAPTER FIFTEEN

she was escorted back. This place was different. It was a small room, barely big enough for Aldith to stand. One wall was a series of windows, which were closed, and a sturdy bed occupying most of the floor space. There was the table, where Aldith placed her armor, and another one with a basin and jug for washing. Everything was locked down and tight. All constructed from heavy dark wood, illuminated by two corpulent candles.

"Where am I?" Tana asked.

"I told you. You're on *Matilda*. First of the Black Ships," Aldith said.

"I-I'm on a boat?" Tana said. She suddenly felt queasy with the up and down and rocking motion, and steadied herself against the bedpost.

"Don't worry, we're still in the harbor. The gentle rhythm is relaxing if you put your mind to it."

"I don't want to put my mind to it. I want to go home," Tana said, sitting down on the bed, and hugging a post for comfort.

Aldith removed her shirt and slipped out of her pants. She wore nothing underneath and was completely naked. She took the jug and poured water into the bowl, and took a cloth and quickly washed her face, neck, her armpits, and finally between her legs. The quick and efficient ablution over, she crossed the room and stood before Tana, comfortable in her nakedness.

"Your breasts aren't very big," Tana said.

Aldith ignored her. "Strip," she said.

"What?"

"You heard me. I said strip. You put it on, now you take it off."

"I'll do no such thing," Tana said, hugging the post for protection now as well as comfort.

"I've wanted you since the solar I first saw you talking with Katla, Tana," Aldith said. She reached down and stroked Tana's hair.

Tana looked up. "You know my name?"

"Of course I do. We have a long night ahead of us, and no time to waste. Now strip off that pretty red dress."

Chapter Sixteen

Carlos : Hetman of the Slagers

Carlos sat at the dresser and stared at his reflection in the mirror. The black mascara around his bloodshot eyes was smudged, and he set about fixing it. His body and left arm still smarted where Jonas Wheeler's blade carved into his flesh, and Perfect Styles's needlework stitched him back together. He was alive and Jonas was feeding the fish and other bottom dwellers in the Basin. The blood stained Hetman of the Slagers gold chain with the crossed cleavers hung heavily around his neck. Behind him, on the ironwood bed, lay the cooling corpse of Cotter Sullivan, his throat gashed open, and his lifeless glassy eyes staring at nothing at all.

There was no remorse in Carlos Grimm. Cotter Sullivan took his pleasure one last time, and as he lay in the post coital sleep of the damned, Carlos seized the solar, and slashed his throat from ear to ear. He watched as the fat pederast gurgled in his own blood and slid into oblivion. Only then did he remove the Hetman chain and place it around his own neck.

Iz a man now, Cotter Sullivan. An' yuz is dead meat.

No remorse, but no plan of action either. Cotter left himself in a vulnerable position, and he simply acted upon it, always the opportunist. Now was the time for thinking and scheming. The time to be bold or perish at the hands of Patch, Black Jack, or Perfect. He sat at the dresser and pondered as the blud on the hetman's chain dried, and Cotter blindly

CHAPTER SIXTEEN

searched for the Ferryman.

It was still early in the morning and the solar was barely up, but the slagers and apprentices went about their business, preparing paranga for their clientele. A few Bully Boys were lying at tables, sleeping off the excess grog from the night before, but most sought other pleasures in the Four Kith and over in the Mutton.

Perfect Styles was working on carving up a heavy carcass on his butcher's block and directing apprentices as they carried away animal parts tightly wrapped up in burlap to be transported to the Burghs, and filled barrels with salted down lesser cuts of meat for the Four Kith. He looked over at Carlos, as he entered the main hall of the slagerhaus and sat in the chair previously occupied by Cotter Sullivan and Mo Dickens before him. He idly fingered the hetman chain around his neck.

"That's a heavy burden you wear," Perfect said, still carving away at the slab on his block, and removing excess fat, which he scraped to one side to be melted down for tallow. Nothing went to waste.

"But wear it I does," Carlos said.

"It takes more than wearin' to be Hetman of the Slagers. Can you hold onto it when others come a callin'?"

"Like yuz Perfect? Do yuz want to be Hetman?"

Perfect smiled as he continued to chop and carve his meat. Carlos had never seen him smile before.

"Not I. I'm just a slager by trade, and Hetmen around here have a habit of passin' too early and in a grave kind of way. There be others in the slager trade who might want the chain now Cotter appears to be no more. Samwell Heap for one. And the Blackmores and the Paisleys."

"Samwell 'as 'is 'ands full keepin' up with Josie Dickens, an' the Blackmores an' the Paisleys are too old an' weak for a fight. Them aside, what do yuz want, Perfect?" Carlos asked, admiring the man's skill with the blade, and thankful he limited himself to the butchery of animals and not men. Still, he was a powerful ally to have when faced with Patch Amstrong and Black Jack Cuttle.

"I want this place to be a real slagerhaus again. I want the fires out durin'

223

the solar, and only lit when the butcherin' is finished. And I want them lot out of here, and no more takin' the choice cuts," Perfect said, pointing his butcher's knife to the sleeping Bully Boys.

"An' if Iz give yuz all of that?" Carlos asked. "What then?"

"I'll be your man, Carlos Grimm. Plain and simple, I'll be your man. And I vouch for my 'prentices too."

Divide and Conquer.

Carlos nodded and the pact was sealed.

Perfect Styles and his apprentices got to work immediately. They roused the sleeping Bully Boys and ejected them one by one from the slagerhaus. Some went easy, still nursing sore heads from the night before. Others put up a fight, and retreated with fresh bumps and bruises. Some went flying to find Patch Amstrong, others scurried in the direction of Black Jack. The fire in the main hearth was extinguished, and the work of washing and scrubbing down the slagerhaus began in earnest. The apprentices went about their tasks with pride to restore the slagerhaus back to the pristine condition they maintained under Mo Dickens.

On Carlos's direction, they also sent Cotter Sullian on his way to the Basin to join Jonas Wheeler and many more before him. Cotter was too obese and heavy to carry out from the bedchamber, so Perfect and his top apprentices worked on the dismemberment where he lay. Heavy limbs were hacked free, and the torso deprived of bloated organs, before the hulking rib cage was shattered and the carcass carried away. Only Cotter's head, chopped loose after three cuts at the neck, remained on the blood soaked bed. One enterprising apprentice saw fit to stick a withered apple core in his mouth for a lark, before Perfect cuffed him about the head and removed it. There was no knife in hand or coin for Cotter Sullivan to pay Jorm for the final ride on his Ferryman's barge. He was deprived of the Onderworld, and would shamble away in the in-between shadow world with other lifeless shades.

Carlos sent a junior apprentice to the Hole to fetch Fleet Dawkins and the mites, and they congregated in the slagerhaus in front of Carlos when Black Jack Cuttle came in. He was carrying a heavy ledger, and accompanied by

CHAPTER SIXTEEN

a gaggle of sullen Bully Boys.

"Where's Cotter?" Black Jack asked when he saw Carlos sitting in the chair of authority and wearing the hetman's chain. He wiped down his bald head with his black rag.

"Gone on 'is way," Carlos said.

"I'll see for myself," Black Jack said, and he and his Bully Boys headed towards the bedchamber.

Carlos held up his hand. "Just Jack."

The pace of the Bully Boys slowed, but they kept moving forward, until Fleet and his mites, knives in hand, blocked their path. The men were bigger and stronger, but they were outnumbered five to one, and although two of them wanted to make a fight of it, Black Jack held them back. He ordered them to stay behind, and entered the bedchamber alone. When he came back out, his face was ashen. The head on the bed and the gore on the floor sent a clear message to the bookkeeper.

"That's a bold move, Master Grimm," Black Jack said, sitting down with his ledger at one of the tables, and wiping his bald pate once again. He gestured to one of the apprentices to bring him some grog. The apprentice looked at Perfect for instructions before complying. It did not go unnoticed by Black Jack.

Patch Amstrong arrived soon after. He burst into the slagerhaus with all of the Bully Boys he could muster on short notice. They were mostly scattered across the Four Kith and the Mutton so their numbers were few. The ones he had were still the worse for wear, though they were quickly sobering up.

"Where's Cotter?" Patch asked Black Jack, who simply shook his head and took a swig of his grog. He glanced over at Perfect Styles, who went about carving his meat and gave nothing away.

Patch turned to face Carlos, who still sat in Cotter's regal chair surrounded by his army of grim faced mites. Carlos saw him visibly shaking as he tried to make sense of what was happening around him. He had been by Cotter's side for five years, and rose through the ranks of the Bully Boys to be second in command. Carlos knew Patch never truly liked Cotter, no one did. However, Patch liked the order of things, and respected Cotter's authoritarian rule. Now a boy sat in Cotter's chair and Patch's world order was falling apart.

"So you fancy yourself as Hetman of the Slagers, and Top Bully Boy, do you?" Patch asked.

"If the crown fits," Carlos replied.

Patch laughed. "Crown he says? This boy has mighty aspirations. King of the Four Kith!"

Patch looked around the room to gauge the situation. The mites were lined up before Carlos, a protective shield if any Bully Boy took the notion of rushing him. Perfect Styles worked at his butchering, but his apprentices were all close at hand in front of him, and they were armed with an assortment of cleavers, hooks, butcher's knives, and skinners. Black Jack and his own Bully Boys sat meekly at a table, waiting for things to play out.

"Are you in on this madness, Perfect?" Patch asked.

"Madness is a dirty slagerhaus. I like mine clean and orderly," Perfect replied.

"So the boy has already bought you off. And you, Jack? What does the Bookkeeper have to say? You've been with Cotter longer than me."

In response, Black Jack Cuttle pushed his grog to one side and opened up his ledger, and took a feathered quill from his pocket. "What's done is done, and the solar doesn't move in reverse. I look at the numbers, and the numbers don't lie."

"And what do the numbers tell us, Jack?" Patch asked.

"Master Grimm's plan is a good one. I've been busy since the fire took the Geroni Bakerhaus and the rest of the block. The Geroni family signed over the deeds to the property to waive Joe's debts, and were happy to be shot of it. Three other families have already signed over their rights for a small sum and a promise of cheap rent elsewhere. We're negotiating with two former landlords. Crews are already cleaning up the debris, and we have builders ready to go to work. We'll have a grand pleasure parlor up and running in three lunars. We'll turn a profit in nine. I've also made some inquiries into the Mutton, and we have a madam who is willing to

CHAPTER SIXTEEN

sign on and run *The Purple Rose*."

"The Purple Rose?"

Black Jack blushed. "It's a working name in progress, Patch. I've always been partial to roses. We can call it whatever you like."

"How about *The Traitor's Bait*? You're forgettin' one thing, Jack. The properties are signed over to Cotter. It's in his name. Cotter owned everythin'."

Black Jack turned a few vellum pages in his ledger, and then stabbed his quill at one particular entry. "Well, Cotter made a small provision for a sister he barely knew. We can honor that as gentlemen, and then write a will, backdated of course, leaving everything to Master Grimm as his chosen heir."

Carlos made his move. It was now or never. "No, not to me. To the four of us. Yuz, me, Patch, an' Perfect. Equal shares in partnership. We can call it *The Brotherhood of the Purple Rose*, if it pleases yuz, Jack."

Iz got 'em now, Carlos thought. *Gild talks loudest, an' Jack an' Patch are all ears.*

The fire and the fury went out of Patch. He worked as Cotter's number two, but it was always a precarious existence, and his reward was always just scraps from the table. Now he would have a seat, a share, and a future. Black Jack beamed with pleasure at the founding of the new partnership, and Perfect gave nothing away.

"There's one problem you seem to be overlookin' in this money makin' scheme," Patch said. "The Swell Daddies are not goin' to take this lyin' down. Puzzle Pete and his Crimpers are not soft idle men. They're stone killers, especially Toby Meyers. They'll make a fight of it. A bloody fight! Are you prepared for war, Carlos Grimm?"

Carlos leaned forward in his chair and stared at Patch. "Iz killed three men already, Patch. Iz can kill more. Are yuz up for it?" It was the command Mo Dickens always used and not an idle request.

Everyone in the slagerhaus looked at Patch and waited for his response. The Bully Boys knew what a war with the Swell Daddies meant and they would bear the brunt of it. However, all of the talk of flesh parlors and more gild to go around had them fired up too. Life was short in the Four Kith and better to flame out than fizzle away. No one wanted to hear old men's stories of what could have been.

"I'm up for it, Carlos Grimm. If it's a war you want, a war you'll have," Patch said.

"Then gather the Bully Boys an' keep 'em close. If this Puzzle Pete is the man yuz say 'e is, 'e'll know soon enough wez steppin' on 'is territory. Then 'e's goin' to come steppin' on ours," Carlos replied. "And send some men to the Slough an' crack a few pickpocket 'ead's for good measure. Word will get around about Cotter, an' some might think to test the waters. Business as normal is the order of the solar."

And just like that, Cotter Sullivan was forgotten. Just one more thug who rose to make his mark, and left only a stain behind on his sorry way out. No one in the Four Kith would mourn him, and many would raise a cheery cup to his demise. Only a sister residing in the Burghs would shed a quick tear, before she counted the pot of gold at the end of her rainbow.

The slagerhaus moved into activity. The main hall was emptied of Bully Boys as Patch proceeded to stamp their authority on the Slough, and Black Jack went back to supervise the clearing of the *Purple Rose* block and the final negotiations with the previous slum landlords. Fleet had a handful of mites stay close to Carlos, in case any Bully Boys had the notion of backstabbing. He took the rest of the mites back to the Hole, and scouted out a new block for firing. Perfect and his apprentices continued carving and packing paranga for the meat market.

Carlos changed seats and sat in Jojo Dickens's old oakwood chair in front of the fireless hearth, and brooded. He was apprehensive about the waiting game. His nature was to jump in first with both feet, and figure things out later. Juan was the planner, and he needed his twin now, more than ever. He longed to reach out to him, to bring him back into the fold, hold his hand, and share his true feelings.

That world is as dead as Cotter. No goin' back now.

He had set the wheels in motion, and had an army at his command, but he had never felt so alone. Perfect was with him for now, but could he

CHAPTER SIXTEEN

truly trust Jack and Patch? He needed more time to watch them. Their partnership was new, and one or both of them were capable of slitting his throat and dumping him in the Basin. For now they accepted his leadership, but one mistake and his mites would not save him.

Carlos was still sitting in the oakwood chair as night fell and the slager work finished for the solar. Two mites built up the logs in the hearth and set it ablaze with enough pyromaniac dexterity to make Fleet Dawkins beam with pride. Carlos had not realized how cold he actually was, lost in his thoughts, until the heat of the fire reached him.

An apprentice nudged him, and handed him a plate with a slab of fresh brood and a piping hot blud sausage, and a tankard of warm black bier to wash it down. He was ravenous and bit into the sausage, with the hot grease running down his hand. He took a hearty swig of the bier.

"A king needs his strength," Perfect called over, as he washed down his butcher's block.

Always workin' that one, Carlos thought. He raised his tankard to Perfect and took another swig.

His blud sausage and brood consumed, Carlos wiped his greasy hands on his shirt, and finished off the last of the thick black bier. He beckoned over one of the apprentices and exchanged a copper coin for a worn hooded cloak, which he quickly put on. He stood up and made for the door.

Off sightseein'?" Perfect asked.

Carlos turned. "Just surveyin' the kingdom,"

"Is it wise to go alone?"

"Best way I know to go undetected," Carlos replied and headed out of the slagerhaus and into the courtyard before Perfect tried to talk him out of it.

It was cold outside away from the warmth of the fire, and there was a light snow flurry, which quickly melted and turned to a thin sheen of water on his cloak. He made his way through the Slough, keeping to the shadows while he could. Patch and his Bully Boys had done their work and the pickpockets and purse cutters were off the streets. He had no doubt a few heads were cracked in the process.

He made his way through the side streets, and followed the bustling crowd of burghfolk and their protectors crossing the narrow corridor to Skank Bridge and over to the Mutton to scratch itches and partake in perversions their wives would not permit. Business was busy as usual.

Enjoy it while yuz can. You'll be in my billeehaus before long. An' I'll own the lot of yuz.

He was anxious he would see Juan on the bridge, plying his trade with Jojo Dickens and his band of thieves. *A pox on 'im*, he thought, put his head down and hurried across the bridge. On the other side, he slid into the shadows again, and took the side streets to get a better sense of the Mutton and his competition.

It was some time since Juan and he first ventured to this side of the bridge, and he vividly recalled their encounter with the Dandy, who took Juan's eye. It was a long slog carrying his brother back with the dead billee in tow, all to satisfy the wanton appetite of Jojo Dickens. He spat. *A pox on 'er too.*

Carlos remembered the orange lanterns and the strange multicolored lights which danced through the fog like grog soaked strumpets, and cast weird sensual shadows in the gloom. The street was vaguely familiar too, as well as the three crones who warmed themselves in front of a brazier. Two took the chill from their hands as they held them in front of the flames, whilst the fat one aimed her huge rear end at the bonfire, which snapped and popped as the wood burned. The hags cackled at him, creatures of chaos with the weird gift.

"We have royalty amongst us," Big Bertha said, with an exaggerated curtsy. She struggled to get back up with the help of her two sisters.

"Twinless he is," Theresa Three Tit said.

"But now he's got three friends suckin' at his teats. Show him how it's done, Theresa!" Long Peg offered, and all three harlots broke into hysterics.

"Death and destruction follows this one," Bertha said.

"War and pestilence is close behind," Peg offered.

"Such is the way of monarchs," Theresa mused.

"All hail the King of the Four Kith!" they shouted in unison. "All hail the

CHAPTER SIXTEEN

Dux of Gastown!"

Carlos slid back into the shadows and away from the unsettling weyward talk, which chased him through the alleyways until he came to an open square where the revelry of the Mutton finally drowned them out. The square was full of alehouses with brightly lit signs, and flanked by buildings with orange lights marking the way to debauchery. Slagmaidens escorted drunk and drugged patrons from the inns and over to their rooms in the flesh parlors, to lighten the load from their ball sacks and purses. As Carlos watched, one did not make it that far, and was escorted into an alleyway where two men went to work with fists and blackjacks before emptying his pockets. The woman took her share, and scurried back to the den in search of another victim.

A small man surrounded by four large bodyguards came out of an inn with the sign of a blind beggar above it. He stopped in the middle of the square, and took a small box out of his pocket, pushed something into his nose, and then convulsed as he sneezed. He wiped his nose, and then continued over to the grandest of the bordellos, a large purple building, bustling with music, light, and laughter. Two heavy set men at the door deferentially moved to each side as he went in as if he owned the establishment, which he probably did.

That's a Swell Daddy! Look 'ow 'e struts.

Carlos did not know why, but he felt a sense of freedom and arousal in the Mutton: a world where anything was permitted. The rules were the ones you made for yourself. It was not the women, or the promised pleasures of flesh parlors which excited him. He had no interest in that direction. It was the control over others he craved. Bending them to his will, making them jump, or cower, or dance if he wanted. And if he could not have the Mutton, he would create his own replica world in the Four Kith, and the Mutton and all the Swell Daddies would come crashing down.

A strong hand slammed into the small of his back and sent him crashing into the wall. All of the air went out of him as his assailant gave him a sharp punch to the kidney, and then spun him around, and pinned him to the wall by his throat. His legs buckled with the pain of the strike, and he struggled to breathe.

The man reached over with his other hand and roughly pulled off Carlos's hood.

"What do we have here then? A badger boy?" he said, staring at Carlos's eye makeup. "Never seen one like you before."

Carlos quickly recovered his senses, but the hand on his throat was exceptionally strong and held him at arm's length. The man loomed large over him. He reeked of grog and other rank odors, and he leered through bloodshot eyes. The same sort of desire Cotter Sullivan showed. He slowly reached for the knife in his pocket, but the thug sensed it, and tightened his grip.

"Now, now. Let's be nice. I won't hurt you, if you play along. Just a taste is all ole Davey wants." He drooled with anticipation.

Carlos had to play for time, until he could reach his pigsticker. He needed some distance between them and the man off guard, and he needed to breathe before he was choked into unconsciousness.

"Alright, I'll play along," Carlos wheezed. "Let me to my knees, an' I'll do for yuz better than any slagmaiden."

The man was hooked. He shifted his grip from Carlos's throat and grasped his hair as he forced him to his knees.

"Mind, no biting," he said as he moved his other hand to his crotch and unbuttoned his fly.

That's it ole Davey, give me somethin' to cut off!

Three shadows hit ole Davey hard from behind. Their hands came back and forth, and blades flashed in them. Again and again they stabbed at the thug's back, kidneys, buttocks, and legs. He let go of Carlos's head, arched his back as if to escape from the stabbing, and grimaced in pain as he was punctured time and time again.

Carlos seized his chance. He pulled his own blade free, stabbed hard into Davey's belly on the right side, and dragged his blade all the way across, up, and free. The ruffian roared as his guts spilled out, and then choked it back as Carlos stabbed him through the heart. He went down in a heap as Carlos pulled his blade loose, and the three cloaked figures fell on him in a

CHAPTER SIXTEEN

stabbing frenzy.

"I think 'es dead now," Carlos said, in between deep breaths.

He looked at his three caped saviors and saw Fleet Dawkins, and his two closest imps, Tipper Hood, and Jugger James. They were small even by mite standard, but Fleet kept them close because they followed orders and could keep their mouths shut. The newly minted killers were all breathing hard too, and there was something different about them. They were all sporting black eye makeup. Not the fancy mascara he used, but soot carelessly smudged around their peepers.

"Wot's this look then?" Carlos asked, pointing at Tipper's face.

"Fleet thought it woz a good idea," Tipper said. "So people know us like."

"An' fear us. Wez a proper gang now," Jugger added.

"Wez just 'aven't come up with a name yet," Tipper said.

Carlos looked over at Fleet to thank him, but the boy was staring down at the dead's man's face. "Don't worry about 'im, Fleet. Just another punter in the Mutton," Carlos said.

"'E's more than that, Carlos. Look at the mark on 'is face," Fleet said, pointing with his bloody knife. "That carve mark next to 'is right eye. That's the mark of a Crimper. 'E's one of Puzzle Pete's boys."

"Then first kill goes to us," Carlos said. He knelt down next to the warm corpse, and went to butchering out the putrid genitalia, which he deposited in the dead man's rank mouth.

Pleasure yourself, ole Davey.

Carlos wiped his blade and his bloody hands on the Crimper's jacket, before he stood up to face Fleet.

"'Ow did you find me, Fleet?" Carlos asked.

"Perfect sent for us when yuz decided it was a gud idea to go a wanderin' by yourself," Fleet said. There was a hint of anger in his voice. "Wez picked up your trail at the Skank Bridge, an' followed you through the Mutton. It's not safe, Carlos. Swell Daddies an' Crimpers will soon know yuz replaced Cotter. If wez can find yuz, so can they."

Carlos nodded his head. "Alright, Fleet. No more wanderin', but I just wanted to see the Mutton before we go to war with 'em. All I want is one last slager's hook at the square, an' wez is back to the Four Kith."

He turned back to look across at the bustling square one more time, and saw a familiar figure next to the slight Swell Daddy. They were standing in front of the flesh parlor and shaking hands like old friends sealing a pact.

Well, well, Patch. What treacherous game are yuz playin'? Carlos thought.

"Things are worse than yuz think," Fleet said, as if reading his mind. "That there Swell Daddy is Puzzle Pete. I'll never forget that mug. He took my sister for a slagmaiden an' we've never seen 'er again."

Carlos turned to the trio. "Not a word of this to anyone, mind. Play nice with Patch until Iz can figure out 'is play."

They put their hoods up and kept their eyes down as they left the Mutton and made their way back to the relative safety of their slagerhaus in the Four Kith. The war with Puzzle Pete and his Crimpers had started.

Chapter Seventeen

Aldith : First Night Second Solar

A gloom settled over Aldith. With the break of a new solar it was time to return Tana to her people and to her husband. A return which ordinarily promised endless toil in the gardens, bearing and raising children, and a final end as her charred remains were cast into the waters of the dead. For now, she held onto her lover in front of her, both naked save for the thick bearskin wrapped around them as they stared out of the cabin window at the sleepy harbor. The Black Ship gently rolled with the tide and soothed them both.

"What does a girl have to do for breakfast around here? Sleep with the captain?" Tana asked.

Aldith hugged her closer and smelled the soft scent in her jet black hair, a holdover from the wedding preparation. It was sweet, spicy, and nutty all at once.

Did I risk too much for this girl? I don't want to let her go. Not yet.

Aldith removed the bearskin from around her own shoulders and covered Tana. It was time to get dressed and face the solar. She quickly slipped on her linen tunic.

"Why don't you go back to bed and rest for a while?" Aldith said, and she worked herself into her chainmail, attached her belt and buckled on her longsword. "I'll have them send you up all the delicious food you want."

Tana went over to the bed and flopped on to it. "Well, we were up all night, and I could use some sleep. I bet my face is a mess, all puffy and red," she pouted.

"Your face is beautiful. Nothing some rest won't fix."

"So it is a mess!" Tana said. "It's all your fault."

Aldith sighed. She did not want to start the solar with a foolish argument. She was tired herself, and so much planning and preparation needed her attention as the fleet prepared for the long sea journey to the lost colony of Agithawald.

"I have a campaign to plan. I'll be back soon," Aldith said.

"Don't you have to return me to Manoj? You've had your night of pleasure. It's time to take me back to my husband," Tana said, but she made no move to get out of the bed. Instead, she lifted up the bearskin and exposed her naked body.

Aldith wanted nothing more than to slide out of her armor and responsibilities and tumble back in with the beautiful Andra girl. However, she was responsible for the security of the realm and duty always called. Tana was her fresh faced lover, but the Duxdom was her old mistress.

"Later," she said sternly, though more as a command to herself, and left the cabin before Tana could entice her to stay.

Once on the deck of her flagship *Matilda*, Aldith took a deep breath, and sucked in the frigid morning air to clear her head. It was still early, but the docks were already in full motion. This was the biggest expedition the Var had undertaken since the capture of Andalayim itself, and all the resources of the Duxdom were mustered. A vast fleet of one hundred Black Ships was needed, each carrying ten Damm Warriors, twenty Red Shadows, and a crew of two hundred sailors, marines, cooks, and craftsmen. The supplies and armament needed for the enterprise were astronomical. A steady line of barrels were rolled along the docks, and across the gangplanks to be safely deposited in the holds. The harbor was not big enough to accommodate all of the Black Ships, and so smaller vessels were utilized to transport the barrels across, and mast yards employed to swing the cargo onboard. Shot and black powder for the ten cannons on each ship

CHAPTER SEVENTEEN

were carefully measured and loaded. Finally, under heavy supervision, the volatile vitali blackfire was cautiously loaded into the reinforced holds. Aldith shuddered at the thought of a mishap with the lethal liquid if it inadvertently mixed with sea water and sent a Black Ship and her crew to the deep abyss and a premature entry into Draugr's Locker.

Food for the journey was primitive at best. Hardtack biscuits made from coarse flour, water, and salt; an assortment of ground cereals and nuts; pickled vegetables and dried fruits; citrus fruit to ward off scurvy; and a daily ration of grog for the crew. Across the ocean, the men were permitted to catch fish to supplement their diet, but the Damm Warriors, and the handful of Konna clerks refrained from eating animal or marine flesh of any kind.

A gaggle of Konna clerks under the supervision of Bursa, the Minister of External Affairs, ensured the vast civil army loaded each barrel to the right ship, and all properties were accounted for. Thievery from the Dux was a death sentence, but it did not stop enterprising lawbreakers testing the system, and risking life and limb for the promise of illicit rewards.

The endless supply of barrels were transported from warehouses, down to the docks, and on to the ships. On and on they rolled, until the Black Ships sank lower in the water line loaded down by their heavy cargo in the hold and the ballast in the bilge. Men suspended over the sides of the ships applied a final coat of black tar to waterproof the vessels for the long sea passage.

Bursa barked a command at a nonchalant docker who rocked a barrel when he should have been rolling. Her tone and manner immediately shifted when she saw Aldith striding towards her. The first of the Damm Warriors towered over the diminutive Konna woman.

"Ah, Lady Aldith. It's such a pleasure to see you so early in the morning. I can assure you we have everything in hand. We've had crews working night and solar to ready the fleet," she said with a humble bow, while clutching at her troubled stomach.

"When can we sail, Bursa?" Aldith asked sternly. She had no time for Bursa's fawning manner. She knew the usefulness of the woman, but her guile was as deceitful as Rafyn's and Aldith longed for straight talk and honest answers.

"Two solars, if we continue at this pace," Bursa said with a weak smile

"Push them harder. We sail tomorrow," Aldith said.

"But Lady Aldith, we could misplace vital cargo if we rush. More haste can lead to waste. I'm sure you appreciate…"

"Tomorrow," Aldith said, and strode off along the docks. She had barely gone ten places when she heard Bursa barking orders again, as she rallied her clerks and harassed the workers to bring in the deadline.

Aldith planned to spend the rest of the solar in the work she did best, preparing her army for war. Drilling was already underway in the training ground as her captains marshaled the troops and tested formations. A series of blares from war horns were used to arrange and rearrange units into different configurations. At present, The Red Shadows were lined up four ranks deep with the butt of their halberds firmly planted in the ground and a boot braced against the base of the angled shaft to form an impenetrable wall. Once the enemy broke, the halberdiers could pursue with devastating effect and strike them down from behind. Damm Warriors with double-handed battle axes were interspersed in the front row to step forward and cut through any enemy who got close enough. More Damm Warriors with their mighty varbows, arrows nocked, stood behind the ranks of Red Shadows ready to rain down missiles. The left and right flanks were protected by Red Shadows armed with lethal crossbows. They did not have the rate of fire or the range of the varbows, but the training in usage was much shorter, and deadly efficient at a shorter range.

Aldith liked what she saw. Her captains knew their warcraft and needed little correction from her. She was confident the Var army was capable of dealing with the savages from the Southern Islands if Agithawald truly was no more and retribution was required.

Her solar was going well until a messenger arrived from Rafyn. Aldith hated family councils and one was summoned in haste. She was wary of her sister Lilith, despised Rafyn, and always felt like a belligerent child when paraded in front of her mother. As head of the family, the Dux

CHAPTER SEVENTEEN

would preside over the kinswoman gathering, and the results were never predictable with an unhinged monarch.

A summons from the Dux meant immediate attendance, so Aldith left the training ground and made her way to the inner citadel and on to the Great Chamber, which both fascinated her and filled her with foreboding. The symbols of Var warcraft, especially Stella's mighty varbow, filled her with pride. As children, Rafyn encouraged her to try and take it down from the wall and examine it more closely. Thankfully, they were caught before they could damage it any further, and suitably chastised. Then there was the artwork of the Old Ones underneath, the strange swirling designs, and intricate spiral patterns. It made her feel as if they were merely sleeping, waiting for their opportunity to rise again and remove the superficial trappings of the Var.

Her sisters were already present, with Lilith occupying Bursa's seat for this occasion. The Dux was on her throne, and below their liege sat her mother, Beira. Aldith made a deep bow to the Dux, and then a smaller one, still showing filial piety, in the direction of her mother before she sat down. Mother and daughter had not talked for six lunars and Aldith preferred it that way.

"Ah, Aldith, good of you to join us at last. I trust preparations for the Varingr are going well?" the Dux said. One of the curs, a particularly fat pug nosed one, sat in her lap while she fed it an assortment of vegetables.

"They are my liege. We sail tomorrow," Aldith replied.

"So soon? That is good news. You know, I still have a mind to join you. Such an adventure we'll have!"

Aldith looked at her mother, who shook her head. "The Duxdom needs you here, sister," Beira said.

"Hrmph," the Dux replied and dropped her black veil over her face. She blew on it a few times and then popped it back up and glared at her sister and nieces. "Why does everyone else have all the fun? I'm stuck here in the palace, Aldith goes off a varingr, and you trek north again."

There was a shuffling amongst the three sisters. Aldith looked first at Rafyn, but she gave nothing away. Lilith looked sheepishly at the floor, so she knew already. "So soon, mother? You just came back. Wouldn't it be wise to tarry longer and provide guidance here in Varstad?"

If leadership was based on ability rather than birthright, Aldith knew her mother and not her aunt would sit on the throne. However, her aunt was the firstborn, and her mother never challenged that authority. At first she acted as advisor to her sister, especially when melancholy moods incapacitated her from ruling the Duxdom. Now she seemed more interested in escaping the confines of Varstad and her true calling, and playing explorer in the north, and leaving the Dux council to manage the affairs of state.

Beira smiled, and Aldith knew a verbal slap was coming her way. "Thank you for your guidance, my child. I'm afraid your costly adventure puts a tremendous strain on the coffers of the Duxdom. We need wealth coming in, not going out. Furs and wood harvested from the north will lessen the burden."

"Besides, my position in charge of domestic affairs doesn't change, and Lilith is more than capable of managing the security of the realm in your absence. However, if you prefer someone else to go in your stead…" Rafyn said with the hint of a sneer.

Aldith often wondered how three sisters from the same mother could be so different. She and Lilith looked alike with their fair complexion and martial stature, and were raised from birth to be Damm Warriors. As direct relatives of the Dux, they also had a guaranteed role in the military affairs of state. However, there was a wanton cruelness about Lilith which set them apart. It was not so much Lilith enjoyed violence, she was simply indifferent to its application. It meant no more to her than a bowel movement. With the remaining Damm Warriors and Red Shadows under her direct command, there was the risk she would apply deadly force without thought to the consequences. As for Rafyn, their physical appearance as well as their nature were in sharp contrast. It was apparent to the lowest chamber boy they had different fathers, some said Rafyn was of mixed blood, but since the matrilineal line was all important, it did not alter the fact they were sisters. They were close friends as young children, but their paths quickly diverged as they matured, and camaraderie turned to animosity and then hate. They were rivals for the Duxdom, as first born rules did not apply outside of direct succession, and Lilith a pawn between them.

"No, Rafyn. It's my duty to go Varingr, you said so yourself."

Rafyn bowed in mock deference to her sister. "Always the First Damm Warrior. Yes, duty calls for all of us."

The cur in the Dux's lap yelped when all of the vegetable treats were consumed. The Dux dropped it down on the ground where it promptly shat, before waddling off in search of the pack.

"It's decided then," the Dux proclaimed. "Beira goes north, Aldith goes south, and Rafyn and Lilith hold down the fort and prepare for the Purge. Time for lunch." The Dux stood up to dismiss the family council.

The family council all stood, but Rafyn had more to say. "Unfortunately, we're not quite finished, my liege."

"Hrmph," the Dux said, and sat back down. She gestured to her family to take their seats.

"It appears we have a disturbance amongst our gardeners..."

Now Aldith knew why the family council had been called with such haste. Rafyn's plan was to humiliate her in front of the Dux and their mother.

"What could possibly be wrong with them? They have such a wonderful time stooping over plants and nurturing the vegetables for us. Why, I have a mind to join them on occasion," the Dux said.

"It appears they've stopped working..."

"Stopped working?" the Dux exclaimed. "Who ever heard of such a thing! We need their hands and green fingers busy for the harvesting. You can't expect me to eat that horrid food we have to import from the Sul."

"Quite so, your majesty. However, it appears Aldith saw fit to borrow one of the brides," Rayfn explained.

"Borrow?" the Dux asked.

"Fyrst Nott," Aldith said, sheepishly.

The Dux pondered on that for a moment, before realization sank in. "Aren't you supposed to select one of the grooms?"

Aldith squirmed in her chair. "My interest lies in another direction."

"Don't you have a Dandy husband?" the Dux asked.

"I do."

"And you visit him?"

On occasion. The experience is … underwhelming."

"Hrmph," the Dux said.

"An unsettling disturbance we don't need at this critical moment," Beira offered.

"Indeed. We were raised to put the affairs of the state before personal enjoyment," Rafyn said, though it was not clear if her intended target was Aldith or her mother.

"I'll pay them a little visit. They'll soon stop this nonsense," Lilith said.

Aldith blanched. Lilith loose amongst the Andra would lead to dead bodies desecrating the gardens, and blood instead of water for the plants. The problem was of her creation. She took Tana for pleasure without considering the ramifications. In that regard, she was no better than her brutal sister.

All I have to do is return Tana, and this ends.

"No, I'll take care of it. My last act before the Varingr," Aldith said.

Aldith knew she should send a troop of Damm Warriors to fetch Tana from *Matilda,* and escort her back to the Andra gardens. She did not have to see the girl herself. She could go back to the final preparations of the Varingr, and sail south without a backward glance. However, something stayed her hand. It was more than lust and the joy of spending more nights with the dark haired beauty. Something else grew inside of her. It was a tiny flame at present, but if nurtured it would grow into a forest fire of love. She needed more time to consider her true feelings, which meant force was required to quell the Andra revolt.

I'm no better than Lilith or Rafyn. The heart must never overrule the head.

She made her way back to the training ground and gathered twenty Damm Warriors as an escort, and a hundred Red Shadows as a show of force to quell any potential rebellion. She also sent for Katla the Konna interpreter to meet them at the gardens. The Andra were a gentle people,

CHAPTER SEVENTEEN

and their only form of resistance was peaceful protest. She needed to stamp her authority on them, make an example, and hold the status quo together for a little longer.

Aldith entered the rainbow colored dome where the communal wedding festivities were held the night before. There was little evidence of the happy celebrations she had so rudely interrupted, save for a few scattered flowers. Katla was by her side and she was flanked by her Damm Warrior escort. The Red Shadows, halberds at the ready, fanned out as before. Aldith looked up at the roof of the dome and the snow melting on contact with the glass.

Such a simple, gentle life they lead. No worries other than caring for the gardens.

The groom was there, sitting on the ground and dressed in the green color of his future in-laws. It appeared as if he had waited all night and into the solar for the return of his bride. The makeup around his eyes was heavily smudged, where his tears ran through it, leaving mournful black streaks on his face. He twisted the hanging man amulet around his neck with a dirt covered hand as if seeking guidance from a higher authority.

As Aldith waited, the Andra gathered. They streamed into the rainbow dome in their various colors: red, green, yellow and orange, earth brown, and the multicolored ones. The families did not intermingle, but stood silently in their respective groups. There was a sadness about them that Aldith knew could only be made whole by the return of Tana.

"Is there another amongst them who can speak the common tongue?" Aldith asked Katla.

The interpreter searched the faces of the Andra until she spotted someone. "Come here, Chandra. That's right, step forward child," she said in the common tongue, beckoning her forward. The young girl hesitated at first, but made her way to stand in front of Katla and Aldith.

The groom got up from the ground and stood with his own people in red. He shouted something in the Andra language, which included Tana's name, that much Aldith understood. The young girl, who had a strong resemblance to Tana, but not quite as striking, did not translate his words.

It seemed she understood her role as the verbal channel between the Var and the Andra and waited for Katla to initiate the conversation with her.

"Tana will not be joining you today. She remains with me of her own free will," Aldith said, and waited for Katla to relay the words in the common tongue, and via the girl into the Andra language.

As the young girl translated, tears rolled down her face, but she diligently carried on with her task. Women wailed, and the groom dropped to the dirt once more, and bashed his fists into the soil and cried out in anguish.

"Tana will be well cared for, have no fear. I promise to look after her and keep her safe," Aldith continued.

Aldith's words did nothing to soothe the Andra. They only served to stir the pot and amplify the grief of the gentle gardeners. The men joined the women in their wailing, and the sound echoed through the dome. Plucking Tana out from the wedding festivities had upended their world, and Aldith felt a tinge of pity, though the Damm Warrior in her could not understand why they gave in so meekly and did not fight back. With that sentiment came a degree of anger.

"Back to your gardens, now. There's nothing else to see here," Aldith said.

The Andra did not move. They were transfixed to the spot in their sorrow, tormented by the loss of one of their own.

Lilith would make an example. Kill a few and force the others back to work. Am I no better? I can't return Tana now and show weakness.

"I said back to your..."

The trajectory of the vegetable was true and it landed squarely on Aldith's upper chest and neck, the flesh and seeds exploding into a sticky mess on her chainmail. The effect was immediate. The Andra stopped their wailing and let out a collective gasp. The Red Shadows lowered their halberds and waited for the order to engage. Ten Damm Warriors formed a protective shield around Aldith, while the remainder pushed into the crowd, swords drawn, and extracted the transgressor. They dragged him before Aldith, pushing him to his knees with his arms forcibly outstretched to the side. One Damm Warrior grasped his hair and pulled his head forward exposing

CHAPTER SEVENTEEN

his neck, while another held her longsword in both hands and awaited instructions from Aldith to decapitate him.

The death of Tana's groom won't solve this.

Aldith waved the swordswoman off. "Take him away. I have a more fitting punishment for him. Now back to work, the rest of you, before I start removing heads!"

Aldith was in a black mood for the rest of the solar. She went back to the training ground, and barked orders at her captains for nothing in particular. She made her army sweat as she pushed them through drills they already knew by rote. She longed to engage in the war exercises, to lose herself in physical activity, and escape from the affairs of state and the heart.

When she could drill her army no further, Aldith returned to the docks and pushed the Konna and the loading crews to greater exertions. Ship after ship was packed with the necessary cargo for the long voyage. Once the hulls were full, the deck hatches were sealed and waterproofed against the elements. For the final night, only skeleton crews were onboard, those men who had no families to speak of. The full complement would ship out with the morning tide, leaving loved ones behind for the best part of a year, if they returned at all.

With night falling, Aldith returned to *Matilda*, but she did not go below deck and visit Tana in her cabin. Time enough for that on the sea journey. She busied herself with the final checks on the seaworthiness of her craft, tasks her captain had already completed. It served to keep her mind occupied and her hands busy. The future of the Var rested with her, and the minstrels would either sing about Aldith the Conqueror, Aldith the Avenger, or Aldith the Unlucky, or Aldith Lackland. Victory or defeat awaited a world away.

The army began to arrive before dawn broke. Each squadron of Red Shadows under the command of seasoned Damm Warriors, were ferried in smaller boats over to the Black Ships. Most had never been to sea before, and the anxiety showed on their young faces. They had signed up to guard Varstad, and retire to the Burghs with riches, take a wife, and raise a family.

A military campaign far from home brought fear, and crossing the ocean induced dread. The crew of grizzled veterans teased them with salty cures for seasickness, how to walk properly on a rolling deck, and spun tales of eight-legged sea monsters they would see along the way, as they pulled them onboard.

There was no fanfare, pomp or ceremony with the sailing of the fleet. Var superstition considered it bad luck to announce the start of a sea journey. It was best to be on your way, before the solar was up, and catch the sea sprites, sirens, selkies, and other maritime elementals sleeping in their watery nests. Aldith did not interfere as *Matilda's* captain went about his work, supervising the men as they cast off the mooring lines, and raised the small sails. Below deck slaafs worked the mighty capstan to generate the power needed to keep the propeller in constant motion. Once out of the harbor, the main sails would be raised and wind power added to the speed. Aldith stood at the stern, next to the sail master at the helm and watched the rest of the fleet moored in the harbor raise anchor and use the morning tide to get them underway.

Free from the safety of the harbor, the pitching and rolling of the ship picked up. Aldith was already feeling queasy and hoped for calm seas until she found her sea legs. The start of a voyage was always difficult and she knew the smell of stale vomit would be a constant feature at least for a few solars. Some men would take readily to the freedom offered by the nautical life, but others would suffer from the confinement, and troubled minds and idle hands was a worrisome combination. Constant work until exhaustion provided the solution.

One hundred Black Ships in orderly formation of squadrons of ten was a formidable sight. Colored lanterns on the mast of the squadron leaders served as the rallying point and held the fleet together for now. As they reached open seas, and squalls and tempests beset them, the hope was smaller groups would stay together, and trust in the captain's navigational skills would see them safely to their final destination. However, a journey of this magnitude, with so many Black Ships to command was fraught with danger.

CHAPTER SEVENTEEN

Aldith had something else on her mind. It was time to visit with Tana, to hold her in her arms, to love her, and tell her she was destined to never see her people again.

Chapter Eighteen

Juan : Confrontation on Skank Bridge

The news of Cotter Sullivan's demise spread through the Four Kith as fast as the Geroni Bakerhaus fire. The tittle-tattle blaze burned bright throughout the solar and into the night as kithfolk gossiped about the reason and offered up their own outlandish theories. Some said the ghost of Mo Dickens stalked the slagerhaus, and his vengeful spirit snuffed out Cotter's warped flame. Others said the Burghmeisters, tired of heavy protection fees for crossing the bridges to the Citadel or to the Mutton, hired an assassin from the south to end his solars. The more fanciful claimed *The Terror* took him in the night, or even the Dux herself had ordered his execution. Few believed a mere boy could take on such a monster and come out victorious on the other side. Juan believed. Juan knew.

Ever since Dismas disappeared in the fog of the Mutton, a melancholy mood hung over Jojo's little gang of pickpockets. Jojo especially took it hard, as if prematurely losing one of her own children to the Onderworld. No one thought Dismas, wracked by a thief's guilt, had run off with the gild. They all knew the boy torn to shreds in the Mutton was their Dismas, but none ventured over to see the remains. Nico was shunned at first for the transgression of missing the purse exchange. He and Gesmas even got into a scuffle over it, until Jojo intervened and told them all they needed

CHAPTER EIGHTEEN

to bond together like a family. Eight thieves working together was better than each one acting alone.

Even pickpockets needed to eat, and Juan led a few excursions out from the safety of their cutpurse nest in Tanner Bank. Pickings were slim, and Jojo had a devil of a time getting even the slimmest shaved coin out of the pawners. It was enough to buy a few scraps of stale brood, and they still had the slop from the Gut to fall back on to stave off hunger for another solar.

"I shud go an' see 'im, wot with Cotter out of the way," Juan boldly announced.

Jojo shook her head. "Things is not the same as before, Juan. 'E's your brother an all, but 'e's changed, an' not for the better, by all accounts. Word is 'e's killed three men by 'is own 'and."

"But it was Cotter who kept us apart, an' Cotter's in the Basin. Don't you want to go back to the slagerhaus an' sit in your chair by a warm fire?" Juan asked.

Jojo closed her eyes, and tears streamed down her face at the thought. "I doz, I doz. But it's not the same without Mo,"

Juan stood up. His anger flowed over. "Nothin' brings Mo back. E's gone, do yuz 'ere! We can't go on livin' like this, Jojo. Nothin' good comes from this life. We deserve better, an' Carlos can help. Our bond is strong."

He stormed out of the derelict building before Jojo could stop him. At the doorway, Flopsie flopped in front of him with a swoon, and Maisie clung onto his leg and implored him to stay with a dramatic flurry. He brushed her off, stepped over Flopsie, and went in search of his twin brother.

It was an exceptionally cold solar in Gastown, and Juan pulled his threadbare coat closer to keep the chill from setting into his thin bones. He shuffled through the lanes and alleys, and past the street vendors, who kept a wary eye on him. The boy with the eyepatch was well known to them, and they kept their merchandise under guard. Juan paid them no heed. He had more important things to consider, such as what he would say to Carlos. Would his brother accept him back with open arms? he wondered. Would there be a hearty meal of paranga, hot blud, and warm brood? Or would he cast him out, back to the Slough, and his only nourishment provided by the Gut? There was only one way to find out.

He stood across the way from the large wooden gateway of Mo Dickens's slagerhaus, close enough to observe, but far enough back to avoid attracting any special attention. Just another mudlark with an empty stomach, and aspirations of stealing meat scraps. He slid a thumb under his eyepatch and rubbed the talisman they had lifted from the country cousin crossing Skank Bridge, the man most likely responsible for Dismas's untimely end. If he could do that to Dismas for lifting a purse, what would he do to get his totem back? He shuddered at the thought, but rubbing the talisman brought him comfort, and he needed a calm mind to summon up the courage to take the first step across the street and into the slager world once more.

The business of the slagerhaus was in full flow as apprentices loaded wrapped meat onto carts, and the prime cuts were sent on their way to the Burghs, whilst the lesser grades, offal, and trimming were offloaded to establishments in the Four Kith. Gastown ate meat, and the slagerhauses were the providers. There were other activities too. A constant stream of small boys, moving at speed and with purpose, went in and out of the slagerhaus. Juan knew a messenger system when he saw one. These mites were an army of spies, the eyes and ears of the network. And then there were the Bully Boys. There were less of them, and they moved with a slower, watchful gait, with heads on swivels, and a defensive mindset. Two of them stood at either side of the gateway, and checked the human traffic on the way in. They were mean looking men with battle scars as testament to their trade. One of them walked with a pronounced limp as they shuffled back and forth to keep the cold at bay.

It was now or never. Juan pulled his coat collar up, and chanced his arm. He waited as three small boys hurried to go inside and tagged along behind them, head down, and moving as if he belonged. The Bully Boy guards were no mugs, as Juan soon found out. A hand shot out and grabbed him by the scruff of the neck. His compatriot blocked Juan's path.

'Just where do you think yuz is goin'?' the grizzled veteran said.

CHAPTER EIGHTEEN

Juan tried to appear confident, but his heart sank. "Iz 'ave a message for Carlos. An important one,"

"'Ave you seen this mug around 'ere before?" The Bully Boy asked his friend.

He shook his head. "Not this one. The eyepatch is a dead give away. "E don't belong to the mites."

"Off with yuz," the Bully Boy holding onto Juan's collar said, as he spun him around, gave him a shove, and a boot up the backside to send him on his way.

"I wouldn't do that, if I was you," a familiar voice said, and Juan looked up to see Perfect Styles, replete in a bloody apron standing in the courtyard, his hands on his hips. He gave a final instruction to an apprentice, before turning back to the two Bully Boys.

"If you rub some of the dirt off, change out the tattered clothes, add some weight, and grow back an eye, you might recognize him. That there is Juan Grimm, Carlos's twin brother. Best let him in, boys," Perfect said.

With a nod of thanks to Perfect, Juan scurried inside before the Bully Boys had a chance to object.

Old memories came flooding back as he stepped inside Mo Dickens's slagerhaus. There was an immediate flashback to the violent confrontation between Mo and Cotter Sullivan, ending in Mo's severed head rolling across the floor strewn in animal bones. Mo's cleaver was still embedded in the pillar as a reminder. Then there was the savage beating at the hands of Cotter's Bully Boys, and the last image of Carlos and the look of fear on his face, before the blackness enveloped him.

Juan was pleasantly surprised to see the paranga operation was still functioning as before. The interior was as clean as you could expect for an establishment dealing with meat, gore, and guts. Blood-soaked sawdust covered the floor, and Juan knew from his own past labors, it would be swept up at the solar's end, the floors washed down, and a fresh covering applied before the butcher's trade began again. The room itself was cold, the way Mo Dickens liked it, and no fire burned in the hearth until night came. Perfect Styles had finished giving directions to the apprentice and was back behind his butcher's block working on dismembering a fresh carcass.

Juan was shocked when he saw his brother. Carlos was standing next to a large bald man who sat at a table, and the two of them pored over spread out papers. The man pointed at one section with a quill, and a smile broke across Carlos's face, until he looked up and saw his twin and the smile vanished. When they were younger, no one could tell them apart, which they used to their advantage. Until the Dandy blade took out Juan's eye and left a permanent marker. Now there was a starker contrast. Juan was bone thin, barely on the plus side of starvation, and dressed with an ill assortment of rags, which struggled to keep the permawinter at arm's length. Carlos was well nourished, bordering on plump, and he was dressed in a wardrobe a Burghmeister tailor would be proud to call his own. Where Juan wore an eyepatch, Carlos sported black eye makeup, which added a sinister appearance.

Juan and Carlos stared at each other in silence, before the large man sitting at the table broke the spell. "Well, well, what do we have here? I see a strong family resemblance, Carlos. A little on the thin side, but I'd say a brother of yours?"

"Why Black Jack, this mudlark be Juan Grimm. 'E's a lost twin of sorts," Carlos said, though he made no move to welcome his sibling.

"A twin you say? Well, I'm sure the two of you have a lot to discuss," Jack said, gathering up the papers, and sticking the quill back in his jacket pocket. "I'll leave you to it. I'm sure there's a degree of catching up to do."

"Oh 'e won't be stayin' long," Carlos said with a sneer. "Probably 'as a pocket or two to pick."

As Black Jack left them alone, Juan noticed the heavy gold chain around Carlos's neck. It was not brightly polished as Mo kept it and was stained reddish brown in places. Dried blud from either man or beast.

"I see yuz become Hetman of the Slagers, an' yuz barely able to carve out a leg joint. It's a nice life yuz set up," Juan said.

Carlos clenched his fists and ground his knuckles into the table, "What does yuz know about my life? Yuz was off laughin' an' jokin' with

CHAPTER EIGHTEEN

pickpockets in the Slough, while Iz was left 'ere with Cotter. My life? Everythin' Iz 'ave Iz took. An' this took it!" Carlos said, pulling out his short blade and stabbing it into the table top.

Juan did not reply. He could see and feel his brother's pain. Carlos was always the one most on edge, and his experience with Cotter had tipped him over. There was a rage about him, which could only be expressed in violence, and never tempered. Peace of mind had been cruelly ripped away from Carlos Grimm, and the shattered remains sought retribution.

"Iz don't need yuz, Juan. Iz don't want yuz around 'ere, yuz 'ear me? Yuz remind me of the older times. This is my world, an' mine alone. It's not for sharin' with the likes of yuz,"

Juan still did not reply and simply stared at his twin, until the anger passed. When it did Carlos sat back down and hung his head. "Best go, Juan. There's a fight brewin' an' it won't be safe around 'ere," he said in a quieter, controlled tone.

"Seems the fight 'as already started. Word is you've killed three men already," Juan said. He wanted to reassure his brother he was here for him, to place a comforting hand on his shoulder and tell him everything would be alright. However, he knew Carlos was not ready to accept his love.

"Four, an' more is comin'. This isn't for yuz, Juan. Go back to your mudlarks and Jojo Dickens, and keep your 'ead down. Go on, best be off with yuz."

Before Juan could reply, an apprentice nudged him, and handed him a slab of brood and meat wrapped in a wool rag. "Perfect says yuz could use this for your journey," the apprentice said.

Juan took the package and left without another word to his twin. Their world was sundered, and Juan did not know how to put it back together again. Time was a great healer, but Juan wondered if they even had a solar on their side. They were both just a misstep away from a ride on Jorm's barge to the Onderworld.

Juan left the slagerhaus and crossed one of the narrow bridges over the Basin. He had sense enough to stick the food package deep in his pocket. Meat and fresh brood was as good as gild in the Slough, and people had died for much less. He would wait until he could find a secluded spot before he ate. He thought about taking it back to their thieves den on Tanner Bank and sharing it with the others, but that idea quickly passed. There was not enough to go around, and he would eat alone and swallow the guilt with each tender mouthful.

Juan was an expert tracker, and could easily stay to the shadows and cover a mark without them knowing it. On the reverse, he knew when he was the intended target, and he picked up the Bully Boy on his tail five blocks from the slagerhaus. The stealth trade was an art form few excelled at, and the Bully Boy was no master. He tried too hard to hide, and moved in quick jerky motions as he jutted in and out of doorways and alleyways, rather than blending with the crowd and seamlessly disappearing in plain sight.

Juan walked slowly to the corner of an old thieves alleyway known as Bunter's Cross, slipped into the darkness and then sprinted the full length, hopped over a body sprawled out on the ground, either dead or dead drunk, and once at the end, looped back around so he would come up behind the Bully Boy. It was too easy. The lug had lost his mark, and Juan was home free to eat his breakfast, and then make a leisurely return to Tanner Bank.

There was another. Juan could feel it in the back of his neck before he picked up the tracker. This one was more professional than his colleague, but a Bully Boy nonetheless. By his gait, Juan pegged him for the one who recently guarded the slagerhaus gateway. No doubt, he had reported on him as soon as Perfect Styles fingered him as Carlos's brother, and someone wanted to know more, or worse, feed him to the fishes. Juan was not prepared to wait and find out.

He moved quickly now, darting up and down side streets, though narrow gateways, across canals, and backtracking to try and get an edge. Despite his obvious limp, the Bully Boy stayed with him all the way, and to make matters worse, he had picked up his companion, and now there were two of them on his trail. He was sweating, despite the cold, and he needed to slow down and think clearly. Simply running was not doing any good, and since they knew he was on to them, it was now more than a simple tail.

CHAPTER EIGHTEEN

Then there were three. Shaking a brace was difficult, but not impossible. Slipping free from a trio was a different proposition, and required a distraction. The way the two Bully Boys deferred to the third man made it obvious he was the leader, and he now directed them to fan out on either side, while he took the more direct center position. Juan saw they made no secret of hiding their presence now. They wanted him, and he had nowhere to run. He remembered the sandwich in his pocket. He was reluctant to give it up, but it was the only collateral at his disposal, and he needed to gather a hungry crowd.

They were all around him, the lost waifs and strays of the Slough. Malnourished boys and girls, who would slit your throat in your sleep for the chance of stealing a stale crust. A fresh slab of brood, and meat they barely saw never mind touched, was a feast known only for a king or a fat Burghmeister. All Juan needed to do was bring them together, and play a variation of the shell game with himself as the pea.

He took the sandwich from his pocket, and resisted the temptation to take a hearty bite. Instead, he placed it on the ground, and gently peeled away the wrapping. "Mudlarks! Breakfast!" Juan said.

They were on it like a mischief of potkans before he had even stepped to one side. They barreled over each other, biting and scratching to get a piece of the brood, meat, or even the wrapping itself to suck on the juices. Juan seized the opportunity, and dove into the pack, rolling and tumbling with them, before popping out on the other side, and sliding into the shadows.

The three Bully Boys saw Juan go into the sandwich melee, but they did not see him come out. They closed in on the pack, pulling mites away, looking for the singular mudlark with the eyepatch. He was not there.

Don't look back!

Juan kept close to the ground, and stealthily made his way to Skank Bridge, resisting the temptation to look over his shoulder to see if he was being tailed. He did not want to go into the Mutton again, but it offered his only refuge at the moment. He could not move as freely there as he could in the Four Kith, but Bully Boys would be on their guard there too, and it was an edge he needed.

Juan froze, and for a brief moment, his legs buckled beneath him. There were five of them coming towards him from the direction of the Mutton. Stone faced men with matching scars under the right eye, and savagery stamped all over them, from the way they walked to the way they dressed. The one in the middle was a giant of a man, carved from the same granite block as Mo Dickens. If trolls were real, this man was a near relative.

He acted instinctively, and slid over the stonewall of the bridge, and hunkered down on the narrow ledge on the other side. The thought of dropping into the icy cold water below gave him added strength as he hung on tightly and waited for the Crimpers to pass. No good would come of their visit into the Four Kith, and Juan wanted no part of it. He held his breath as they got closer to his position, and was filled with dread when they stopped directly across from him. There was a gap in the stone wall, and Juan peeped through it with his one good eye. They were not alone. The three Bully Boys blocked their path.

"Nice of you to come and meet us, Patch. Saves us a walk into the Four Kith," the troll said.

"What does Crimpers want in the Four Kith, Toby? We did our business the other night," Patch replied.

The mountain of a man named Toby stepped closer to the man he called Patch. He towered over him, but the smaller man did not show any sign of fear as he held his ground on Skank Bridge, although his two companions were not so self-assured. Juan could tell his first tail was on the point of bolting. Other travelers across the span gave the two groups a wide berth, while the more cautious ones simply turned around to avoid the impending confrontation.

"Things took a turn for the worse, Patch. You see, while you were talking' with Pete, some of your boys were putting a stabbing to ole Davey. Carved up real bad he was, with his junk in his mouth as a message."

Patch shook his head. "Not my doin', Toby. I told Pete, I want no trouble, and things back to how they were. Bully Boys stay in the Four Kith, and Swell Daddies and Crimpers have the Mutton. We have no business settin' up a pleasure haus on our side of the river. The boy is ambitious, but we'll

CHAPTER EIGHTEEN

rein 'im in. We was chasin' after his twin brother, as collateral like, before we ran into you Crimpers."

"Ole Davey was a particular favorite of Pete," Toby said, as if he had not heard a word Patch just uttered to him. "Looked after him and showed him the ropes as he was just starting out. Pete had a soft spot for the ole bugger."

"I've told you, Toby. I want no trouble. Davey's demise was not my doin'." Patch replied, his confidence quickly evaporating.

"Pete's a vengeful man when he thinks he's been wronged. And pity the pug who takes him for a fool," Toby snarled.

Patch held up both arms, palms facing towards Toby in a gesture showing he wanted no bother. All his previous bravado left him in an instant. "Please, Toby. We had a deal."

"Pete wants a body, and the body is yours!"

Toby's left hand shot out fast for a lumbering giant, and seized hold of Patch by the throat. Patch's arms froze in mid-air in the gesture of peace, love, and misunderstanding, and were incapable of moving. Juan did not see the blade, but Toby's right hand punched forward three times towards Patch's heart, and he immediately went limp. At that moment, his arms collapsed to his side, his legs buckled, and his chin sagged to his chest, as the big man continued to prop him up with one hand. Juan knew death had cast a veil over Patch, and one more feared Bully Boy was making an early entrance to the Onderworld.

Toby's actions set the Crimpers into motion. Two instantly squared off with the limping Bully Boy, and knives flashed on either side. It did not last long, though the gimp tried to make a fight of it, and the Bully Boy was finally dispatched as he lay in a bloody heap on the ground. The remaining Bully Boy immediately grasped the unevenness of the situation, and bolted as if gravity refused to hold him down. The two Crimpers thought about chasing, but when they saw the speed of the rabbit, they simply shrugged their shoulders. One of them did make a passing stab at the now dead Bully Boy, who limped no more, as an act of participation, and just to get his blade wet.

Toby passed Patch's warm corpse over to two Crimpers, who took him by the arms.

"Heave him over the side, boys!" he ordered.

Juan clung tightly to the side of the stone wall on the outside of the bridge, as first Patch's body, and then the dead lamer went sailing over the side and into the icy waters below. They hit the surface with a splash, and sank like stones into the blackness.

"We go after the Grimm boy now?" one of the Crimpers asked.

"No, let him stew on his fear for a while. With no Cotter or Patch, the Bully Boys have no true leader. At least no fighting man at the front. We'll go in when Pete says, and take over the Four Kith. Looks like ole Davey passing did us a favor after all."

Juan waited until he was sure the Crimpers were back on their way to the Mutton, and the bridge foot traffic moved freely again as if nothing had happened. Feet trudged through the snow and mud, and quickly churned any remaining blud into the sludge. He slid back over to the right side of the bridge, startling one elderly gentleman, and hurried back to the Four Kith to warn Carlos.

He moved quickly on his way back to the slagerhaus, but still with a degree of caution. The Bully Boys were not his friends, and he stayed in the shadows as best he could. Hunger and all of the excitement, which drained his energy, got the better of him now, and he wished he still had his sandwich to munch on. He slowed his pace as he wondered how he would get past the Bully Boy guards at the slagerhaus entranceway without Perfect Styles to grease him through.

When he reached his observation spot across from the slagerhaus, he was surprised to see no guards on duty. With a fight brewing with the Crimpers, security was lax. Still, it provided him with the opportunity he needed, and all he had to do was walk in and explain to Carlos what he had seen. Someone called Pete was coming for him, and it was time to give up the charade as Hetman of the Slagers, and escape into the relative safety and obscurity of the Slough. Being a pickpocket came with drawbacks, but it was preferable to facing an assassin's blade. At least they would be

CHAPTER EIGHTEEN

together again, like old times.

Juan cleared the gateway, but before he could enter the hall, a mite a little younger than him and sporting a burn mark in his scalp, blocked his path. He was flanked by two smaller boys. They all had black soot smeared under their eyes, and there was a look about them that screamed pending violence.

"Iz need to see Carlos," Juan said.

The boy shook his head. "No Slough mudlarks in 'ere,"

Juan tried to move forward, but was pushed back, and the two wing boys pulled out knives. "Yuz don't understand. I just saw someone called Patch killed on Skank Bridge. A limpin' Bully Boy too. They're comin' for Carlos. Iz 'ave to let 'im know."

The mite stood his ground. "Carlos already knows. Now be off with yuz, before we make yuz leak. Wez 'is brothers now, an' 'e don't need the likes of yuz."

Juan could see it was no use, and he was not getting back into the slagerhaus on this solar or any other. If the mite was right, Carlos already knew what was coming, so the danger was crystal clear. He turned on his heels and ran off back to the Slough.

Chapter Nineteen

Kasha : The Recovery

Her head was on fire, as if she had plunged it into a cauldron and let the intense heat sear her brain. Her skull throbbed as if two tiny blacksmiths were beating a steady tattoo on the inside, trying to break out. Her body was not much better. Her face was puffy and swollen on one side, two fingers on her right hand were obviously broken and bound together with a leather strap for support, and the pain in her ribs made it difficult to breathe, though no ribs were broken. At least there was no discomfort between her legs. Wherever she was, she had not been violated.

Kasha wanted nothing more than to close her eyes again and drift back into the foggy sleep offered by the sweet liquid someone intermittently poured between her cracked lips. She fought it hard, and slowly pushed up on her elbows, struggling against the pain caused by simply moving. She lay naked in a comfortable bed covered with a warm fur. Her clothes, washed and neatly folded, lay on a chair beside her. She reached out a hand and touched her tunic, and felt the tree brooch still attached. There was no sight of her purse, and the silver coins she needed to survive in Gastown. Her weapons were missing too.

She remembered the fight outside *The Copper Coin*, the slight man with the sneeze, who Berric insulted, and the thugs waiting to pounce at his command. They fought hard, and kept them at bay for a while, but the

CHAPTER NINETEEN

numbers were against them. Then Berric was stabbed and went down. She could only remember fragments after that. Blackness, and then helping hands. Vague memories of being bathed in a secret pool, drowning, and then the sweetness which brought a peaceful sleep.

Berric!

She had just found her brother, the first relative she had met outside of Tornar, and now he was gone. They would not journey north together and reunite with their father. That dream was ripped from them, gone in a short burst of senseless violence.

Men are so arrogant and stupid. Why can they not hold their tongues, or turn away and swallow their pride?

She craved to be a waheela again, to escape the stench and noise of Gastown, and slip back into the *Machala,* the frozen grasslands, and run free. There all she had to care about was her next meal, and as an apex predator, there was no short supply of prey.

"Rest easy, my child," Beira said softly as she entered the room. She sat down on the bed beside Kasha, and laid a gentle hand on her arm. "You were badly hurt, and we worried the knock you took to the head would cause severe swelling to your brain. Luckily with rest and treatment, it subsided."

Beira reached up a hand and touched Kasha's forehead. "You still have a slight fever, but not raging high like before."

"Where am I, how did I get here, and for how long?" Kasha asked. Her voice was hoarse, and barely audible. Her jaw hurt, and talking was difficult.

Beira stood up and walked over to a nearby table. She took a pitcher and poured water into a wooden beaker. "Here, drink this," she said, as she helped Kasha take a sip.

Kasha wanted to drain the cup, but even a small swallow caused her pain. She drank slowly with Beira's help.

"You're in a safe place, so no need to worry. Drest brought you here and has been watching over you for five solars like you were his own. Quite fortunate really, some of our crew were celebrating in the Mutton and came across you lying in the snow. You're lucky to be alive. I warned you, Kasha. Gastown, and especially the Mutton, is no place for a young woman."

"And my brother? Did they find him too?" Kasha asked.

Beira took Kasha's hand between her own. "They found him."

"He's dead, isn't he?"

Beira shook her head. "No, child. He's still with us, but he hangs on by a thread. It was a killing blow for most men, but it seems Tornar's children are made of sterner stuff."

"Alive? He's here? Can I see him?" Kasha asked, trying to get up. Beira gently pressed her back down.

"He's in the room next door, and you can see him in good time. He's not awake, Kasha, and you must prepare yourself for the possibility he could still slip away. We gave him the White Tears to ease his suffering and to let him rest peacefully. He needs many lunars of bed rest to recover."

Kasha lay back down and tears welled in her eyes.

We've failed our father. I've failed. How can we reunite now? Gastown is a world of thieves and killers. I must take Berric far north to the Faratha to be with his people again.

It was as if Beira read her thoughts. "There's nothing for you here in Gastown, Kasha. Come north to the *Opplanda* with me and leave this behind. I can use your help in the Wildlands. We'll bring your brother too. The fresh air will do him good, and we can move him carefully. We'll take you both home where you belong. Now rest, and gather your strength. We'll have a long journey ahead of us."

Kasha could not rest. She had one more task to complete before she left Gastown forever. On Tornar's instructions she needed to reunite with her foster parents, and bring something of importance back with her. It was the reason Berric was there to assist with a safe passage. She had no idea what that could be, though she would find out in due course. If her foster parents were still alive.

"Alright, Beira. Berric and I will come to your *Opplanda*, our *Faratha*, with you. But I have something I need to do first."

CHAPTER NINETEEN

Beira misunderstood her intentions. "Revenge won't make things right, Kasha. Don't go back into the Mutton and try to find the man responsible for this. Let it go."

Kasha shook her head, and pushed herself up into a sitting position. The fur slipped away exposing her nakedness, her scars, and her inked skin. The waheela tattoo as her talisman, the ice bear representing her direct lineage with Tornar, the intricate spiral patterns, and the wheel of thunder. All applied by her father's own hand.

"I'll never let it go, but now is not the time. I need to see the people who raised me before I go north to my father. One last time."

"I can see your mind's made up on this one, Kasha. But please be careful, and keep your movement slow. Your body is still recovering."

Beira stood up and placed a small pouch next to Kasha's clothes on the chair. "You'll need this too. It's not much, just some copper coins to get by. I'm afraid the thieves in the Mutton stole your silver coins. There's a knife, and a small hatchet by the door. Hopefully, you won't need them. And there's a new pair of kamiks too. Your old ones have seen better solars. They should fit nicely."

"Why are you doing this, Beira? Kasha asked. "Why are you helping me?"

Beira smiled down at her. "Let's just say you remind me of someone."

Kasha wanted to leave immediately, but Beira insisted she ate some turnip stew first. A servant woman placed a tray beside her bed along with a hunk of warm brood and a beaker of thick black bier. Kasha knew she was weak, five solars without nourishment takes a toll, but eating was difficult and painful. She took a few spoonfuls of the thin stew, but refrained from chewing the vegetables due to the pain in her jaw. She could not chew the brood either, so she dipped it in the broth until it was soggy and sucked it up. Two gulps of the bier went straight to her head, so she left it mostly untouched.

Getting dressed was a bigger challenge than Kasha realized. Small movements were fine if she went slow, but pulling on her pants and tunic required much more effort, and the heavier fur jacket weighed her down. Once she pulled on her kamiks, she was forced to sit on the bed and regather her strength. Her breath was labored, her side ached, and her spinning head took a moment to settle. Five solars of inactivity meant her joints were stiff, and she could only stretch out with small motions until her ribs healed.

As a waheela I'd do a morning stretch and crack everything back into place. Why is this human form so weak?

She needed to see Berric before she sought out her foster parents. Beira said he was in the room adjacent to hers, so she left her own bedchamber on unsteady feet, and went into the room next door. She was shocked when she saw Berric lying prone, and unmoving. His face was pale from loss of blood, and it looked as if he was laid out on his deathbed rather than a recovery cot.

Kasha sat in the chair beside her brother and gently peeled back the fur covering him to examine the wound in his side. It was heavily bandaged, and blood stained. She touched his forehead, which was warm beneath her fingers, and held his hand, which was deathly cold. She glanced at his tattoos, and saw many similarities to her own. She recognized her father's work. There were others too, which Kasha could not decipher, intricate spirals, celestial bodies, and depictions of Berric's life journey. There was room for more on his human canvas, and she knew Berric would add to them once he fully recovered.

Berric. You were so strong, and now look at you? We're all just one blade strike away from the Dreambringer. I'll take you home, I promise. Away from this filthy place. Home to the Faratha and our people. Back to father.

She left him then. Alone with his dreams in a stranger's bed, drifting in the shade world between the living and the dead.

Kasha exited her brother's bedchamber and made her way down the wooden staircase to the ground floor of the vast warehouse. Men and women milled around, carrying in supplies and stacking them under the command of small women in gray cassocks. Barrel after barrel were stacked high, and boxes of trinkets for barter with the northern tribes were stockpiled to one side. Men burnished the runners for the sleighs and sledges, while others greased the slides with oil. Some polished or

CHAPTER NINETEEN

repaired the wooden chassis. In one corner, a blacksmith's forge was in full operation as smithies worked on runner repairs. No one paid Kasha any notice. They had work to do, and a tall girl in outlander furs meant nothing to them.

Once outside the warehouse, it took Kasha a moment to gain her bearings. She grew up near the docks as a child, running and playing with the harbor urchins, though never more than a stone's throw away from her adopted mother's watchful eye. The docks were relatively safe, as long as you avoided falling into the cold waters. Kasha did once, and held her best bonnet high above her head to keep it from getting wet as she was drowning. A sailor plunged in to rescue her from a watery grave, though the scolding from her mother made her wish she sank like a stone.

Kasha knew from an early age she was different from the other children and from her parents. She towered over the boys and girls her own age, and could out wrestle all of them. While she was a tall redhead, her parents were short stocky people of a darker complexion. They were kind enough, and loved her in their own way, but there was always a divide between them. The reason why became obvious when they took her outside of Gastown to meet Tornar for the first time. Her mother cried incessantly as she left with her real father, but there were no regrets for Kasha. She was exhilarated to be going off on an adventure, and leaving behind a world where she never truly belonged. That was five years ago, though it felt like a lifetime.

She wondered if her adoptive parents still occupied the same small house on Mariner's Lane. It was just off the main thoroughfare, and sheltered from the winds, which could sweep through the harbor. It was a small house for three, but cozy and comforting, and her mother kept it neat and tidy. And there was always a pot of stew on the stove for her father when he came home from working a long solar at the docks. It was a simple life, but one free from the violence and turmoil of the Slough or the vices of the Mutton.

Kasha quickly found her bearings as she navigated the familiar pathways of her childhood. The old Miller house, which the children said was haunted by the spirit of an old sea captain, was still there on the corner. Only Kasha was brave enough to go in, but she ran too when the wail from an old drunk got the better of her. There was Butter Row, where she dueled the Bratworth brothers with makeshift wooden swords to an exhausting standstill, until the call for supper ended the clash of junior arms. Blind Pete was still carrying his tray of handcrafted lucky mariner charms to ward off all kinds of evil for superstitious seafaring men. He lifted the bandage covering his seemingly sightless eyes to stare at Kasha as she strode past his station.

Kasha turned the corner onto Mariner's Lane and saw her childhood home. It was even smaller than she remembered. It was respectable on the outside, though a little more rundown from exposure to the elements. Kasha stared down at the deeply polished red front step, half expecting to see her foster mother on hands and knees, scrubbing away to show the neighbors they were not poor. The door was open and she could see a fire burning in the hearth. She hesitated before she went in.

What will I say after all these years? How will they react?

She took a deep breath and passed through the doorway, wiped her feet, and stepped back into her old life.

Her foster mother saw Kasha first. She was standing by the hearth, stirring stew in a large black iron pot dangling over the fire. She stood up, though there was still a stoop in her back, and placed a hand over her open mouth. The other hand held on tightly to the wooden spoon. Kasha was surprised to see her adoptive father there too during the working solar, but she saw the cause. He was sitting in a chair with a cane in one hand, a clay pipe in the other, and a heavy bandage on his right leg. Losing labor through injury was a constant fear for all dock workers and their families. No one could afford the loss of a wage in a hand to mouth existence.

Their given names were Frank and Molly, though they never used them when addressing each other. Their hardscrabble life was reflected in their appearance. Even as a child, Kasha thought her parents were ancient when compared to the other couples in the docklands. Now they were truly wizened, and all they could look forward to was an end of solars in the

CHAPTER NINETEEN

dockworker's poor haus. A grim life with a grim end.

"She's been fighting again, mother," Frank said, communicating through his wife, and never directly to Kasha.

"Leave her be, father. She's come back to us. My little Kasha," Molly said, putting her wooden spoon down on a table. She wiped her hands on her apron, and then dabbed at her eyes with a corner of the cloth.

"She's not so little now, mother. I dare say she could outlift most of the men at the docks."

Molly moved closer to Kasha and took hold of her large hands. Molly's hands were much smaller in comparison, though her grip was surprisingly strong. "Come closer, Kasha. Let me get a better look at you. My, you do have bruises on your face. Couldn't you talk it out without fighting?"

"Not this time, mother," Kasha said.

"Come, sit next to the fire, and I'll make all of us a cup of herbal broth. It will do you good," Molly said, pushing Kasha towards her own chair closest to the fire while she sat on a short stool, which made her appear even smaller.

"Will she be staying long, mother? Her old room is the same as the solar she left us. You've kept it the same, down to the little hobby horse Jasper the carpenter made. I dare say the bed is a little on the small side for her now."

Kasha shook her head. "I can't stay. I stopped by to see how you were faring … and to pick up something my father… Tornar said was of importance."

At the mention of Tornar's name, Frank and Molly stared at each other.

"Tornar. Both a blessing and a curse," Frank said.

"Hush father. Don't go upsetting the child," Molly chastised.

"He brought joy into our life when he left Kasha with us, and broke hearts when he took her away."

Molly stared at her husband, and then dabbed at her eyes again to wipe away the last of her tears. "We had eleven good years, father. And she's back to see us now. It can be like old times again, if just for a short while."

They sat in silence then. The three of them lost in their own thoughts, the only sound the occasional crack of wood in the hearth as the fire consumed the logs, and the soft sucking noise as Frank worked to keep the tabak in his clay pipe smoldering.

Kasha brought the tranquil moment to an end. "Why did Tornar choose you all those years ago?"

Frank savored a mouthful of smoke, and then blew it out up to the rafters of the small cottage. "You can tell it best, mother."

"Not before we all have some herbal broth," Molly replied, as she eased herself up from the stool. She scooped three beakers into a barrel, placed them on the table, and then plucked a poker out of the fire. One by one, she plunged it into the liquid in the cup, and watched as it hissed and boiled. She handed a cup to both Kasha and Frank, and left her own on the table as she recounted the tale for Kasha.

"We lived in the Wildlands back then, trying to make a go of it as homesteaders. The Dux encouraged it, to expand the reach beyond the walls, and push out the northern tribes still lingering in the south. It was not an easy life, but we tried hard to carve something out for ourselves. Father built a cabin with his own hands, not much bigger than this cottage, but it was home. We trapped and traded with the merchants and butchers in Gastown. There were still some old growth trees back then, and we harvested them too. We scraped by as best we could, as we waited for our children to arrive. There was only one, and she was a sickly child. She only blessed us for a few solars before she was called back to the other side of the veil, though long enough to leave grief in our hearts.

That's when Tornar came into our lives. The sight of him terrified us, a giant of a man from the North. But he carried a tiny bundle in his arms, and was ever so gentle with you. It took some of his fearsomeness away, if only for a moment, and we listened to his proposal. He'd heard about a mother who lost her child, and he needed a nursing woman for his own baby daughter. You see, your own mother died in childbirth, and he'd lose you too, if he couldn't find you milk. There was gild for us if we returned to Gastown, and raised you as our own. He needed you safe and out of harm's way, though he never said why you were in danger. So we came

CHAPTER NINETEEN

here, and bought this cottage with his gild, and father took to working in the docks. Tornar said, he'd come back for you when you'd grown, and at an age to understand who you really were. No disrespect to him, but we clung to the hope that solar would never arrive. When it did, our hearts broke again. He sent word to us through another homestead family, and for us to bring you out of Gastown to meet with him. He couldn't set foot inside, you see, on account of his enormousness, and the Dux would have him put to death. We considered ignoring his call, and going on as best we could. But a pact is a pact, and father said we had to honor it, or we'd have to answer for it on the other side when the reckoning came, and our life's tally is counted. So we took you out to meet with your real father, and to set you on your true path, away from the drudgery of Gastown. And now, here you are, back with us."

Kasha remembered the solar well. One moment she was playing with the other dockland children, and the next, her mother was scrubbing her face, and pulling a comb through her long red hair. Tears accompanied the cleansing, though her mother would not say why she was so sad on a bright and cheerful morn. She was bundled into her best dress, and a garland of fresh flowers was placed in her hair. Then the family of three left Gastown, and only two returned.

"And the thing of importance?" Kasha asked.

"Ah, yes. I almost forgot about that. Tornar gave it to us for safekeeping, for when you entered womanhood. A family heirloom of sorts, though on his instructions, we never looked at it. Where did you put it, father?" Molly said.

Frank took another puff from his pipe, and then pointed the stem towards an earthen jug on the top shelf. "It's where it's always been, mother. Tucked away in the granny jar up yonder."

Molly glanced up at the shelf, and then climbed on her stool to reach it, though it was just beyond her grasp. Kasha stood and stretched out for it, and winced at the pain in her ribs. She placed the dusty jar on the table, and pushed a hand inside to pull out a worn leather pouch.

"That's it, mother. That's the thing of importance Tornar left in our keeping. It would be nice to see what it is after all these years," Frank said leaning forward on his cane.

Kasha glanced at her adoptive parents and their eager faces. She pulled on the drawstring and poured the contents into her hand. She held it up for them to see. The chain itself was not much to look at, roughly made metal rings, more to carry the weight than for grace and elegance. The stones were something else. There were seven in all, and their deep rich color pulled in the light.

"Would you look at that, mother? Black Diamonds. And to think just one of them could buy all of Gastown."

She left them then, after placing the small bag of copper coins on the table. It was not much for all of the kindness they had shown her, but it was all she had. Tears welled in her eyes as she stepped out of the cottage and made her way back to Beira's warehouse. Her childhood under Frank and Molly's protection was a happy one, and she would miss them dearly. However, she had a new life now. She was a woman of the north, who discarded frivolous things like comfort and safety. She had a mission to complete and Tornar was calling her back.

Chapter Twenty

Justin : The Apotheka's Apprentice

Justin pondered on how his life had changed so dramatically since the fateful solar in the Dandy Great Hall and his rage got the better of him. Striking fellow Dandies was a transgression they would not allow, and he was banished from their ranks. One moment, he was content with his studies, and Petra the Pythoness was considering access to the Tower of Tomes. The next, he was dragged away by Damm Warriors, and locked up for the common good.

He was still a prisoner in the castellated tower, but his accommodation was upgraded after his fateful meeting with Rafyn. He took the old bearskin, and the daronite rock he named *Safwan*, as keepsakes from his dungeon cell, and of course, he still had the silent gaoler who brought his meals. He had everything he needed except his freedom, and Rafyn promised him that would come in time, provided he upheld his side of the bargain. He had little choice in the matter, but first he needed to hone his studies on a particular subject matter.

Rafyn ensured he had access to everything he required. His writing supplies and handmade papers were brought over from his previous chamber in the Dandy Great Hall, and were carefully arranged in his new quarters. There was ample room, and though the cell was still on the chilly side, he made do with the smelly bearskin wrapped around his shoulders for creature comfort.

Despite her threat to burn the books in the Tower of Tomes, Rafyn proved to be a scholar in her own right. She understood the language of the Ma'din to make book solicitations to Petra the Pythoness, who was amazed by her sudden interest in the subject of herbal prescriptions, medicinal compounds, and measurement systems for precise weighing. Most surprising was a sudden interest in the varieties of tabak for healing purposes.

Justin requested books and papers by the Apotheka's dozen, and they came in short order. Some were already translated into Varic, such as *Fundamental Herbs,* by Aslam, and *350 Treatments and 800 prescriptions from Medicinal Plants,* translated from the initial works of the Sul scholar and great healer, Zhang. Justin would have dearly loved to delve deeper into Zhang's *Internal Medicine,* and the art of needle placement, but there was no time for that. Instead, he kept to potions, poultices, prescriptions, and steam distillation of plants. He became a master of the uses of billeewort for stomach cramps, motherwort for alleviating menstrual discomfort, witch hazel for treating sore muscles and inflammation, and milk thistle and devil's claw for soothing gout.

Most times, the tomes were delivered by Konna apprentices under the tutelage of Petra. However, on occasion, Rafyn made the delivery, and stayed long enough to quiz Justin on his progress. She never talked about the family connection, and Justin never asked, though from their obvious resemblance, he surmised they were siblings. It was simply a business relationship. Justin would get his freedom of sorts, in exchange for information picked up within Gastown.

"It won't work, you know. Who will come to someone as young as me for their treatment," Justin complained, as he casually flipped through *The Apotheka's Secret Lore* by Claudis, until he came to the section on the healing properties of dragon bone. He took a scribe and quickly jotted down the translation.

Rafyn watched him work. "You know it's a pity you were born a Dandy. A mind as sharp as yours deserves to be in a Konna body."

CHAPTER TWENTY

She examined one of his drawings of yarrow, and nodded in satisfaction at the clear crisp representation of the flowering plant. "And it will work, Justin. You're to be an Apotheka's Apprentice, under the tutelage of Habala. A very apt name, don't you think? No one sees your master, of course, and you relay all messages back and forth between the patient and your imaginary teacher. Plans are already in motion, and I've purchased a small building in the heart of the Four Kith in Habala's name. The plant and potions you requested are being assembled as we speak, at no small expense, I might add. All you have to do is watch and observe, and pass on everything you hear to me."

Justin looked up from his studies and stared intently at Rafyn. He was struck again at the similarity in appearances. The black hair, the gaunt, stretched features. Even some of their mannerisms were identical. "I'm no Apotheka, and you expect me to treat people? They'll chase me away at the first misdiagnosis. And what of your plans then?"

Rafyn held his gaze, until Justin was forced to look away. "There is no Apotheka of worth in the Four Kith since Master Culpepper died and his apprentices looted the building, down to his death sheet and candelabra. The ones left are hacks who rely on superstition and placebos. You know more about apotheka secrets than all of them combined. People will find you, and business will boom. Trust will build and secrets will spill. And I want to know it all. You'll be my eyes and ears in the Four Kith. Justin the Apotheka's Apprentice will be a friend to all, and my fly on the wall. Isn't that a fair price to pay for your freedom?"

"Freedom? What freedom? You'll have me dangling on a string, more puppet than man!"

"I could have you returned to your dungeon quarters if you like. Along with that stinking bearskin and the glowing rock you talk to like a friend. And no access to any books," Rafyn hissed.

"That would be a waste of my considerable talents."

"Then we have an agreement?"

"What about security? By all accounts the Four Kith is a very dangerous place. I won't survive a lunar!"

"Apotheka's are healers. Even the lowest form of human life does them no harm. No guards," Rafyn said. "I ask again, do we have an agreement?"

Justin nodded his head. "I'll dangle for you. Until I give out the wrong potion, or whisper the wrong secret. Then I'll dangle at the end of someone else's rope."

"Until that fateful solar, the Apotheka's shop is yours."

Rafyn turned to leave, and then stopped at the cell door. "Tell me, Justin. Do you hear voices in your head when you sleep at night?"

Justin hesitated before he answered. "Just one."

"And the voice speaks to you in Ma'din?"

Justin nodded.

A former Red Shadow, a ramrod straight individual who now made a living offering security to Burghmeisters, met Justin at the citadel gates and escorted him across the Bridge of Broken Souls to his new abode in the heart of the Four Kith. Justin cast a wistful glance back at the citadel as he crossed the bridge. It had been his home for the past seventeen years, and his sanctuary. Now he was expected to fend for himself in the rough and tumble world of the common folk. He felt both scared and excited at the same time. He was a free man and yet still a prisoner. He was also masquerading as a healer and a spy.

They stopped in front of an old worn building, which leaned precariously over the street. A sign proclaiming *Habala The Apotheka* hung above the doorway. Since most of the folk in the Four Kith could not read, a picture of an ancient healer with long white flowing locks and a white beard surrounded by herbs and potions, clearly marked the proprietor's business.

So you're Habala in the painted flesh. Nice to meet you, Master.

Without a word, Justin's guide and protector handed him a large key to the building, turned on his heels and left him all alone, the sole proprietor of the Four Kith's latest apothekaria.

The great unveiling was somewhat of an anticlimax for Justin, as he inserted the key, and stepped into the gloom. In his mind's eye, he saw shelf upon shelf of all the ingredients he had requested, neatly stacked and

CHAPTER TWENTY

labeled based on the ordering system he had devised. In reality, the shelves were empty, and the barrels and boxes were a mishmash of dried herbs, old bones, dying plants, and poorly blended potions.

Justin wasted no time in getting his apothekaria in order. None of the ingredients were labeled, so he divided them out by type. Tabak to the left, herbs to the right, bones, whole and ground to the back, and medicinal plants to the front. His plan was to label and stack the ones he could easily identify, and then spend a little more time on the ones where he was a little unsure. A misidentified herb, or a wrongly blended potion, could lead to the illness or death of a patient, and a swift end to his budding career.

He started with the tabak, as the least invasive and likely the easiest to identify. Using Maratha's *Tabak for Medicinal Uses and the Pleasure of the Smoke,* as his guiding light, he pinched, smelled, examined, and tasted each one. There were cases of Old Burley, Latak, Peri Peri, and even the hard to come by dark fired Sol. There were some medicinal uses for stomach cramps when steeped in hot water, but mainly they were for enjoyment. The Barri, Lolo, and Ma could also be used for lightheaded pleasure, but medicinally they helped ease anxiety and stress, and were especially effective when combined with a sweat bath.

Separating the bones was a trickier proposition. The horn of the kombo, and the tusk of the wooly mamont was relatively simple. Dragon bone, and tiger teeth came next. However, testing some of the powdered bone was extremely challenging. The bitter taste of one casket led Justin to believe it belonged to antlers of the giant poro. However, he was not entirely sure, so he put it to one side. He was sure one casket was a hoax, and contained the ground bones of an assortment of tundra animals and nothing remotely exotic. Its only purpose was to feed plant growth, and that was a rarity in the Four Kith.

Justin enjoyed his time identifying, separating, storing, and labeling the herbs and medicinal plants. By the end of it, his palate was shot, and his sense of smell was lost to the heady aroma of the combined bouquet. At the end of the fragrant expedition, he had lavender, witch hazel, billeewort, yarrow, burdock, valerian, rose petals, cinnamon, lemon balm, peppermint, rosemary, dux basil, and the prize of all, a small pouch of golden strands of the much sought after man-root, dandra.

Justin had a few more tasks to complete before he could consider his work done, and settle down in the small bedchamber in the upper story of the house. He moved the distilling equipment for steaming and extracting liquid into a small room off to the side, and used another small room for blending herbs, mixing potions, and shaving plants. Next, he set up the front parlor for meeting with clientele. A simple bench for waiting patients, and a private chamber for consultations. Finally, he set about working on Habala himself. As a special request to further his own anatomical studies, and not really related to the work of an Apotheka, he asked for a fully functional human skeleton. He did not ask where Rafyn procured it from, but was happy to see the flesh was completely removed. He put it to use as his makeshift master. He sat the skeleton in a chair behind a desk, and used wire and cordage to hold it firmly in place. He wrapped the bones in his old bearskin, not to keep warm, but to bulk out the figure, and placed a black scholar's cap on his skull. He rigged up a contraption of sorts, which would blow out a steady stream of tabak, as if the old man was deep in thought within his aromatic cloud.

After consuming a bowl of mushroom soup he had made himself in the back kitchen, Justin finally lay down on his bed. It was the first time in many a lunar he did not wrap himself up in his old bearskin to keep the night chills at bay, and he missed the familiar musky smell. Only then did he realize how exhausted he was, and the enormity of the task in front of him. His knowledge was book bound, and not from practical application. He was an imposter in a world where a simple transgression led to violence, and spilling secrets was certain death. Life was freedom in an Apotheka's gilded cage.

When the dead of night came, and he slipped into the dream state, he listened once more to the secret voice in the lost language of Ma'din. The voice told him to be confident and to continue with his studies. Customers would soon look past his young age, and respect him for his knowledge. He was there to help and they would seek him out. And they would confide

CHAPTER TWENTY

in him.

No customers came on the following solar, or the one after that. Justin whiled away the hours reading, transcribing, and concocting some ancient herbal blend from *The Lost Secrets of Herbal Lore*. Other than he had nothing to report to Rafyn, it was not such a bad life. He took to talking with Habala for company.

"No one today, Master Habala. I suppose they haven't heard of your healing powers just yet. Give it time, master."

The bell above the door rang as it opened, and a young waif of a girl stepped into the parlor. She furtively glanced from side to side, and considered bolting from the strange room, and back to the relative safety of her own bleak world outside.

"Step forward child," Justin said, deepening his voice to sound more mature. He towered over the girl, which did nothing to put her at ease. "What ails you?"

The girl looked up at him, and held out her hand. "Iz 'as a scorcher. Right raggy."

Although Justin saw the girl's ailment, and could readily prescribe the necessary treatment for a burn, he realized his knowledge of the common tongue was academic, and the vernacular application, especially from a denizen of the lower reaches of the Four Kith, was currently beyond his ken. He would need a crash course in gutter speak. He was about to reach for the ingredients, when he realized the subterfuge of consulting with Master Habala was required.

"Let me consult with my master," Justin said, and disappeared into the back room for a moment, and stood before the skeleton and the bearskin, which was hidden from the young girl's eyes. He popped back into the waiting room, and beckoned the girl to take a seat. "Master Habala recommends a blend of honeycomb and the dried yellow petals of the calendula, wrapped in a gauze covering. Now make sure you keep it covered, and don't lick it off."

GASTOWN

The girl nodded her head, and sat patiently, as Justin first cleaned her wound, and then applied the sticky treatment to the palm of her hand, and carefully sealed it in gauze. By trial and error, he learned from the girl, a storekeep had applied a hot poker to her hand as punishment for looking at his merchandise. She was adamant she was not trying to steal anything, though Justin had his doubts. Still, it was harsh maltreatment and would leave a permanent scar.

As Justin finished wrapping the wound, the young girl held out a shaved copper coin as payment, which he politely refused. "You are Master Habala's first customer in the Four Kith. Tell your friends and neighbors about us."

Two long hours passed before the bell rang again, and the second customer entered the apothekaria. This one was in marked contrast to the young girl, and had an air of arrogance and self importance about him. He was not alone. As the customer lowered his stout frame into the nearest chair with the aid of a walking stick, and elevated his right foot onto a nearby stool, the bodyguard stood by the door.

Justin entered the parlor and placed a cup of herbal tea beside the gentleman, and offered a second cup to his escort, who ignored the kind gesture. He turned back to face the corpulent man sitting in the chair, who was now wiping his sweaty brow.

"How may we be of assistance, good sir?" Justin asked.

"I've been to every apothokaria in the Four Kith, and no one can help. I dare say, I'm wasting my time here too. Fakes and charlatans, the lot of you!" the Burghmeister growled.

"I can assure you, Master Habala offers the finest care available. Now, if you'd be so kind as to explain your symptoms?" Justin asked.

"Send your master out then, and I'll deal directly with him."

Justin smiled meekly. This was the first real test. Would patients accept dealing with the apprentice while the master stayed veiled behind the screen?

"I'm afraid my master no longer ventures on this side of the curtain. I relay the symptoms to him, and he prescribes the remedy. He's very

CHAPTER TWENTY

accurate."

There was silence for a moment, and then the Burghmeister shuffled in his chair. Justin was worried he was going to get up and leave, but he was simply positioning himself better to remove his right boot. When he did, he exposed a big toe which glowed like a daronite rock.

"Aches something awful when the gout is upon me, so it does," the Burghmeister groaned. "Nothing, I repeat, nothing helps."

Justin thought about advising the tubby fellow to change his diet and refrain from eating so much rich food, but he held his tongue. "Let me consult with my master, and I'll be right back."

"And what's that fine smell while we're at it? Old Burley if my snout doesn't deceive me, and it seldom does," the Burghmeister said.

"You have a fine nose, sir. Old Burley it is," Justin replied.

"Well, if you're selling tabak too, I'll take twenty bowls with me."

Justin left the room to consult with his imaginary master, and reappeared with a basin of hot water, a towel over his shoulder, and bowl with a host of ingredients. First, he placed the gouty foot in the water, and then wrapped it in the warm towel, while he mixed the components of ginger, milk thistle, devil's claw, and burdock root together into a fine paste. Once completed, he removed the towel and applied the poultice to the offending hallux. The relief for the Burghmeister was profound and he let out a sigh of relief.

Two satisfied customers was a recipe for success, and word quickly spread about the validity of the latest Apotheka to grace the Four Kith. No one knew exactly where he came from, and rumors abounded. Some said he came by ship from the southern kingdoms, others said he arrived by caravan from the west, though no one had made that journey for an age. Whatever the origin story, all agreed the master was a healer, and his tall apprentice patiently applied the results of his diagnosis.

In short order, the apothekaria was a thriving concern, and Justin was having difficulty managing the crowded waiting room and the extra line outside. He got word to Rafyn he needed help via the drop box method she recommended, and the silent guide from his first sojourn into the Four Kith was hired to keep things orderly and the herd under control. Justin treated everyone as equals, and Burghmeisters were not permitted to jump the queue ahead of mudlarks. Each paid according to their means and conscience. The tabak trade was a thriving concern too, and Justin soon ran short of supplies. Standard shipments from the south were set up.

Justin used the gild raised to purchase more herbs and medicinal plants. He also let it be known he was a collector of information too, and would pay for it in free treatment or coin. Mudlarks, fisher wives, and dockworkers did not know why he was interested in the everyday gossip of the Four Kith, but they were happy to share. Everything, no matter how trivial, made its way back to Rafyn.

The waiting room was suddenly quiet and Justin soon found out why as he escorted a tailor's wife with a flatulence problem out of the private parlor. She clutched the bag containing a mixture of peppermint, chamomile, caraway, anise, and fennel tightly to her chest, as if worried the mites who now poured into the apothekaria were here to steal her cure and condemn her to a leaky gas existence. They paid her no heed as she hurried out of the door and back to her sewing.

There were five of them in the room. Menacing boys with smeared black makeup around their eyes. Four of them were dressed for the streets, shabby clothes and scuffed boots. The fifth, who ignored Justin and sat down in one of the chairs, wore a tailored outfit. His boots were freshly polished. Justin could tell he was the reason for the visit. The eyes behind the makeup were bloodshot, there was a rigidity in how he held himself, and he was having some difficulty in breathing, though he tried his best to conceal it.

"I'm afraid there's no jumping the queue. You'll need to wait your turn. I believe Mr. Willoughby the chandler was up next," Justin said, trying to sound in charge, though failing miserably.

One of the mites stood before Justin and looked him up and down with a sneer on his face. Justin towered over him, but he knew the boy was a born killer, and he could only push things so far. He also smelled of smoke and char, and the mark of his trade was evident in the burn scar running through his scalp.

CHAPTER TWENTY

"The chandler decided 'e 'ad wax to mold at 'ome. Same with 'em other fishes outside. So wez not claim jumpin', on account everyone else 'as bounced," the mite said.

"Well, if you put it like that, what can I do for you?" Justin asked. "I'm assuming your friend over there is the reason for this visit?"

The mite jabbed a thumb in his own chest. "I'm Fleet Dawkins." He pointed the same thumb at the boy sitting in the chair. "That over there is Carlos Grimm." He waited, as if the names would mean something to Justin. They did not.

"'E's come to see the Apotheka, on account of some 'eadaches, 'e's 'avin'. Nothing more. Just give 'im some powders an' the like, an' we'll be on our way," Fleet said.

"I'm afraid there's a little more to it than that. First, no one sees Master Habala directly. I'lll discuss with Mister Grimm, in private of course, and relay the information to my master. Then he prescribes the necessary course of treatment."

"We came all this way to see the Apotheka, not the bleedin' apprentice," Fleet hissed. "Now get out of the way afore I do for you." He pulled a knife from his belt and brandished it at Justin to emphasize his point.

"Fleet, let 'im be, and do as e' says. Yuz know the rules about no 'arm to healing folk," Carlos said. His voice was muted, but still carried authority.

Fleet reluctantly lowered his blade.

Justin turned his back on Fleet and faced Carlos. "If you'd like to come this way, we can get started," he said, gesturing towards the private parlor.

Carlos stood up on shaky legs, and for a moment, Justin thought he would need to reach out a helping hand. However, he instinctively knew Carlos was struggling not to show any further weakness, so he let him enter the parlor under his own steam. Once inside the room, Carlos virtually collapsed into another chair. He held his hands to either side of his temples, and pressed hard as if attempting to squeeze out the pain.

"How long have you been having headaches?" Justin asked.

"A couple of lunars."

"And they're getting steadily worse, and for a longer duration?"

Carlos nodded his head.

Justin reached out a hand and took hold of Carlos's right wrist. He checked his pulse with three fingers, and counted. Next, he placed a hand on Carlos's chest, and listened to his breathing. Finally, he checked his eyes.

"Your pulse is racing, your breathing is fast and shallow, and your eyes are unfocused. There's more too. Uncontrollable fear hits you all of a sudden, and you black out, don't you?"

Carlos looked up at him. "No one knows about 'em. They've only 'appened twice."

"But you feel as if you're not in control, an imposter, and you can't have that. Perceived weakness will be the death of you."

Carlos nodded. "Can you do anythin'?" At that moment, he was just a vulnerable adolescent seeking help.

"Rest here for a moment, and let me consult with Master Habala. He'll know the remedy."

Justin left the private parlor and entered the back room. He stood before his seated makeshift master, as if they were in deep consultation. It gave him time to formulate his diagnosis. The physical symptoms were obvious to him after reading Chosi's *The Body and the Mind Connection* from cover to cover, and back again. The blackouts from panic attacks were a likely progression and his educated guess. Carlos Grimm was manifesting symptoms from childhood trauma brought on by physical or sexual abuse, and there was the overlapping suffering caused by witnessing or engaging in violent acts. Chosi examined countless soldiers returning from war, and the majority were stuck in a permanent state between fight or flight. The real cure was changing the environment, and removing all of the negative influences. However, Justin suspected that was not an option for Carlos Grimm. Weakness in the Four Kith meant certain death. All he could do was offer a temporary solution to manage the inner pain, and dampen down the raging demons.

Justin returned to the private parlor and his patient with a pipe stuffed with the finest Ma from the south, and a lighted taper. He handed the pipe

CHAPTER TWENTY

to Carlos, and instructed him to suck on it, while he applied the flame. The room soon filled with the smoke, and the accompanying musky, woody, peppery aroma. It was an acquired taste, and not one to Justin's initial liking.

"It's not like ordinary tabak. Don't swish the smoke around your mouth for the taste alone. You need to inhale and suck the smoke down into your lungs for the best results," Justin said.

The effect on Carlos was instantaneous. He sat back in his chair and immediately relaxed. His pulse slowed down, his breathing stabilized, and his eyes abandoned the lost soul stare. There was even the glimmer of a smile on his lips.

"It's not a cure, of course. But it does alleviate your symptoms. I'd recommend only one bowl a solar, and an extra one only when the pressure builds. It can be addictive, and also lead to more mellow moods, which might not fly in your line of work, whatever that is. Thirty bowls should be enough for now, and I can set up a standing order. Mister Dawkins or one of his associates can pick them up for you. Now, if you don't mind, after you finish that pipe, I'd like to see if my other patients will return."

Return they did, in droves. Word of mouth coupled with successful treatments, was a very potent marketing tool, and Master Habala's eminence quickly spread to all corners and crannies of Gastown. Success brought a steady stream of customers, both new and repeat, which meant Justin had to turn people away as darkness came and he dropped exhausted into his cot. Some cried, some shouted, and others threatened physical violence, but they came back the following solar, and left as converts to the healing powers of the Apotheka. There were disappointments too. An old cripple was dismayed when Justin had no potions to help him grow back his lost foot, and a Burghmeister's wife was livid when there was no elixir available to make her daughter beautiful. He did offer an herbal blend to assist with weight loss, and a recommendation to put a lock on the pantry door. An indignant mother and daughter waddled away with a vow never to return.

The waiting room was empty again, and Justin was about to chastise

Fleet Dawkins for gratuitously removing patients when the thirty bowls of Ma were packaged, sealed, and ready for pickup. However, there were no mites to face. Instead, he was confronted by a colossus of a man who took up half of the room by himself. He had two accomplices, not nearly so large, but equally menacing. They all bore the same scar, which depicted the letter *kaun* in Varic and *kenaz* in the common tongue under their right eye. The symbology, which obviously represented some gang affiliation fascinated him.

"Whom do I have the pleasure of addressing?" Justin asked. His mouth was as dry as his words.

"My name's Toby Myers, and we've come for the Apotheka. And who be you?" the giant asked.

"Justin, the Apotheka's Apprentice."

"No family name to offer us?"

"Just Justin."

"Well, Just Justin, lead on," Toby said, gesturing towards the back room with a meaty paw.

"I'm afraid you don't understand. It doesn't work like that…"

"Really?" Toby said, and grabbed hold of Justin by the collar and escorted him, his feet barely making contact with the ground, into the back room and the inner chamber of the apothekaria.

Toby stared at the skeleton with the hat on his head at a jaunty angle, and the old bearskin wrapped around his shoulders. The pipe contraption on the desk billowed tabak smoke into the air at regular intervals.

"A bit on the thin side, isn't he?" Toby said. "You have some explaining to do boy, and be quick about it. I know a shell game when I see one."

Justin had a cover story he had worked out with Rafyn if their ruse was discovered before they could send Habala off on a respectable retirement, and the apprentice stepped into the master's shoes. He relayed it on to Toby now as he dangled from the man mountain's grip.

"I'm afraid Master Habala passed away on our journey to Gastown. He was over a hundred years old, and he simply went in his sleep. We'd already sent gild ahead to purchase the store, and everything else was tied up in the

CHAPTER TWENTY

supplies. I was close to the end of my apprenticeship, having been with my master for fifteen years, so I figured I could consult with him as I always did, only this time the answers were in my own head, and I could hand out the remedies."

Justin waited anxiously for the big man's judgment. His time in Gastown and the apothekaria experiment could be over in an instant. He would be exposed as a fraud, or worse, bludgeoned to death, stabbed, or strangled. The possibilities for his demise were endless, and equally alarming. Alive or dead, he'd be of no use to Rafyn, and the game of spies and subterfuge would end, and with it his freedom or life.

Toby released his grip. "Who knows about this con?"

"Just you and I," Justin lied.

Toby shrugged his huge shoulders. "Makes no difference to me, as long as the cure works, and Pete's satisfied. If it doesn't…"

"Pete?" Justin asked.

"Puzzle Pete. The top dog Swell Daddy in the Mutton, and leader of us here Crimpers. Now grab your bag of tricks, boy, and let's be off."

"Wait, it's not that simple. I have to have an idea of what ails Pete. It would be easier if he came here, and I have everything at hand."

Toby shook his head. "Pete don't step foot into the Four Kith. There's a war started, and he don't leave the safety of the Mutton."

A war? Rafyn will want to hear about this.

"Can you give me anything to work with?"

Toby scratched his head, as if he had a delicate subject he did not want to touch upon. "Well, it's like this. Pete has a fondness for the ladies, and he's not too careful about where he puts it, if you catch my drift."

Justin's heart sank. Venereal diseases came in all shapes and sizes, and infected all shapes and sizes without exception. For the treatable ones there were remedies with rosemary, basil, oak bark, soma, honeysuckle, ox knee, and even a paste made from moldy brood. There were some quack cures by pushing trace metals into the infected member. However, the results were generally fatal, and in this case, would be fatal for him too. He preferred to stick with the Apotheka's course of treatment. If bad luck prevailed, and it was identified as a permanent infection, then there was no solution Justin could recall from any of his research. He could alleviate symptoms, but provide no remedial action.

Justin took a canvas traveling bag and filled it with as many herbs and plants he thought would cover all bases, and the necessary equipment to weigh ingredients, blend a salve, or mix a powder. The thought of touching Pete's putrid phallus, or cupping contaminated scrotum filled him with horror. The alternative was to throw up his arms and accept his fate here and now at the murderous hands of Toby Myers.

"Shall we go then?" Justin said.

Chapter Twenty One

Chandra : The Purge

Life in the gardens was not the same since the Damm Warriors carried off Tana, and seized Manoj on the following solar. The Andra, ever a peace-loving people, returned to their work in nurturing the plants, and abandoned their nonviolent dissent. Only a handful of the Erupu young men, in solidarity with Manoj, stamped on red peppers and covered their hanging man talisman in the juices as symbolic blood, a gesture of defiance the Var never saw.

Chandra missed Tana. Even her spiteful stinging words were preferable to her absence. Her parents took it harder still. Father lost his smile, and spent long hours sitting alone, wallowing in paternal grief. Mother cried often and her joy of cooking left her so the food she prepared was loveless too. Only Amma accepted Tana's fate, as the wheel turned. Little Sri went on as before, pulling weeds, and silently and delicately snipping plants with his shears.

No one knew the fate of Tana and Manoj since the Damm Warrior broke the vow and refused to return the bride after *Fyrst Nott,* and no one talked about it. Some of the other families shunned Chandra and her family, as if the disgrace of losing their first born brought shame on them all. Chandra hoped the couple were somewhere in the citadel, united again as husband and wife. However, she could not feel her sister's life essence so close. It was still there, though a faint echo of her vibrancy. As the solars passed, it drifted even further away.

Chandra continued with her language learning. She was accompanied by two other girls, one from the Preena, and one from the Narinja, as they studied at the feet of Katla. However, Chandra did not respect her teacher the same way. She was still kind and gentle as before, but Chandra now regarded her as an overseer, and she was only instructing them in the common language to serve the twisted needs of the Var. Chandra was a gifted student, like Tana before her, but the exhilaration of learning dissipated with the Var betrayal.

Chandra looked up with a start as a Damm Warrior stood behind Katla and stared down at her and her two fellow students. At first she thought it was the Lady Aldith, the one who came and snatched Tana away, and returned again for Manoj. There was a great similarity in the size and facial features. However, the eyes were different. One was blue and the other a milky green, and there was no emotion behind them, only hollowness and a soulless depth. There was no flicker of excitement, the way Lady Aldith gazed upon Tana. Chandra shuddered at the thought of being carried away by this one.

The Damm Warrior spoke to Katla in the common tongue. "Teach them well, Katla. They have important work ahead of them." She turned and limped away with a cane for support without waiting for a reply.

The whistle blew and the Andra finished their garden work under the protection of the glass domes for another solar. Chandra helped her Amma over to the blanket where they sat and ate the family meal. It was an uninspiring sambar, which lacked flavor and passion. Her father was as silent as Sri as he dolefully ate his evening repast. Her mother's tears diluted the stew. Her cousins played music in the background, bereft of joy or spirit. No one danced.

"What's to become of us, Amma?" Chandra asked.

"Whatever do you mean, child? We'll go on as before, as we always do. Working in the garden and nurturing our charges. The wheel turns," Amma

CHAPTER TWENTY ONE

replied. She dipped bread into her bowl of thin stew and slowly chewed. "Shall I tell you about *The Long Journey* again?"

Chandra shook her head. She had lost her appetite, both for food and stories, and pushed her bowl away. "It feels different, Amma. As if Tana and Manoj leaving us was just the start of something bad happening."

"Hush child. Gloom and doom serves no purpose. Sad thoughts bring sad endings. Focus on the here and now, and maintaining life in the garden. That's our true purpose."

"Is it, Amma? All we do is serve the Var. They take our food, they take our people. They have a word for it in the common tongue: *Slaaf*. That's all we are, that's all we've ever been. We have no free will of our own, and we live to serve our mistresses."

Amma smiled and gently tapped the side of her head with the tips of her fingers of both hands. "We're free up here, Chandra. It's not such a bad life if you don't let anger and hatred consume you. We're blessed with the gardens, we have full stomachs, we have each other, and the wheel turns. Be good in this life, and you'll be rewarded in rebirth."

Chandra stood up. Anger did consume her. She was angry at the Var, and now she was angry at her Amma too. "A spoke in the wheel broke when they took Tana and Manoj." She kicked over her bowl and left the family to wander in the garden alone.

Chandra was full of remorse for how she had talked back to her Amma. Was she becoming like Tana? Sharp-tongued and spiteful? She could not bring herself to apologize and ask for forgiveness. Instead, she avoided her amma as best she could, and lost herself in her garden work and language studies. She hoped time would be a healer, and they could return to their lives as before. But the wheel had turned, and the path was set.

Before Tana's wedding solar, her father had talked about her own courtship with a boy from the Preena, and she had relished the thought of a new life working with the spices and aromatic herbs each and every solar. That dream was at an end. Her father lost interest in pursuing a suitable hand for her, and the family in question moved on from the shame of association with them. If time was a great healer, Chandra wished for the solar and lunar to spin faster and end their grief.

They came just after work had started for the new solar and the Andra were already out working in the gardens. Red Shadows, hundreds of them with their long halberds, poured into the glass dome, and fanned out behind them. There were Damm Warriors too, and at their command, the heavily armed men lowered their weapons, trampled over the vegetables and plants with no respect, and herded the Pacca towards the entrance of the dome. Children cried, women wailed, and the men frantically asked what was going on in a language the Var and their soldiers cared not to understand.

Chandra was swept up in the human wave, and pushed along with the others. She was able to take hold of Sri's hand, and grip it tight. She looked into his eyes, and saw fear and uncertainty. She had no doubt the same look was in her eyes too, but she had to stay strong for her brother. She squeezed his hand firmly, and moved forward with the press. One of the old men fell to the ground, and people stepped over him as best they could, unable to stop to help. Two Red Shadows pulled him roughly to his feet, and pushed him along behind the throng.

The other clans were being herded too, out of their domes and down towards the River of Life, where the dead were cremated on funeral pyres and the ashes pushed into the waters to drift away on this life's final journey, before the rebirth. The Erupu, Narinja, Banda, and Preena, all mixed with the Pacca in a sea of confused colors as they were driven forward by the Red Shadows and their Damm Warrior mistresses.

The funeral site was not meant to hold so many people at one time, and the Andra were tightly pressed together by the relentless drive of the Red Shadows. Chandra could feel her chest tightening as she shuffled forward within the squeezing mass of people. It was worse for Sri and the other children who could not see what was going on, and were crushed down low within the human wave. Some of the young men pulled themselves out of the jam, and climbed the stone walls on either side of the walkway. The Red Shadows did not stop them, as long as they moved forward and down with the rest of the Andra.

CHAPTER TWENTY ONE

Chandra saw their final destination ahead, but did not understand the purpose. The Andra had never been paraded in front of the Var dignitaries before, but she was certain that was who they were. Her people came to a stop in front of a raised stage, guarded by a thin line of Red Shadows in front. In center stage, there was the Dux, a small round woman encased in a black dress, sitting on a majestic throne. A gold crown, which seemed a little too big for her head, perched at an angle which threatened to topple over. In one hand she held a heavy orb, and in the other a scepter. Her ministers of state were on either side. Small dumpy women like herself, as well as tall Damm Warriors, and another tall woman also in black, who seemed to be in charge of the proceedings. Katla was there too, taking instruction from the woman in black.

Chandra glanced over at the River of Life to her right. No funeral pyres were in sight, and no charred remains were in readiness to be spilled into the waters and away from the gardens.

Why bring us here?

The Andra went silent as they waited to understand their fate. It was not long in coming. The woman in black stepped forward, and unrolled a scroll. Katla stood by her side, and searched the crowd for her charges. She spotted Chandra not too deep in the crowd, and beckoned her forward.

"Chandra, Saanvi, Nithya! Push through to the front. We need you to translate for your people," Katla said. There was a friendly smile on her face, which Chandra no longer trusted.

Chandra moved through the front ranks as politely as she could, though she never let go of Sri's hand.

"What is she saying?" an Erupu man asked as Chandra went by. She ignored him. Time to pass on the Var declaration soon enough.

"That's right, come on through," Katla said, as her three interpreters finally made their way to the front. "Chandra to the middle … with her little brother, I see. Yes, stand just here. Saanvi, over to the left please, and Nithya, to the right. Good. Good. Now remember to raise your voices, and make sure the people at the back can hear. This is a very important solar for us all. Lady Rafyn will read a proclamation. I will convert to the common tongue, and please translate to your people as accurately as you can. You were all wonderful students, and I thank you for your diligence and hard work."

Were? Why did she use the past tense?

With a bow towards the Dux, Rafyn began to read, and via the common tongue, it was translated to the Andra, who waited anxiously to hear why they had been gathered at the River of Life for some sort of proclamation.

"In the presence of the Dux, first of the Var, ruler of Varstad, Assaborg, and Varlanda beyond the walls, we bid you welcome." Rafyn paused to make sure the translations were relayed smoothly and then proceeded.

"We give thanks to the Andra. We brought you here over three hundred and fifty years ago at the commencement of the Great Year. Long have you toiled in the glass domes to provide sustenance for Varstad. Now another Great Year is upon us, and the cycle renews."

"The wheel turns," someone in the crowd shouted, and there were murmurs of agreement.

"Our Pythoness, our stargazer, has made all of the necessary calculations. The heavenly bodies are aligned, and the charts show it is time for the Andra to return from whence you came."

A cheer went up from the Andra closest to Saanvi on the left. "We're going home!" they cried. Men and women dropped to their knees and kissed the ground. "A new Long Journey!"

"What is happening over there?" An elder from the Preena asked Chandra. "What did they hear that we didn't?"

"I translated as heard," Chandra said. "The Andra to return from whence they came."

"Which could mean we're going home, or…"

Rafyn continued. "All possessions, all crops, will be consumed. Fire is the great cleanser."

Some people at the back of the crowd, and then the men high up on the walls, pointed behind them. Shrieks of anguish grew as more people turned to see the commotion. Red Shadows carrying flaming torches moved from hut to hut and through the gardens igniting everything.

CHAPTER TWENTY ONE

"They're burning the gardens! Our possessions too. Everything is in flames!"

Even from the front, Chandra could see the smoke billowing upwards. She held tightly to Sri's hand, and continued to translate the words passed to her from Katla, as Rafyn raised her voice.

"We purge the land with fire, and we purge the people with water, the greatest purifier of all!"

Purge?

Chandra did not know the word, so stopped her interpretation. She pulled Sri closer to her and hugged him tightly.

"What did she say, Chandra? Please, explain!" a Pacca neighbor asked.

Chandra remained silent. There was nothing else to say. The Andra were simply chattels of the Var. They were there to be used as beasts of burden. Nothing more, nothing less. The Var did not break their word. They knew from the beginning the fate of the Andra. Now their time was at an end and the wheel would turn no more. Time to give up these bodies and seek a better life in the next incarnation.

The steam whistle from the clock tower blew louder than ever before. The Andra, shocked by the noise, covered their ears and dropped to the ground. Family members hugged each other tightly, relishing what could be their final embrace. Even the Var nobility were shaken by the high-pitched shrill sound. The Konna women stuffed fingers into their ears, and the Dux discarded her orb and scepter and covered her own ears. Only the Damm Warriors remained stoic.

The whistle served as a signal, and four teams of Red Shadows, two on either side of the makeshift stage, moved into position, wheeling forward large contraptions with long hoses attached. The line of Red Shadow who had been covering them, moved three paces behind. With a signal from Rafyn, the hoses came alive and high velocity streams of water blasted into the Andra. Other Red Shadows opened sluice gates which caused the water current to increase.

Men, women, and children, old, and young, were bowled off their feet as the water cannons mowed them down, and pushed them towards the fast flowing River of Life in a tangled mass of bodies. Clothes were torn off as the force of the water disrobed many. An Erupu man was blown off the wall and hit his head on the hard ground. He lay there, unmoving, as the water carried his blood down towards the river. The screaming was pitiful as people cried in desperation to be saved. Some of the Andra tried to run back towards their former homes and gardens. However, water cannons were now there too, and pushed them back into the soaking multitude There was no pity or remorse from the Var. High on the stage, the Dux bounced on her throne and clapped her hands in excitement at the aquatic show.

Chandra's breath was taken away as the first stream from a water cannon hit her in the chest and neck. The shock from the cold and the intensity of the water pressure was immediate, but she managed to hold onto Sri as the two of them were knocked off their feet, and tumbled and turned with their sodden kinfolk on their forced passage towards the River of Life.

She could hear the screams and heavy splashes as bodies, living and dead, made contact with the turbulent water. Some plunged like stones, some in their panic, clung onto neighbors and dragged them under as they vainly tried to save themselves. Others managed to keep their heads above the surface and thrashed their arms and legs as the current carried them away.

The sheer ferocity of the drenching pulled Chandra's dress off, and she rolled naked, head over heels into the river. The initial blast of the water stream was one thing, but the shock of the cold river water encompassed her whole being and paralyzed her senses. She tried desperately to hold onto her little brother, but the crashing of bodies forced her to let go. Her last contact was the touch of his fingertips as he was pulled from her grip.

The press of bodies all around her forced Chandra down into the depths of the river. Someone kicked out, and she felt a blow to her stomach, which forced out the remaining air she had left in her lungs. There was a light above her, and she thrashed her arms and legs to push up towards the surface. She broke through, and sucked in air, before a desperate soul landed on top of her and pushed her under again.

The river current was strong, and she was stuck in the middle of the

CHAPTER TWENTY ONE

flow, where it ran the fastest. She went under constantly, but managed to break through to the surface, and suck in life saving air. She moved past other Andra who struggled in the flow. Many simply gave up and went under for the last time, downward to feed the bottom dwellers. The cold seeped into her bones, and it was difficult to think or move her limbs. All she could focus on was just one more breath, to survive a little longer.

The night sky was above her now, and she could see the stars for the first time without the protection of the glass domes. Snow was gently falling, and she thought how beautiful it all was even as she felt her life slipping away. For a brief moment she thought of Tana, drifting far off in another world.

People lined both banks of the canal, as the Andra floated by, human jetsam discarded by the Var. Some managed to reach the sides, and raised a hand for help. Two men pulled a naked woman from the river and immediately carried her off. A man and woman pulled out a boy, not much older than Sri, and took him away after inspecting his teeth. A young man still wearing his brown Banda robe reached out a hand to be pulled up. As he managed to get a foothold, a heavy stick wielded by a heartless beast crashed into his head. He fell back into the water, and disappeared from sight.

They're only taking the women and children!

All along the canal bank the same scene repeated itself. The old and infirm were offered no assistance, the healthy men were pushed back into the river, or bludgeoned to death. People even fought over women and children as they pushed and pulled them from the waterway. Bodies of the Andra drifted on by, out towards the sea. Returning to whence they came.

The women of the Burghs were also out in force. They were stern ladies, aided by a few converted men, who railed against the demon drink, the sins of the flesh, and the general corruption endemic to mankind. Salvation came at a price, and saved souls would work long hours for the Burghmeisters in exchange for a life dedicated to repentance for the wickedness of others.

Chandra knew if she was to survive she had to get out of the strong pull of the current and over to the canal bank. Who knew what her fate would be, but if she remained in the freezing waters much longer, death was certain. She kicked and kicked her legs, and windmilled her arms. And then she was free from the pull of the tide, and she drifted over to the left side. She reached up an arm for help, and the act caused her to sink once again. Then a hand grasped her by the hair, and another hand roughly pulled on her arm. She was heaved upwards onto the ground, and a blanket placed around her shoulders.

She sat there, shivering under the protection of the blanket, and trying to catch her breath. She had made it out of the river, but what came next? All she knew was she had survived for a moment, but what was her fate? What of her father, mother, Amma, and Sri? Her people were no more, her family were no more. Was the grief worth living through? However, she had no tears for them.

A man was looking down at her. A slim man with wild hard eyes and a thin mustache. He reached down and pulled open the blanket to stare at her nakedness.

"You'll do nicely, my pretty. I might even keep you for myself." He turned his head to one side and sneezed.

Chandra was unaware, but not all of the inhabitants of Gastown acted with blatant self-interest. Although late to the Purge, there were acts of altruism from various quarters. A small army of apprentices carrying fire torches and clubs and led by a little woman and a strong-armed son, descended on one section of the crowd to liberate their frozen captives.

'PUT THAT CHILD DOWN!" she said, and her voice reverberated around the canal. "HAUS HEAP APPRENTICES, RESCUE THESE PEOPLE!"

Marshaled by Samwell Heap, they tore into the rabble, and pulled as many of the Andra free as they could find and wrapped them in life-saving blankets.

The fishermen and dockers were active too, driven to action by kind-hearted beefy wives who would not stand for injustice. They battled with the lowlifes and secured women and children. They also put their fishing nets to good use, and pulled the last of the Andra, including the old and the last of the men, from the frigid waters. Frank and Molly, Kasha's foster parents, were at the forefront and adopted another young girl into their household.

    The Andra were crudely discarded by the Var after generations of loyal service, but not totally abandoned by those further down the social ladder. In time, they would forget their old ways, and the glass domes and the gardens, and add vibrancy to the collective gene pool of Gastown.

Chapter Twenty Two

Aldith : The Black Ships

The winds were favorable since the Black Ships left Varstad harbor and consistently blew in a southerly direction. Aldith stood on the quarterdeck of *Matilda*. next to the captain and the helmsman, and admired how the two men went about their craft. There were no barking orders, salty threats, or acts of violence. Both men were professionals and worked seamlessly together, as the captain checked the direction with reference to the sun and visible landmarks, and the helmsman adjusted the course based on the captain's subtle hand signals. Each ship in the fleet had their own captain and helmsman, but they all took their lead from *Matilda*. One hundred ships sailed in unison to the southern islands and the lost colony of Agithawald.

Aldith relished the journey more than the final destination. Sailing at the head of a magnificent armada out on the ocean, trumped the stifling responsibilities of command and control as Domina, Minister of War, back in Varstad. Here she was free from constant decision making, and could enjoy the simple pleasures, like the wind at her back, the billowing sails, and the seabirds flying high above who followed the fleet. She knew her sister Lilith should have led the Varingr and not her, and her absence from the citadel left Rafyn unbound to increase her influence over the Dux. However, Rafyn would plot regardless, and dealing with her half-sister

CHAPTER TWENTY TWO

was for another solar. When she came back victorious, everything would change. For now, she was unfettered from the chains of authority, and could enjoy the passage. And there was Tana.

Tana. There were two sides to Tana. Once the seasickness abated after a few solars and she found her sea legs, and could keep food down, she settled into a routine. When the solar was up, she was all vinegar, with more harsh words than a fishwife. Tana berated everyone, from the cabin boy who did not clean the quarters to her satisfaction, the cook who did not know how to prepare food to her liking, the helmsman for not steering straight, and Aldith. Aldith the most. Aldith for separating her from her family, Aldith for being Aldith. However, when the lunar illuminated the night sky, it was all honey. Brackish words subsided, the language of love reigned supreme, and they wore each other out.

Tana was by her side now, and Aldith could feel the tenseness creeping over her own body. She looked down at the dusky, beautiful woman with the sultry eyes and pouty lips, and wondered why she had developed such a spiteful tongue. If she barked so well in the common language, then her biting discourse in Andra would be something to behold. A mute version of Tana would ensure eternal happiness.

"When are we going ashore?" Tana asked.

"Not until we reach Agithawald," Aldith said.

Matilda hit a swell and then sank down over the heavy wave into a trough. Tana lost her footing and steadied herself against Aldith, who moved smoothly with the rocking motion.

"You there! Keep this boat steady. I almost fell over," Tana barked at the helmsman.

"It's not a boat. *Matilda* is a ship," Aldith replied. "And you can't control the seas, you just roll with the waves as best you can."

"Whoever heard of giving a name to some pieces of wood patched together. And why aren't we going ashore?"

Aldith took a deep breath. "The Sul rule over there," she said, pointing to a land mass on the right they could barely see. "If we put ashore, they will see us as a threat. One hundred Black Ships can't sail through their waters without being challenged. We're set for a Varingr not trade. They would stop us, and confiscate our vessels."

"They have the power to do that?" Tana asked. There was wonder and fear in her eyes.

Aldith nodded her head. "The Sul Empire is vast, and has suzerainty over many kingdoms to the south. Even we pay tribute in hides and wood to their emperor. So we stay outside of their territorial waters and sail to Agithawald, or what's left of it."

"There must be other lands the Sul don't control. Can't we go there? You can't expect me to stay on this floating crate for much longer."

"Yes, there are others. After the Sul Empire, we sail past the Sun people and the Forbidden Islands."

"Forbidden?"

"We traded with them once, when the islands were divided between warlords and they fought amongst each other. Then a single ruler united them, and banished all outsiders. To go there is certain death. Even the Sul leave them alone."

"Then we shall not go there. And beyond?"

"The Sindhal continent, where your people came from over three hundred and fifty years ago."

Tana pulled on her arm, and looked up with puppy dog eyes. "My people? We go past the Andra homeland? Please, Aldith. Please, please. Just for a solar."

Aldith shook her head. "You wouldn't like it. Fierce horsemen from the north hold sway. Your people are just chattels to them. They take all of their food, and occasionally their women too."

Tana let go of her arm, and the vicious tongue returned. "Sounds like you have a lot in common."

Aldith watched her go as she stormed off to their cabin on wobbly sea legs. No doubt she would sulk alone, and throw the occasional object to see how it held up against the heavy oak beams. Nighttime would soften her mood, and they would hold each other in a loving embrace. Until the morrow.

CHAPTER TWENTY TWO

Aldith knew from the outset making landfall before they arrived at the southern islands was not an option. The crew, the warriors, and the soldiers steeled themselves for an arduous sea journey, and the result of being ship bound for such a long time. Three full lunars, if the weather remained in their favor, was an eternity to be cooped up in close proximity. Martial training was essential to burn off excess energy and keep the fighting edge. The Damm Warriors trained the Red Shadows excessively on the main deck, much to the amusement of the crew. At first, they had difficulty moving in unison with the ocean, so they spilled about the ship, careened into each as they broke formation, and did it all again at the behest of the Damm Warriors. Chainmail was the first and constant casualty in the battle with the maritime elements. After the morning drills, the afternoons were spent cleaning away signs of rust, and greasing the metal in animal fat for the Red Shadows, and linseed oil for the Damm Warriors. The evenings were free for relaxation and petty squabbles, driven by boredom and base human nature.

Discipline aboard a ship was essential to maintain control and harsh punishment was meted out to transgressors for all to witness. Crew and soldiers were subject to the same rules, and infractions were swift and severe. One Red Shadow picked a fight with a crew member, and was given twenty lashes. A crewman took more than his fair share of grog, and paid the price with fifty strokes from the spiked billee tail. Capital punishment was rare, but when a sentence was passed, there was no reprieve.

A skeleton crew stayed in the rigging, a lookout man in the nest above, and the helmsman at his post. The rest of the crew, and the Damm Warriors and Red Shadows, gathered on deck. The first mate, a kinsman of the captain, was on trial for improper relations with a cabin boy. The first mate, with chains around his ankles and wrists, stood defiantly before his two accusers, who caught him in the unnatural act. The cabin boy, a slight youth with black ringlets and sad eyes, cringed on the deck between them. The captain stood stoically, listening to the grave charges brought against his cousin.

Aldith stayed on the quarterdeck so as not to be seen as interfering with the captain's authority. She knew the charges, and knew the sentence the captain must pass to honor the naval code. The trial itself was a formality. Everyone knew it, including the first mate, but they all played their part in the charade.

Tana came up on deck, looked at the crowd and then made her way to stand by Aldith's side.

"What's going on? Why is Auggie crying?" Tana asked.

"Auggie?" Aldith replied.

"Our cabin boy. Don't you know the servants' names?"

Aldith shook her head. "Not one. Why should I?"

"I was calling for Auggie to bring me some fruit, and he didn't answer. Is he in trouble?"

"He's a player in this drama, but no, he's not in immediate danger."

Tana linked her arm in Aldith's and leaned against her. "My head is a little silly this morning. You'll have to explain it to me."

"The first mate, the large man in the chains, was caught with your Auggie, bent over a barrel."

"Did Auggie consent, or was he forced?"

"They're professing love for each other."

"Well then. Go down there and put a stop to this."

"The captain has jurisdiction. It's punishable by death onboard a ship. The first mate is the giver, so he pays the price."

"What will happen to him?"

"Watch."

The captain passed sentence and made a speech for the gathering crowd, which Aldith and Tana could not hear up on the quarterdeck. It obviously amused the first mate because he threw back his head and laughed. His large belly bounced up and down with each guffaw. Auggie wept at his feet.

Four sailors seized hold of the first mate and dragged him over to the left side of the ship, while others used a yardarm and ran a rope through an iron ring, around the stern and through another iron ring on the other side. They tied one end of the heavy rope to the first mate's hands and the

CHAPTER TWENTY TWO

other to his feet.

"What are they doing?" Tana asked.

"It's called *kielhalen*. They drag him under the ship and up on deck on the other side. He's lucky I suppose. We cleaned the hull before we sailed and removed most of the barnacles. At least he won't be completely cut to pieces."

With a command from the captain, the men on the opposite side took up the slack and pulled on the rope attached to the first mate's hands, and hauled him over the side. The men holding the rope fastened to his feet let it play out.

The crew and soldierly contingent remained in place and silent, as the rope was slowly pulled under *Matilda's* hull.

Tana tightly squeezed Aldith's arm. "Can't they go any faster? No one can stay under that long."

The men kept pulling the rope until the first mate's bound hands were visible over the rail, and then they seized hold of him and dragged him onto the deck. He lay there motionless for a while, blood oozing from barnacle cuts, and then spewed out seawater and coughed as he filled his lungs with air.

Tana let go of Aldith's arm and clapped her hands together. "He made it! Now he can go free and be with Auggie again."

"Not quite," Aldith said.

The first mate was dragged roughly to his feet. A rope was wrapped around his body, binding his arms tight to his side. A noose was placed around his neck, a cloth in his mouth, and he was hoisted into the air. He swayed back and forth with the motion of the ship, his legs fluttering, as his life was squeezed out of him. At the final moment, as death beckoned, his bladder emptied and he pissed on the assembled crew below, a golden shower as his closing statement on maritime justice.

The first mate's body was lowered to the deck, and four men set to work removing his bindings for another solar and another prisoner. They each took hold of a floppy limb, carried him to the side, rocked him back and forth three times to build momentum, and unceremoniously heaved him over the side.

Auggie let out a scream, and before anyone could stop him, he leapt over the side to keep his dead lover company. His plight did not last long. Sharks, attracted by the blood left in the water by the first mate's kielhalen, made short work of the cabin boy. He was no more than a snack in their huge jaws as they tore him to sheds.

"I don't understand," Tana said, after she finally opened her eyes, temporarily averted away from the carnage. "Why can't a man and boy be together?"

"They can in Varstad. It happens all the time in the place they call the Mutton. And our own Dandies strike up long term relationships."

"And we're together too."

"Yes, but it's different for women. The rules aboard a ship are clear. Every man knows them, and understands the consequences."

Tana thought for a moment. "With Auggie gone, who will bring my fruit?"

Aldith knew the weather would not remain in their favor for the whole journey. Rounding the Sindhal continent and the storms which plagued and tormented the seas was for the future. For now, their nautical challenge was becalming. The winds ceased blowing, and with it, any respite from the oppressive heat. The sails were trimmed, but still the Black Ships moved along although at a much slower pace. Sailors dragged a piece of wood behind the stern, and counted the knots in a rope for a measured amount of time to calculate the speed. Aldith did not need to see this to realize how slow they were actually moving.

"This heat is stifling. Can't we go ashore and rest under the shade of a tree?" Tana asked.

Aldith bristled, as she always did when Tana crept up on her and lodged her first complaint of the solar.

"No, we can't," Aldith said tersely.

"It was never this hot back in the glass domes," Tana said.

"The glass domes were a luxury for your people. The Andra who live in these lands deal with the sweltering heat, the incessant storms which tear up the land, and the heavy rains which last for lunars at a time. Count your blessings!"

"My blessings? I didn't ask to be dragged away from my family, my husband, my life. I didn't ask to be your plaything, when I should be happy working in the gardens and looking to raise children. I didn't ask to be bundled up in a carpet and stolen away by a thief in the night!"

Aldith rounded on Tana, seized her roughly by the arms. "Your people are no more. That life is no more. Don't you understand? I saved you." Aldith regretted her words the moment they left her mouth.

Tana's legs buckled and Aldith lowered her to the deck. She sat down beside her and waited for the verbal storm.

"What do you mean … no more?"

Aldith took a deep breath. How could she explain the ways of the Var to an outsider when she barely understood them herself. On the surface, the loss of vital resources, and the disruption to their livelihood seemed unnecessary. However, the customs of the Var were clearly recorded, and rigid obedience was required.

"My people have a tradition which requires a cycle of change. We see it as a rebirth, as a way of purification."

"I don't understand."

"We believe our food determines who we are. Over time we get weak, and sickness creeps in if we don't purge and start afresh."

"Purge? I don't know this word.

"It means we remove the people who are no longer desirable and replace them with others. We have fresh people with fresh food working the gardens for us. The Andra are purged. Your people are no more."

Tana let out a pitiful shriek, which reverberated around *Matilda*. Crew members stopped working and stared. Superstitious sailors had a hard enough time with women on board, but one wailing like a banshee was destined to bring bad luck. They spat over the side as their personal offering to the sea and to ward off evil spirits and unseen monsters lurking deep below.

Tana gained enough composure to speak, but she only had a look of hatred for Aldith. "You cast us off like broken husks. No more? I have to go back to my people. Where did you send them?"

Aldith shook her head. "There is no turning back. You have to accept your people are gone. The Andra gardens and belongings were burned. The people were expulsed into the canals. Most would have died in the cold waters, and drifted out to sea with the current, or simply sank to the bottom like human stones. Those few who did survive will be slaafs for the lower denizens of Assaborg. I saved you from that fate, Tana."

"Saved me? For this? This is no life! I want my people!" Tana screamed as she hammered her fists onto the deck, and tore out her own hair.

Any sympathy Aldith may have felt evaporated like morning sea mist, and was replaced by an immediate resentment for her beautiful companion. As she looked at her now, all she saw was a harridan in the making, a shrew of a woman who could turn water to vinegar, and sour milk as it left the teat. She hoped for love, but it would not grow out of her lust.

Aldith stood up and grabbed hold of Tana by the hair, and lifted her to her feet. "You want your people? I'll show you what's left of your people!"

Aldith pulled up a hatch revealing a flight of stairs down to the bowels of the ship. She took the steps down, dragging Tana behind her. Down they went, towards the mechanical sound of gears turning. They stopped in front of a heavy door, and Aldith banged on it with her fist, until a guard opened it up.

The smell hit them first. Human odors, human filth. Both Aldith and Tana instinctively covered their mouths and noses. There were men inside, all naked and covered in their own waste. They were chained to a rotating wheel where they walked at a constant pace following the beat of a drum. This was the means of the ship's propulsion when the wind did not fill the sails. Men walked the wheel and powered the screw at the stern of the hull.

Aldith roughly pushed Tana into the room. "Look. That's what's left of your people!"

Tana stared at a naked man with the hanging man amulet around his neck. He looked straight ahead, lost in his own madness as he walked

CHAPTER TWENTY TWO

to nowhere and slowly pressed *Matilda* on to the southern islands and Agithawald. The wheel turned.

"What do you have to say now?" Aldith demanded.

Tana looked at what was left of Manoj, his wild matted hair, his nakedness, and his exposed manhood. She looked up at Aldith. "He's smaller than I thought."

The tempest came as Aldith knew it would. The wind picked up to aid their passage around the tip of the Sindhal continent, and then collided with competing winds to whip up the seas and pound the Black Ships into submission. There was no holding the fleet together in such a squall, and every ship, captain, and crew, fought their own personal battle against the elements.

Aldith refused to stay below decks, despite the pleas from the captain, and stood next to the helmsman to add strength in keeping the bow pointed into the waves and steering *Matilda* through the eye of the storm. Below decks, Manoj and the men on the wheels walked their death march to the steady beat of the drum and provided the only form of locomotion to counterbalance the wild force of nature. The skies were black and furious, wave after wave crashed over the ship, and the winds whistled a furious tune of encouragement to the deadly waters, while doing their own part to crush the maritime trespassers.

The captain was able to get men topside and furl the sails from top to bottom before the worst of the storm enveloped them, but there was no respite for the crew. Men worked feverishly to pump excess water from the bilges, while others secured loose ropes and threw jetsam to the waters to lighten the load for added stability and appease the sea gods for the superstitious. One man went overboard, and his crewmates were unable to offer assistance as he bobbed in the dark waters for a few heartbeats before disappearing from sight.

Aldith put all her strength into assisting the helmsman in keeping *Matilda* on a true course. Her clothes were soaked through with the cold sea water, the swirling wind made visibility challenging, and her muscles burned with the continuous effort. Then on the port side, another Black Ship came barreling out of the gloom and cut a path directly in front of *Matilda*. The captain had decided to trim his top sails, but the mainsail was still up as he raced with the wind behind them, carving a path through the waves like a demented mariner. It was a dangerous game to play, and Aldith held her breath as the stern of the passing vessel inched past their bow and just avoided contact.

Other craft were not so lucky, or the captains were not so skilled. One Black Ship lay overturned in the frothy sea with the mast broken free. Men clung onto the shattered timbers in the water, or any flotsam which would hold their weight. Many frantically waved their arms to the *Matilda* for assistance, but there was no stopping in the storm. She sailed on by, and her crew looked away in shame, and in relief they were not being consigned to a similar watery grave.

In the distance, a ball of fire illuminated the night sky, followed by a mighty explosion. Aldith surmised the holding tank containing the vitali blackfire had ruptured, and quickly mixed with sea water for a deadly combination and unholy eruption. There would be no survivors from that detonation.

The storm ravaged the fleet for another three solars, though there was no light in the sky to indicate when a new cycle would begin. There was no rest for the crew either, and exhausted sailors toiled away under the captain's command to stay the course. Quick swigs of water, and hardtack was the only sustenance they had, but they persevered and battled their natural enemies. Aldith promised herself she would suitably reward the captain if they made it through to the other side.

The fury broke in an instant, as if the winds and the sea had decided their collective temper tantrum was over, and the ships were now free to go on their way. They provided a light breeze and a gentle swell to aid in the rest of the journey with no hard feelings and a standing offer to come back and play on the return voyage.

Aldith and the helmsman gave up steering duties to a substitute, and the captain reset the course before handing over responsibilities to the

CHAPTER TWENTY TWO

newly elevated first mate as he retired below decks for a much needed rest. Aldith did not immediately go to her cabin. The solar was up and she preferred to stay clear of Tana's serrating tongue and incessant questions for a while longer. Her chief concern was the fleet, and how many ships she had left to continue with the Varingr. As she scanned the surrounding seas she was heartened to see Black Ships with sails raised on all sides. They came together in clusters and formed up as best they could to constitute an armada once again. Their numbers were depleted, and the storm took its bounty, but there were still enough Damm Warriors and Red Shadows to meet the challenge ahead.

Aldith stood at the stern of the ship, and let the breeze, which gently filled the sails, blow some of the weariness from her head. The first leg of the journey would be over soon, and she would have to go back to being the leader again with everyone reliant on her for direction. Agithawald would rise again, and the Var dream of a vibrant southern colony in the warmth of the full solar with an abundance of natural resources would be given new life.

The ocean came alive around them. Hvalr in their thousands swam around the Black Ships, all on a similar journey south to their feeding and mating grounds. Spouts of water broke the waterline as the giant creatures surfaced and expelled air from their blowholes. Others breached the waters and splashed down hard on the surface in a display of aquatic gymnastics. There were hvalr of all size, color, and shape swimming in family groupings, large and small. There was a huge white bull with a head the size of a mountainous iceberg surrounded by smaller cows and cubs. Even larger hvalr were blue in color, though fewer in number. The majority were smaller in size, and various shades of gray. They showed little interest in the Black Ships as they swam by.

Damm Warriors and Red Shadows, putting the terror of the storm behind them, came deckside to point, smile, and marvel at the majesty of the kings and queens of the southern seas. Aldith remembered stories of the Sun people of the Forbidden Islands putting to sea to harvest these noble creatures for their bone, flesh, and oil. She hoped they were free of such practices this far south, far away from the human menace.

The hvalr pods moved faster than the Black Ships, and soon the last of them swam out of sight. The sailors returned to their duties, and the Damm Warriors and Red Shadows returned to martial practice to shake off the rust and occupy idle hands.

Aldith noticed the captain was on edge, and scanned the horizon. He sent word to the lookout above to be extra vigilant.

"What concerns you?" she asked.

"Hvalr species never swim together unless they're looking for safety in numbers. When there are pods of this size, a hunter follows. They no longer frequent the northern waters, but they still exist in the southern seas: *Kormgundr,* the giant sea serpents. They feed on whales, and kill ships for pleasure," the captain said.

"Sea tales told by superstitious sailors to scare cabin boys," Aldith said, though she could see the captain was serious. She had been around him long enough to know he was not easily scared, but there was fear about him now.

The lookout above shouted to get the captain's attention, and pointed far out on the port side.

The captain cursed. 'We'll keep the Black Ships close together. We must rely on safety in numbers."

Aldith stared into the distance and saw a huge shape breach from the waters, and come down with a mighty splash. It was five times larger than the biggest whale they had seen, and moved with tremendous speed, straight towards the fleet.

"She has our scent," the captain said, and sent a command to signal the Black Ships to sail in close formation.

"Can we outrun her?" Aldith asked.

The captain shook his head. "Not with a tempest behind us. I'm afraid she's on a course to kill."

The Kormgundr came closer, carving a serpentine path through the choppy waters, as she swam parallel to the Black Ships. Her hide was made of overlapping scales, and covered with the ancient dark green slime of the sea. Her head was the size of a Black Ship, elongated, with mighty jaws, and teeth larger than the tallest man. She was a primordial beast and few survived to bear witness to her maritime atrocities.

The colossal sea serpent submerged, and left a giant whirlpool in her wake. There was an eerie silence as the expectant crews waited, and then she breached the surface and came crashing down on a Black Ship which was slow to close ranks with the rest of the fleet. The ship completely disappeared from sight, as if she had never existed.

As Aldith watched, four Black Ships broke off and sailed towards the Kormgundr.

"Whose half squadron is that?" Aldith asked the captain.

"*Shadow* is in the lead," he replied.

"That's Kari's command. She's not one to make foolish decisions."

"She's buying us time, distracting her away from the fleet."

Shadow and her three sister ships sailed side on with the Kormgundr, and a cannon volley erupted. Aldith saw the plumes of smoke before she heard the delayed sound, and saw black balls hurl towards the sea monster. The fire was in haste, and erratic. Stone shot plowed into the ocean, but one or two made contact with the hard hide of the beast but bounced off. The Kormgundr dived deep.

There was an uneasy calm as the Kormgundr stayed under, and the frantic crews ran around the decks, and looked over the side for their deathbringer. The rest of the fleet sailed on, lengthening the distance away from their sacrificial sister ships and their nemesis.

The Kormgundr surfaced in front of the bow of *Shadow*, and her monstrous head burst from the waters. The fire crew were ready, and a stream of vitali blackfire made contact with the sea and burst into a liquid pool of flames. There was a horrific roar from the Kormgundr, as the fire surrounded her, and she dived again. *Shadow* spun in a circle in the wake of the sea serpent, and vitali blackfire spurted all around her in a blazing ring.

Shadow was still spinning when the Kormgundr surfaced again in a mighty upsurge from the water, and crashed over the Black Ship. Her coils wrapped around the vessel, and snapped it in half. Men and women were in the water, screaming as the flames consumed them. Most went down with the ship as the Kormgundr tore it to pieces.

Two Black Ships collided into each other as they tried to maneuver away from the sea monster, and the third lost its sails as the Kormgundr's tail whipped out of the water and shattered the mainmast.

The Kormgundr circled the stricken vessels, and then there was a violent eruption in the waters close by, and another serpentine head broke the surface. The three ships were temporarily forgotten as the two sea monsters crashed into each other and fought for supremacy. They twisted and coiled together, and inadvertently destroyed the ships which occupied their watery battleground. The rest of the fleet was of no consequence as the duel to the death played out.

The Black Ship fleet sailed on, and left the conflict behind them. Aldith made a silent prayer to Frotha to take Kari and her Damm Warriors into the fold. She would see them again in the Great Hall reserved for Var fighters. She returned to her routine of sorts, staying busy in the solar hours, and engaging in lustful pleasures with Tana when night came, and her mood softened, and all thoughts of abandoning the Andra beauty were forgotten. She knew it would not last. Once on shore the Domina would reappear and there would be no time for frivolous behavior. She would need to devote all of her energy to Agithawald.

The captain's course was true, and again Aldith marveled at his maritime skills to sail from Varstad to Agithawald under the direction of the solar, the stars, and the infrequent coastline. One degree off and they would sail on past the southern islands to who knew where. The end of the earth perhaps where sea monsters waited to devour the hapless, or ships plunged into the great abyss. The Old Ones claimed you came once again to your original embarkation point, but that made no sense to Aldith. You went there and back again, not round in a circle.

The natural harbor was vast, and seventy Black Ships, beaten and battered, sailed into the bay, and the protection it offered from any pending storm. Twenty five ships were lost to the tempest, and Aldith hoped some of them would limp in later, or find their way back to Varstad. Most she knew would never be seen again, and it was a heavy price to pay for an abandoned colony. Ten ships stayed further out to provide a protective line, while the remaining sixty vessels anchored closer to the beachfront. Longboats were dispatched to go ashore. Despite the risk, Aldith was in the lead boat. Tana too. Once she heard they had made landfall, nothing would keep her aboard *Matilda*.

The longboat reached the beach, the sailors stacked oars, and two of them jumped ashore to pull the craft further up, and secure it in place with a small anchor. Aldith stepped down into the surf and steadied herself on uneasy legs. She still felt the rocking motion of the ship beneath her, and waited for it to subside. Tana, in her impatient haste to reach dry land, leapt down and promptly planted her face in the wet sand.

Other boats quickly followed, and a party of Damm Warriors and Red Shadows formed a protective ring around Aldith as she made her way up the beach and on towards the wooden palisade of Agithawald. The main gate was open, and intact. There was no sign of a struggle, but no sign of life. Agithawald truly was a ghost colony.

Chapter Twenty Three

Justin : The Yaobai

There was a buzz around the Four Kith as word spread down from the citadel the Purge was coming. Most did not know what it meant, and those who did shook out the old myths and legends and gave them a new spin. It also caused many to reflect on their own origin stories as they looked at their neighbors with fresh and sometimes jaundiced eyes. The people of Gastown were a mishmash of races and fragments of creed. They were light skinned, dark skinned, blue eyed, and black. They had sallow features, or pale skin. Thick or thin lips, tall and slender frames, or stocky and short bodies. Many fled from other lands for the economic opportunity the rise of Gastown offered. Others were subject to the Purge themselves, though from what bloodline they could only guess.

Justin heard all of the stories from his customers as they waited for the fateful solar. They talked about nothing else. He also had the added advantage of access to the Tower of Tomes library, and the strict laws laid down by the founders of Varstad. Justin wondered what twisted minds came up with the notion of purging farmers every three hundred and fifty years when it impacted twelve generations in the future. He knew it was based on a constellation alignment, and Petra the Pythoness would have double checked her calculations for the auspicious solar, but beyond that he could see no purpose. Superstition and blind obedience to the founder's

CHAPTER TWENTY THREE

wishes meant the ethnic cleansing of a people, and the partial addition to the collective gene pool, if any managed to survive the ordeal. Justin had not had contact with the Andra during his time in the citadel. He was secluded with his books, and they existed in their glass domes. However, he knew they were gentle, peace-loving people who deserved better.

Justin considered staying indoors and taking inventory of his tabak supplies when the solar of reckoning arrived, but curiosity got the better of him. He wrapped himself in a heavy cloak over his customary cassock, and he followed the excited crowd down to the canal. Some of the kithfolk got there early and staked out picnic areas to feast, drink, and observe the show. Enterprising merchants set up stalls to feed the masses with a rich assortment of delicacies one could eat on the go, from meat pies, pickled fish, pig's trotters, and chicken feet, as well as an assortment of overly sweet, and decidedly unhealthy, confectioneries. Naturally, prices increased for the occasion. Then there were the men and women who sought to profit from the misery of others. They came armed with boat hooks and nets to fish out prizes from the cold waters, and clubs to beat down the unwanted for sick sport and savage amusement.

The crowd lining the canal banks were already six rows deep by the time Justin arrived, so he settled for a position on higher ground where he could watch the human disaster about to unfold. He did not know what really drew him, though there was a sense he could help in some way. Perhaps he could save one Andra life, and offset the guilt he felt on behalf of his own kind.

High above Gastown, the three arms in the clock tower aligned, and completed the three hundred and fifty year cycle. The steam whistle, whose shrill call punctuated the beginning and end of the working solar, opened up its metal throat to full capacity, and audibly assaulted the multitude. Hands covered ears to offer some protection. Justin, forewarned, had plugged his own ears with waxed cloth, which dampened the piercing wail. He knew he would be treating patients for ringing in the ears for solars to come.

The steam whistle abated, and there was a pause as the masses waited, some patiently, some not, for the human jetsam to be forcibly ejected from the citadel, and down through the canals and out to the open sea beyond. The turbulent waters were the first signs of activity as the volume and flow increased. People pointed as the first bodies came into view, twisting and turning, tumbling and spilling through the deluge. They went under, arms raised high for help, and bobbed up again to grasp for air to fill failing lungs. Lifeless bodies floated down the waterway with the living, some offering a raft of sorts as their kinsmen clung on to save themselves.

Justin wept. The inhumanity of it all, and the savagery of Gastown left him cold, and he wondered why he was treating these people. One Andra man reached up a hand to be pulled from the canal, only to be clubbed unconscious and pushed back into the water. Blood oozed from his head wound as he floated away. The children and young women were the sought after prizes. The children for servitude and the women for pleasure. The old and the infirm were left to make their final journey out to sea, the men who sought to scramble ashore were clubbed and stabbed as a pastime. No hand of friendship was offered. Two rough men plucked out a woman and dragged her into a nearby alleyway as they removed what little clothes she had left to cover her modesty. On the other side of the canal bank, a man pulled out a naked young girl by her hair, and covered her with a blanket. Justin was gratified to see some semblance of humanity, until he saw Puzzle Pete, flanked by Crimpers, standing over her. Her fate was sealed, and Justin wept some more.

Then there was a commotion around the canal. On the far side, men and women carrying torches, as well as an assortment of makeshift weapons, pushed into the crowd and sought to free the Andra who were being seized. Justin hoped to see the Andra girl recently pulled out of the frigid waters by Puzzle Pete's Crimpers rescued too. However, she was already spirited away, as were many of the other captives. Nevertheless, a handful were liberated and led away to safety. Men cast nets into the canal and pulled out stragglers, including the last of the Andra men.

On Justin's side of the river, another group had the same intention. A little middle-aged woman was shouting orders to her provisional army, though Justin could not hear a word as his ears were full of wax. Men fought back when they realized their human prizes were being rudely taken from them, but the clubs in the hands of the liberators had a way of making them see the error of their ways.

Justin was not a fighter, but he intended to help as best he could and he made his way down to the canal bank as the crowd dispersed. Four young boys, denizens of the Slough, based on their shabby dress and wraithlike appearance, were throwing stones. Justin was horrified to see their targets were three prone bodies lying in the mudflats. He yelled at them to stop, and one boy turned to throw a stone in his direction, until he waved his arms in the air and chanted some incantation fragments in Ma'din to frighten them away.

Justin stepped down into the mud to examine the bodies, The first, a man with his skull shattered was a hapless victim for being male. He had little to offer his killers other than the thrill of dispatching a helpless soul. There was nothing Justin could do for him other than to light a candle in remembrance. The second was an old woman. Her lifeless eyes would never lovingly gaze on her grandchildren again, her hands would never again tend to the garden. Another candle. The third was a naked boy who lay on his side, clutching a pair of shears in his hands. Justin leaned down and checked the pulse on his neck. He was surprised to find there was a faint beat. The boy clung on to life, and Justin knew he had to save at least one of the Andra.

He moved swiftly, placing the boy on his stomach and pumping his ribcage to expel any water trapped in his lungs. After three pushes, water oozed out, and he began to breathe again. His body was icy cold, and Justin knew he had a short window to save his life. He took off his cloak and wrapped the boy in it, and carried him back to the apothekaria. Two candles and one saved soul was the price to pay in atonement for witnessing the Purge.

The healing process was an arduous one, but Justin poured time and energy into helping the Andra boy recover. Treatment was compounded by the fact the boy could neither speak nor hear. Justin did not know if the shock of his loss and the plunge into the icy waters caused his muted condition—he had read case studies in Chosi's masterpiece, where men returning from the hell of war experienced similar symptoms—or if he simply entered the world that way. He suspected the latter, since the boy seemed at ease with perpetual silence.

First, Justin went to work on healing the body. The boy had a broken right tibia, which he reset and wrapped in a poultice of healing herbs. There was no putrid smell associated with the onset of gangrene, so there was no need for amputation. Justin was relieved on that point, since he did not possess the skills of a sawbone, which were few and far between in the Four Kith. Most folks were forced to rely on the local slager as a substitute surgeon. Other physical wounds were superficial, a few cuts and bruises easily treated with healing salves. The boy's mind and spirit were something else. Most nights resulted in violent dreams punctuated by silent screams, and the solars were spent in listlessness. He barely touched the meals, mostly vegetable soups, Justin put in front of him, and ate only enough for base sustenance.

Change did come over time. The boy had one thing he cherished and always kept close at hand, his little gardening shears, which Justin used to his advantage. At first, Justin worried about the boy holding on to a potential weapon, either as a threat to him, or self infliction. However, he showed no signs of aggression, and Justin encouraged him to use them to work with the herbs. The boy showed a natural talent for pruning, and in time, it helped him to regain a new lease of life. He was in his own garden again. With his mind now focused on a familiar task, his body healed too, and he ate everything Justin put in front of him.

Justin remembered a tome he had briefly leafed through called, *The Art of Sign Language and Hand Symbology,* and he put in a special request via his handlers for a temporary loan from the Var library. He received a quizzical look since it had no bearing on the work of an Apotheka, but they complied with his wishes. When it arrived, he set about meticulous study and quickly mastered the basics. He made notes, and even improvements with simplified shortcuts. Teaching the boy was a laborious process, and

CHAPTER TWENTY THREE

Justin started with hand signs for two names, Justin and Samal, the silent one. At first, the boy's concentration was not there, and he refused to put down his shears. However, once he mastered his new name, perhaps the first time he had one, he embraced the dexterous exercises. He even showed Justin a few simple signs of his own, which they incorporated into the lexicon.

The apothekaria continued to grow, and with Samal's extra hands and sharp shears, they serviced clientele from all of Gastown, from the Burghs, the Four Kith, including the Slough, and the Mutton. Word quickly spread Habala the Apotheka was a fair man, who showed no preferential treatment for the richer members of society. He treated all with the same level of respect, and received payment according to their means. The Apotheka's Apprentice followed the same creed, and over time he took over more and more responsibilities from the master, who increasingly busied himself with mystical studies.

Justin continued to provide all information to Rafyn, whether he deemed it relevant or not, as a key member of her spy network. He relayed choice stories from Missus Markle about the amorous attachment between an immoral baker and a baker's dozen of female customers, and the strange tale of Constantine Crabbe, the cabinetmaker, who many considered to be *The Terror* of the Mutton. He informed her of the growing conflict between Carlos Grimm and Puzzle Pete, and his role in administering treatment to both of them. Most importantly, there was also the reaction from the folks who relied on the Gut as their only source of nourishment. Since the Purge, there was no slop to distribute, bellies were empty, and the mood was turning ugly.

Justin was just closing up shop for the night, and was looking forward to a steaming bowl of leek and potato soup, and perhaps a toke of special tabak, when two Crimpers appeared with a summons from Puzzle Pete. He groaned, but knew there was no turning down this request. He packed his bag with all of the necessary treatments for venereal diseases, smiled at his simian minders, and followed their lead into the Mutton.

Pete's bordello was shifting out of the sleepy solar mode, and into the wildness and debauchery heralded by the arrival of night. Orange lights blazed above the entranceway, and illuminated the windows above, where the slagmaidens were already taking up residence to display their bodily wares. Two Crimpers were stationed in front of the building, but they let Justin and his two minders through with a simple nod of the head and a tip of the hat as a greeting. Justin recognized one of them as a customer at the Apotheka in desperate need for a bowel movement. Jonah Barrow was his name, and he had been backed up for nearly a lunar. Justin concocted an extra strong mixture of aloe, frangula, and rhubarb root, and the Crimper immediately dropped weight, and his disposition improved.

The main parlor of the bordello was already waking up, and a few slagmaidens paired off with early customers. Others sauntered down the stairs and took up residence in the plush chairs, and poured cheap drinks at a premium price for gullible punters who would leave with lightened scrotums, and even lighter purses. Business was thriving for Puzzle Pete and his Crimpers.

Justin glanced over at the bar area and saw the man mountain Toby Myers talking with the barkeep. He held a thin glass with a bright green liquid in his hand, which he finished in one gulp and held out for a refill. He saw Justin, and gestured towards the staircase. One of the Crimpers escorted Justin up and passed a couple of curious slagmaidens, and stopped outside a bedroom door. The Crimper knocked, and then opened the door for Justin to go inside.

The large room was dimly lit, and the window shutters were already closed. Justin could make out four figures in the extra large four post bedstead, which dominated the room. He momentarily forgot the task at hand, and moved closer to examine the fine carving and delicate painting of the nearest bed post. He reached out a hand and caressed the wood, which was carved with naked men and women in various forms of the carnal act.

"You're admiring the wooden version when I have three beauties in the flesh beside me?" Pete asked.

Justin continued to stroke the wood, and marveled at the craftsmanship.

CHAPTER TWENTY THREE

"It's the finest old growth oak, and the carving of the woman's form is exquisite. Truly the work of a master."

"Ah, so there's more to our Apotheka's Apprentice than we realized," Pete said. "More light please, so our artisan can study."

One of the naked women climbed out of the bed and lit a fresh candle from the stump of another. She went about the room and lit four more bringing forth illumination. Justin glanced at her, slightly aroused by her bare form before he could check himself, and then looked at Puzzle Pete as he lounged between two other beauties who sat up on either side of him in the huge expanse of the bed. One was a very attractive brunette with pendulous breasts. The other was a slim dark girl with rouge on her lips and nipples, lustrous black hair, and sad green eyes. Justin recognized her as the girl Pete's associate had pulled from the canal on the night of the Purge. Another Andra lived, but Justin pitied her for the existence she was forced to endure. Life with Pete meant certain infection, but it was preferable to the hardscrabble existence other Andra women were now facing.

Justin did not know why, but he felt a strong attraction to the Andra girl. There was something more to her than the physical beauty on full naked display. He felt as if they had met before, though his scientific mind did not believe in tales of karmic reincarnation. He simply stood there and stared, until Pete interrupted his gawking.

"A lightning bolt just found its mark," Pete said, and broke the spell on Justin.

Pete shooed the three women out to a connecting room, climbed out of the bed naked. He opened a silver box, and sniffed a pinch of powder into both nostrils. A moment later he let out a hard sneeze, followed by another. He walked over to Justin and sat at the foot of the bed.

"Did you bring your bag of tricks? What delights do you have for me today? Salves to burn, and poultices to peel away my flesh?" Pete asked.

Justin looked down at the small, slight man. He towered over him, and in his black cassock he resembled the angel of death more than a healer. Despite Pete's diminutive size, there was an air of authority and menace about the man. Justin was in no doubt he could kill for himself, or have someone dispatched in a moment with no sense of guilt. His world followed his rules, and everyone else was simply there to do his bidding, or suffer the consequences. Unlike Carlos Grimm who killed for revenge or simply to survive, Puzzle Pete was a homicidal slayer.

Justin knelt down and opened his bag. "You know you could wear protection of sorts. The sheep's intestine cover I recommended. I could make you one," Justin said.

"When I want to go inside an animal, I'll shag a sheep. It's the bareback life for me."

"It's not just you, you know. You infect the women, and they in turn infect you back. I can't cure you, if you continue to be a repeat offender. And there are some venereal strains no treatment can cure."

Pete laughed. "You have a point there. Perhaps I'll let you treat my favorites too. Chandra for instance. The Andra girl. I saw how you looked at her. Would you like to examine between her legs, Justin the Apotheka's Apprentice."

Chandra. Her name's Chandra.

Justin flushed, and ignored the comment. Instead he focused on preparing his salve. He made sure to add in a burning ingredient to aid in the healing process, and to cause Pete some added discomfort. He moved closer to Pete, pushed his knees a little wider apart, and leaned forward to examine his manhood.

"Please warm your hands this time," Pete asked. "Last time my nuts shrank from walnuts to pines."

Justin quickly rubbed the palms of his hands together to generate some heat, and then grasped the bundle to check for inflammation and lumps. Pete winced.

"Do you still feel a burning sensation when you urinate? Are you ejecting any pus?"

"No and no."

"The herbal drinks. Are you still taking them twice per solar?"

"Yes, yes, as regular as I copulate. The bitter taste is almost enough to

CHAPTER TWENTY THREE

make a man renounce jumping bones. Almost."

"Good, good. There is some healing going on. Now if you could only take a break from fornication for a lunar or so, we might have a breakthrough."

"A lunar? Why don't you cut them off right now and be done with it. A life without humping is no life at all. Apply your ointment and be done with it ... Argh!"

Pete gritted his teeth as Justin slapped a salve on his scrotum. It burned fiercely until the heat sensation subsided.

"If I had an inkling you did that for savage amusement, I'd have Toby tear off your limbs."

Justin returned to his healing bag and pulled out a poultice he had prepared. He carefully unwrapped it.

Pete groaned. "Not that again."

"It's for your own good," Justin said as he quickly wrapped it around Pete's flaccid penis.

Pete's whole body tensed as he struggled to deal with the momentary pain as the combined poultice ingredients seared his phallus. He slowly inhaled and exhaled as Justin had instructed to control the warning signals to his nervous system. In time, the pain subsided.

"You're enjoying this, aren't you?" Pete said.

"Not at all," Justin lied. "Unfortunately, there's a price to pay for your pleasure."

"Speaking of pleasure, hand me that silver box," Pete said gesturing behind him towards a table near the bed.

Justin retrieved the box from the table and handed it to Pete. He held onto it a moment before releasing his grip.

Pete looked up. "What? You're going to tell me this is bad for me too?"

"Tabak in all its forms can be detrimental to health if there is overconsumption."

"You're just a bundle of laughs, aren't you?" Pete said, as he flipped open the lid, took a pinch of the powder and sniffed it up his left nostril. He paused for a moment, with mouth open and eyes closed, and sucked in a mouthful of air before he sneezed. He repeated the process with the right nostril, and followed it with another nasal expulsion.

"There's one other thing you can do for me before you go, Justin the Apotheka's Apprentice."

"Yes?"

"A little dove in the Four Kith tells me Carlos Grimm paid you a visit. What ails him?"

"I'm afraid I can't divulge privileged client information," Justin said, trying to sound as professional as possible, with the hope Puzzle Pete would not press the issue.

"You do know we're at war?"

"I do."

"And any inside information gives me an advantage."

Justin gulped. "I can't tell you about his treatment, any more than I can tell him about yours."

"I could have you killed."

"You certainly have the means to do so. But then who would light up your member and bring fire to your testicles?"

Justin left the bordello, and the two Crimpers who escorted him to the Mutton saw he made his way safely back to the apothekaria. Little Samal was already asleep, and Justin sat in the kitchen and ate a bowl of hearty leek and potato soup and a slab of stale brood, which softened when he dipped it in the creamy liquid. After his meal, he sat in front of Master Habala and took a pipe of Old Burley tabak. He held the bowl of his pipe in his left hand and blew out a steady stream of smoke. His right hand reached out for *safwan*, his glowing rock and he casually played with it as he pondered the predicament he found himself in. One moment, he was a prisoner with only his bearskin and daronite rock for company. Next, he was an Apprentice Apotheka to a dead master, and a forced spy for Rafyn, caught between two factions who sought death and destruction for the other. Then there was the growing dissent in the Slough, which threatened to ignite all of the Four Kith.

"This is a fine mess we have for ourselves, isn't it Master Habala?" Justin said, blowing out another stream of tabak smoke.

CHAPTER TWENTY THREE

Master Habala was silent.

The commotion outside emptied the apothekaria waiting room in short order. Justin finished up with a patient who had an infected hand with a misplaced fish hook and went out to see what was going on for himself. Little Samal, though he could not hear the ruckus, sensed something was happening and joined Justin in the street. The two of them followed the crowd down to the main thoroughfare. Red Shadows lined the causeway on both sides from the main gates all the way to the Bridge of Broken Souls, and the pathway to the citadel itself. Justin had a strong inkling of what was occuring. He had read *The History of the Var: from the Conquest of Andalayim to the Present* by the Konna historian Dagmar Bodilsdottir. Justin found her prose to be too flowery and a tad melodramatic. However, she did capture the spirit of the times, when the Andra arrived in Varstad via the Black Ships three hundred and fifty years ago, in turn replacing the Lankati people. For three lunars, the inhabitants of the citadel fasted during the solar, and subsisted on pickled vegetables along with the grains imported from the south when the fresh supplies dissipated. Until the first new crop of vegetables bore fruit. The inhabitants of the Slough were not so lucky, and starvation took hold as the secondary purge decimated the poor and infirm. Some sought to steal what they could from the more affluent areas of the Four Kith. Riots broke out, which were savagely repressed by the Damm Warriors and Red Shadows. Once the vegetable sludge flowed again, the depleted population of the Slough went back to their hand to mouth existence.

The chandlers, carpenters, tailors, and coppersmiths of the Burghs; the dockworkers, fishermen, fishwives, and laborers of the Four Kith; the ragamuffins, pickpockets, and beggars of the Slough; and even the early rising slagmaidens, draymen, and publicans from the Mutton, abandoned their own self-imposed social standing, and formed a large heterogeneous collection eager to catch a glimpse of the fresh arrivals. This was their one and only time to view the new people who would live out their lives in the glass domes of the citadel, before their descendents would be forcibly expelled generations in the future.

If the Gastown multitude were expecting a band of merry farmers, decked out in their best clothes, singing happy songs of the joy of working in the gardens and tilling the soil, they were sorely disappointed.

Justin, with little Samal perched on his shoulders for a better view, felt as let down as the rest of the watchers. He was anticipating a celebratory parade, and what he saw was a rag tag army of small dour peasants, who looked in need of a bath, a change of clothes, and a good meal. He could not distinguish the men from the women, as they pushed and pulled their heavily laden handcarts up towards the bridge and on to their final destination in the citadel. From what he could tell, their earthen colored jackets and trousers were made from fibrous plant material, possibly hemp, their footwear was carved wooden clogs, and they wore wide brimmed conical hats on their heads, which they kept bowed down as if concealing their faces. From what Justin could tell based on drawings he had seen in *The Ethnic Diversity of the Heavenly Kingdom,* they were inhabitants from the southern reaches of the Sul empire. Farming stock for sure, but more suited to the heat of the south than the frozen landscape of the north. What struck Justin, and the crowd too, was their disheveled appearance. Their clothes were a collection of patches, and yet still full of holes. In places, dark brown stains surrounded the ruptures in the cloth. They walked awkwardly in their wooden clogs, perhaps the result of the arduous trek, or difficulties maneuvering in the hard mud and slush. There were no Sul guards accompanying the farmer's caravan, just a lone court official, who looked out of place in his fine silks, scholar's cap, and a long beard down to his waist.

"Would you look at that lot! Mudlarks in the Slough dress better," a slagmaiden jeered.

"Probably use their own waste as fertilizer, I'm guessing," a self-important Burghmeister offered.

"Take 'em back to where they belong. No one will eat their slop!" a vagrant barked.

A mudlark in the rear threw a stone in a wide arc over the heads of the

CHAPTER TWENTY THREE

crowd, which made hard contact with a farmer's hat. The man momentarily looked up, and Justin saw a look of anger, and the need for revenge in his hard eyes. He was not expecting that from a downtrodden peasant, who was probably used to slights all of his life. Then the head ducked back down, and the son of the soil moved on.

One enterprising guttersnipe saw an opportunity to profit from the passing peasants, and reached a hand past a lax Red Shadow guard and seized hold of a conical hat from an unsuspecting head. He yanked it free, and bolted back through the Gastown spectators, offering to sell it to the highest bidder. Later in the solar, when no buyer had materialized, and the boy grew tired of wearing the strange headgear, he tossed it into a side alley where it became the nest for a resourceful potkan.

The crowd lost interest in the proceedings long before the last of the farmers made their way across the bridge, and divided again into their respective classes and went about the business of the solar. Justin moved closer and stood just behind the line of Red Shadows. A dumpy Konna woman dressed in gray was taking a tally.

"Excuse me, who are these people?" Justin asked.

The bookkeeper kept her head down and made another entry into her book.

"I asked a question. Who are they, and where do they come from?" Justin asked, this time in Varic.

The Konna looked up with a start. She was not expecting to hear Varic come from someone in Gastown, and she was even more surprised when she saw a tall Dandy dressed in a black cassock, with what appeared to be an Andra boy sitting on his shoulders. The boy was playing with a pair of shears as if giving the Dandy an imaginary haircut.

"W-who are you?" the Konna asked.

"My name is Justin, and I answer to Rafyn. Who are these people?"

The Konna was flummoxed. All she could think to do was answer the question and quickly move on. "They're called the Yaobai. Farmers from the far south of the Sul Empire."

"Ah, yes. The Yaobai. If I remember correctly, they will provide cabbage, mustard greens, lotus root, bamboo shoots, snow peas, radishes, and eggplant. All good healthy vegetables," Justin said with a smile.

"Quite," the Konna replied and moved on before Justin could question her more.

Justin watched as the rearmost of the Yaobai crossed the bridge and disappeared inside of the citadel. The Red Shadows filed away, and Gastown went back to work.

Chapter Twenty Four

Juan : The People's March

There was no food from the Gut, the feeding hall of the destitute, for more than a lunar, but still the dwellers of the Slough gathered in front of the locked doors and eagerly waited for the flow of slop to resume. The chimes of the edentime bells did not help, but added to the discomfort of the drooling crowd, who clutched at distended bellies. Those who had refrained from already eating their belts, tightened them one more notch.

The Slough was completely cleaned out of scurrying potkan in short notice, and over fishing in the Basin cleared out the bottom dwellers who fed on the unfortunate souls who were thrown, or fell in the murky waters. Bully Boys and former Red Shadows guarded all of the slagerhauses, bakeries, and confectionary stores, so even stealing a stale crust of brood was likely to result in a broken head. Risking it all for a blud sausage meant instant death. Even the street vendors added their own protection, and stayed well clear of the Slough. So the occupants on the lowest rung of the Gastown social ladder slowly starved to death.

The Burghs, as always, were off limits to the occupants of the Four Kith, and the Burghmeisters nocturnal visits to the Mutton were severely reduced while they waited for the Slough to return to its normal thieving ways and an acceptable level of criminal behavior. Those who did travel across Skank Bridge added extra security as the necessary price for an illicit encounter. Blue Jackets, the constabulary of the Burghs, worked overtime to protect the borders, and even moonlighted in the better heeled areas of the Four Kith while the overtime pickings were good.

Juan gathered outside of the heavy oak doors of the Gut along with Jojo, Maisie, Flopsy, Gesmas, Topwell, and Shadduck. Nico had left the little band of thieves not long after the murder of Dismas, overcome with his grief at missing the purse handoff. Juan liked to believe the rumor he had gotten a fresh start cleaning out dirty stables, but the more likely truth was he ended his days at the bottom of the Basin.

As the band of companions huddled together, two mirror-image cripples, one missing a left leg and the other the right and no crutch they could call their own, propped each other up as they took turns bashing a rock against the heavy lock securing the door to the Gut. They were getting nowhere.

Juan could stand it no longer, and pushed through the crowd who waited eagerly to gain access, and stood before the two creepers. "Let me give it a try," Juan said.

The missing lefty stayed his hand, but held his rock close just in case Juan had any inclination of stealing it. "What makes yuz think yuz can wield a stone any better than uz? Be off with yuz, before I find a better use for it!"

"I don't need your stupid stone. I 'as my 'ead, an' this," Juan replied, pulling a metal toothpick from his pocket. Ignoring the two cripples, he knelt down before the lock and went to work at picking.

Gesmas, Topwell, and Shadduck moved forward and stood around Juan, in case the rock owners got any ideas of clubbing him out of sheer malice. Jojo, Maisie, and Flopsy stayed back, though Flopsy made it clear she was ready to swoon at a moment's notice if a distraction was required.

Juan worked fast, and smoothly. The lock was of an intricate design, but he managed to work the tumblers, and in the time it took to pick a Burghmeister's pocket, the pivoted hook sprang free. He stood up with a satisfied smile on his face and addressed the two cripples.

"Gentlemen, the honor iz yours," Juan said, gesturing to the heavy oak doors.

CHAPTER TWENTY FOUR

The legless paupers looked at each other, and then they both leaned on the doors, left and right, and pushed them open, and promptly fell on their faces.

The crowd did not wait, and streamed into the Gut. Someone produced a flame, and the candles sprang into life and illuminated the ice cold chamber. The Gut was as spotless as the solar Jaguar Drummel, the Dux's own appointee to manage the great hall, closed up, and the flow of slop was put on hold. The hungry mob ransacked the building, looking for any scraps. A fight broke out between two mites when one thought he found a piece of a vegetable, but it turned out to be a green pebble, which they took turns in sucking. Some nostalgically sat at their previously allotted seats at the wooden benches, waiting for the missing Etenmeister to summon them to the trough. Others licked empty bowls, and reminisced of the time they were full of earthy slop. One crazed man mimicked Jaguar Drummel, and stood ramrod straight with his hand on the lever to release imaginary vittles down the chute.

"Alright, my unwashed lovelies. Dip!"

Some of the crowd played along, and dipped their wooden bowls into the empty trough, sat down at their benches, and ate with dreamy gusto.

"Step aside, now," the Slopmeister's doppelganger barked. "Make room for the second rank. Dip!"

Jojo tugged on Juan's sleeve. "This is madness, Juan. It's barren. There's no food of any sort to be 'ad. Let's be off out of this."

Juan shook his head. "Iz 'ave a plan, Jojo. We can use this as a base. It'll be nice an' warm, once we get a fire goin', an' we 'as a ready made army."

"An army? Wot's we want with an army, Juan?" Jojo exclaimed. "Best be off with our little gang, an' fend for ourselves."

Juan had other ideas. "People power, Jojo. An army means we 'as numbers. Wez can force things. Iz don't know about yuz, but I'm tired of the starvin' life. Iz want a full belly an' Iz want it now! These 'ere mudlarks are goin' to 'elp us get it."

"Iz know that look in your one good eye, Juan Grimm. No good comes from the fight yuz are rushin' into. Let's just go beg from Carlos until these times are past. The rest of the Slough can starve."

"Not this time, Jojo. Not this time."

Juan stood in front of his brother with literally his cap in hand. He fumbled with it as he waited for Carlos to make his declaration. They were in even starker contrast than before. One emaciated twin in rags and a worn eyepatch. The other was well fed, and moving to the wrong side of portliness, dressed in a fine silk tunic with black mascara around his eyes. He sat in Jojo Dickens's old chair and stared into the fire as he twirled his Hetman of the Slagers chain, lost in deep thought.

It was not easy getting an audience with Carlos. With the territorial war raging with the Crimpers from the Mutton, security was extra tight, and Fleet Dawkins and the army of mites were protective of their leader. Once again, Juan only managed to get a meeting with his brother after Perfect Styles intervened on his behalf.

Juan's proposal was a simple one. He was not asking for the choicest cuts, or even the paranga which went into the manufacturer of blud sausages. All he asked for was the last of the scraps, the cast off bones, and the discarded fat. If Carlos would provide the butcher's largesse, then the other slagerhauses would follow suit. Their reward was the good wishes of the Slough dwellers, and a dampening down of any potential revolt in the Four Kith. Once the slagers stood up to be counted, it would be an easier task to shame the bakers to provide their cast off stale brood. Juan's plan was to use the Gut and make an animal based slop of his own. Anything and everything which could provide sustenance would go into the pot, and the brood would mop it up, and fill bellies. It would not be much, but enough to keep the Slough alive until the vegetables flowed once again from the citadel.

"Why should Iz help?" Carlos said in a voice barely above a whisper. He did not address his brother, but continued to stare into the fire.

"'Cos you can," Juan said.

"'Cos I can. And what's in it for yuz, Juan?" This time he did turn his head and stared directly at his twin.

CHAPTER TWENTY FOUR

"They're our people, Carlos. I'm just tryin' to keep 'em alive, is all."

"Our people? Iz dragged myself out of that gutter."

"But the gutter remains, and the people need feedin'. Are yuz up for it, Carlos Grimm?"

Carlos Grimm was up for it, and he provided a wagon of offcuts, scraps, broken bones, and the white offal discard, which generally ended up in the Basin. Perfect Styles even included a poro liver for Juan himself, but it ended up in the pot along with everything else. Food for one was food for all. It was not much, but it was a start. The smell of the stew was enough to make a gong farmer gag, but the Slough came in droves to consume it and survive another solar.

Once Haus Grimm made the donation, the other slagerhauses felt compelled to provide their cast offs too. Haus Heap made a sizable donation of their own, despite the protestations of Josie Heap, who recommended they eat appelflap instead. However, her mother-in-law and Samwell, her husband, were of a more compassionate nature. Then the bakers shared stale loaves, and even the Mutton brewers flowed rank bier into the Slough. For the most part, the Burghs remained aloof. One charitable organization decided education was the way out of poverty, and offered a bowl of cold carrot soup for each solar spent learning to read and write the common tongue. Attendance was thinner than the broth. The Dux and the citadel remained silent, and there was no sign or hope of an outpouring of nourishment.

Once they had the ingredients, Juan now set about the task of organizing the system of cooking, and feeding the masses. They had a good blueprint to follow with the Gut, and Juan assembled a group of volunteers to rig up cauldrons over fires, and cooks to stir the stew, which came to be known as *slagermush*. Juan was prudent enough not to dismantle any of the inner workings of the Gut for the future solar the slop flowed again. However, he did utilize the troughs, and the system for feeding the masses in ranks, bowls in hand for scooping. He even roped in the Etenmeister's mimic to shout out commands, and keep a semblance of order.

Juan sat with his six companions at one of the benches in the Gut. "It's not right," he said, as he held his nose and spooned the last of the slagermush into his mouth.

'It's not so bad. Iz 'ad worse," Shadduck said.

"When?" Topwell asked.

"That time we 'ad no fire, an' ate the potkan raw, tail an' all. Or the rotten dead fish we scooped out the Basin."

"Alright, don't remind us," Gesmas said.

"That's the point," Juan said. "We can't go on like this. We deserve better, an' them folks up in the citadel need to provide some of what they keep for themselves."

Jojo put down her spoon and stared at Juan. She was a shadow of her fat self who spent time in her chair in front of Mo Dickens's fire, eating blud sausage, drinking a steady flow of black bier, smoking her tabak pipe, and spitting tabak juice into the flames. Her hair was matted, and the last of her teeth had fled from her odorous mouth.

"You've done wonders to get food into needin' bellies, Juan. Don't be spoilin' it now. Those folks in the citadel aren't for messin' with. They bring death an' destruction if yuz challenge their ways."

"Challenge their ways, I doz. They haz everythin' an' wez 'as nothin'. We need to set out our demands, an' make 'em share."

"Make 'em? Yuz not makin' sense, Juan. How doz we make 'em?" Jojo asked.

"Why, we 'as an army 'ere in the Slough. We write out our demands, a charter they call it, and march it to 'em across the bridge."

"Iz can't write," Gesmas said.

"Nor I," Topwell offered.

"I can scratch an X," Maisie said. "The gud woman from the Burghs sez it spells Maisie."

"Can yuz write?" Flopsie asked Juan.

Juan shook his head. "No, but Iz can find someone who doz. The important part is comin' up with our charter."

CHAPTER TWENTY FOUR

Juan did find someone who could write, and Justin closed up the apothekaria for the afternoon and visited the Gut for the first time. He even brought a canvas bag with him to administer some off the cuff medicinal support for those in the most need. He took one look at Jojo Dickens and handed her a small jar of a sage, turmeric, and clove compound to rub on her bleeding gums. He gave Flopsy some calendula to apply to her bruised knees from all of the falling down. An assortment of treatments for the down and out soon diminished his herbal supplies. Justin promised he would visit again, as time allowed, but they were all more than welcome to visit him at the apothekaria.

Juan waited impatiently for the tall young man in the black cassock to finish up with his ministrations, and to get to the work for which he was truly summoned. Justin obliged, and took out a roll of parchment paper, which he proudly announced he had created himself, and a quill and ink to record the words. He sat down at one of the benches, directly across from Juan, while the rest of the companions hovered around. Only Jojo sat a little further back, as she happily puffed on a pipe filled with tabak courtesy of Justin.

"What do you want me to write then?" Justin asked, rolling up his sleeves, and dipping the quill in the black ink. "I think a title is required first. What is the name of your document?"

Juan thought for a moment. *"The Charter,"* he said.

"The Charter," Justin wrote in his most flowery penmanship.

The companions leaned closer to stare at the words.

"That's wot it says then? The Charter?" Juan asked.

"It does indeed," replied Justin.

"How about, *The Gastown Charter*," Topwell offered.

"Alright," Justin said. He crossed a line through *The Charter,* and wrote out *The Gastown Charter* in its place.

"Wez don't speak for all of Gastown. Not even the Four Kith, just the Slough. Make it, *The Slough Charter*," Nico said.

Justin drew another line through the title, and wrote out the latest iteration.

Juan shook his head. "The Slough Charter ain't grand enough. We need somethin' the nobs will take seriously."

"May I suggest *The Great Charter*?" Justin offered.

Juan slammed his fist down on the table. "That's it! 'The Great Charter.' They 'as to pay attention to them words."

The companions nodded their heads in agreement and Justin wrote down, *The Great Charter* as the duly nominated title for the covenant.

"Now we've established The Great Charter, what main points do you want to convey?" Justin asked, quill at the ready.

Juan scratched his head. "Well, we 'asn't given that too much thought. Firsters, I'd say 'All men are equal.'"

"Excuse me!" Jojo said, blowing a plume of smoke in Juan's direction. "What about womenfolk? Last I checked, the Dux is a woman hisself, an' the Gentry are ruled by women, so they are."

"I can attest to that," Justin said.

"Wot about animals? Isn't they equal as well?" Maisie offered.

"Tell that to your slagermush! Thems equal parts in there!" Gesmas said with a laugh.

Juan patted Maisie's arm. "We'll look out for the animals as best we can, but this 'ere charter is for the people. 'All people are equal.' That's our first rule," Juan said, and Justin duly recorded it.

With one right recorded the companions fell into a brooding silence. They were at a loss on how they wanted to express their grievances with their current existence. Justin broke the peace.

"I'd recommend you have at least seven rights. How about 'No taxation without representation'?" Justin offered.

"Wot's taxation?" Flopsie asked.

"Wot's representation?" Gesmas inquired.

Justin put down his quill and looked at his nonplussed audience. "Well, taxation is a levy the Dux and her ministers place on the Burghs. For instance if a merchant sells a bolt of cloth for five gild, one gild goes to the Dux."

"For doin' nothin'?" Flopsie asked.

CHAPTER TWENTY FOUR

"For allowing the trade to occur," Justin replied.

"That's nowt but stealin'," Topwell said. "Anyways, we don't pay no taxes in the Slough on account wez don't make anythin'."

"An' representation?" Gesmas inquired again.

"Well, representation means you have a say in the governing of things if you pay your taxes. Even setting the limit of the taxes themselves."

"Looks like representation don't apply to us either," Gesmas said with a dismissive sniff.

"Food is a common right, starvation is wrong!" Juan said firmly, and with that the aphorism flood gates opened.

"What we steal fairly we keep!"

"Warm beds an' blankets for the poor!"

"Brood an' bier for all!"

"Turn back on the slop, an' add more carrots!"

"Free tabak for ole tarts!"

Justin scribbled furiously, and once he had finished, he held up the Great Charter for all to see, though none of them could read. They marveled at the majesty of the document they had created, and touched the words, when Justin pointed out the lines they had plucked from their egalitarian imaginations.

"I'll create another copy for you, so you can keep one here at the Gut, and present the other one to the Dux's ministers, though I've no idea how you'll go about that."

"I 'as a plan," Juan said.

After Justin made a copy on a fresh piece of parchment, Juan took the original, borrowed the rock from one of the cripples, and a rusty nail from an old roofer down on his luck, and hammered The Great Charter to the oak door of the Gut for all to see. The Slough folk stared in wonderment at the words, but no one could read, so at regular intervals, Juan left the sanctuary of the Gut and recited the seven rules for all to hear. They listened and learned, and made the rules their own, chanting them in unison.

The following solar, and after the last of the slagermush was consumed to sustain them on the march to the bridge, Juan assembled the Slough army. They were a ragtag assortment of dipsters, pilferers, footpads, lurchers, harlots, orphans, cripples, mudlarks, inebriates, and at least one old tart with no tabak. The collective tangy bouquet from so many unwashed bodies in close proximity rivaled the stench from the slagermush. If their demands and show of force did not force the Dux's hand, the assault on her delicate snout would surely prevail.

Juan gathered with his six companions before he addressed the eager crowd. He had never intended to be a leader, but circumstances had pushed him in that direction. He was scared of the likely outcome, but he knew he had to proceed. The alternative was a slow death. He stared at the grinning Gesmas, Topwell, and Shadduck. All three of them were wearing eye patches, Gesmas and Topwell covering the right eye, and Shadduck the left orb.

"Wot's this then?" Juan asked.

"Why, it's a shell game," Gesmas explained. "Yuz stick out with the missin' lamp, an' they'll surely single yuz out in the crowd."

"Now, when they give unnatural attention to yuz, duck down, and one of us pops up, an' draws 'em away," Topwell continued.

"It's a dangerous game yuz are playin' boys," Juan said.

"Wez all up for it, Juan. One for all, and all for all," Shadduck offered.

Juan grinned. "Come on then, let's get this swarm movin.'"

Juan turned to face the crowd, and when he saw their eager faces, on tenterhooks for him to speak the words, his mouth went dry and his knees buckled. They were waiting on him, Juan Grimm, to lead them out of starvation, and the hope of a better life. They did not want much, not a fancy haus, a life of indulgence, or baubles and curios beyond their grasp or vision. They simply wanted a full stomach at the end of the solar, and a pinch of dignity.

Juan took a deep breath and searched for inspiration.

Wot doz I say?

"All people are equal!" Juan shouted, holding up a clenched right hand.

CHAPTER TWENTY FOUR

The crowd roared. "All people are equal!" they echoed, punching up their own right fists into the air.

"Food is a common right, starvation is wrong!" Juan yelled, punching his fist again.

"Food is a common right, starvation is wrong!" they chanted.

Juan had them now. He held up both of his open hands and gestured for silence. The crowd immediately settled down. Behind him, Gesmas stepped forward holding up a long pole with the Great Charter parchment nailed to a crossbeam. The masses gazed up in wonderment, as if it was a list of magic incantations. Some reached up their hands, as if touching it would cure them of any ills.

"Iz give yuz The Great Charter! Wez are goin' to march on now, across the bridge an' up to the citadel. Wez goin' to plant this 'ere Great Charter next to the Dux's door. These 'ere are your demands! These 'ere are your rights! Are yuz up for it?"

"Wez up for it, Juan!"

"Lead us to the bridge!"

"Death to the Dux!"

Juan shook his head at the last cry for action. "No! No death chants. This 'ere is a peaceful protest. No violence!" Juan shouted. "Now are yuz ready to march with me?"

"Wez ready, Juan!"

"Ready, willin' an' able!"

"Lead on, Juan. We'll follow yuz to the Onderworld if that's the path!"

As Juan moved forward, the crowd turned in the direction of the Bridge of Broken Souls and followed. People wanted to carry the Great Charter, so Gesmas handed it off, and first a harlot, a thief, and then a cripple took turns holding it aloft.

"All people are equal!" they chanted.

"Food is a common right, starvation is wrong!" they cried.

"Turn back on the slop!"

"Don't forget the carrots!"

"Free tabak for ole tarts!" Jojo squawked.

Juan's flock were in a happy, playful mood as they followed him through the Slough and onto the bridge. Some of the folks from the Four Kith even came out to see what all the commotion was about, but they were sensible enough to watch from a distance. This was not their squabble, but the distraction offered free entertainment. A handful of street vendors thought about hawking their meat pie and blud sausages, but given the nature of the demonstration, and the chant of 'What we steal fairly we keep,' they decided to shut up shop.

The crowd stopped when they reached the bridge. A lone figure confronted them and sought to stop their progress across and on to the citadel. It was Jaguar Drummel, the Slopmeister himself, and he stood ramrod straight as always. He was in full regalia, in his chef's green toque hat and sharply pressed green apron. He held out a wooden spoon in his right hand, the one bestowed on him by the Dux herself. It was his symbol of authority, and by default, the Dux's sovereignty. Jaguar Drummel held up his wooden spoon for all to see. He pointed it at the Great Charter, as if warding off great evil.

"You shall not pass!" Jaguar bellowed.

The Slough hesitated. Until Juan broke the spell.

"All people are equal! Food is a common right, starvation is wrong! Onward!"

A roar went up from the throng, and they surged forward.

"You shall not pass!" Jaguar yelled again, brandishing his spoon.

The crowd ignored him, and tried to walk around the Etenmeister. Soon, the push from behind was too strong. Jaguar Drummel went down, and dirty feet walked all over his once pristine green apron. They moved on over the bridge, a journey most of them had never taken. Crossing towards the citadel was forbidden territory reserved only for the burghfolk who were allowed to work for the Var.

Juan's heart beat faster as the Slough folk surged onward towards the citadel and the intent of planting their post at the very gates for all to see the Great Charter and their list of demands. He did not know what the result would be; he had not thought that far ahead, but the exhilaration

CHAPTER TWENTY FOUR

of leading his people and the unity of folk who would generally kill each other for a shaved coin, was worth any potential risk to life or limb.

Juan's army never made it to the gates of the citadel, or even to the other end of the Bridge of Broken Souls. As they crossed the arch of the bridge, they saw what was waiting for them on the other side and stopped dead in their tracks. Three ranks of Red Shadows with halberds lowered, spanned the width of the bridge. Behind them on a raised platform was a rank of Red Shadows armed with crossbows, and directly behind them stood the tall Damm Warriors with their varbows at the ready. A tall woman in black stood in the center of the back rank, flanked by a tall Damm Warrior leaning on a cane, and a smaller woman in brown, who stood on a wooden block to match the height of the other two.

"They knew we woz comin'. Some mudlark told 'em," Juan said.

"Best be gettin' out of 'ere, Juan. I don't wants no free tabak anyways," Jojo said, though the press of the crowd stopped her going anywhere.

Juan looked up at the Great Charter nailed tightly to the post. He felt pride for what they had accomplished, even as they were stopped by a wall of spears.

"Disperse this unlawful gathering, by order of Lady Rafyn, Minister of Domestic Affairs, and Lady Lilith, acting Minister of War. Return to your homes, and only your leaders will be punished for this transgression," the small woman in brown announced.

"We 'aint got no homes!" a harlot yelled.

"All people are equal!" Juan shouted, and raised his right fist.

"All people are equal!" the crowd responded, though their chant was lackluster, and only half raised their fists in counter salute.

The woman in brown unrolled a scroll. "Yes, yes. We have your list of seven demands here. All people are equal. Food is a common right, starvation is wrong. What we steal fairly we keep. Warm beds and blankets for the poor. Bread and beer for all. Turn back on the vegetable stew, graciously donated by the Dux. Free tabak for old ladies."

"Ole tarts!" Jojo corrected.

"All of your demands are unacceptable. The Dux rules with singular authority, and her word is law. Disperse, I say, or suffer the consequences!"

"All people are equal!" Juan shouted again. This time the response from the Slough was decidedly muted.

The tall woman in black leaned over and whispered something to the woman in brown, who nodded her head.

"One more thing. There will be no mercy for Juan Grimm," the woman in brown declared.

The crowd gasped, and a few heads turned to look in Juan's direction.

"Don't give 'im away, yuz mudlarks!" Jojo hissed, and pulled Juan's hat down to conceal his eyepatch.

Gesmas pulled off his hood for all to see his eyepatch. "I'm Juan Grimm!" he cried.

Over on the other side of the bridge, Topwell did the same. "I'm Juan Grimm!" he yelled, as Gesmas ducked back down.

Shadduck responded in kind, though his patch covered his left eye and was not fooling anyone. "I'm Juan Grimm!" he bellowed.

A rock, previously in the possession of two cripples, sailed over the head of the crowd and made violent contact with the helmet of the woman identified as Lady Lilith, who removed her helmet and examined the dent. She barked a command, and the rank of Red Shadow crossbowmen let their bolts fly into the front row of the crowd. The quarrels made no distinction between man, woman, or child. Chainmail and armor plate offered scant protection against the lethality of the crossbow, and the people of the Slough had none. The front row collapsed as metal punctured flesh, and the cries and shrieks from those behind signaled to the crowd death was coming.

As the Red Shadow crossbowmen, fresh bolts held firmly between the teeth, lowered their weapons to pull back on the strings to reload, the Damm Warriors pulled back on their mighty bows and sent a shower of arrows high into the sky to descend on those in the rear.

On Lady Lilith's next command, three Damm Warriors focused on the people around the Great Charter. A cripple, using the pole more for his own support than acting as the standard bearer, took an arrow shaft to the throat. He clutched at it as the blood gurgled in his gullet, and he collapsed to the ground. A brave harlot seized the pole and stood defiantly for all of three seconds, until three arrows thudded into her chest. No one else sought the privilege of championing the Great Charter, and it fell to the ground, a forgotten emblem of a lost cause.

The Red Shadows unleashed another volley of bolts, this time into the backs of the fleeing crowd. The Damm Warriors continued shooting volley after volley, and indiscriminately slaughtered the cut and run flock. The arrows and bolts took their toll, but more folks died trampled under foot as unity was abandoned for self preservation.

Juan was no exception. As his Slough army disintegrated around him, he kept his head down, crouched even lower, and climbed and pulled his way through the dying and the dead. He glanced over to see Gesmas standing tall with his face exposed.

"Get down you fool!" he hissed.

It was too late. The three Damm Warriors singled out the boy with the eyepatch, and peppered him with arrows. One shot was low and went through his liver. Another pierced his heart, and the third went clean through his eyepatch.

"They've killed Juan Grimm!" the cry went up, and if the rabble needed any further excuse for taking to their heels and a return to a slower death and starvation in the Slough this was it.

The Slough army was no more, and no threat to the Var. The shooting stopped and the wounded and dying were left to fend for themselves. Juan ran on in full retreat, but to where? He knew he could not return to the Slough. They would never forgive him for bringing the punishment of the Var down on them. He paused at the end of the bridge to catch his breath, and then darkness took him.

Chapter Twenty Five

Josephine : The Bridge of Broken Souls

For once, Josephine was up early, and could take a more leisurely stroll to her work as she masqueraded as her dead brother, the Assameister's Assistant in the depths of the citadel. She stopped off at Andersen's Hotshop and basked in the joviality of the happy establishment as she ordered a fresh meat pie for her lunch to augment her brood and cheese. Mister Andersen was in fine form, and despite the early hour, he precariously balanced on a wobbly stool, and entertained his patrons with a fine rendition of, *A Passing Wind,* which he performed with flatulistic perfection.

   The respite was as fleeting as Mister Andersen's gas, and Josephine's thoughts soon returned to the recent disagreements with her father. She tried to be a dutiful daughter and respect his wishes, but nothing seemed to get resolved and with her father's deteriorating health, they were running out of time. Although she relished working in the assachamber and perfecting her skills, she wished she could do so openly. The Var women could rule Varstad with an iron fist, but the women in Gastown were relegated to second class citizens, and she would never be accepted as her father's replacement. A more satisfactory solution was required, but it remained elusive.

   Josephine and Castor Willow locked horns about everything these solars, and Nell Barley, their housekeeper often acted as peacekeeper in an

CHAPTER TWENTY FIVE

increasingly fractured household. Josephine politely pushed back on her father's request for more time to sort out the family secret and how to deal with her dead brother. They were also on opposite ends of the spectrum in reaction to the Purge. Josephine had been passionate for more involvement from the Burgh folk to come to their rescue and rally forth and provide aid. Castor Willow had been adamant they should not get involved in the business of the Four Kith, and in the end he forbade Josephine from leaving the house on the tragic night. The delicate relationship between father and daughter was further strained when the magnitude of the lethal event unfolded.

Josephine was in a sullen mood as she walked with the other workers on her way to the citadel. On top of a disruptive family life, there were no more secret trysts with Ori in the hidden alcove to offer spiced kisses at the end of a solar. All she had left from that brief encounter was bruised ribs.

Her cap was pulled down, and she was almost on the Bridge of Broken Souls before she saw the signs of the carnage up ahead. The people's march of the previous solar had been abruptly terminated and the poor folk who survived the indiscriminate slaughter had gone back to their lives of destitution and hardship. Most of the dead and wounded were cleared away, either carried back to the Slough, or tossed into the frigid waters, so Josephine was spared that sight. However, the remnants of the conflict were still on display. Reddish-brown bloodstains smeared the snow in irregular patterns, and discarded clothes and the odd worn shoe littered the causeway. Broken arrows and bent crossbow quarrels lay in evidence as to how the Var dealt with anyone challenging their authority.

There were still Slough folk on the Bridge of Broken Souls, which lived up to its name on this solar. Those who were near to death, and those who lacked the ability to move, or friends to assist with life-saving transportation. A tall young man in a black cassock moved amongst them, offering help where he could. He bandaged wounds, and applied salves, and frantically passed instructions to two hired men pulling a cart who carried off the most recently treated, as if he was personally responsible for redeeming everyone.

The sight of the recent slaughter was bad enough, but what concerned Josephine the most was the indifference shown by her fellow workers, who streamed across the bridge, heads down, and on to earn their crust from the table of the Gentry, or back to their warm beds in the Burghs. No one stopped to offer assistance. No one paused to provide solace to their fellow man or woman in need. No one challenged the Var. Josephine stared up at the imposing citadel which dominated all of their lives, and she felt hatred well up inside of her.

The whistle sounded calling men to work, and Josephine stopped in her tracks. *Not on this solar.* She would face the wrath of her father later, but now she was called to help as best she could. She opened her lunch pail and broke the brood, cheese, and hot pie into smaller bite sizes, which she distributed to the needy. They took it with grateful nods, and devoured the slim pickings. She took her flask and moistened parched lips and soothed dry throats. She respectfully listened to their narratives of the peaceful march, which had turned into an orchestrated bloodbath. She held the frozen hand of one old dear, until she slipped away, and Josephine cried as if her own grandmother had traveled on to the Onderworld.

By the time the solar was at the midpoint, there was nothing more Josephine could give, and she was emotionally spent. She wanted to help with delivering the wounded back to the Slough, but she was shrewd enough to know it was too dangerous an undertaking. Going on to the citadel was now out of the question as the heavy gates were firmly closed barring access to all latecomers. There was no alternative but to head back to the Burghs and her own warm cottage, and dwell on the inhumanity of it all.

Josephine crossed back over the small sliver of the Four Kith, conscious she did not have the security of the returning workers to hide within. Safety in numbers gave way to singular flight, and she furtively glanced about even as she moved at a quicker pace, expecting to be accosted, robbed, or murdered at any moment. Her fear subsided when she passed the border into the Burghs, and the sight of two Blue Jackets on patrol meant she was

CHAPTER TWENTY FIVE

safe. They gave her a quizzical look as she touched her cap in greeting as she walked on by, and whispered about what form of punishment the Assameister would impart to a workshy apprentice.

Josephine approached their two-story cottage at the end of the lane, and steeled herself for the inevitable questions Nell would pepper her with, before sitting her down to help craft a story to partially placate her father. She took a deep breath, opened the door, and stepped into Nell's kitchen.

Nell was not engaged in the usual busy activity of preparing the Willow evening meal, washing up pots and pans, or stocking up wood for the kitchen fire. She sat in her familiar chair, with a wooden casket on her knee and tears in her eyes.

Josephine immediately forgot about her own tribulations, and went to comfort her housekeeper. "What is it, Nell? Why are you so upset?" she asked, as she crouched down and took her hand.

Nell came out of her stupor, and took a moment before she seemed to comprehend Josephine was there.

"Oh, my! Have I been sitting here all solar? Your father will be home soon and there's no dinner prepared," Nell said, wiping her eyes with a crocheted handkerchief.

"It's still the middle of the solar, Nell. But no mind to that now, what made you so upset?"

"A man came to see me today, name of Jack Cuttle, and he left this casket. It's a gift from my brother," Nell said.

"I didn't know you had a brother?"

"I don't any more. He's dead, you see."

"Oh, I'm sorry, Nell," Josephine said, forgetting she was still wearing her dead brother's soiled work clothes, and tightly hugged her housekeeper.

"We were never close, and he was a bad sort. But he did a kind act in the end, and it got me to wondering how he went down the crooked path he did." Nell opened the casket on her knee and showed Josephine the contents. "It's a pot of gild."

Josephine was astonished at the amount of gold and silver coins, more than she had ever seen before. "Why, Nell, you're rich!"

"I guess I am. Strange how life takes twists and turns. I'm not complaining, mind you. I landed in a happy place ... that's before young Joe passed. But it was a struggle getting here. Cotter ... that was my brother's name ... Cotter Sullivan. Sullivan was my name too, before I married the dearly departed Jacob Barley. Well, Cotter had no one to keep him in hand and raise him the right way. There was only our tired mother, you see. And she was too busy washing and cleaning to keep us fed. There was no man of the house for discipline and teaching the right way of things. So Cotter ran with a mean crowd and did wicked things. He even gave me this burn scar..." Nell said, touching the old white wound on her cheek. "That's all I had to remember him by, until this casket showed up."

"Well, he can't hurt you any more, Nell," Josephine said.

"No, or anyone else for that matter." Nell snapped the casket lid shut. "I can't accept this! Who knows how he came by it. Thieving and killing and the like!"

She put the casket on the floor, and pushed it under a chair with her foot as if the very sight of it would cause her pain. "I'll return it immediately. What was I thinking about taking it in the first place? As soon as he mentioned Cotter's name I should have shown him the door!"

"Or you can use the gild to do some good. Help the poor and those in need. If Cotter did bad things in life, he can do good from the Onderworld. That can be his redemption," Josephine offered.

"I wouldn't know how to go about such a thing!" Nell complained.

"I can help, Nell. I can help," Josephine said, getting all excited about providing some good at last, even if it was with someone else's newly received nest egg.

Nell patted Josephine on the cheek and kissed her on the forehead. Then it dawned on her that Josephine was home in the middle of the solar and all was not right with the Willow world.

"Oh, my! Why didn't you go to work? Your father will be furious when he gets home."

"I can explain, Nell."

"Well, get yourself upstairs first and out of those smelly work clothes

CHAPTER TWENTY FIVE

and into your dress. I'll make us both a nice herbal broth."

Josephine knew there was no arguing with Nell, and she would have to postpone her explanation until she was suitably attired as the dutiful daughter of Castor Willow. She went upstairs, and paused before her dead brother's room and private mausoleum, and placed a respectful hand on the door and said a silent prayer. She did not go in, she never did. Nell kept the only key in her apron pocket, and Joe remained alone in his shroud with never a familial visitor.

Poor Joe! What would you have made of this cruel world?

Josephine quickly changed into her plain haus dress, and put away her brother's clothes for another solar, though she wondered if she would ever wear them again, or even if she wanted. In part, that would depend on how her father reacted when he came home.

The two women sat around the small kitchen table and nursed their hot drinks. Nell had stacked the fire with new logs while Josephine was changing, so the kitchen was a cozy haven. She waited patiently for Josephine to explain the events of the solar, and why she seemed to be disobeying her father at a time when he needed her the most.

"It was terrible, Nell. I didn't see the worst of it, but they just shot them down and all they were after was food for empty bellies. I had to stop and help as best I could. I gave them the little food I had, and a comforting hand where needed."

Nell missed the point. "Oh, you poor dear. You must be hungry. Let me fix you some brood, pickles and cheese," she said.

Josephine shook her head. "I have no appetite, Nell. I wish I could have done more. It's not fair some people suffer while we sit here in the Burghs and act like no wrong is going on outside our borders. Burgh folk walked across the bridge today as if nothing had happened. And the Gentry? They're cruel, merciless people! First they discard the poor farmers and push them into the canal, and then they slaughter the poverty-stricken for the crime of having nothing to eat! Better we burn them all down and start fresh!"

Nell put a hand to her chest, as if the very words caused her pain. "Don't say such things, Josephine! If you speak out against the Gentry, even in private, dreadful things will happen. They have spies everywhere!"

"But we have to do something, Nell. We can't just sit here and drink hot broth!"

"You're not the first to have such thoughts, Josephine. And I dare say you won't be the last. But let me tell you a cautionary tale of the last one to follow this dangerous path. His songs and poems are out of favor now, but when I was a girl, *The Ballade of Tyler Straw* was still something we recited, though our childish minds couldn't comprehend the meaning behind all of the words. Tyler was a minstrel, a handsome man by all accounts, who wooed Gentry, Burghmeister's wives, kitchen maids, and harlots in equal measure. He turned up in Gastown one solar aboard a Black Ship. He started in the taverns in the Mutton, but also drew a crowd in the Four Kith, and was even invited to perform in the Burghs. His songs were about love, life, laughter, betrayal and jealousy. But many had a deeper meaning too, and people sang them at first without truly understanding the hidden message. The words were powerful, and they weaved their way into people's hearts until they believed them as their very own. Words like: equality, freedom, liberty, and justice. Soon people were stirred up, without truly knowing why, and Tyler Straw openly talked about challenging the authority of the Gentry and marching on the citadel. Of course, the Gentry got wind of it, spies and all and at least one jealous husband, and Tyler Straw was arrested before things got out of hand. For his troubles, he was cut into pieces, and his parts hung up all over Gastown for everyone to see, and understand what challenging the Gentry truly meant. However, heroes aren't allowed to die, and stories abounded about how he was rescued from the block by a Damm Warrior lover, who spirited him away to sing elsewhere. And to perhaps return when the people are truly ready to listen."

"I'm ready to listen!" Josephine said.

"Tosh posh. You're missing the point, Josephine. The true message of this tale is mind your own business, and keep your pretty head down. Stirring the pot brings unwanted attention. Best to forget the likes of Tyler Straw and the trouble they bring down on us all."

CHAPTER TWENTY FIVE

"But there are things I can't forget, Nell. Cruel things done by cruel people. I don't want to work for the Dux and her Gentry any more!"

"We need the assa too, my dear. Without it, Gastown freezes."

"Then let us all freeze and be done with it!"

"And what's the good in that?"

"We live in a cold-hearted world, so let's have an end to it."

"Tosh posh, Josephine. You're not making sense. There's good in this world too. You just have to look very hard to find it. But it's there. Small act of kindness can go a long way," Nell said.

Nell stood up and smoothed down her apron. "Now let's have something to eat, and put this nonsense behind us. I'll make us some fresh scones, and we'll top them with fruit preserves and cream. Not a word of this to your father, mind."

Josephine sat at the dining table along with Nell and her father. She had helped Nell to make her father's favorite meal: thinly sliced poro meat dipped in batter and deep fried, and then smothered in a rich white sauce, and accompanied by buttered baby potatoes. They sipped mulled wine, as if it were a special occasion. On the surface, it was a comfortable setting, but the only warmth came from the fire in the hearth. No one spoke, and everyone ate sparingly. Josephine kept her head down and avoided eye contact with her father.

Nell broke the awkward silence. "Is the meal not to your liking, Mr. Willow?"

"It's fine, Nell. I just don't have much appetite these solars," Castor replied.

"I have a nice butterscotch pudding to follow it with, provided you have some room."

"You spoil me, Nell."

"I try, Mr. Willow. I do try."

There was another inconvenient pause in the stilted conversation before Castor Willow addressed Josephine's absence from the assachamber and the dereliction of her brother's duties.

"I needed you there, Josephine. There was trouble with one of the boilers, and I had no one to take over the general running of things while I fixed the problem," Castor said.

"I had something to attend to," Josephine said, as she pushed a potato around her plate.

"More important than watching over the assa and keeping the citadel and Gastown warm?"

"On this occasion, yes!" Josephine said.

"Now Josephine, we said we would handle this differently. No point upsetting your father," Nell gently chastised.

"I'm sorry, Nell, but I have to speak my mind."

"Did I raise you to have a silent tongue?" Castor asked.

"You raised me to be a daughter, not a son," Josephine said.

"I thought you like working as an Assameister's Apprentice?"

"I do, but I can't go on masquerading as Joe. And I can't work for the Gentry! Did you see what they did on the bridge?"

"There was a rebellion they had to put down."

"It was a peaceful march by hungry people, and they were slaughtered!"

"Affairs of the state, Josephine, and managed by the Dux and her council. The Burghs don't get involved and we're left alone to run our business as we see fit."

"As long as we pay taxes, provide our young men as Red Shadows, and keep the boilers running."

"There are worse ways to live."

"I know, there's life in the Slough!"

"Then be thankful for what you have!" Castor said, raising his voice.

Josephine dropped her cutlery on the table and stood up. "I have a dead brother upstairs who needs a proper burial, and a father who is dying!"

Josephine's words hit home, and her father fell silent. He got up from seat at the table, and sat in his comfortable chair by the fire, and pulled out his favorite tabak pipe and lit it up.

"No butterscotch pudding, Mr. Willow?" Nell asked, trying to restore the peace.

CHAPTER TWENTY FIVE

Castor Willow did not answer. Instead, he consoled himself by puffing on his pipe and sending smoke rings up to the rafters of the low kitchen ceiling.

Josephine helped Nell to clean away the dishes from the table, and washed and dried the plates, cups, and cutlery. It gave both her and her father the chance to calm down, and approach their problems with cooler heads. The tasks completed, she went over to her father and stared down at the wizened old man. He had aged so much since Joe's death, and he was a shell of his former self. He was never a large man, and his diminutive size was reflected in his surname. However, he was also resilient, and bent under pressure but never broke. Until now.

Josephine dropped to the ground, put her head in her father's lap, and gently wept. She wept for poor dead Joe, she wept for her dying father, and she even had a few tears to spare for herself.

"What are we to do, father?"

Castor Willow stroked his daughter's head with one hand, and held his pipe to his mouth with the other. "I just need time to sort things out. Just a little more time."

However, Josephine knew time was in short supply, and if her father did not make a decision soon, their imperfect circumstances would surely dictate the outcome.

Chapter Twenty Six

Carlos : The Trial of Juan Grimm

Carlos sat in the heavy oak chair on the raised platform. Although he wore the Hetman of the Slager chain of authority, Perfect Styles sitting to his right was the true butcher, and his hands moved nervously, away from his block and the comfort of cold steel in his grasp. Black Jack Cuttle, his accountant and financial architect of the illegal enterprise, sat to his left, mopping his brow with a black handkerchief, which went in and out of his pocket like a magician's rabbit. It was only a few lunars since Carlos himself was the one on trial, and Cotter Sullivan sat in the exalted chair, Now, he was the judge, jury, and potential executioner for another Grimm; his twin brother Juan was on trial for his life.

Once word reached Carlos of the people's march on the citadel, he knew no good would come of it. He had sent Fleet Dawkins and a handful of mites to watch the proceedings from a safe distance, and bring back word as the disaster unfolded. Fleet went one better, and brought Juan with no more than a lump on his head.

The slagerhaus was full, but not with an audience to Carlos's liking. There were far fewer Bully Boys in attendance, and their numbers had dwindled since the advent of the conflict with Puzzle Pete and the Crimpers. He made up for it in recruiting more imps and mudlarks to take their place, and Fleet Dawkins now commanded a small army of undersized soldiers.

CHAPTER TWENTY SIX

However, he needed fighting men at his side if they were to prevail. There were others there too on this special solar, denizens of the Slough called to witness.

Carlos greeted the solar with another blinding headache, and it took two bowls of the special tabak for the pain to subside, and a mellowness to wash over him. He knew it was a dangerous game to play, and he needed his savagery and cunning to survive. Relaxation and calm was a perceived weakness in the under belly of the Four Kith, and misfortune stalked the frail of mind and the feeble of body.

Juan stood before the high table, cap in hand and head bowed. As Carlos looked down, all he saw was a broken, wraith-like, one-eyed shell of himself. A guttersnipe in rags, a pickpocket, a rabble rouser, and a former leader of a failed protest. Whatever bravado he possessed to temporarily pull the starving Slough together had evaporated with the slaughter on the Bridge of Broken Souls.

"Mister Cuttle, be so kind as to read the charges against, this 'ere mudlark," Carlos ordered.

Black Jack flipped open his book, and read aloud. "Juan Grimm, you are charged with upsetting the natural order of things in the Four Kith, and bringing the wrath, and unwanted attention, of the Dux down on our heads. As a result of your selfish actions, over five hundred souls crossed the river, and many more are maimed and crippled. What do you say, Juan Grimm? Guilty or Not Guilty?"

"We woz starvin'," Juan muttered.

"Speak up, boy. We can't hear you," Black Jack said.

"We woz starvin', is all," Juan said in a louder voice.

"Quite. We'll record that as 'Not Guilty,'" Black Jack said, dipping a quill into a bottle of ink, and duly recording the plea.

"But yuz wasn't starvin' no more," Carlos said. "Yuz came cap in 'and for paranga, an' wez provided it free of charge. The other 'auses did the same, so grub was on your table."

"Wez 'ad bones, white organs, an' putrid scraps. Slagermush stank, an' woz 'ard to keep down," Juan said.

355

"The vittles weren't to your likin', but yuz weren't starvin'," Carlos snarled. He gestured to Black Jack. "Write down 'we woz starvin' in the ledger, and strike a line through it."

Black Jack took out his black handkerchief and mopped his bald head, before recording the words, and striking them out with a flourish of his quill.

"Time to call sum witnesses, don't yuz think, Perfect?" Carlos said.

Perfect Styles nodded his head, and gestured to two slager apprentices at the rear of the hall. They escorted a woman, on the wrong side of her prime, to a designated spot between the raised platform, and where Juan and the members of the audience were allowed to sit for the occasion.

"Name, and occupation?" Black Jack asked.

"Nancy Throgbottom. Gentleman's companion," Nancy said.

"Nancy Throgbottom. Harlot," Black Jack recorded in his book, much to the chagrin of the woman on the stand. "Now tell me Nancy. How do you know the witness?"

Nancy pointed an accusing finger at Juan. "'E's a devil, that one. 'E spoke 'em words which cast a spell on us all. Wrote 'em down too, to hold us in 'is powers. Then, 'e made me carry them. But that pole woz too 'eavy, on account of me weak arms with all of the washin', and Iz 'anded it off to me sister, a strappin' lass, who's 'ere' no more!" Nancy said, and broke down in a flood of false tears.

"Someone get this lady a cup of black bier," Jack ordered.

"And a nice piece of meat?" Nancy requested.

Black Jack leaned forward. "Black bier, or water if you prefer?"

Nancy brushed away a tear, and wiped her nose with the back of her sleeve. "Bier it is."

"Now, do you have anything else to add?"

"I curse the very solar 'e came among us. 'Undreds died on that bridge, 'cos of 'im. *Juan's Folly,* we now call it."

"Write that down too, Jack. *Juan's Folly.* 'E's famous. They named a bridge after 'im." Carlos said.

While Black Jack wrote, a slager's apprentice handed Nancy a cup of

CHAPTER TWENTY SIX

black bier, which she promptly downed as she was led away.

The next witness was escorted to the stand, and he leaned heavily on his own slager's apprentice for support, on account of his left leg was missing and he had no crutch to call his own.

"Name and occupation?" Black Jack asked again.

"Albert Kilmartin. Cripple," Albert said.

Black Jack looked up from his book. "A cripple isn't an occupation, Albert."

"It is if yuz only got one leg."

"Occupation … beggar," Jack said. "Now tell me Albert, what do you have to say about all of this?"

"Same as the 'arlot. I rue the solar he picked the lock to the Gut…"

"Yuz was tryin' to break in with a rock!" Juan said, indignantly.

"Silence!" Black Jack shouted. "There will be no interrupting witnesses. Go on please, Albert."

"As she sez, 'e used powerful words to trap us. Made us repeat them back to keep the spell strong. An' 'e stole my rock!" Albert shouted.

"That's a lie!" Juan said.

"Stole it an' threw it at the 'ead of the Damm Warrior. Only an 'elmet saved 'er skull. And then the arrows came, and poor Eddie, me left legged mucker, took one to the throat."

"That was yuz!" Juan shouted.

"Did you steal this man's rock?" Black Jack asked Juan.

"I-Iz borrowed it for a moment to 'ammer in a nail. But I gave it right back," Juan said.

"Stole the man's rock," Carlos said. "Write that down too, Jack."

There were no more questions for Albert from Black Jack, and Juan simply glared at the cripple, with no interrogation of the witness in his defense. Albert hopped away with the support of his slager's apprentice, spilling some of his own black bier with each bouncing step.

The next witness to take the stand caused Juan to perk up and take notice. Jojo Dickens had spruced up for the occasion as best she could with her limited wardrobe, which was now a few sizes too big for her steadily shrinking frame. Her dress was more patchwork than the original material, and the mangy fur of a long forgotten animal covered her frail shoulders. She somehow managed to powder her face, so she resembled a baker after the end of a long shift, and rouge covered her thin lips, which accentuated the cavernous hole of her toothless mouth. She had done the best she could to improve her hairstyle by cutting out the tangled knots and pulling a broken comb through what remained.

"Name and occupation?" Black Jack asked.

"Jocelyn Jolana Dickens. JoJo for short. Occupation? Hetman of the Slagers's wife," Jojo said, boldly.

"Mo Dickens is no more. Iz is Hetman of the Slagers, an' yuz is no wife of mine!" Carlos snarled.

Black Jack looked perplexed. They could not proceed without a stated occupation. "What do I write down?" he asked.

"Put down cutpurse an' fence," Carlos said.

Jojo looked shocked, and put a hand to her chest as if her heart would stop beating with the shame of it all. "I'm no cutpurse," she gasped.

"No, but yuz 'ave little fingers do the pullin' for yuz," Carlos replied. "Write it down, Jack, write it down. Just as Iz said."

Jack complied, and scribbled in his book. He looked up and asked Jojo the first question. "Tell us, Jojo. How do you know the accused?"

Jojo relaxed and smiled, displaying her blackened gums. "Why, Iz practically raised 'im as my own. Yuz too, Carlos. Tell 'em, Perfect. I was a second mother to the little mites."

Perfect lowered his eyes, but sheepishly nodded his head.

If Jojo was expecting any special treatment from Carlos, she got none. It was as if Carlos had bundled all of his hatred and anger since the events after Josie Dickens's wedding, and blamed Jojo for his misfortune.

"Now 'e cribs for yuz?" Carlos asked.

"We doz what we can to get by," Jojo replied.

"The suspect is fingered as a thief. Write that down too, Jack."

"And what was your role in this little rebellion?" Black Jack asked, addressing the charges at hand.

CHAPTER TWENTY SIX

Jojo adopted the persona of the heavily aggrieved once more. "Oh no! Iz 'ad no role in it. Tell 'im, Juan. Didn't Iz say no gud would come from it all. Them's my very words, no gud at all. Why, Iz sez go an' see Carlos. 'E'll do gud by us an' provide vittles. An' so yuz did, bless your 'eart. Slagermush kept us goin'. No use upsettin' 'em on the 'ill. Only death comes down from there. Them's my words."

Black Jack unfurled a damaged parchment, the charred remains of the Great Charter nailed to the door of the Gut. "Free tabak for old tarts?" Black Jack read aloud. "Did that particular call to action come from you?"

"Well, they already 'ad six others. Iz just added a line as a joke, like. Yuz know, keepin' to the 'umor."

"I see no humor in over five hundred dead, and many more maimed for the little life they have left," Jack said sternly.

"It wasn't my fault," Jojo said meekly, wringing her hands together.

"Then whose fault was it?" Jack asked.

Jojo bowed her head and tears coursed down her painted face, leaving clear streaks behind. "Juan's," she said, and hung her head in shame.

Jojo was escorted from the makeshift courtroom, though there was no black bier for her. She sat in a corner at the back of the room and cried her eyes out. Nobody came to console her.

With no more witnesses to call to the stand, Black Jack invited Juan to make a plea in his defense.

"Juan Grimm. You've heard the charges laid out before this court, and you've heard the damning evidence even from one who says she all but raised you. Do you have anything to say in your defense, before we pass judgment?"

Juan straightened up, and took a moment to compose himself. When he spoke he directed his words at Carlos.

"Iz didn't mean for anyone to die," Juan said.

The look of grief on his face did little to soften Carlos's mood.

"But die they did. Them fine Damm Warriors an' their kept men may 'ave fired the arrows an' bolts, but your fingers was on the triggers and bowstrings. Yuz killed 'em as soon as your foolish 'ead came up with the plan to march on the citadel an' present your demands. The *Great Charter?* No more than words from a slick goose to trick bird brains!" Carlos snarled.

Juan hung his head in shame. "Iz didn't mean for anyone to die, is all," Juan repeated, and fell silent.

With the trial concluded, Carlos, Perfect Styles, and Black Jack Cuttle huddled together to discuss the merits of the capital case. The discussion was over in short order, and the evidence was damning. Black Jack banged a gavel on the table to bring the courtroom to order, and once there was silence in the slagerhaus, he proceeded to read out the sentence. Before he did so, he wiped his bald pate one more time, and then placed the black handkerchief on top of his head.

"Juan Grimm. You have been found guilty by this tribunal of the crime of leading an insurrection, which resulted in the death of over five hundred innocent souls. The witnesses clearly outlined your role as the instigator, and how you manipulated them to go along with your devious plan. You offered no words in your own defense. There can be only one sentence for such a heinous act. Death."

There was an audible gasp from the crowd.

Juan's face, which was already pale due to malnutrition, went three shades whiter. He wobbled on unsteady legs.

Carlos stared at his twin, though his eyes gave nothing away. "'Owever, given that yuz me brother … wot's the word Iz lookin' for Jack?"

Black Jack leaned over and whispered in Carlos's ear.

"Commuted, that's the word. Fine word," Carlos said. "Given that yuz me brother, an' as Hetman of the Slagers, an' with final say. Iz commute your sentence to banishment. Yuz to leave Gastown in a few solars never to return!"

As the crowd dispersed, the slagerhaus returned to business as usual. Perfect Styles donned his apron, and went back to work, cleavers in hand, carving paranga and chopping through bones. The slager apprentices, with no more witnesses to escort, carried meat and offal, and discarded bones and gristle.

CHAPTER TWENTY SIX

Carlos sat with his brother, a cup of black bier in hand. Behind them, much to Carlos's chagrin, Jojo Dickens sat in her old chair in front of the fire. At her feet sat two boys, a year or two younger than him, and two diminutive girls: the remnants of Juan's companions. They all had cups in hand, and chewed on blud sausages, courtesy of Perfect Styles's soft hand. Carlos glanced over at the chief slager, who was content chopping through bone and separating out the best cuts of meat. He wished his own world could be so singular and simple.

"A spy spoiled your plan an' saved your miserable life," Carlos said.

"Iz don't understand," Juan replied, though still in a daze after his death sentence and quick reprieval. His own blud sausage and black bier lay untouched beside him.

"They were waitin' for yuz at the bridge. Yuz didn't invade their world, so they were content with a bit of killin' to send a message. On the other 'and, if yuz surprised 'em, an' marched on the citadel, a great slaughter would 'ave come of it. Not just for the Slough, but the rest of the Four Kith as well. There's more."

"More?"

"They said your name at the bridge. Called out Juan Grimm. They don't know they killed another in your place, but the spy will soon let 'em know the truth of it. Juan Grimm, Carlos Grimm. Guilty by association. Iz can't have that, Juan."

Juan stared hard at his brother with his one good eye. "What will yuz do with me?"

"Banishment. Yuz can't go back to the Slough. A knife will cut your throat the first night. Yuz can't stay with me, cos the Gentry will come callin'. Iz need things as normal in the Four Kith, with no involvement from above. They get the taxes from the Burghs an' tame men to work in the citadel, an' to keep the docks operatin'. The common folk go about their business as before."

"Banishment to where?" Juan asked.

Carlos grinned. "That's the best part. There's a caravan goin' north in a few solars. Harvestin' wood, furs, an' the like. They'll be away for at least six lunars. Time enough for people to forget all about Juan Grimm and his little rebellion. Iz 'anded over a purse of silver coin for yuz to go along with 'em. You'll work for your passage. Yuz 'as a new name too. John Bucket. Iz expect yuz will carry a lot of 'em."

Juan bristled. "Why don't yuz just kill me an' 'ave done with it?"

Carlos smiled. "I can't do that. When yuz die, a part of me does too. Yuz were ever the smart one, Juan. But soft too. This little trip will toughen yuz up. Now eat your sausage, an' drink your bier. I 'as work to do."

"Is this 'ow it ends between us, Carlos?" Juan asked. There were tears in his one eye.

"Be thankful yuz is still above ground. Many in the Slough can't say the same."

Carlos left his brooding brother and went in search of Fleet Dawkins, who was not hard to locate. He found his captain of mites instructing two new recruits on the finer points of rapidly deploying a blade and picking the most lethal sticking points. Carlos waved him over, and Fleet dismissed his charges with a parting kick.

Fleet grinned. "Five new recruits this solar. Our army is growin'."

"But we need Bully Boys to match the Crimpers, an' they're on the verge of dissolvin'."

Fleet spat. "A pox on the Bully Boys. All they're good for is guard work, an' shaggin' the slagmaidens wez gatherin'."

"They're fightin' men, when not runnin' scared of Puzzle Pete and Toby Meyers. We need somethin' to lift their spirits, is all."

"Yuz 'as a plan?"

Carlos nodded. "Iz a plan. But first, we need to deal with that nest of thieves," he said, gesturing over toward Juan's companions. "The two mudlarks can join your mites. Iz guessin' they know how to use a blade already. Take the two doxies to me chambers. Iz a use for 'em."

"And the ole tart?"

"Look at 'er, sittin' in me fire chair like she still owns the thing. As soon as me brother is out of 'ere, dump 'er in the Basin."

CHAPTER TWENTY SIX

Carlos put his plan into motion as soon as Juan was out of the slagerhaus and no longer his responsibility. He paid a small fortune to a proprietress of a rundown bordello in the Mutton, one who was being unduly squeezed out of her profits by Puzzle Pete, to rent the penthouse suite of her establishment. She had no idea where the gild was coming from, just another rich Burghmeister who wanted privacy to fulfill his unnatural fantasies. Maisie and Flopsy were used to bait the honey trap, and the madam was under strict instructions to let no one else sample the wares. The girls were nervous at first, but Carlos promised no harm would come to them, and it was simply an acting job. Once she heard that, Flopsy brightened up, and practiced her swoons with renewed gusto. Carlos cleaned them up too. Their restrictive diet living in the Slough was not a hindrance, since the prospective target was known to like his girls young and undersized. However, they were in dire need of a bath and scrubbing, which they fought like hellcats to avoid. The makeover was completed when a new wardrobe was provided for them to squabble over. Nothing fancy, but ten steps up from the rags they usually wore.

The girls were escorted to the bordello in the Mutton, and ensconced in their room with strict instructions from Carlos to behave.

"Remember, no liftin' purses while yuz iz there," Carlos said. "Yuz is to wait until we point out the mark, then take 'im up to the room."

"Wez know 'ow to behave, don't we Flopsy?" Maisie said.

"Wez certainly do," Flopsy answered, putting the back of her hand to her forehead and dropping into a swoon.

Maisie promptly caught her on the way down, and looked up at Carlos with doe-like eyes.

"An' none of that there flopping, do yuz 'ear! Just a straight actin' job."

Flopsy opened one eye. "An' yuz promise to come in time?"

"Iz'll be there, don't worry."

Carlos sat in the plush velvet chair in the main entertainment room of, *The Haus of Syn* bordello. In his own acting role he was a toy boy for hire, but he never left his chair to go upstairs with amorous clientele. Those solars were over with the death of Cotter Sullivan. However, it allowed him to watch and observe anyone entering the brothel. Fleet Dawkins was there too, working behind the bar washing out cups and flagons, and complaining about the damage all of the water was doing to his hands, which were more at home playing with fire. The rest of the mites huddled outside, waiting on Carlos's orders to storm the room.

That was three solars ago, and still their target had not shown up at the bordello. Carlos was beginning to think he would never show, when in walked the man mountain Toby Meyers, Puzzle Pete's henchman and number one killer. He paid no attention to Carlos, or the slagmaidens on display, and headed straight to the bar.

"How's business, Synthia?" Toby asked the madam, who was on the other side of the bar.

"Better before you came into my life," Synthia replied, as she poured a green liquid into a glass for the big man, who took it and downed it in one.

"Now, now. No need to be like that. Pete just wants his honest share."

"Honest and Pete in the same sentence is a stretch."

"Best hold that tongue, Synthia, or it will be put to uses you thought you'd give up years ago."

"You don't scare me Toby Meyers."

"I should Synthia, you silly old Molly Queen. Now tell me, any new quails on the premises I should know about?"

Right on cue, Maisie and Flopsy walked down the stairway arm and arm, and into the main parlor. As Toby turned to look, Fleet replaced Toby's empty glass with a full one, and nodded at Carlos.

"Well, well. What do we have here?" Toby said.

"Off limits, Toby. Those two are on ice for a rich Burghmeister," Synthia replied.

"We'll see about that," Toby said, gesturing for the girls to come on over.

"Ordinarily, I never pay on a point of principle. How much to sweeten the pot for the brace?" Toby asked.

"More than you can afford," Synthia said.

"Pete's cut for a week."

"A lunar."

CHAPTER TWENTY SIX

"Done."

To Carlos's relief, Toby turned and drained his second glass. Fleet had doctored it with a potion they had procured from the Apotheka, with clear instructions to use sparingly, since a full portion would stop the heart. Fleet dumped it all in as directed.

Toby towered over Maisie and Flopsy, and held out a hand to each of them. They reached up to hold on, but could barely wrap their small mitts around his index finger.

"Ladies, shall we?"

Maisie and Flopsy turned, and the three of them, the mountain in the middle, walked back up the stairs to the room at the top.

Carlos waited for less time than he planned, before jumping out of his chair and racing up the stairs. Fleet had already left the bar, and went to gather the rest of the mites. There was a secret passageway at the back of the bordello, constructed for important visitors to bypass the main entrance, which led straight to the penthaus. Fleet would use it to breach the room.

Carlos took a deep breath before opening the door, and stepping inside. He closed the door behind him. Maisie and Flopsy were on the other side of the large bed, clutching tightly to each other, fear in their eyes. Toby was sitting on the corner of the bed, and he had already removed his jacket and shirt.

Fear hit Carlos as he stared at the monster's broad back. It amplified as the man stood up and Carlos saw the bulging muscles in the front of his body, and the knife scars which criss crossed his torso. Killing Joe Geroni was easy. The drunken man was prone in his bed and rage drove him on. Jonas Wheeler's demise was more luck than skill with a knife, and ending Cotter Sullivan took no more effort than dragging a blade across the sleeping pederast's throat. Gutting ole Davey required the timely assistance of Fleet and his mites, and Carlos needed them again. Even then, Toby Meyers might prove too much for them all.

"What do you want? I don't need boys. Be off with you!" Toby growled.

At that moment, Flopsy fainted, either the best acting job of her short career, or a genuine swoon brought on by the fear of engaging in the coitus dance with Toby. Maisie caught her sister.

Toby turned his attention away from Carlos and back to the girls. "What's wrong with her?"

"Just a case of dropsy, sir. She'll be better with a splash of water," Maisie said.

"Hurry up and bring her round. I need you both back here sharpish," Toby said. He turned back to face Carlos as Maisie carried her sister out of the bedchamber and into the adjoining room. "You still here? Last chance to leave, boy."

Fleet and four mites, three of his most trusted lieutenants, and the new boy Shadduck, who seemed to show some skill with a blade and was eager to prove himself, stepped out of the side room and into the bedchamber. They were all armed with an assortment of knives. Fleet grasped one in each hand. Carlos pulled his own pigsticker and held it out in front of him.

Toby's head swiveled, looking at the five mites who fanned out, and back at Carlos. "So that's your game. I know a honey trap when I see one." He pointed a finger at Carlos. "I'm guessing you're Carlos Grimm, and you've come with your alley potkans to do me harm. Better men than you have tried."

The plan was for Carlos to engage Toby at the front, and the mites to charge in and stab repeatedly at the Crimper until he fell down in a bloody mess. However, once they came face to face with the colossus, everyone hesitated.

"Wez come to avenge Patch Armstrong," Carlos said.

Toby threw back his head and laughed. "Avenge Patch? He sold you out before I sent him on his way. Did a deal with Pete to doublecross you. Wanted things back to normal, he said. You should be thanking me, not threatening with knives."

"Then say 'ello to Patch when yuz see 'im next. Come on boys, let's do 'im," Carlos said, gritting his teeth, and taking a step forward. The mites still hesitated.

Toby put a hand to the side of his head, and steadied himself against the

CHAPTER TWENTY SIX

bed as his legs buckled. "What's this then? Poison?" he slurred.

Shadduck saw his opportunity, and charged in to stab at Toby, but the effects of the drug had not yet robbed him of his senses or a fraction of his power. He lashed out a right fist, which heavily connected with Shadduck's left temple, and sent the boy crashing into the wall. He made contact at an awkward angle, and the impact was followed by a sharp cracking sound. He fell lifeless to the floor.

Toby went down on one knee, and Carlos dove in and stabbed him in the left shoulder. Toby grunted and swung his right fist again, but his power was waning, and he only caught Carlos with a glancing blow. It was enough to dislodge the knife and send Carlos staggering back.

Fleet Dawkins screamed and jumped forward with both his blades repeatedly puncturing the giant's back. Again and again he stabbed in a frenzy of knife blows. Deep wounds opened up on Toby's torso, and his blood flowed. The other three mites joined the fray, and their own blades rained down on the big man, and gashed, slashed, and hacked him to shreds.

Toby still had some fight left in him, despite the drugs and the four ferocious mites. He let out a roar and swung a back handed blow, which sent them bowling over. Carlos, his head now clear, retrieved his knife, and moved in to deal the killing blow with a stab to Toby's heart. There was a look of shock on Toby's face as the knife penetrated his chest, as if he was in disbelief a mere boy could take him down. The melee was over, and Toby crossed to the Onderworld to meet all those he had sent on ahead of him. He slumped forward on his knees, his arms hanging by his side, his head bowed, and Carlos's knife still impaled in his ruptured ticker.

Carlos looked around at his four mites. They were all breathing heavily, and were covered in Toby's blood. He guessed he looked the same. Maisie and Flopsy peered around the corner of the adjoining room, hands to their mouths at the sight of the carnage.

"Did yuz bring Perfect's cleaver?" Carlos asked Fleet.

Fleet went into the side room, past Maisie and Flopsy, and came back with a large meat chopping blade, which he handed to Carlos.

"Time to give Puzzle Pete a strong message," Carlos said, and went to work with the butchering of Toby Meyers.

Chapter Twenty Seven

Aldith : Agithawald

After three lunars of the maritime life, with rough seas, a constrained diet for sustenance rather than enjoyment, and brackish water to wash it down with, the crew and the military arm of the expedition were eager to step ashore. Aldith needed to maintain discipline, and instructed her captains to stagger the landside excursions and keep the Black Ships in a state of military readiness. The orders were not received with enthusiasm, and one crew rebelled against the restrictions, until two of the ringleaders were flogged into unconsciousness.

There were no signs of human life, not from the former occupants of Agithawald, or from the local population. Aldith sent out search parties to locate pathways to adjacent villages, seek out sources of freshwater, and to harvest from the land. They quickly found food and water, but no dwellings or people. For the Damm Warriors and Konna, there were vegetables they had never seen before, purple root vegetables and green leafed produce with a spicy aftertaste, which became a staple. The men hunted large flightless birds which were easy to trap, and ducks and their eggs closer to the shoreline. There were fruits to enjoy too. A brown hairy ball with a delicious green interior, and red, black, and purple berries for the taking.

Aldith approved of the original choice made in selecting the location for Agithawald. The natural harbor offered protection to the fleet, and the triangular stockade dominated the surrounding landscape. A small force could hold a much larger army at bay. There was some disrepair, which Aldith quickly rectified, but the bones of the fort were strong. The chilling aspect was that the quarters were replete with clothing, personal belongings and mementos from home. Pots and pans filled the kitchen and the armory was well stocked. It was as if the people had just walked out one solar and left everything behind.

Runa the Stewardess had been busy since the founding of the colony. Trees had been cleared around the stockade, and there were signs of fields planted with seeds from home. However, it was not the same as the glass domes of Varstad, and there had been no Andra to work the gardens. There were no crops now, just weeds in their place as the land reclaimed lost ground. A rudimentary dock had been constructed at the shoreline. It was large enough for a squadron of Black Ships to moor alongside, and for much needed timber to be loaded and shipped back to Varstad.

"This is a strange dark place. I don't like it," Tana said, as she took another spoonful of the delicious stew the cook had prepared. She sat across the table from Aldith in the quarters of the old Stewardess. Her belongings still occupied the room, and Aldith refused to pack them away in the hope she would return.

"Better make the most of it. We'll be staying for a while," Aldith said.

Tana dropped her spoon on the table and pushed her bowl away. "It's too hot, and sticky during the solar. And it rains too much. I prefer the glass domes where everything is regulated."

"You were a pretty bird in a cage. Here, you're free."

"Free? I can't go five paces without guards shadowing me. And that tall one with the crooked eye keeps staring like he wants to undress me," Tana pouted.

"I admire his taste. But if it bothers you, I'll have him replaced. The guards are a precaution until we figure out what happened here."

"Were they killed?"

Aldith shrugged her shoulders. "There's no sign of a struggle, and the

CHAPTER TWENTY SEVEN

local tribe were friendly at first. Then something changed. Runa, the Stewardess, was a cautious woman, who didn't take unnecessary risks. It would have been difficult to take her by surprise."

Before Tana could offer an opinion on the good sense, or lack of it, of the Stewardess, the eerie sound of horns blowing interrupted the evening repast. There was a deep resonance to the call, and as one extended note faded away, another rose to take its place. The wailing was a primordial echo of the natural world, and its purpose was to terrify those who did not belong.

Aldith was on her feet and out of the chamber before Tana could ask what was going on. She quickly made her way to the top of the defensive wall where the Captain of the Guard was on duty.

"Over there," the captain said, pointing towards the rocky outcrop on the other side of the bay. "There's at least ten of them making that racket."

As they watched in the gloom, fires were lit on the cliffs, and two more spang up in the distance.

Tana came up, slightly out of breath, and clung to Aldith's arm. "Are you going to send someone out and make them stop? I can't possibly sleep through the night with all of that noise."

"I'll lead a party myself in the morning. No one is going out tonight."

They stood a while longer, staring at the shadows of men dancing in the firelight, and listening to the reverberation of the horns.

Aldith went out before the solar rose, and left Tana sleeping, despite her claims of not being able to shut her eyes. The disruptive dissonance went on most of the night, but stopped abruptly just before dawn. They made a strong show of force, and a combined troop of one hundred Damm Warriors and Red Shadows, traversed along the shoreline, and up the steep incline to the top of the rocky outcrop. There were signs where the fires had burned and black scorch marks remained on the stone. There were also two symbols. The face of a fierce looking man within a circle was crudely carved into the rock face. Beside it was a broken varbow.

"What do you think it means?" the captain of the Damm Warriors asked

Aldith.

"They're telling us we're not welcome here. That bow belonged to Runa, so we can guess what happened to her command," Aldith said. "No tracks to follow on this outcrop. Best we make our way back to the stockade, and start sending out war parties."

There was someone waiting for them when they returned to the fort. A middle-aged man dressed in a grass skirt, with a bird feather cape draped across his shoulders, stood just outside the main gate. He was not especially tall, despite what Aldith had heard about the local inhabitants, but he did display the black tattoos which covered his torso, legs, arms, and even his face. There were intricate swirling designs, geometric shapes, and the stylized representation of mythical animals. Five Red Shadows stood guard around him, which seemed to amuse their visitor, and the Captain of the Guard was waiting to report to Aldith.

"Who is this?" Aldith asked.

"A messenger from the local chieftain. He says he'll only speak his words to the new Stewardess," the captain replied.

"He speaks our language?"

The captain nodded. "He has a rough command of the common tongue. Enough to say he wouldn't step inside the stockade on account of the bad spirits who live there."

"Then we'll converse outside."

Aldith approached the man, and gestured to the Red Shadows to step to one side. She was a head taller than the man, and though she was heavily armed it did not appear to concern him. He placed his right hand over his heart and bowed slightly.

"I'm Lady Aldith, Domina of the Var. Who am I addressing?"

"My name is Tanema, the messenger. I talk for Okakara, the chief of the Taramoa in the northern island, and now chief of the Raratoa in the southern isles too. Okakara, the Great Unifier," Tanema said.

"How did you learn our language?" Aldith asked.

"My chief, Ataranga, ordered me to learn so we could trade with the Var. It amused one of the small women to teach me. Then Okakara came and took Ataranga's war club and his wives, and now I speak for him."

"And where are my people? I found the broken varbow you left for us. It belonged to Runa, the Stewardess."

Tanema bowed. "I'm not permitted to talk of it. Those are words from Okakara directly to you. I will lead you to his pah, his village. It's not too far from here, along a hidden path."

Aldith sensed a trap. Leading her away from the stockade was a smart maneuver, and would split their forces. Divide and conquer was always a sound military tactic. This chief Okakara had already proven himself in war with the conquest of the southern island, and Aldith had no way of knowing she could trust his word.

As if reading her thoughts, Tanema pulled out a small carved wooden object from the top of his skirt, which he handed to Aldith.

"This is a token for safe passage. Okakara pledges it to you. Bring as many people as you need to feel protected, but you will not be harmed in his village."

"I need to consult with my captains first," Aldith said.

"As you wish. I will be waiting here for you," Tanema said, and promptly sat down on the ground.

Aldith returned to the main hall of the stockade and summoned her four Damm Warrior captains. Although she would listen to their counsel, her mind was already made up, and she would lead an expedition to Okakara's village. She clutched the wooden token in her hand, and wondered how much faith she could place in it for protection. It was not just her life at stake, but the future of Agithawald, and the Var foothold in the southern isles.

Aldith quickly laid out her plan, and waited for her captains to offer their opinions.

"It's madness to split our forces when we don't know what we're facing," Hildr, the grizzled old captain said. She was never one to be afraid of speaking her mind, but Aldith knew once the final order was given, she would follow it to the end.

"I hear you, Hildr. But we have to find out what happened to Runa and the others," Aldith replied.

"What if it's a trap?" Tove, the newest captain asked.

"Then we'll fight our way out of it," Aldith said grimly.

"I want to know. My sister was Runa's captain," Gyda said.

"And you, Siv? What do you have to say?" Aldith asked her last captain.

"Orders are orders. Let's get on with it before the solar drops further," Siv said..

"Good. Hildr, you and one hundred Damm Warriors come with me. No Red Shadows. I want to move quickly if we need to. Siv brings up the rearguard, Gyda holds the beach, and Tove the stockade, and our last line of defense. Now, let's go find our messenger and pay this chieftain a visit."

Tanema led the way out from Agithawald and the stockade, and into the rainforest. He moved quickly for an older man, but the Damm Warriors were chiseled for war, and the hardships of a fast paced march was nothing new for them. Each one carried a varbow, with a longsword by her side, or a battle axe slung over the shoulder, and all wore chainmail. One hundred Damm Warriors was a formidable force, and Aldith knew they would fight to the last woman.

The path through the rainforest was narrow, and the dense coverage overhead filtered out most of the light. There was no sign of wildlife, but Aldith could feel eyes, whether human or otherwise, watching them every step of the way. It was the perfect location for an ambush, and Aldith was acutely aware Tanema could simply be leading them out into the wilds and then abandon them. Finding their way back would be difficult, and Aldith ordered her warriors to leave visible signs to help guide them on the reverse journey.

An hour into the trek, the troop were soaked, whether from their own sweat, or the moisture from the foliage. There were no breaks, and the Damm Warriors took sips of water from the water bags strapped to their waist while on the move. Tanema kept them moving at a fast pace, as if he was eager to reach the village and be done with his task.

Up ahead, Aldith could see more sunlight, and an opening. Once they came though into the clearing, there was the Raratoa village. It was a vast

CHAPTER TWENTY SEVEN

construction, with wooden palisades surrounding the large communal houses within. Aldith guessed it was at least four times larger than their own stockade. She wondered how her scouts had failed to locate it.

As Hildr formed up the Damm Warriors, six Taramoa champions came out to greet them. They were huge men, both in height and width, and they towered over the tallest Damm Warrior. They wore loincloths to cover their manhood, but nothing else. Like Tanema they were covered head to foot in exotic tattoos, and each of them carried a large wooden war club with sharpened obsidian shards embedded. They advanced on the Damm Warriors, and brandished their clubs, stamped their feet, stuck out decorated tongues, and made fierce faces.

Two Damm Warriors instinctively notched arrows in answer to the threat.

"Hold!" Hildr ordered, and looked to Aldith for a command.

"No need to worry," Tanema said. "This is a traditional greeting for honored guests."

"I'd hate to see what welcome they had for enemies," Aldith said, and gestured to the two Damm Warriors to lower their bows.

"Come, come, Okakara is waiting," Tanema said, leading Aldith and her Damm Warriors past the fierce welcoming party and through the main gates of the village and into the open space of the compound. Men, women, and children stood and stared at the heavily armed women warriors. Some were of the same smaller build as Tanema, but most, including the women, were large, and heavy boned. All were tattooed, and even the young children had a smattering of ink designs. There was no hostility from them, just curiosity, and none of them were armed.

Tanema led them over to a covered area, and instructed them to sit down on woven grass mats. Aldith sat in the front with Hildr, and five Damm Warriors on either side. The rest sat behind in four rows, with the rear row facing in the opposite direction in case anyone decided to come at them from behind. Aldith and Hildr removed their helmets, but the rest remained battle ready.

Women laden down with baskets of fruits and vegetables came up to the mats and placed them in front of their guests. Two men carrying a whole roasted pig, fresh from a fire pit, placed it in the center position on the floor. None of the Damm Warriors ventured to eat.

Without any ceremony, a titanic man with a colossal belly appeared at the makeshift table, flanked by four equally heavy set men. He was past his prime, and his beard was already gray, but Aldith could tell he was still a formidable fighting man. Battle scars marked his thick arms and legs, and Aldith had no doubt his upper torso, covered with a fur cloak, also bore signs of warfare. His hair was tied back in a topknot, and three feathers were stuck in place for decoration. He carried a small ceremonial war axe with a smooth green obsidian blade, obviously a sign of authority. His four chieftains were similarly dressed, but they carried carved war clubs, signifying their respective roles. Without a word to their guests, they all sat and immediately began to eat.

The chieftain reached over and took a large piece of pork meat and crackling, and followed it with a handful of berries. He said something to Tanema who translated.

"Ranga Okakara asks why you are not eating? It shows disrespect to your host," Tanema said.

Okakara gestured to one of the women who brought over the bowl of berries directly in front of Aldith. Okakara dipped a meaty paw in and stuffed a handful of black berries into his mouth. The woman replaced the bowl, and Okakara pointed to it.

"Okakara says eat," Tanema said.

Aldith picked up one berry from the bowl and popped it into her mouth. She chewed twice and swallowed. "Good," she said.

Okakara threw back his head and laughed heartily, as his belly bounced up and down. "Good," he said in the common tongue.

His chieftains joined in the laughter, and soon all of the people were laughing in unison. When Okakara stopped they all broke off. One man continued laughing a little too long, which caught Okakara's attention. He gestured to the men beside the offender, and two of them immediately seized hold of the man's arms, and forced him to his knees. Another man

CHAPTER TWENTY SEVEN

stood over him with a heavy club in his hands, and brained him. One blow and his head broke open, and his life ended. They dragged him out of the compound by his feet leaving a trail of blood behind. No one intervened or made a noise of protest. Aldith surmised it was a normal occurrence at the whim of a tyrant. She looked back at Okakara who was eating again, as if nothing out of the ordinary had happened.

Okakara spoke again and Tanema translated into the common tongue. "Why do you come to our land?"

"To trade with you," Aldith replied.

"No trade. Trade was for the Raratoa. The Taramoa don't give up our sacred trees. We don't allow pake ... foreigners, to take our land."

"We come in peace," Aldith said.

"You come armed. You come to steal our land. If I allow you to stay, your trading post will become a fortress. Soon, thousands of you will invade and take everything from us. Go, take your ships home and leave us be," Okakara said, and Tanema converted into words the Damm Warriors could understand.

"And our people who were here before? What happened to them?" Aldith asked.

"We invited them to a feast like this one. Then we ate them," Okakara said, taking another large chunk of pork and popping it into his mouth.

"You ate them?" Aldith said aghast.

Behind her the Damm Warriors bristled. Aldith heard swords loosened in sheaths.

"Stay those hands," she said to her warriors.

"The small chunky ones were tasty like this pork. But the tall warriors like yourselves. They were lean, too much strong muscle, and not as good. Too hard to chew."

Aldith's jaw dropped open, and she could barely process what she was hearing.

"Don't worry, we killed them first. We're not savages. I killed the leader myself. Crushed her head in and broke her bow after she put an arrow through Aputa's leg. Here, look," Okakara said, as he grabbed hold of the limb of the chieftain sitting to his right and showed them the puncture wound.

"Why? When you have all the food you need. Was it some way of taking the strength of an enemy?" Aldith asked, trying to reason out the atrocity. She knew at least one of the northern tribes in the Wildlands had a similar culture.

Okakara threw back his head and laughed once more, quickly joined by his people. "No, it's a sign of disrespect. We put them in one end, and shit them out the other."

Aldith stood up, and her Damm Warriors followed suit. "We have nothing else to discuss here." She held up the carved stick Tanema gave her for safe passage. "I'm assuming you'll honor your word, and let us go back to our ships?"

Tanema smiled. "That's just a child's toy I thought would add to the game. You can go back to your ships. If you can reach them. We'll give you a headstart, so better run fast!"

Aldith threw the stick to the ground. She thought about ending it there, with a volley of arrows aimed at Okakara and his chieftains. Cut off the head of the snake and the others might wane without a leader. She looked down at Okakara, who continued to eat without a care in the world.

He's not afraid to die. That means others will take his place. I led us into this trap, I need to lead us out.

Aldith and her Damm Warriors left without another word, but they looked about them apprehensively as they made their way through the crowd of people and to the gateway. Aldith expected a rush of fighters at any moment. It did not come.

Outside the main gates of the compound, Hildr formed the Damm Warriors up into a column of twos and they marched to the path back through the rainforest. Aldith glanced back and the women and children filed outside to see them go. There were no men present except for Tanema who had the audacity to wave them goodbye.

Aldith turned towards Hildr. "Once we're out of sight, run them back at double speed. Keep it controlled," Aldith said.

CHAPTER TWENTY SEVEN

"We could go faster if we ditch the armor," Hildr replied.

Aldith shook her head. "We'll need chainmail when we make our stand. It will give us an edge in the fight. One last thing before we go."

Aldith notched an arrow and quickly took aim. She sent the missile flying and pinned Tanema to the wall of the compound.

Aldith and Hildr joined the Damm Warrior column, and once they were out of sight of the village, they double marched along the path. Once again, Aldith could feel eyes watching them through the foliage, but no attack came.

The Damm Warriors were sweating heavily from running in chainmail and fully armed, but they kept an even pace. All their lives they trained for battle, even when they saw little of it in Varstad. Their military discipline, and physical and mental toughness was like tempered steel.

The horns blew. First one, then joined by many others. It was followed by the roar of men, thousands of raised voices lusting for the chase.

"Here they come!" Aldith yelled. "Hildr, quicken the pace!"

The Damm Warriors picked up speed, but they were at their limit without breaking into a full sprint. Behind them they heard the sound of a fast moving army on their heels. Heavy feet thundered through the undergrowth and closed the distance. They were not just directly behind, but on either side too.

"There's more than one path. They're trying to get ahead of us to cut us off," Aldith shouted.

Onward they ran, panting heavily now, and Aldith knew they could not outpace their adversaries. For all their size, the Taramoa men were fit, strong, and fast, and unencumbered by armor. Their only hope was for a rearguard action to hold up the main force, and allow the majority of the column to make it back to the stockade.

"Rear ten to me," Aldith shouted, and stopped running. The back ten Damm Warriors immediately stopped too, and caught their breath as they waited for Aldith's instructions.

Hildr came running back. "Domina, let me hold them," Hildr said.

"I got us into this mess," Aldith said.

"And you'll get us out of it too. Now go, we need you at the stockade!"

Aldith stared at her grizzled captain for a moment, then clapped her on the shoulder and took off after the column without another word.

"Line up, and make every shot count!" Aldith heard Hildr shout.

On they ran, getting closer to the stockade with every labored step. The clash of battle was behind them, followed by the roar of men, and the chase was on again. On either side, they could hear heavy steps in parallel with their own. A spear came out of the treeline, and slammed into a Damm Warrior. She went down, but was helped up by two companions, her chainmail saved her, but her running was now labored. More spears came through the foliage, and the Damm Warriors dodged or deflected them as best they could.

Varbows were too long and cumbersome to fire on the run, so Aldith stopped in her tracks, planted her rear foot, and pulled her bowstring taught. She caught sight of the shadow of a man, and let fly. There was the sound of the contact with flesh, a grunt, and then a body hitting the floor. Aldith was off and running again.

The Damm Warriors followed Aldith's lead. One by one, they stepped off the path so as not to hinder those running behind. Loosed off an arrow, and then rejoined the running party. Bodies dropped, but Aldith knew it was only a handful, and the bands on either side were now ahead of them. Before long they would close in the horns, and cut off their retreat. Then the chasing force would slam into them from the rear and it would all be over.

A Taramoa warrior came charging out of the vegetation and cut directly through the column. As he passed he impaled a spear into the neck of a surprised Damm Warrior. Then he was through and disappeared into the treeline on the other side. Twenty paces on, another Taramoa tried the same tactic. This time, a battle axe decapitated him before he reached his intended target.

There was a loud commotion on either side of the retreating column. Weapons clashing, battle cries, and men screaming. Aldith looked to the front, and her heart sank. She knew it was all over. The Taramoa were

CHAPTER TWENTY SEVEN

ahead of them.

Chapter Twenty Eight

Aldith : Battle of the Southern Isles

The men blocking the path were not Taramoa. They were Red Shadows, and their weapons were steel halberds and not wooden clubs. Then she saw Siv, grim-faced Siv, with her party of one hundred Damm Warriors and two hundred Red Shadows.

Aldith stopped before her captain as the rest of her exhausted warriors made their way through the ranks, and took the opportunity of the brief rest to suck in air.

"We'll hold them here, Domina, and fight a withdrawal action. On to the beach. Gyda is waiting there, with a little surprise for our friends," Siv said.

"Don't be too long in coming, Siv. We need your varbow," Aldith said, and stepped through the line of Red Shadows and on towards the safety of the shoreline and the stockade.

Aldith formed up her small group once again. They were down Hildr and the ten Damm Warriors in the rearguard, and three others were dropped by spears on the run. They still had some way to go before they reached the beach, so Aldith took them at double speed again.

They heard the fury of battle behind them as they continued to run, and then they broke through the treeline, and into the open clearing of the beach. They let out a spontaneous cheer as they saw Gyda's army lined up behind a series of sharpened wooden stakes. They held up their weapons

CHAPTER TWENTY EIGHT

and answered their returning sisters.

The bulk of Aldith's forces were lined up on the beach. Tove held the stockade with ten Damm Warriors and one hundred Red Shadows, as the last line of defense. The remaining four hundred and ninety Damm Warriors and roughly twelve hundred Red Shadows were prepared to battle in the open, and test the willingness of Okakara and his Taramoa to fight to the death.

Aldith and her exhausted party passed through the stakes, and through the combined ranks of the Damm Warriors and Red Shadows. They made their way to the rear to regain their strength and replenish their arrow supply before rejoining the ranks for the coming fray. Aldith sought out Gyda, who held the command point in the center of the small army.

"Well done, Gyda. We can thin their numbers out here, and retreat to the stockade if we must," Aldith said.

"How many of them, Domina?" Gyda asked.

"More than enough to go around. They'll be here soon enough for us to count them."

"And Hildr and Siv?" Gyda inquired.

"Hildr didn't make it. She went down holding the rearguard to buy us time. Siv has orders to make it back to us. I expect her to carry them out."

Aldith surveyed her army and contemplated the battle plan once more. She looked behind her, where Tove stood on the wall above the gates with eight Damm Warriors all lined up to provide additional fire support with their varbows. The Red Shadows, along with their Damm Warrior officers, guarded the gates themselves, ready to close them as needed. Out in the harbor, the Black Ships would play their part too. Ten held the line, anchored further out to protect the rest of the fleet which was at anchor. Five ships were angled to bring their cannon to bear on the shoreline. The land army itself was formed up in the traditional Var battleline. Red Shadows, marshaled by their officers, were four ranks deep and held their halberds at the ready, an impenetrable fortress of steel. The sharpened stakes in front of them would help to slow down any charge. Damm Warriors, those who favored the mighty battle axe, which they would swing with both hands, augmented the front rank. Their role was to provide a cutting edge and to add resolve to the Red Shadows if they showed signs of wavering. The rest of the Damm Warriors were to the rear, where they would bring the lethal capabilities of the varbow into play. They would also form up into flying wedges to smash through enemy strongpoints, and bring chaos to their foes.

Aldith was anxious, and she breathed deeply to steady her nerves. Although she had trained in martial ways all her life, and facing death with an unwavering spirit was instilled in her since childhood, she was painfully aware she was about to engage in a fully fledged battle. She was untested in actual warfare, and her army, for all of their intensive training, were facing real combat for the first time. Fear was not the way of the Var. She would remain calm, in control, and would lead by example. She glanced around at her Damm Warriors, and they exhibited the same grim determination. The Red Shadows were a different proposition. There were grizzled veterans, but men near the end of their term, and looking forward to an easier life in the Burghs. And beside them were the newly installed recruits. It would take a firm hand to keep them from breaking when the fighting began.

A cheer went up, and Aldith looked to the front. Four Damm Warriors, swords drawn, and three Red Shadows minus their halberds, broke through the tree line, running for their lives. Siv was with them, though she was limping as she ran, and blood ran from a wound to her thigh. Her helmet was missing, and more blood ran down the side of her head, and across her left ear. A Taramoa warrior put on a burst of speed, and caught up with the Red Shadow to the rear. He brought down his war club with a vicious swing, and crushed in his enemy's back. The Red Shadow went down, arms extended, and the Taramoa fighter stood over him and rained down heavy blows.

"That man!" shouted Aldith, and in reply a rain of arrows arced from the rear and peppered the warrior and the now dead Red Shadow, though they were more than three hundred paces away.

A large group of Taramoa warriors broke through the treeline and gave

CHAPTER TWENTY EIGHT

chase to the remnants of Siv's command. They were a formidable sight, tall, muscular men with long flowing hair, and tattoos displayed on all available skin. They carried an array of clubs, spiked with shark's teeth, and sharpened stones. They moved fast and closed the distance.

"Covering fire!" Aldith yelled.

Another volley of arrows clouded the sky, and thudded into the Taramoa. Five of them went down immediately, with shafts in their heads or upper torsos. Many more took wounds to arms, and legs. They all stopped in their tracks and hobbled back to the relative safety of the treeline.

Siv and her group reached the Var line, and the Red Shadows made room to let them through the ranks. Blood soaked Siv sought out Aldith to make her report.

"There were too many of them to hold back. We took down four times our number, but they kept coming. They're formidable fighters. Lucky for us, they only have primitive weapons, and no armor. Armed with steel, they'd almost be the equal to us," Siv said.

"You bought us time, Siv. For that I'm grateful. Now go back to the stockade, clean up your wounds, and come back to us. As I said, we need your varbow," Aldith said.

There was a lull as Aldith and her Var army waited for the Taramoa forces to arrive, and then the heavens opened. There was no cover, and the rain soaked them all, but it quickly passed, and a rainbow filled the sky. Aldith wondered if the Taramoa took it as a favorable sign, because once it burst across the heavens, they poured out of the rainforest, and lined up on the beach. There were thousands of them, and they kept coming.

A group of thirty Taramoa broke off from the rest and moved a hundred paces closer to the Var. They were unarmed, and as Adlith wondered what would happen next, they lined up in formation, and began to dance and chant in unison.

"I think they're challenging us," Gyda said.

"Their rules, not ours. Let's see if they can dance through arrows," Aldith replied, and gave the command for another volley.

Many of the dancers went down, but those who did not continued despite their wounds. One more salvo took them all down but one. He performed solo until he closed out his chant, and then slowly drew his thumb across his own throat, as if symbolizing what would happen to his enemies when he got close. He stood there defiantly, despite an arrow through his bicep and another in his shin. He turned and strode back to the massed Taramoa.

"Another volley?" Gyda asked.

Aldith shook her head. "Save our arrows for more targets. There's plenty of time left to kill him."

With the ceremonies over, the Taramoa prepared for battle. A thousand of them formed up and advanced across the sand. Men beat on their own chests, others roared challenges, all of them readying themselves for conflict.

"Wait until they reach the dead dancers then let fly," Aldith shouted to her archers.

Twenty more paces and the Taramoa were in optimal range, and Siv, who was now back and in command of the archers, signaled for them to fire. Three volleys in quick succession poured down on the advancing warriors, and many went down. Wounded men writhed in pain in the sand, and the dead littered the ground. The advance did not stop even as two more volleys decimated their numbers.

Aldith looked at the Red Shadows lined up in front of her. Some were shifting uneasily, and Aldith knew they were thinking of breaking. They were adequately trained for warfare, but they had never faced a foe in battle. The Taramoa moving towards them were fighting men, and they would take no prisoners.

"Red Shadows! Remember your training, and hold the line. Stick them, and stick them again! Any man who falls back answers to me!" Aldith shouted.

At one hundred paces, the Taramoa let out a tremendous roar, and broke into a charge. It was a fearsome sight, as the close to eight hundred fighting men barreled towards the Varic army.

The Taramoa made violent contact with the sharpened stakes, and the ranks of the Red Shadows. The force of the impact buckled the line in

CHAPTER TWENTY EIGHT

places, and Aldith could feel the surge of energy from the collision, but they held. The press from the Taramoa in the rear pushed men onto stakes, and they hung there, impaled as if sacrifices to some perverse deity. Others were pushed, or ran headlong into the spikes on the top of the halberds. The men in the second rank swung the heavy polearms, and used the thick blades of the halberds to slice through flesh. All along the line, Taramoa fighters stabbed with spears, or battered at the helmeted heads of Red Shadows and Damm Warriors with war clubs. The fighting was fierce, and men went down on both sides, but the wall of halberdiers and the advantage of armor prevailed. A Damm Warrior, the battle fever upon her, swung her battle axe and cleaved through flesh and bone time and again, before a spear pierced her eye and into her brain. Aldith watched it all unfold from deep in the ranks, and longed to be free of command and in the thick of the battle.

High on the hill above the stockade, horns blew. The Taramoa pressing forward from the rear backed up, and then the whole force slowly retreated. The blood lust was on the warriors, and they pointed their spears and waved their clubs, and offered taunts to the Red Shadows to step out and fight them. A roar of triumph went up from the Red Shadows, and they waved their halberds in the air. They had survived their first test.

"We've beaten them!" men cried.

"Hold your noise! They'll be back," Aldith shouted. "Wounded to the rear. Get those dead off the stakes, and dispatch their wounded. Use the bodies as an extra barricade. Be quick about it, we don't have much time."

Aldith looked at the battle scene, and the dead bodies scattered across the beach. The heady aroma of combat filled the air. The stench of iron-rich blood, shit, piss, and the rank odor of sweat: the bouquet of death. With the arrows and the close quarter fighting, about five hundred of the Taramoa made it back to their ranks. Only twenty Red Shadows and Two Damm Warriors were lost in exchange.

They're brave men, but they don't fight as a unit. Each man wants his own personal battle. We can hold them.

The horns sounded again, and as Aldith looked up at the hill above, she saw Okakara and his chieftains, pointing spears.

"They're directing the attack from up there," Aldith said to Gytha. "That first wave was to test our strength, probing for weaknesses. The next strike will be stronger. Get them ready."

Across the beach, the Taramoa were coming again. This time, double the number than before. Two thousand battle hardened men began the death march towards the Var army.

Aldith signaled to Tove on the stockade battlements, and immediately two of her Damm Warriors waved flags. The answer came from the five ships patrolling the shores. Cannon roared, and stone balls whistled through the air towards the Taramoa. The first salvo was long, and sailed into the rainforest. Despite their bravery, the Taramoa instinctively ducked as the projectiles whistled past high above their heads. The second salvo was on target, and crunched into the assembled warriors, bowling them over like rag dolls and decimating their ranks. Broken, and headless bodies littered the ground, but they still advanced. One more volley wreaked havoc, and then the Taramoa were too close to the Var line for the Black Ships to risk another fusillade. However, now the Taramoa came under the deadly fire of the varbows once again. Three quick volleys littered the beach with Taramoa corpses, and the critically wounded, who were left to fend for themselves.

This time, the Taramoa did not break into a headlong rush at one hundred paces, and instead continued their measured advance until they were within thirty paces of the Var, then stopped.

"What are they doing?" Gytha asked.

"We're about to find out," Aldith said.

Suddenly twelve huge men surged from the ranks of the Taramoa. They stamped their feet, rolled their eyes, stuck out their tongues, foamed at the mouth, and gashed their own bodies with stone blades. They raged like furies before the fearstruck Red Shadows, their battle madness in full display.

"Shock troops," Aldith said. She had heard of the legends from her own people, battle crazed warriors who lived to die in combat, but not before

CHAPTER TWENTY EIGHT

they blazed a deadly trail through their enemies. All feared them. Shunned them in time of peace, but revered them in war. These men were of the same mold. Men who drew supernatural strength from animals, and killed anything in their path.

The Taramoa fighters were too close for Siv's archers to bring their firepower to bear. However, Tove had a clear line of sight from the stockade walls, and her Damm Warriors used their varbows to lethal effect. Two of the giants were riddled with arrows, and went down before they could display their fighting prowess. Two others took hits, but continued with the assault.

The remaining shock troops charged as one, and crashed into the front ranks of the Red Shadows. As Aldith watched, a Damm Warrior named Freydis, took up the challenge and stepped out of the ranks. Her mighty battle axe slashed into the arm of one of the beserkers and severed it at the elbow. In reply he stabbed his spear through Freydis's throat, and left it there as he picked up his war club from his own hacked off hand. He dove into the ranks of the Red Shadows, and battered in heads, even as his body took stab after stab. The ten refused to go down, and killed anyone in their path, cutting a bloody swathe in front of them.

With the line breached in places, the Taramoa let out a battle cry and charged forward into the waiting blades of the Red Shadows and axes of the Damm Warriors. Aldith could feel the swing in fortune, and knew she had to steady the line, or all would be lost. She drew her sword, and pushed forward through the Red Shadows to battle herself. Gyda sent twenty Damm Warriors with her, and they hacked back the Taramoa.

A rabid fighter held a group of Red Shadows at bay. They surrounded him with a ring of halberds, but no one was prepared to step forward and challenge him. He bled from more wounds than one normal man could take and still be alive, but he stood strong and swung his war club. Finally, a Red Shadow moved in and drove the point of his halberd into the man's side. He grunted with the impact, smashed the polearm with his club, and then crushed in the skull of the brave Red Shadow. Aldith stepped into the circle and confronted the giant. He swung his club, which she deflected, and then spinning in a circle, she sliced her sword though his neck and sent his head flying. A Red Shadow stuck his spike into it, and sent the bloodied trophy soaring back at the Taramoa.

The battle crazed titans fell, but not before taking many lives with them. They had served their purpose, and allowed the Taramoa to breach the line and gain a foothold, and now they could go to work. Out of formation, the Red Shadows were no match for the Taramoa fighters. Their size, strength, agility, and a willingness to fight without fear made them formidable opponents.

"To me!" Aldith called to her twenty Damm Warriors, and they formed a wedge, with Aldith at the tip. They went forward, slashing and stabbing at the Taramoa, and cutting a path through their ranks. It gave strength and courage to the Red Shadows, who formed up behind them, and closed the breach. Damm Warrior wedges pushed through in two other places, and steadied the line.

High on the hill, the horns blew again and the Taramoa began to fall back.

Aldith gasped for air and steadied herself on her bloody sword after all of the killing. Bodies were all around her, and men and women lay writhing in pain. The dead were everywhere, and this time there were many Red Shadows and Damm Warriors amongst them.

Gyda came up to Aldith and offered her a flask of water, which she gladly took.

"We'll be hard pressed to hold another assault. Perhaps time to retreat to the fort?" Gyda asked.

Aldith shook her head. "Not yet. We hold them once more. We retreat now and we give them the upper hand. We still need to thin their numbers."

"Ours are thinning too," Gyda said.

"We'll hold them," Siv said, hobbling forward, and using her varbow as a makeshift crutch.

"That's the spirit, Siv," Aldith said. "Same as before, dispatch their wounded, and get ours back inside the fort. And form them up again. We'll have quite a barricade with all of their dead."

CHAPTER TWENTY EIGHT

"And our dead?" Gyda asked.

"Put them in the wall too," Siv said. "They're not dismissed even in death, and they still have a job to do."

The Var army was weary after fending off two vicious assaults, and Aldith was under no illusion the Taramoa were ready to withdraw back to their villages. She looked around at those who remained. They were blooded now, but the aftermath of conflict made warriors and soldiers react in different ways. Some were calm and prepared for the next assault, others stared into space, and had to be cajoled into activity. Some were visibly shaking and Aldith knew they were the ones on the point of breaking. They needed time to physically and mentally recover, and time was not on their side.

On the other side of the killing ground, the Taramoa formed up once more for the final assault.

"They're all coming this time," Siv said.

"Must be five thousand of them," Gytha replied.

"I suspect Okakara held his veterans back for this charge. They'll be fresh and eager to fight. The Black Ships have their range now, and should cut down their numbers," Aldith said, confidently.

"I hope so. We're down to five volleys left before they hit our lines," Siv said.

"Then make every shot count," Aldith replied.

Aldith watched as the five thousand chanting warriors closed the ground. They were a fearsome sight, and Aldith knew this was a fight to the death. No prisoners would be taken, and she vowed to take as many Taramoa with her as she could.

"Why are the ship's cannon not firing?" Aldith said. "They're within range now."

She got her answer. Out beyond the harbor there was a fearsome explosion, and a huge fireball went high into the sky. One of the ten Black Ships guarding the fleet detonated, and parts of the ship and men shot up as if fired from their own demonic cannon. The other nine ships were under attack too. Huge double hulled canoes with a large fighting platform in the middle sailed around them. They were powered by twin triangular sails, and men lined either side, furiously digging in their paddles. They moved fast, and harassed the Black Ships. Taramora flung grappling hooks to attach themselves to the ships, and swarmed up the sides. They were too close to repel them with vitali blackfire or cannon shot, and the crew were only armed with a smattering of crossbows and their small curved swords. They stood little chance against the ferocious warriors storming their decks.

"The fools! They were watching the battle ashore, and not looking out to sea," Aldith said.

One by one, the ships began to burn. Another Black Ship exploded, sending friend and foe to their deaths, and sinking two large Taramoa canoes in the process. Flames spread across the sea water, and burned the men who had jumped overboard to escape the fighting. The other Taramoa war parties were more cautious now. As Aldith watched, they slaughtered the crews before setting the Black Ships ablaze, and jumping back to their canoes in search of another target.

Aldith looked on in horror as ten double hulled canoes came into the harbor. There were no sails, or men paddling to provide power. There were no men on the fighting platform either. In their place were stacks of burning wood.

"What's driving them?" Gyda asked.

Black and white hvalr popped up around the canoes and propelled them forward. Each had a Taramoa warrior riding on their backs, and guiding them forward. Hvalr and man went under water, and came up again, always driving the fire canoes on. The Black Ships anchored in the harbor had no way of escaping, and no means of defense. One ship tried to engage with vitali blackfire, but only succeeded in adding to the inferno, which soon engulfed their own vessel. The canoes struck home, and the Var fleet burned. As Aldith watched, *Matilda* went down in flames.

"Look! They're turning tail and leaving. The cowards!" Gyda screamed pointing towards the five Black Ships who were previously providing fire support on the shoreline.

CHAPTER TWENTY EIGHT

"They're not cowards. They're trying to save what we have left of our fleet," Aldith said. She watched as the Black Ships turned, and headed for the open sea, chased by Taramoa war canoes.

With the fleet lost, Aldith had no choice but to focus on the battle at hand. Their only chance was to hold firm, and blunt the assault. However, after watching the destruction of the fleet, and faced with a determined foe, her army was on the point of breaking.

"Across that ground is all you need to focus on," Aldith shouted pointing her sword in the direction of the Taramoa. "A man comes in front of you, you kill him! Then the next, and the next. You keep killing until there are no more. There is nothing else to think about. No past, no future. Be in the present, and kill! The glory is ours on this solar!"

The Taramoa army was in optimal bow range now, and Siv commanded her archers to unleash a volley. As the arrows arced down, the Taramoa stopped and raised canoes, hidden by the front ranks, above their heads, and ducked under them for protection. Not all of the men had cover, and arrows made their way through. However, the death toll was light.

The Taramoa stood up, and let out a battle roar pointing their weapons at the Var, and on they came. Another volley, and the Taramoa went under the canoe cover once again.

"Hold your fire, Siv," Aldith commanded. "We'll save them for their retreat. It's hand to hand now."

The Var army lined up as before, with rank upon rank of Red Shadows with halberds at the ready. However, more Damm Warriors than before stiffened their ranks, and some even used halberds to show the men they were prepared to fight side by side with them. Varbows were discarded for now, and Damm Warrior battle wedges formed ready to plug breaches in the line, and drive the Taramoa back.

The Taramoa advanced. A sweaty, raging, roaring mass of men who shouted and taunted, and brandished their weapons of war at an enemy they were about to annihilate. They stopped ten paces in front of the barricade of stakes, and dead bodies, and the groups advanced, and threw the canoes against the blockade and held them in place. Lithe warriors immediately sprinted forward, ran up the canoes, and vaulted into the ranks of the Var army. Halberds stabbed out at the Taramoa holding the canoes, and others stepped forward to take their place. One leaping Taramoa was pierced in midair, and impaled on a halberd spike. Others landed on top of Red Shadows, and slashed and clubbed.

The whole Taramoa force surged forward, and once again, Aldith felt the shock wave as the two armies collided in a fierce hand to hand struggle. Halberds stabbed and axes cleaved, and war clubs and spears went to work in thinning out the ranks of the Red Shadows.

Aldith prepared to charge into the thick of the battle when Gyda pointed behind them. "They're inside the stockade!"

Aldith looked behind and saw Tove and her Damm Warriors battling with Taramoa on the ramparts. At the gateway, the Red Shadows were trying desperately to hold back the attack, but their formation was already broken, and in single combat they stood little chance.

"Siv! Two hundred with me. The rest in wedges. Gyda! You must hold them until we take back the stockade. It's our only chance," Aldith said, and without waiting for a response, she charged her small force back towards the gates, and the Taramoa warriors inside the fort.

The Damm Warriors hit them hard in the initial rush. Aldith stabbed her sword, and impaled a man through the heart. She placed her boot on his stomach and kicked to pull her blade free, and then immediately hacked into the exposed neck of another. He dropped his club, and his hands shot to his wound as if to stop the blood from gushing out, but the cut was fatal.

All around her, Damm Warriors engaged with Taramoa, and pulled the remaining Red Shadows back into the fight. The Taramoa did not back down, and fought to the last man.

Aldith instructed twenty Damm Warriors to secure the gate with the last of the Red Shadows, Siv, to clear the battlements, and she led the remainder of her small force to clear the compound. There were few Taramoa remaining, and they were quickly dispatched. Aldith ran on, checking each room, and witnessing the slaughter the Taramoa left in their wake. All the non-combatants were butchered, from the Konna, to

CHAPTER TWENTY EIGHT

the carpenters, cooks, and serving men. The wounded, brought to safety from the battle outside, were clubbed to death in their cots. There was no quarter given to anyone, and blood and gore decorated the stockade interior.

Tana!

In the heat of battle, Aldith had not thought of Tana once. However, now the fight was inside the stockade itself, her attention went to her lover. She raced to her quarters, fully expecting the worst, to see her broken and violated body, but Tana was not there.

"Tana!" Aldith yelled.

She ran outside, and a Taramoa warrior charged into her, knocking her to the ground. He stood over Aldith and raised his club. She stabbed up her sword into his groin, and stopped his attack. As he fell to the ground, she got back to her feet, and beheaded him.

"Domina, over here," a Damm Warrior called, and led Aldith over to a small building at the rear of the stockade. "They came through here. There's a tunnel under the wall."

"Seal it, and post guards," Aldith commanded.

"Yes Domina."

Aldith ran back to the main gates. Outside, the fight was raging, but the tide of battle had turned, and not in favor of the Var. The Taramoa had breached the barricades, and were forcing Gyda and what little troops she had left back toward the stockade. On the battlements, Siv was doing her part to hold them back. At close range, her bowwomen could pick out single targets, and each arrow counted.

Aldith looked up at the hill towards Okakara and his chieftains, but they had already gone.

You've beaten us, and can't even stay around for the finish!

Overhead, the skies blackened, and the wind picked up. A storm was blowing to batter the contending armies. Rain began to fall, and came down in sheets. Lightning flashed across the darkening heavens, followed closely by the roar of thunder. The competing Gods of War fought their own battle.

Aldith marshaled her rain soaked troops at the gate, shouting harsh commands to encourage the Red Shadows to hold their ground as best they could, and deal with the press from the Taramoa. It was a losing proposition, and Aldith knew it. The best she could hope for was to get as many inside the stockade, and force a closing of the gates.

"To me!" Aldith cried, and led a wedge of Damm Warriors forward into the mass of Taramoa. She reached Gyda's side, swinging and stabbing her blade at angry faces and exposed bodies. One man went down with a stab to his open mouth, another when a slash took out his throat. Taramoa blood covered the front of the wedge, and the rain did its best to wash it away.

"Gyda! Get your warriors back inside and close the gates. I'll hold them here," Aldith shouted.

"No, Domina. It's my fortune. I'll hold the gate," Gyda said.

"Gyda, it's an order!"

"You can't deny me this, Domina. A warrior's end. Have them sing songs of the battle of *Gyda's Gate.* Now go!"

The Damm Warriors slowly gave ground to the advancing Taramoa, but the line did not buckle, as they retreated step by step to the gate. Siv and her archers unleashed a tremendous volley with the last of their arrows, and cleared a space between the two armies. Gyda and twenty of her comrades let out a yell and charged forward, and the gates closed behind them.

On the other side of the gate, Aldith heard the final clash of battle, intermingled with the intensity of the storm. She stuck her sword into the muddy ground, sank to her knees, and let the rain mask her tears.

Okakara and his chieftains sat on mats on the ground under a canopy. They had positioned themselves in the open in front of the stockade to show good faith. There was a litter to the side of them, and Tanema lay on it. There were no Taramoa warriors in sight, and except for Okakara's ceremonial blade, they were not armed.

Three solars had passed since the last of the fighting, and the battlefield was cleared of bodies, both Taramoa and Var. Women wailed when they

CHAPTER TWENTY EIGHT

identified fallen loved ones, but there was no violence exacted against their enemies. The mood of the Taramoa was more one of reverence for those who chose to die in battle. The remnants of the Black Ship fleet was a charred and broken wreck in the harbor, and a sorry reminder to the Var in the stockade of their lost escape route.

Aldith came to meet them alone and unarmed. Siv protested she take a guard, but if it was a trap she could not afford to lose more Damm Warriors, and they would be needed for the final assault. The defeat, and the shame of it, was hers alone. Okakara had outmaneuvered her every step of the way. From luring her into his village, killing vital Damm Warriors on the run back, the destruction of the fleet trapped in the harbor, invading the stockade through tunnels, and outsmarting her in the battle on the beach. The stockade protected them for now, but for how long? she wondered. There were only fifty five Damm Warriors left, half were wounded, and three would certainly die. Hildr, Gyda, and Tove: all were dead. Only Siv stood by her side. Thirty two Red Shadows were now combat veterans, but they hung their heads when Aldith walked past. And the five Black Ships? They sailed free of the harbor, but Aldith had no idea if they had escaped the Taramoa trap.

Aldith sat down on the open mat across from Okakara and his chieftains. As she did so they all bowed their heads as a mark of respect. Okakara pointed his green obsidian blade at Aldith and waved it as if offering a blessing.

"Ranga Okakara says you fought bravely, and he is honored to call you his enemy," Tanema said, propped up on his litter. His face was pale with loss of blood, and his shoulder was heavily wrapped in blood stained leaves.

"What did you do with our dead? Are they part of some monstrous feast?" Aldith asked.

Tanema translated from the common tongue, and Okakara shook his head and replied.

"We didn't eat them. The womenfolk dressed their bodies, and wrapped them in flax leaves. We weighted them down with rocks, and buried them at sea. They're not of this land, so we can't place them in the earth like our own warriors. They fought well, and no one ran away. Noble deaths. We'll sing songs of their bravery," Tanema said.

"Thank you," Aldith said, bowing her own head.

Okakara spoke again through the mouth of Tanema. "You killed many of my bravest warriors, but I have many more. I can kill you all, don't you agree?"

"It will come at a heavy price," Aldith replied.

"I don't want you dead. You see, if you don't return to your people and tell them what happened here, and how formidable the Taramoa warriors are in battle, more of your kind will come. This is our land, not yours. Go with a warrior's blessing, but don't come back," Okakara said.

"And how do we leave?" Aldith asked.

Tanema smiled. "We let five of your ships escape the harbor, but we're watching them closely. They can come back and take you home. Five ships should be enough for the warriors you have left."

Aldith stood up to go.

"One more thing," Tanema said. "Your arrow was true, and I'm dying. This is my last task for Ranga Okakara. In the future, he will have a new translator, if ever needed. She learns our language very fast, especially the harsh words. Our chief took her as a wife too, though he may come to regret that. Her name is Tana," Tanema said.

Tana. So you're alive. Time to put playthings behind.

"She's of no consequence to me," Aldith said, and turned around and walked back to the stockade.

Aldith stood next to Siv at the stern of *Svanni*, her new flagship, as they watched the stockade burn behind them. Agithawald was a short lived dream of a new land, a colony where the Var could grow and expand. Now they were ice bound again, cold people destined to live out their solars in the frozen north.

"Okakara was right, Siv. We didn't come to trade. We came to take their lands. If he didn't make a stand, no matter how many warriors it cost him, we would have destroyed them in the end," Aldith said.

CHAPTER TWENTY EIGHT

As the five Black Ships sailed out of the harbor and into the open ocean, a lone Taramoa canoe sailed close to watch them go. A warrior onboard saluted them as a mark of respect. In response, Aldith gave the command to unleash vitali blackfire, and sent them into oblivion.

"What now, Domina? Do we sail back to Varstad with our tails between our legs?" Siv asked, as they watched the canoe burn.

Aldith shook her head. "The Var are vengeful people. It's time to go Varingr. Okakara is in the southern isles with his warriors, but he comes from the northern isle. Let's go and pay his villages a visit. Let's kill and burn, and leave our mark. We can't return to Varstad. Our life there is over. We're true Var now, and we return to the old ways."

Chapter Twenty Nine

The Great Trek

There was no formal ceremony for the caravan to commence the great trek north. Beira made one last visit to see her sister, the Dux, and to presumably receive final instructions. However, Kasha was not privy to any of that. Her main concern was Berric, and to see he was as comfortable as possible for the journey. Beira gave over one huge sledge for her sole use, more a house on rails, requiring eight giant snow shovelers to pull it. The sledge was fitted out with a bed for Berric, and extra cushioning to soften the passage. There was also room for Kasha's quarters, and an alcove for a servant Drest promised to provide. Kasha's only request was to make him small enough to fit the pocket, and to make sure he bathed each lunar.

Kasha had watched over her brother for almost two lunars since their fateful encounter in the Mutton. She fed him, washed him, tended to his night soil, and cleaned up his bed sores. Although still weak, and a long way from full recovery, Berrric was awake more often than sleeping. He had been an obnoxious patient, and barked at Kasha when he should have thanked her for her sisterly care. He would always apologize later, and promised Kasha he would be a better brother once he was out of the cot.

Transporting Berric from his bed in the warehouse to his new lodgings in the covered house on the sledge was painfully slow, and Kasha lost her

CHAPTER TWENTY NINE

temper with one carrier, who stumbled and bounced the stretcher. Berric cursed too, and promised the culprit he would pay him a visit in the dead of night when the lunar was full.

Berric frequently requested the White Tears so he could sleep at night, and Kasha feared he was dependent on the substance, and it contributed to his bursts of temper. Under its influence, he was a shadow of the brother she met in *The Copper Coin*, and he drifted in and out of the nether gloom. He clutched at his neck in his fevered dreams, and muttered about his lost pendant and the *Tarb Dreag*, the airstone, while Kasha mopped his brow. Kasha was instructed in both from her father, but she failed to see the connection, and Berric would not elaborate when he returned to consciousness. He smiled and told Kasha not to worry, and everything would make sense once they reached their father in the north.

There was a knock at the door, and Kasha left her sleeping brother to see who was visiting. She opened the upper section and peered out. Drest was standing there, a block of a man with no ears, and he held a skinny boy with a missing eye by the collar.

Kasha stepped down from the sledge and stood hands on hips while she inspected Drest's charge. He was so malnourished Kasha wondered if he could make it out of Gastown, nevermind survive the harsh expedition. He was a bag of bones wrapped in filthy rags.

"What's this then?" Kasha asked.

Drest let go of his temporary ward, and roughly pushed him over to Kasha. "Servant," he said, and trudged off.

"I didn't ask for a ragamuffin guttersnipe. I asked for someone to help take care of my brother!" Kasha called after him. "Come back, Drest, and bring me a proper hireling!"

Kasha looked down at the boy in front of her. She could not tell his age from the size of him, but she suspected he was older than his frame indicated and likely close in age to herself. Unfortunately, she was downwind of him, and he reeked like rotten vegetables, stale sweat, and raw sewage, mixed together in a pungent odor only the Slough could blend.

"What's your name, boy?" Kasha asked. She towered over him, and adopted an aggressive stance.

"Iz John. John Bucket," Juan replied, using the false name Carlos had bestowed on him.

"That's the language of the gutter, and we don't speak it here. Not 'Iz,' but 'I'm called.' Now you try it."

"I-I'm called John," Juan replied.

Kasha nodded her head. "Good. At least you can take instruction. Now tell me John, have you ever cooked?"

"Sum. Iz ... I can mix things in a pot, an' put fire to it," Juan said, trying his best to improve his diction.

"Good. Good. Soups and stews are needed. Now, your main task will be looking after my brother, Berric. You'll help feed him, bathe him, empty his pans and clean away the night soil. I'll take you to meet him soon enough. But first, we need you out of those rags, and into some furs, or you'll freeze to death in the north. Before that, you need a bath to wash away years of Slough grime and filth. I don't know where Drest found you, or why you agreed to come on this land voyage. You're probably tied up in that slaughter on the bridge I'm guessing. Well, you're here now, and you best do as I say," Kasha said, making sure to stamp her authority as early as possible. Wild dogs would bite the hand that fed them if you did not show an immediate hierarchy.

"Yes, mi lady," Juan said, cap in hand.

"Not *my lady*. Save that for Beira, the mistress of this expedition. I'm just Kasha. I'll be fair with you, but I'll beat you black and blue if you step out of line. Do you hear me?" Kasha said, waving a fist in his face.

"Yes, Kasha."

"Now make yourself useful, and listen out for my brother while I go find you a new wardrobe. He barks a great deal these solars, though he hasn't bitten anyone recently," Kasha said, and strode off.

Left alone, Juan cursed Carlos for the new life he had thrust upon him. He had thought about running away, but he knew he had nowhere to go. Carlos had rejected him and the sanctuary of the slagerhaus was denied. After the tragic People's March, every hand in the Slough had turned

CHAPTER TWENTY NINE

against him, and all he could hope for there was a quick ending. So he would leave Gastown, and trek north and play the part of a city dweller scared of his own shadow in the Wildlands. He would bow and scrape, polish his words, and hold his tongue. Although he vowed to himself he would stick Kasha if she so much as put a hand on him. Then there was the reckoning with Carlos when he eventually returned. He would use the time away to harden his body, learn to fight, and strengthen his resolve. He took out his pigsticker and spat on the blade and made a promise to himself to exact revenge. Finally, he touched his eyepatch and the talisman behind it for good luck, though it had brought precious little of that so far, and wondered what had become of the country cousin who was the previous owner.

The largest caravan ever to make the great trek north moved through the gates of Gastown and out into the wildlands of Varlanda, the forested *Viorlanda,* and the *Opplanda* beyond. There were at least one hundred sledges of various sizes and functions in the convoy. Some were laden down with wool blankets, glass beads, and cooking pots for trading purposes. On the return journey, they would transport timber and pelts. There was also a heavily secured sledge rumored to contain a strongbox full of silver arm bands, which the local chieftains coveted to decorate their womenfolk and display their own power, though no one other than Beira and Drest were permitted inside. Smaller sledges were the guard dogs, who protected the convoy from wolf packs of all kinds. They were filled with fighting men Beira recruited, former Red Shadows, or proven killers Drest sniffed out from the Four Kith, or outlanders who were used to the wild ways of the *Viorlanda.* Renegade scouts from the northern tribes helped guide the convoy and assist with delicate negotiations.

The sound of women and children crying followed them, as their menfolk embarked on a perilous six lunar excursion to ensure their families lived in relative comfort. It was a dangerous undertaking, and some would not make the return journey. However, they all knew Beira was fair, and the families would receive their just share. As long as Beira herself returned

GASTOWN

with a bounty from the Wildlands in tow.

Beira was at the head of the column as usual, in her quick sleigh expertly driven by Drest. Out in the Wildlands, she would send out men in smaller sleighs to scout ahead. For now, the power show for Gastown was all important. Kasha and Juan sat next to their own driver, somewhere in the middle of the caravan, which snaked through the gateway and out into the thick packed snow. Furs and fire were the source of comfort out there as they left the warmth of the city and the underground heating behind.

Kasha looked back at Gastown, and saw Juan doing the same. "You're wondering what you have got yourself into, and if you'll ever see Gastown again, aren't you?" Kasha asked.

Juan had resisted a bath, but Kasha had two men strip him and hold him down while another scrubbed him clean with hard soap and cold water. He was all skin and bones, but surprisingly strong for his malnourished state. He was a fighter too, which Kasha appreciated. Dressed in hand me down furs, he looked two sizes bigger than the boy Drest had first presented.

"Somethin' like that. What about yuz?" Juan asked.

"'You,' not 'yuz.' Not me. My true home is in the *Faratha*, or running free in the *Machala*, the *Steppenlanda* in the common tongue. I hope I never have to come back again."

Juan gave her a quizzical look. "You run in the *Steppenlanda*?"

"It's complicated," Kasha said.

The first lunar of the journey north was uneventful. They passed a few homestead families, who were grateful for news from Gastown, but there was no contact yet with the northern tribes. Juan quickly learnt his chores and performed them without complaint, even when Berric was at his worst. In spare moments, Kasha even instructed him in the rudiments of combat. He was proficient with a knife, but had difficulty with axe and sword. Instead, Kasha showed him how to wield a quarterstaff and he quickly mastered the basic strikes and counters.

Kasha relished the fresh air once again, away from the stench of city life. She longed to leap off the sledge, strip off her clothes, and run free as a waheela. Cooped up all this time in her human form made her feel

CHAPTER TWENTY NINE

diminished, and unfulfilled. There would be time for that later. Now she had to focus on her brother's steady recovery, and assisting Beira in dealing with the tribes.

The caravan halted for the night, and the sledges and sleighs circled up for protection, though this far south the tribes were not generally hostile. The snow shovelers were released from their harnesses and allowed to graze as a herd. The herdmasters stayed close, and men armed with crossbows and hatchets guarded the perimeter. The snow shovelers were precious. Without them the expedition ground to an immediate halt, and no one wanted to walk the snow trek back to Gastown.

Kasha and Juan sat around their own little campfire and warmed themselves. While there were cooks who boiled up gray meat in a rich gravy, known as hunter's stew, augmented by snow hares and anything else they could catch in the wild, Kasha preferred to make her own fare. That way she could ensure Berric did not suffer from a dose of hunter's belly, though he constantly grumbled about the lack of a heavy slab of meat. Juan stirred the small pot, and was about to scoop out a plateful to feed Berric, when a howl made him jump.

"It's just a wolf calling to the pack. About three leagues away," Kasha said, as other wolves answered the call.

"They don't sound so friendly," Juan said.

"There are many out there more dangerous than wolf packs. Direwolves are twice as big and more fierce. Then there are waheelas, bigger still, and my personal favorites. There are also giant ice bears, snow cats, and ice worms."

Juan looked up, and Kasha saw fear in his one eye. "Ice worms?"

"Yes, they make tunnels under the crevices, and unsuspecting creatures fall into their lair. They suck you up whole, and slowly squeeze the life juices out of you until all that's left is the skin and bone."

Kasha was enjoying herself now. "Then there's the weather. You think it's cold here, John Bucket? Just wait until we reach the true north. Blizzards come out of nowhere, and you can't see your own hand. Up here they have twenty words to describe snow, and twenty more for ice."

Juan shuddered. "Who would want to come up 'ere with danger all around?"

"That's only the half of it. This is the land of the seven tribes of the Cathulla. If they ever unite, there will be no more caravans heading north, or settlers in the Wildlands. Then in the deep boreal forests we have the *Skovenmen*, who live in the giant trees and carry men off to eat their flesh, and make towers out of their skulls. And we have the *Chuchana*, the great snow beast. Part ape, and part man. No one sees them, just tracks in the snow, but if they get on your trail and lock on your scent, there is no escape, just a hideous death."

"Old wives' tales," a voice behind them said.

"Then there's Drest. The most fearsome man out here," Kasha said, looking up at the short, squat man.

"If you've finished scaring the boy, Beira wants to see you," Drest said, and turned to walk back.

Kasha stood up, and gave an order to Juan. "Take a plate to Berric and see he eats it all. And then stay by the fire, if you know what's good for you."

Kasha followed behind Drest until they came to the campfire where Beira waited. She sat in a wooden chair with an extra fur around her legs, and sipped something hot from a wooden cup. She gestured to the empty chair beside her.

"Come sit, Kasha. I want to talk with you. I've been so busy of late we haven't had a moment to catch up."

Kasha looked at the flimsy chair. "Will it hold my weight?"

"It's stronger than it seems. I had them specially made by one of the finest woodworkers in the Burghs. It folds up so you can store it away. Try it."

Kasha sat down, and eased into the comfort, then remembered she needed to be strong in the Wildlands and not give in to soft ways of city life, and sat up straight on the edge of the chair.

"How is your brother doing? I hope the journey is not too tiring for him," Beira asked.

CHAPTER TWENTY NINE

"He grumbles too much, but he's slowly getting better. Another lunar and he'll be back on his feet," Kasha said.

"I'm glad to hear it. When we first found him in the Mutton, I thought he was destined for the stone mounds of his ancestors."

Kasha started intently at Beira, but said nothing.

"Are you surprised I know something of the origin story of the Cathulla?"

"We don't speak of such things," Kasha said. Tornar told her the stories were not to be shared, but kept close to the heart, and secure behind a guarded tongue. People only knew fragments, and the little they knew brought fear.

Kasha remembered her lessons with her father when he returned and educated her on the ways of shapeshifting, the language of her people, the ways of tribal warfare, and her unique heritage.

It started with Cathul, from a race of giants, the clan folk referred to as the Realta Duin, Star People. It was a time long before the Tarb Greag, the airstone, struck the earth, and the solar retreated for eons, and the permafrost surged down from the Faratha, enveloping the vast western plains, the Machala, the forests and scrubland, the Snacoilltean, and the valleys, and rich pastures, the Gleann. Over time, the southern world recovered, but the north remained locked in a frozen grip.

Cathul was twice the size of normal men, and he came amongst the scattered northern clans and united them. He ruled by fear and took clan chief daughters for his wives and they bore him seven sons. Many did not withstand the ordeal of giving birth to their own giant offspring. The sons were not as tall as their father since they were half bloods, but they were distinguished by their double rows of teeth, large heads, and extraordinary strength. Cathul created seven tribes out of the clans, and named them the Cathulla. Each tribe was ruled by one son and his descendents, and all answered to Cathul.

Cathul ruled for over one hundred years, but even he could not overcome the challenges of time. The Cathulla created a huge stone mound in his honor, and buried him sitting up on a granite throne, with his ten best warriors at his feet, ready to rise for the Cathulla in their time of need. His eldest son, Bridem MacCathul, took his father's right hand, and made a crown and seven diadems with the bones and embedded precious stones. He ruled the seven tribes with an iron fist, and when his time came to pass, another stone mound dominated the landscape. More followed.

When the airstone hurtled down, everything changed. It glowed brightly in the sky, and then hit the earth with tremendous force, burning down vast forests, and banishing the solar and the lunar from the heavens. Ice and snow held sway, and thousands died of hunger before they learned to adapt to a harsher environment. Those who remained, led by a Darachan, a shaman with magical powers, blamed the descendents of Cathul, and drove them out of their villages, or killed them while they slept. No one knows when the curse of shapeshifting overcame them, though it was claimed the same Darachan laid a curse when his daughter was spirited away. Tornar declared shapeshifting was a gift bestowed on all of the distant sons of Cathul. Now a daughter too, Kasha always added.

Tornar MacLorn was the true king of the Cathulla, but only a handful of tribesmen, steeped in the old lore, and willing to endure Darachan persecution, accepted him as such. Most shunned him as he moved from village to village. Now the seven tribes were separated, some with chieftains, others with elder councils. They made war amongst each other, and disunity made it easier for the Var to transgress on their lands. Homesteads now littered the southern Machala, the land once held proudly by the Nechtana, and the great caravans snaked north for furs and timber.

When the Old Ones came and built their mighty citadel of Andalayim, and tamed the great worms with their magic, they traded equally with the Cathulla. They did not covet their land, but stayed in their city, and the oceans beyond. The Var were different. They were people who murdered and stole, and took what they wanted. Once the tribes were united again, the Var would be cast out forever, and their citadel broken down, stone by stone.

"As you wish, Kasha. No more talk of Tornar MacLorn, the King of the North. We'll save that for another solar. For now, how much can you tell me about the Nechtana? I'm assuming that's not off limits?" Beira asked.

Kasha shrugged. She knew she had to offer something in return for joining the trip and with Berric in their care. She also owed Beira for their lives. The cost was not cheap, and it seemed information was the price.

CHAPTER TWENTY NINE

"Some still follow the old ways. Old Uradec of the Nechtana is one of them, and he fed us and provided shelter when we passed through. Most kept their distance out of fear of the Darachan finding out. The Nechtana are peaceful enough, though they have a violent past. They're not given to raiding homesteads like before," Kasha said.

"We make sure to gift them when we pass through their lands. However, this trek is different."

"How so?"

"Usually, when we approach the first meeting place, the Nechtana will come and receive their gifts for allowing us safe passage. It's ceremonial, of course. This time, they won't come."

"It's not like their chieftain, Uuid, to pass on free bounty. He's a greedy man, and his wives covet the silver arm bands," Kasha said.

"Yet he stays in his lodge. My spies also tell me a Darachan has been seen in the south, and the northern tribes will refuse us passage.

Kasha bristled. She threw a stick on the fire, and she deliberated on her reply. "The Darachan haven't been this far south for some time. It could mean they plan to stop you."

"The trek is hard enough without fighting our way up to the great forests," Beira said.

"I wasn't expecting to fight my own people."

"I hope it doesn't come to that. Just stay close to your sledge and in the middle of the pack, and you'll be safe enough."

"I wasn't thinking about safety. I'm no coward."

"No one could ever say that about you, Kasha," Beira said with a smile. "I hope I can depend on you when needed, but for now I'd prefer you leave the fighting to others, and just provide me with counsel."

"I can do that," Kasha replied.

Something caught her eye on the other side of Beira's campfire. There was another fire surrounded by a group of tall women. Four were dressed in the usual garb of the Damm Warriors, with thick woolen clothes, and a heavy cloak over their shoulders. Kasha was sure their chainmail was stored away in their sledge, in easy reach in case needed. There were three other women too, tall like their compatriots, but dressed in white cotton clothes, and a white fur over their shoulders to protect them from the cold. Two of the women were older with graying hair, which was similar in length to Beira's in contrast to the sharp bowl cut customary to the Damm Warriors. The other was in her prime, a tall confident woman who seemed to be in command. Her hair was also longer than the regulation short style Kasha had come to expect from the Var women.

"I thought Damm Warriors weren't needed for these treks," Kasha asked.

"They aren't. That's Adis, a former Captain of the Dux's Guard, and her most trusted companions. They're going on the final journey to the Three Sisters," Beira said.

"I don't understand," Kasha said.

"When the Var first came to the citadel and liberated it from the Old Ones, we left our sacred grove far behind. At first, those who felt the calling, traveled back to the old country. However, once the ice and snow came, we were cut off from that land journey, across the *Steppenlanda*. Then Gerd the Mighty, had a vision of another sacred grove in the *Opplanda* to the far north. She made the trek with her two sisters, and an honor guard from the Dux herself. Only one came back, but she reported they had found the grove, now known as the Three Sisters, and Gerd and her siblings had made the ultimate sacrifice to honor Frotha. Now, when Damm Warriors experience the calling, they accompany the caravan north," Beira explained.

"They give themselves up freely?"

"They are the Chosen Ones. It's a great honor."

Kasha remembered Beira had used the same term on their first meeting, and a chill came over her. Before she could ask another question, there was a commotion and a herdsman came running up, his bearclaws churning up the snow. Kasha and Beira stood up, and the heavily panting man stopped in front of them, pointing back towards the direction he had just come.

"They're attacking the herd!" he said.

Without a word, Beira drew her sword and charged off in the direction of the snow shoveler herd. Kasha quickly went back to her own sledge, and tied on her bearclaws, and put her axe and short sword in her belt. She

CHAPTER TWENTY NINE

picked up another set of bearclaws for Beira.

Juan popped his head out from the sledge. "What's goin' on?" he asked.

"Stay with Berric. Guard him close!" Kasha ordered.

Kasha had not gone far, when she came across Beira floundering through the heavy snow. She tossed her the spare pair of snowshoes.

"Here, put these on," Kasha said. She did not wait for Beira and ran on toward the herd, axe and short sword now in hand.

Kasha could hear fighting up ahead, and ran towards the thick of it. The herd was still intact, and the snow shovelers huddled tighter together as wolves howled all around them. Kasha saw two bodies in the snow, with arrows sticking out of them. One was a herdsman, the other a snow shoveler he gave his life to protect. Other men surrounded the herd, and fired crossbow bolts at anything that moved outside their perimeter.

They're shooting at shadows!

Kasha came across another dead snow shoveler, and she stopped to examine the wounds. Its throat was torn out, but none of the flesh was consumed.

It's a death hunt. They're not here to feed.

Kasha heard the growl and felt the charge, and instinctively dropped to the snow. A figure sailed over her and she stabbed up her short sword, and heard a grunt as she pulled the blade through guts. She rolled to one side, and came up beside the body on the ground, and crashed her fighting axe into the skull.

Beira closed up on Kasha. She was not used to wearing the bearclaws, and she was breathing heavily. She leaned on her sword, and looked down at the broken body.

"Wolf?"

Kasha placed her weapons back in her belt, reached down and flipped the carcass over. It was the dead body of a man, naked except for the wolf skin wrapped around his torso, and wolf claws in his hands. His skull, encased in a wolf's head, was crushed in, and his innards seeped out, where Kasha's blade had disemboweled him. He was short of stature, but powerfully built, and blue ink tattoos of intricate spirals and animal figures dominated by the wolf, covered his frame. Even in the gloom, Kasha recognized him. It was Maelchron, Uradec's son who had stalked her as she entered the old man's camp on her journey south to Gastown.

"A Nechtana wolfman," Kasha said.

"Shapeshifter?" Beira asked.

"He's no shapeshifter. Just a man in wolf's clothing playing the part. The Nechtana are a wolf clan. They raise them to do their bidding, and wear their skins for power. They're attacking your herd because they know you're lost without them."

Drest and twenty men armed with crossbows came skiing out of the night. He stopped before Beira, but waved the men on to chase away their enemy.

"You shouldn't go off alone," Drest chastised his mistress.

"A momentary madness," Beira said. "Besides, I had Kasha to protect me."

Drest looked at the corpse of the wolfman, and then up at Kasha. "She'll do," he said.

When the solar came, they tallied the dead. The picket line was broken in two places, but the Nechtana had failed to drive the herd away. Four herdsmen paid with their lives, and five snow shovelers perished. Men were already butchering the animal carcasses, so nothing went to waste, and the deceased herdsmen were buried in the snow with little ceremony and no markers. Other than Maelchron, there were no more Nechtana corpses or wolves to be found, though blood tracks in the snow suggested the wounded or possibly the dead had been dragged away.

Kasha knew they were lucky and said so to Beira. The Nechtana attack was more a probe than a full on assault, as if they were appeasing someone, but not willing to risk the full wrath of the Var. Being so close to Varstad, they would bear the brunt of any reprisals, and Uuid, their chieftain, was not a man to take unnecessary risks. If confronted, he would put the blame on a handful of renegade warriors, and make an example of them.

Beira's caravan always traveled with a surplus of snow shovelers. The

CHAPTER TWENTY NINE

herd suffered losses along the way, and the dead always provided a ready supply of fresh meat. However, it was rare to lose this many so far south, and so Beira ensured they doubled the night guard for the rest of the trek. For the next few solars, Drest dogged Beira's every step, until she promised never to go off into the night alone again. Only then did he give her some breathing room, but he always kept her in sight.

The caravan moved on further north, and out of the territory of the Nechtana. The howls of a wolfpack, or men imitating the sound, echoed behind them. Now, they were in the no man's land between the Nechtana and the fierce Fidacha tribe. It was a wide expanse of open ice land, largely barren of life, until the boreal forest leagues ahead. Frigid storms came out of nowhere, and the elements tried to kill anyone who ventured through. The harshness of the terrain and the difficulty traversing it kept a tenuous peace between the tribes, and gave occupants of the caravan time to ponder on what lay ahead.

The winds lashed them from the west, and pushed snow storms across them as they continued north. Kasha sat next to her driver with John Bucket by her side. They were bundled up against the cold, and could barely see the sledge in front.

"How do they know where their goin'?" Juan asked.

"The Var use a solar stone to point the way. It shows the position even when you can't see. The Cathulla read the land, and follow the natural weather cycles. It's all patterns if you know what you're looking for," Kasha explained.

"Will the next tribe let us through?" Juan asked.

"Who knows. Beira will send a scout ahead to find out. If he comes back we'll have safe passage, if he doesn't..."

The next solar, the storm lifted, and though there was still a deep chill in the air, visibility was good. After a quick breakfast, the caravan trudged on again, and Kasha and Juan took their usual position next to their silent driver. He flicked his whip at an errant snow shoveler, who tried to stop in search of grazing, and kept the sledge moving.

"What's that over there?" Juan said, pointing at a large rock outcrop, which seemed out of place in the flatlands.

"That's the burial mound of Fidach himself. First chieftain of the Fidacha, and Cathul's second son. Believe it or not, but this used to be fertile lands, and snow shovelers and giant poro grazed here. That's when we had four seasons like the kingdoms to the south. Before the permafrost came, and covered everything in ice."

"I wish I could go south, an' feel the warm solar on my skin," Juan mused.

"Perhaps one solar you will, John Bucket. For now, it's north for us, and more ice and snow."

The scout did not come back, but they did find his headless body nailed to a lone frozen tree. The message was loud and clear: turn back, or face the consequences. Beira looked up at the body, and Drest and Kasha stood by her side.

"Probably not a good idea to send a Kelturan tribesman to talk with the Fidacha. Cailtram, their chieftain, still holds a grudge for his great great grandmother being carried off long before he was born. They don't forgive easy in the north," Kasha said.

"I can see that," Beira said. "What do you propose we do, Kasha?"

"I'd say keep moving at a steady pace. Don't let the scouts roam too far ahead, circle the sledges at night with the snow shovelers inside, and wait."

"Wait?"

"They'll either let us pass through, which seems unlikely. Or they'll attack at night. The Fidacha are not like the Nechtana. They have greater numbers, and they revere the direwolf, much fiercer than the wolves we left behind."

"Waiting for someone else to make the first move doesn't sit well with me, but I'll listen to your advice. For now," Beira replied, and left as Drest instructed his men to bring down the remains of their former scout.

Berric was in another foul mood, so Kasha decided to feed him his supper of snow hare broth rather than have him take his anger out on John Bucket. Berrric took a few spoonfuls, but pushed his bowl to one side.

CHAPTER TWENTY NINE

"Enough of this thin soup. I need a poro steak and a black bier!" Berric complained.

"In good time. For now you need to be careful what you eat. Just ten more solars and you can be up and about and we'll add red meat to your diet."

"Then give me more White Tears so I can sleep before I die of boredom!"

Kasha looked at her brother and wondered if she would act the same if she was in his position. They were both raised and trained for a life of activity, and idleness and immobility were a warrior's bane. She was also disturbed by her brother's physical appearance. Although he was healing, his body had wasted away, and the White Tears dulled his appetite and mind, and sharpened his tongue when the potency wore off.

"Are you sure you need more?" Kasha asked, though she knew the answer he would give.

"Just pass the bottle, Kasha and spare the sisterly advice!"

Kasha hesitated for a moment, and then handed the bottle to her brother. Berric pulled the cork loose and took a swig. Gone were the solars when he took a sip from a spoon.

The effect was immediate, and Berric lay back down with a relaxed expression on his face, and his eyes closed. Kasha stood up to go, and to leave him with his dreams.

"Kasha ... there's something I need to tell you," Berric said. "It's about my mission..."

"Your mission? Don't you mean our mission?"

There were voices outside. "Kasha! You need to come and see this!" Juan shouted.

Kasha left Berric and stepped down from the back of the sledge. She did not need John Bucket to tell her what was going on, the fires burning all around the circle of sledges told her what was happening. Within the protective barrier, men were running in all directions, positioning themselves as instructed by Drest. They were heavily armed, with axes, swords, and crossbows. The Kelturan scouts had short bows too, the kind favored by the tribesmen, and the kind they would use to good effect against the Fidacha, spurred on by the murder of their brother. Herdsmen worked frantically to settle down the herd, and ensured the pack leaders were hobbled, so the others remained close.

Kasha had no assigned task or defensive position from Drest, so she sought out Beira to stand by her side during the skirmish. She armed herself with her axe and short sword, and went in search of the snow queen of Varlanda. She was not difficult to find, commanding cooks, carpenters, and loggers, in preparation to put out fires. The Damm Warriors were close by, the four in chainmail and helm, and three still dressed in white, but now armed with long swords. Kasha knew they would make short work of any Fidacha tribesman who penetrated the inner defenses.

The Fidacha started the confrontation and broke their truce with the Var. Fire arrows came in from all sides, and peppered the sledges. One stuck in the flank of a snow shoveler, until a herdsman pulled it free and burned his hands in the process. He immediately applied a moss poultice to the wounded animal and settled it down.

Beira's fire watchers scurried within the enclosure, running from sledge to sledge, and scooping snow onto the flames to quickly extinguish them. Black arrows came next, and the men seeking to extinguish the fires were the intended targets. Whistling arrows were interspersed with the black ones. Their sole purpose was to instill fear into the men inside the caravan enclosure.

Beira was no fool, and had paired her men up. While one dealt with the fire, another held a makeshift shield, cobbled together from buckets, stools, and slats from the sledges. It was no guarantee to keep the arrows away, but if offered the man dealing with the fire the comfort of knowing someone had his back. A cook forgot the instructions and acted alone. Perched high on top of his wagon, snuffing out two fire arrows, he was an inviting target. Five arrows pin cushioned him to the top.

"They're all around us. There must be thousands of them," Beira complained.

"Unless they've united all of the tribes, they don't have those numbers. It's an illusion. They're moving men quickly around the perimeter on

CHAPTER TWENTY NINE

skis. They're probing for a weakness. When they find one, they'll send a diversionary attack on one side. When you move to deal with it, they'll attack in force from the other side," Kasha explained.

"How do you know all this?" Beira asked.

"Tornar taught me well."

"In that case, let's make it easy for them to find what they're looking for."

Beira passed on instructions to Drest and he held back the snow carriers from extinguishing a blaze which had taken hold of a scout sleigh. He massed his men behind it, and waited for the attack. Beira, accompanied by her own men, as well as the seven Damm Warriors took up position on the other side, and waited for the diversionary attack.

There were no battle cries, or yells to instill courage from the Fidacha tribesmen as black shapes poured over the sledges and made their way towards Beira and her small group. Kasha stood ready, axe and short sword in hand. She could feel her own battle rage building, and held on to stop the war madness overtaking her. Now was not the time. She looked at Beira beside her, sword drawn, and a determined look on her face. She was a Damm Warrior at heart, and Kasha knew she would give a good account of herself.

Before the Fidacha got closer, Beira's men unleashed a torrent of bolts from their crossbows, reloaded, and fired again. Tribesmen went down in droves, as the quarrels struck home, but the remainder did not falter and came on. They were small, dark haired tattooed men, naked from the waist up, and armed with crude battle axes, short swords, and spears. They all wore snowshoes for easier movement. A handful climbed atop the sledges, and fired their black arrows down on Beira's group. One arrow took a Damm Warrior in white in the throat. She went to her knees, and stuck her sword into the ground. Her head dropped forward as she died. Her four companions in chainmail swung their varbows free, and cleared away the Fidacha archers.

The Fidacha came at a run and locked for close quarter combat. With Beira's men, that was single combat, but they had never faced Damm Warriors before, and they fought as a group. Swords drawn, they advanced on the tribesman, and hacked through limbs, bodies, and heads. Each one watching out to protect their sister. Some blows got through, but they rang against chainmail, and the reprisal strike brought death. Kasha stood side by side with Beira, and they towered over their adversaries. A tribesman stabbed his spear at Beira's abdomen, and she easily parried the blow. Kasha swung her short axe, and crushed in his left temple. Another came at her right side, and his short blade just missed striking at her ribs. Kasha blocked that blow with her short sword, and Beira's sword took off the top of his skull.

As quickly as they came, the Fidacha retreated, and disappeared into the night. Beira left her men to guard the rear, and went with Kasha and the Damm Warriors to join Drest for the main assault.

The scout sleigh was still burning, when it was suddenly pulled out of the line by a series of hooks attached to ropes. Once it was free, the Fidacha charged through the opening. Drest was waiting for them. His men were lined up in a wide arc with their crossbows leveled. There was more. A battery of stingers, heavy crossbows held in place with a ground beam and cross beams, and operated by three men, were armed and ready for the tribal assault. As soon as the first rank of Fidacha passed through the breach and into the fire zone, the bolts were unleashed. The heavier bolts from the stingers did the most damage. At close range, they passed cleanly through the first man, and impaled two more behind. They quickly reloaded, and killed again. Broken bodies piled up in the gap between the sledges.

Between the stingers and the crossbows, the Fidacha had no chance to close with Drest and his men. They backed up, and disappeared into the night. Behind them, the torches went out, and the only illumination came from within the caravan circle. The sound of the dying, and the broken corpses were all the Fidacha left behind.

Kasha could sense his presence rather than see him, but she searched the mountains in the distance. There was a noise behind and she turned, weapons at the ready. It was Berric with a bloody sword in hand, and propped up by John Bucket holding his quarterstaff.

CHAPTER TWENTY NINE

"What are you doing?" Kasha asked, turning on Juan.

"He insisted. Said he'd come alone if I didn't help," Juan explained.

"He's here. Father's here. I've brought you home, Kasha," Berric said, before he collapsed.

Chapter Thirty

Gastown Confessions

Little Samal was tucked up in his bed for the night and already fast asleep. His night terrors had subsided, and he was adapting to his new life as an Apotheka's Assistant. Justin was glad to have the boy for company. He was the one bright spot in the false narrative of his life in the Four Kith.

Justin left the soup bowls on the table, and promised himself he would take care of them first thing in the morning. He sat in the chair, once occupied by the counterfeit corpse of Master Habala, and filled his pipe bowl with the last of his Ma. Between Carlos Grimm and himself, they had gone through the final jar. He knew it was a bad Apotheka who consumed his own stock, especially one as potent and mind numbing as Ma. However, since the slaughter at the Bridge of Broken Souls, now adaptly named, *Juan's Folly,* he wanted to escape reality.

They should call it Justin's Treachery.

In his more logical moments, Justin reasoned he had not pulled the trigger of a crossbow, or sent arrows arcing overhead to impale the helpless paupers whose only crime was to seek sustenance. However, his report to Rayfn was the catalyst for the carnage and he could not shake the sense of responsibility, plus the fact he did indeed have blood on his hands. How could he provide much needed treatment to the Slough dwellers on the one hand, and end their lives with the stroke of a pen on the other?

CHAPTER THIRTY

There was more troubling Justin. Ever since he had seen Chandra, the Andra girl, sitting up in Puzzle Pete's bed, he could not keep her out his thoughts. Her flowing black hair, her sad green eyes, her lips, and her rouged nipples. In his mind's eye, he had tried not to look, but his gaze alway fell to her exposed breasts. He wanted to cry for her, to rescue her, to take her in his arms, and hold her close. He took another pull from his pipe, and let the calmness wash over him.

He had finally put the charade of old Master Habala to rest, and retired the skeleton to a closet in the back of his room. The old musky bearskin was back on his bed, where it belonged. He adopted the name Master Habala himself, and no one seemed to mind or notice. Only Puzzle Pete's Crimper bore witness to his secret, and he had been abruptly removed from service at roughly the same time. Justin was now a fully fledged Apotheka, and he was miserable.

Justin finished a detailed report to Rafyn, and promised himself it would be his last. Whatever the consequences, he was done with being his sister's spy. He outlined the number of dead, and the wounded he still treated after the disastrous march on the citadel. He included the Slough rumor Juan Grimm was still alive, and the one-eyed boy killed on the bridge was an imposter. He wrote about the death of Toby Meyers, the Crimper in the employ of Puzzle Pete. His body was full of stab wounds, and his head was hacked off, and stuck on a pole outside of Pete's own establishment. Carlos Grimm was the obvious assassin, and the Bully Boys, who seemed to be on their backfoot, were now emboldened, and came back to his side in droves. There were a few more casualties in the turf war, mostly along the borders, but the lines were drawn between the Four Kith and the Mutton, while Puzzle Pete and Carlos Grimm figured out their next treacherous move to gain the upper hand. Whatever they did was no longer his concern.

Justin rolled up the scroll with his report to Rafyn, and made the snap decision to hand it to her himself. It was a bold move to try and gain entry into the citadel at night, but he was a Gentry by birthright, if not by choice, and he was confident he could talk his way past the nightguard. If he claimed he had an urgent message for Rafyn herself, who would be foolish enough to turn him away until the next solar?

He felt a degree of negligence leaving Samal all alone in the apothekaria, but he was sleeping soundly, and if Rafyn was reasonable, he would be back in his own bed in a few hours. If Rafyn was not fair-minded, and threw him back in his jail cell, what of Samal then? The boy would be all alone in a hostile world. Justin hesitated for a moment, and then his resolve hardened, and he prepared for what could well be his last journey. He left the keep with his bearskin and *safwan*, his daronite rock. He took them now for comfort, and as trusty companions if a life in captivity beckoned.

As Justin stepped out of the apothekaria, his path was blocked by two mudlarks. At first, he thought they were chancers out to rob him, then he noticed the black soot about their eyes, and he knew they were part of Carlos Grimm's extended family.

"Wez come for the package," one mite said, while his companion casually picked at his rotten teeth with a rusty knife.

"I'm afraid I'm all out of Ma. The next shipment isn't due for another lunar. Tell Carlos to slow down his consumption," Justin said.

"Tell 'im yourself," a voice said from the shadows, and then Fleet Dawkins came forward.

Justin was significantly bigger than the fire mite, and wrapped in his old bearskin, he dwarfed him. Yet something about the boy was unsettling. Like Carlos Grimm, death and destruction had smirched him, and shone through his killer eyes. He always smelled of rank smoke, soot and fire grime were ingrained in his clothes, and the burn mark on his face advertised he was no stranger to the hazardous flame.

"Carlos is here?" Justin asked.

"No, dombrain. The streets is too dangerous for 'im to be walkin' about. 'E wants yuz over at the slagerhaus, sharpish," Fleet hissed.

"I can't possibly do that right now. I have a prior engagement," Justin protested, though it fell on plugged ears.

"Sharpish, Iz said. An' bring some of that special tabak, an' an extra pipe. Though it looks an' smells like yuz 'as 'ad an 'ead start in the game. Sharpish, or this fine establishment of yours will make a nice bonfire."

CHAPTER THIRTY

Justin felt a tinge of guilt for consuming the last of the Ma, but there was still a healthy supply of Barri and Lolo on hand. He found the Barri a tad spicy, and left a bitter taste in the mouth. The Lolo was not as potent as Ma, but the natural sweetness was more pleasing on the palate. He took ten pouches for Carlos's later use, and another for them to share in the confines of the slagerhaus.

They moved at a fast pace through the streets and alleyways, always staying in the shadows. One of the mites was on point, the other by Justin's side, and Fleet Dawkins brought up the rear, only a sharp knife thrust behind. They reached the slagerhaus before Justin realized he still had the scroll intended for Rafyn buried inside the folds of his cassock. It was a death sentence, if Carlos decided to search him, and had anyone on hand to read it.

The fire in the hearth of the great hall was blazing, and Justin found Carlos sitting in a heavy oak chair close to the flames. Fleet and the two mites grabbed tankards of bier, and went to join their companions at the long tables. A somber man stood at a butcher's block, sharpening his knives. He nodded as Justin moved closer to Carlos and the fire. There was a chair waiting for him, and a small table between them with an empty pipe and a fresh taper on it.

Justin took the stash of Lolo from his pocket and deposited it on the table. He picked up Carlos's long pipe, and filled it to the brim, lit the taper in the fire, and applied it to the tabak. He puffed three times until the contents of the bowl were burning, and handed it to Carlos.

Carlos only had eyes for the flames, but he accepted the offered pipe, and took an extended pull, sucking the smoke deep into his lungs. He slumped back into his chair and let out a long, satisfying exhale. He was back in the land of the living, and the reality of his current existence. Justin could almost see the heavy weight he carried on his juvenile shoulders and the temporary relief the Lolo brought.

"That ole bearskin's seen better solars," Carlos said.

"It comforts me," Justin replied, as he flopped down into his own chair. Between the blaze from the fire, and the burden of the bearskin, he was sweating profusely, though he dared not take it off for fear of exposing Rafyn's intended scroll.

"Are yuz not joinin' me?" Carlos asked.

"In a little while," Justin said.

"Ah, I see. It's a poor Apotheka who smokes all of 'is wares in secret. Or a guilty one."

Justin did not reply. He filled his own pipe from the open pouch, but left it unlit on the table.

"Tell me, Apotheka. 'Ave you ever killed anyone?" Carlos asked.

"Not directly," Justin replied.

"Iz wielded the blade myself, but only five souls fell under it. If a man 'as the power of words to send five 'undred to the Ondeworld at one stroke, who is the true killer?"

"I would say they're both equally guilty," Justin said. He brought life back to the taper, and applied it to his own pipe bowl, which he held in a shaking hand. Perspiration ran in rivulets.

"We've all done things we're ashamed of. No one is truly good or bad. It's about having a moral compass and course correcting when you shift off track," Justin said.

"Wot's a compass?"

"Oh, just somethin I'm working on."

Carlos took another pull on his pipe. "Tell me, Apotheka. Did yuz meet my brother, Juan?"

"You know I did." Justin exhaled and let the calmness envelop him.

"An' yuz 'elped 'im with that Great Charter?"

"I recorded the words for posterity."

"And those grand folks in the citadel got a fresh copy of their very own, an' was waitin' on the bridge. I dare say Slough folks would be keen to know the source of that betrayal. Traitor's blud would flow."

"I dare say it would."

Carlos took another pull from his pipe, and pointed the stem at Justin. "Do yuz know where Juan is now?"

"I'm sorry for your loss, but didn't he die on the bridge? I'm told they

CHAPTER THIRTY

named it after him. *Juan's Folly* it's called," Justin said. He knew full well Juan did not perish there, though he had not been seen since.

Carlos coughed as a mouthful of smoke went down the wrong way. "*Juan's Folly* it is, but that mudlark of a brother didn't go down under arrows. That was a foolish decoy who took the 'it for 'im. Name of Gesmas. Fleet an' the boys rescued my brother, an' brought him 'ere."

"So you have him safe?" Justin said, and he felt a sense of relief truly knowing Juan at least escaped the carnage on the bridge.

"That would be guilt by association, an' the 'igher ups would pay dearly for that information."

Justin continued to sweat, although now it was not just from the heat, but from Carlos's close scrutiny.

He knows it was me. If he finds the scroll, he has all the proof he needs.

"No, Juan isn't 'ere. It cost me a bag of silver, but I sent 'im aways up north, an' out of Gastown."

"Then he's safe."

"An' another bag of silver to make sure 'e never comes back. The Gentry will eat that up too. Carlos Grimm can be trusted to keep Four Kith troubles aways from the citadel. Out of sight, an' out of mind."

"You would kill your own brother?" Justin said incredulously. For some reason, despite everything he had seen and heard in the Four Kith and the Mutton, the shock of Carlos assassinating his own twin truly shocked him. Then the thought crossed his mind, Rafyn could do the very same thing to him.

Carlos turned away from Justin, and stared intently in the fire as he took another calming hit of Lolo.

"Too much smoke 'as addled your brain, Apotheka. Not kill, settin' free," Carlos said. "This is no life we lead in the Four Kith, and worse in the Slough. The burgh folk an' the Citadel Gentry might live long an' 'appy lives, but all wez do is suffer. Starvation an' disease for most, the blade and the Basin for the damned. I'm settin' 'im free for the both of us, never to come back to Gastown. Iz dare say in time, 'e'll become Lord of 'em Wildlands."

After Justin left, Carlos sat alone in front of the fire, and filled his pipe with one more bowl of the special tabak. It was not as strong as the previous supply from the Apotheka, and he needed one more hit to help him fully relax.

Kill my brother?

In truth the thought had crossed his mind, and a word to Fleet would have set it in motion. However, he could no more kill Juan than he could kill himself. Banishment and a new life far away from the filth of Gastown was a suitable punishment. Juan was always the smart twin, but he was now the one pulling the strings for the both of them. He needed Juan out of the way, and not a bargaining chip for the likes of Puzzle Pete to manipulate. Now there was no one who could be used against him, and he could concentrate on the war with the Crimpers. The Bully Boys had come back to him and he had an eager army at his command. Men who were previously hesitant to follow a boy would willingly take orders from the killer of Toby Meyers. However, Carlos knew Puzzle Pete would not give up on the fight, and he would have to act soon to press his advantage.

Then there was the Apotheka. He needed him for medicinal reasons, but he could not be trusted. Carlos knew he was the one who betrayed Juan and the Slough folk marching on the citadel. Their conversation all but confirmed it. Still, he could use a spy reporting back to the Var as an asset, and feed him false information. There would need to be a reckoning at some point, and Fleet disliked the Apotheka as much as he did Juan. His blade would deal with the problem, but that was for a later time.

Deep in the Burghs, Josephine was restless in her upstairs room in the Willow household. She had gone up relatively early to continue with her studies on the dangers of assa emissions, though she did not take an extra candle on this occasion. She could not concentrate and struggled with the assignment as her thoughts were elsewhere. Her father had not come home, despite his promise to lessen his workload given his poor health, and Josephine wondered if she was the cause of his late night hours in the assachamber rather than spending time arguing with his daughter across

CHAPTER THIRTY

the dining table.

Josephine closed her book, took her candle, and went down the stairs to wait. She was not surprised to see Nell sitting in her favorite chair with her embroidery in her lap. She was still working on her Willow design, which never seemed to finish.

Nell looked up when Josephine came into the room. "You should be sleeping already. No need for the both of us to wait up."

"I can't sleep, Nell. Something doesn't feel right, and father should have been home by now. Everything was fine with the boilers when I left, and it's dangerous to be passing through the Four Kith this late."

Oh, everyone knows the Assameister. Mr. Willow won't come to any harm, unless they want their heating turned off for good."

"I should go to him, Nell. He might need me," Josephine said.

Nell put her needle and thread down. "Tosh posh! I won't hear of such a thing. A young lady can't go out at night."

"I'll go as Joe, silly. I can move fast through the Four Kith corridor, and I'll be on the bridge before anyone notices."

"And just how will you get into the citadel? Answer me that? The guards won't let you pass."

"I'll figure that out later," Josephine said. Her mind was set. She went back up to her room and changed into her dead brother's work clothes.

Outside of the slagerhaus, Justin felt free himself. Free and clear on the choice he had to take. The crisp freshness of the night air cooled him down, and Carlos had let him go, expecting he would deliver the information on to the citadel. Perhaps Carlos would send on an assassin one cold night when he was back in the apothekaria, if Rafyn did not dispatch him first for defying her. That was for the future, and he had no stargazer's ball to see the way. He knew he was done with spying and he was ready and willing to pay the piper for his crime. On to the citadel and a reckoning with his dark sister.

The snow which fell throughout the solar and into the early part of the evening had passed, and the night sky was clear, and the brighter stars were visible despite the light pollution Gastown cast on the heavens. Justin wondered what it would be like to be further north, where the firmament could be freely observed, or even in the great Sul observatory rumored to be atop Jade Mountain. He remembered his celestial studies back in the Tower of Tomes. There was *Frotha's Wagon*, the mighty constellation of seven stars, *Njall's eyes*. the twin stars formed when Tiv cast the giant's orbs into the cosmic abyss to placate his angry daughter, *The Great Bear, The Little Bear, The Blue Star, The Morning Star,* and his favorite, *Loti's Toe,* which peeped out of a heavenly blanket and froze, and was snapped off and cast up in a fit of rage.

As he watched, a shooting star briefly blazed a path, before burning out. He thought about another shooting star eons ago, the *loftsteinn*, the airstone from the Bull Constellation, which had not flamed out. Instead it had landed in the far north and brought the permawinter. Legends said the remnants of the sky rock were still there, and guarded by shamans.

Justin craved to be away from the responsibilities he had surrounded himself with in Gastown, and far away from Rafyn's orbit. Freedom. Freedom to travel, study, survey, or simply live without spilling secrets.

The Four Kith was not a safe place at night for a lone traveler, and Justin put his faith in two things to keep himself safe. The bearskin filled out his skinny frame, and coupled with his height he presented a menacing appearance in the dark. He was also well known as a healer in the Four Kith, and anyone seeing him up close might allow him gratis passage. If all else failed, he gripped *safwan* tight in his hand for self defense.

Justin made his way to the Bridge of Broken Souls and the gateway to the citadel without incident. He paused at the bridge to pay silent respect to the hundreds of Slough souls who gave their lives for the want of a vegetable stew. He treated many of the wounded who had made it back from that fateful solar, and his guilt did not allow him to take payment.

There was one final act he needed to accomplish before he faced Rafyn and his undecided fate. He took the scroll from out of his cassock, unfurled it, tore it into shreds and dropped the parchment fragments into the waters below. He would deliver his last report verbally, and make no mention

CHAPTER THIRTY

of Juan Grimm on his trip north. Juan Grimm had died on the bridge he was now standing on, along with the Great Charter, and that was all Rafyn needed to know.

What if she has other spies?

There were footsteps behind him, and Justin turned expecting to see a cutthroat. Instead, he saw a slight young man walking across the bridge towards the citadel. He passed Justin, keeping his head down and his hands in his pockets.

"You're wasting your time. They won't let you in at night," Justin called out. His tone was friendly so as not to unduly alarm the man.

"What's it to you," the young man muttered.

"Just offering some friendly advice," Justin replied.

"I don't need friends."

The young man continued to walk along the bridge to the citadel and Justin walked silently a few paces behind. The man stopped and turned to face Justin.

"I'd prefer it if you didn't walk behind me," the man said.

Up close, Justin could see he was no more than an adolescent boy. "Totally understandable. Crossing from the burgh to the citadel can be a dangerous undertaking. I mean no harm. I'm Habala the Apotheka, and I come in peace," Justin said with a smile, and an exaggerated bow. It served to break the ice.

"I've heard of you. Nell, our housekeeper swears by your remedies for the flux and a touch of arthritis. And half the Burghmeisters smoke your Old Burley tabak. I would have expected someone older with a long white beard. You look a little on the young side to be an Apotheka," the boy said.

"Looks can be deceiving," Justin said, as he stared intently at his new acquaintance. "There's no protruding brow, or square jaw. The eyes are not deep set, and definitely larger. The eyebrows are not straight and bushier, and somewhat higher. The cheeks are rounder and softer, the nose is slightly upturned, and the lips are fuller. And there's certainly a lack of a laryngeal prominence. All physical representations of the feminine gender."

The boy shifted uncomfortably. "Do you always talk like that?"

"Apologies, I don't mean to pry, and we all have our secrets. It's just in my line of work, I'm an observer of the human condition. Tell me, what brings you out here? Risking life and limb, and conversing with a strange Apotheka in a smelly old bearskin?"

"I've come to find my father, the Assameister. He's not in good health, and he should have been home hours ago. I'm Joe, by the way. Joe Willow. And you? What brings you to the citadel?"

"I've come to deliver a report," Justin said.

"They won't let you in. You said so yourself," Josephine said.

"Ah, but I have a friend in high places. Getting in isn't my concern, it's getting out again."

"Then if you don't mind, I'll tag along with you."

The two of them made strange companions, as they walked side by side across the span of the bridge. The tall gangling Apotheka wrapped in a bearskin, and the slim girl, who tried desperately to pass as a boy. Justin was content to remain silent, and not press the issue, though he wondered who Joe was fooling. Everyone was entitled to their secrets.

"I've seen you before," Josephine said. "On this bridge attending to the wounded."

"That was a very sad solar indeed. The people were cruelly slaughtered, all for the wont of a vegetable stew," Justin said mournfully.

"It's not right. There is plenty of food to go around. No one should starve and we should help each other."

"Noble words, Joe. Unfortunately, we live in a cruel world, and the Var are vengeful people."

"What if the Var weren't here? What then?"

"I would keep those thoughts to yourself so close to the citadel. Walls have ears, and I have it on good authority that spies are everywhere."

They had reached halfway across the bridge, when there was a loud, thunderous noise from within the citadel itself, which stopped them in their tracks. Smoke and flames sprang up from one of the interior buildings, and then other fires quickly followed. The sound of fighting and ringing

CHAPTER THIRTY

bells filled the air.

Chapter Thirty One

Varstad Burns

They moved quietly in the night. Silent killers: men, women, and children. There were only a handful of their traditional weapons to go around: the short recurved composite bows, and the nomadic sabers, secreted away inside the seed barrels. They were reserved for the most seasoned warriors amongst the men and women. The rest of the clan used anything at hand from small knives, hammers, garden shears, and even sharpened sticks toughened in the fire. They had one chance to take control, or die trying. It was not about glory, or power, or riches. It was all about survival.

There were no guards outside of the glass domes and the fighters formed up into their three war parties, each numbering close to four hundred. They moved quietly out into the corridors and hallways of the citadel. All of them had discarded their wooden clogs, so they made little noise as they glided barefoot across the stone floors. The few archers were in the lead of the first group, and the veteran killers followed close behind in the second unit. A ragtag army, some of them old men in their dotage, or children as young as five, brought up the rear. There was no doubt they would kill when the time came. They were raised to butcher from an early age. As soon as they could hold a knife they had to dispatch animals, and they constantly nicked the necks of livestock to drink the warm blood for sustenance. They even practiced their archery on prisoners and hit

CHAPTER THIRTY ONE

assigned bodily targets before the final death shot ended the captive's misery.

Chimeg rounded a corner and came across the first great chamber and was gratified to see there were only two guards on duty. It was obvious the Var never considered anyone would attack them inside their own mighty citadel, because the approach to the barrack doorway was partially concealed.

Chimeg was striking to look at, with the combination of her father's green, angular eyes, and her mother's silk black hair, high cheekbones, and lithe figure. While she inherited her father's ability to lead and to fight, she also took on her mother's jealous nature, and her tongue ran rampant, especially where her older brother was concerned. Her father, Jargal, doted on her.

The discipline of the Damm Warrior guards was strong, and they stood ramrod straight and alert. Both women were in full armor, though their longswords were sheathed. Chimeg waved her twenty archers forward, and they took aim, while six warriors stood ready to rush in. At a signal from Chimeg, arrows flew and found their targets. Two missiles ricocheted off chainmail, which made Chimeg wince as they bounced to the ground, but the others found open flesh in necks and faces, or penetrated their armor at close range. The distance between them and the guards was short, and the six warriors sprinted forward, and caught the bodies before they collapsed. Weapons were in short supply for Chimeg's fighters, and armor was non-existent. However, there was little they could strip from the dead women. The chainmail was too heavy, and the longswords were too cumbersome to wield for fighters used to a faster blade. Two knives were all they were able to liberate.

Chimeg took a deep breath and entered the great chamber with her silent slayers. There were no candles burning, and the only illumination came from the natural light of the lunar streaming in through stained glass windows. It shone onto the rich tapestries which covered the walls. Row upon row of beds, and sleeping women upon them, lined either side of the barrack room. A wooden chest was at the foot of each billet and on top there were rolled up chainmail, a helmet, and a longsword or battle axe. Long varbows hung horizontally on the wall behind each bed, accompanied by a quiver of arrows.

At the far end of the chamber, there was a curtained area, and Chimeg suspected this was a privilege of rank, and the resting place of the troop commander. She quickly made it to the far end of the chamber, slipped the curtain aside, and stared down at the woman sleeping on her back. It was an older face, with short cropped hair, and a scar under her right eye. She was gently snoring. Chimeg pulled her knife free, clamped a hand over the woman's mouth, and stabbed her three times in the side of the neck. The Damm Warrior's eyes opened wide in surprise and then glazed over.

Chimeg wiped her dripping blade on the bed cloth, and then exited the private quarters. She took up position beside another slumbering Damm Warrior as her fighters did the same, two next to each sleeping figure. With a signal from Chimeg, the slaughter began. Knives and sabers, stabbed, slashed, and butchered two hundred warriors. Women who trained all their lives for combat were dispatched without lifting a finger in their own defense, and died without knowing who held the assassin's blade.

The brutal slaughter in the first great chamber was over, and Chimeg was amazed at their total success. She longed to seek out her father and proudly boast he had made the right choice. She wanted both his praise and his forgiveness. Her brother Altan would have failed miserably and alarm bells would already be ringing out across the citadel. However, there was more killing to do, and other chambers to clear.

They had spent a lunar masquerading as the Yaobai farmers in the warmth of the domes, clearing away the burnt crops from the previous occupants, setting up makeshift shelters, and doing their best to look industrious planting seeds at regular intervals in the tilled soil as they secretly prepared for combat. Keeping down the pickled vegetables, provided by the Var as their only source of sustenance, was almost as painful as farming. They collectively yearned for a diet heavy in lamb, goat, or horse flesh, and the sweet and sour taste of the fermented mare's milk. Some of the older

CHAPTER THIRTY ONE

men suffered at first from withdrawal symptoms from the latter, and their hands had shook and their hearts had beaten a little faster until they recovered. The time for deception was now over. They were the Kuruk and the destruction of the Var was at hand.

The Kuruk were masters of the surprise attack and counter ambush. Usually, they charged in on horseback out on the *Tal Kheer,* their open grasslands to the southwest, and hit their enemies with a hail of arrows, and then feigned a retreat, until turning back around and devastating their opponents with volley after volley. They did not have the luxury of horses, and their bows were in short supply. This attack required stealth to silence the sentries, and to murder the majority while they slept in their beds. They would bring bushels too, and use the flame and smoke to their advantage if needed.

Jargal, the leader of the clan, was a tall, heavyset man for a Kuruk, and a sturdy horse was required to carry his weight. In his younger years he was a champion wrestler and broke the backs of lesser challengers. Now he commanded others to do his killing. His two blood brothers, Gan and Oktai were on either side of him, steely-eyed, hard-faced men, tough as the sacred Iron Mountain of their birth land, who would give their life for their Khagan without hesitation.

The many warring tribes of the *Tal Kheer* were finally united under Jargal's leadership, a struggle which had taken him a lifetime to achieve. It came by strength of arms, cunning in battle, guile in politics, and outright deceit when needed. He murdered his own blood uncle who took him in as a child and seized control of the immediate clan as a springboard to greater achievements. His final act of tribal unification came with the death of his beloved, hot-tempered blood brother, who had led a revolt, coaxed by an overly ambitious wife. However, that was in the past, and all he could focus on now was the immediate survival of his family.

Jargal changed his plan of attack after they came upon the first great chamber. As soon as Chimeg and her fighters went inside, he waved the archers forward along the long corridor. They rounded another corner and stealthily approached another two Damm Warrior guards. The bowmen disposed of them in similar fashion, and his fighting force entered the barrack room to silently kill the occupants.

Chimeg came up to her father as he exited the kill zone of the second chamber. Both of them were splattered in the blood of their victims.

"Altan?" Chimeg whispered, fearing her father had sent her brother on to the third great chamber, where more Damm Warriors slept.

Jargal shook his head and pointed to the rear, where his son stood impatiently with the old men, slow women, and anxious children.

Chimeg smiled. "Time to clear out another nest."

Jargal nodded, and his savage daughter went to work again. He had to admit she was ruthlessly efficient, and he had a sense of paternal pride in her ability to kill on command. But how would she react when the advantage was lost? he wondered.

Chimeg quickly dispatched the two guards in front of the third chamber, and entered the sleeping quarters for another silent killing. She was enjoying herself now, reveling in the easy decimation as she ended lives with a well-placed sharp blade. She exited the room, now thick with the smell of recently released fresh blood, and waited for her father.

The guards to the fourth chamber were no hindrance, and Jargal and his fighters entered the chamber as silently as before. They streamed in and took up killing positions. However, one warrior was late to his assigned target, and as he sprinted to get into place, he made sharp contact with a foot locker, and went sprawling across the stone floor. His saber came loose from his hand, a death sentence for a Kuruk warrior, and clattered across the tiles. He also upended the Damm Warriors helmet, which bounced loudly, and sent the longsword rattling to the ground.

All around the room, Damm Warriors sat up with a start. The Kuruk were a practical people, and did not wait for a command from their Khagan for the killing to commence. They sprang into action and delivered death with knife and saber. The Damm Warriors were fighters in their own right, and they fought back with hands against steel. One took a stab to the ribs, but kicked her assailant back, snatched up her longsword, unsheathed it in one quick motion, and decapitated the Kuruk fighter.

CHAPTER THIRTY ONE

There was shouting and screaming through the chamber as fighting erupted. Most of the Damm Warriors went down quickly, but a few were able to scramble free from their beds and reach their longswords. They fought like furies and sliced and hacked through the unarmoured Kuruk. A Damm Warrior whirled in a circle, gutting one Kuruk fighter, and slicing through the jawbone of another. A Kuruk female leapt on the Damm Warrior's back, wrapped strong legs around her torso, pulled back her head with one hand, and slashed open her throat with a razor sharp knife. The two women hit the floor hard, and the Kuruk rolled free, and immediately sought out another target.

At the far end of the chamber, the Damm Warrior commander emerged from her enclosed sleeping quarters. She was wearing her chainmail and helm, and carried a double-handed battle axe. She bellowed a challenge and strode forward.

Two Kuruk fighters armed with sabers charged ahead, and engaged her from either side. One lunged with his saber while the other tried to get behind. The mighty battle axe came crashing down, and smashed through the head of the man to the front, almost splitting him in half. The Damm Warrior twisted her blade free as the broken body crumpled to the floor. The other Kuruk fighter seized his chance and stabbed his blade into the side of the commander, and stared in amazement as the point of his blade broke against the chainmail. A backhanded blow from the battle axe sent him to join his brother.

Jargal and his two blood brothers, and self-appointed bodyguards, closed in on the commander. A head on assault would not take her down, so they had to use guile and position to end the conflict. It was like three wolves taking on a mighty ice bear. They nibbled and snapped, but did not overcommit, and sought to create an opening. As Jargal moved forward to draw a strike from the battle axe, Gan slid to the floor behind the Damm Warrior, who had not taken the time to don her boots, and sliced clean through both achilles tendons. The Damm Warrior suppressed a scream, but the pain of the crippling attack was plain to see on her face. She dropped to her knees and braced herself with her battle axe. This was the opening the Kuruk needed. Oktai clattered his saber against the commander's helmet, momentarily stunning her, and Jargal drove the point of his blade deep through her left eye and into her brain.

"Grab the longbows from the walls! We'll need them now!" Jargal shouted to his fighters.

Jargal exited the fourth chamber. He was breathing heavily now, and cursed he was no longer in his prime. His own personal discomfort was forgotten when he rounded another turn in the long corridor, and saw the fight now raging up ahead. Damm Warriors, still in their nightshirts, streamed out the fifth chamber and engaged with Chimeg's force, longswords and battle axes swinging into action. A handful, armed with varbows, scurried further back to gain distance, and fired over the top of their own sisters into the Kuruk ranks.

Jargal ordered Gan and Oktai forward to hold the line, while he pulled his daughter to one side. "You should have entered the fifth chamber as soon as the noise started and we lost the element of surprise! Go on now and find the men, Leave the last of the women to us!" Jargal said angrily. "And take bows, as many as you can find. We need firepower!" He did not wait for a response and joined his own fighters in the savage battle with the last of the Damm Warriors.

The Kuruk had the superiority of numbers over the Damm Warriors, and Jargal was gratified to see they did not have the benefit of chainmail. Still, the women were fierce fighters, and did not give ground. The battle axes were causing havoc amongst the Kuruk, and many warriors were decimated by the lethal blows in close combat. Jargal ordered his archers to target them, and the axe women were silenced one by one.

The width of the corridor was too narrow for the Kuruk numbers to have a true advantage. There were thirty abreast on either side, and the struggle continued as they pressed into each other and tried to gain the upper hand. The Kuruk ranks were deeper, but the Damm Warriors held the line. There were shouts, screams, and battle cries as they fought furiously, and those who went down were crushed underfoot.

A singular horn blew from the fifth chamber and thirty Damm Warriors in chainmail emerged through the doorway. They were formed up in a wedge formation, and aimed at the center of the line. The women in the wedge grunted in unison as they moved forward, and their sisters in nightclothes, many now soaked in blood, parted to let them through.

The ironclad wedge was unstoppable, and they cut through the Kuruk ranks with ease. However, their success depended on the rest of the Damm Warriors following close behind them, and that course of action was denied.

"Let them through! And close ranks behind them!" Jargal bellowed.

The wedge pressed forward, but the Kuruk let them pass. The front Kuruk ranks closed the gap, and held the rest of the Damm Warriors in place. Now they could bring their numerical superiority to bear.

The Kuruk surrounded the separated wedge, and gave ground as the Damm Warriors moved onward. Then a gap opened in the Kuruk ranks, and twenty bowmen fired volley after volley at close range. The impact was devastating, and the Damm Warrior formation collapsed. Now it was singular close quarter combat, and although the Damm Warriors took many Kuruk fighters with them, they perished to the last woman.

Only sixty Damm Warriors remained, and they were too few to hold the line in the corridor, and the weight of the Kuruk fighters forced them to give ground. They knew they were doomed and no quarter would be given, so they retreated as best they could into the chamber, and twenty tried to hold the Kuruk back, while the remainder scrambled back to get to their varbows.

Ten of the Damm Warriors managed to make it back to the far recesses of the chamber, and string their bows, but the rest were cut down in the savage fighting. Arrows flew, and a number of Kuruk paid the price. The Kuruk engaged with their own archers, and many also tried to use the varbows too. However, the latter were not used to the longer bows, and were wildly inaccurate with their aim. The Kuruk rate of fire was faster than the varbow, and one by one the Damm Warriors fell. The battle for the fifth chamber was over, but the Kuruk had paid a heavy price and over one hundred fighters lay dead, and many more were wounded.

Chimeg was furious with herself for hesitating, and her father's words stung her into a blinding rage. She rounded another corner at a sprint, and almost ran directly into a group of fifty men lined up with their halberds lowered. Behind them others poured out of their adjacent chambers, and moved along the corridor and out a set of wide doors to the open courtyard behind.

The Red Shadows formed a reluctant but determined rearguard. They had heard the sound of fighting from the Damm Warrior section of the citadel, and watched anxiously as their comrades made it outside to the courtyard and relative safety. They had no Damm Warrior officers to lead them and bolster their confidence with grim determination and threats. However, there was a bold Sergeant-at-arms who ensured they held firm, despite the screaming horde forming in front of them, baying for blood.

If Chimeg was expecting the Red Shadows to fold on impact, she was sorely disappointed. She led her four hundred fighters forward, and charged into the thin red line. One Kuruk woman ran headlong into the halberd spike and impaled herself, but the other fighters were more skilled, and parried halberds to one side. Halberds in the rear rank swung down and crushed heads and bodies. In close quarter fighting, the Kuruk were the more skilled fighters. As the Red Shadows tried to push back with their longer blades, sabers and knives went to work underneath. The Red Shadows went down to a man, but they held the Kuruk back long enough to allow their comrades to organize their battle formation.

Altan led his army in search of the Var men as soon as the commotion erupted from the fourth chamber. He was the oldest sibling by three years, and a strong warrior in his own right. He was neither handsome nor ugly, but plain faced with flat features, and deep set black eyes. He still lacked the ruthlessness a true Kuruk leader required, and his father hoped that necessary characteristic would still develop in time. His strength was in his cunning nature, and he was a man who planned for the long game, unlike his headstrong sister. His mother was a concubine, and so many Kuruk considered him unworthy to succeed. Chimeg was the offspring of Jargal's first wife, and although she was female, this gave her standing with the elders Altan would never achieve. However, she overcompensated for her gender by acts of outright cruelty, and she lived in the moment. Despite her mother's intrigues, she would never be accepted by some of the male-dominated subordinate clans and so she had vowed to crush them at the first opportunity. Jargal could nominate a successor, and in his lifetime his people would accept his decision for the most part. However, he was wise enough to know the strongest would take control after his death, whatever the proclamation, and so he preferred to encourage them to squabble, and scheme, and fight for the succession. It was the Kuruk way.

Altan scratched at his side, and his nimble fingers plucked another flea from the inside of his infested jacket. He inspected it for a moment, and then crushed it between finger and thumb. He cursed the dirty Yaobai farmers and their filthy clothes, and then offered up another obscenity, dedicated to Chimeg, who was the cause of their current predicament. Angry Chimeg, who alternatively begged and wailed before their father for the plum assignment in the Var extermination, while he was left to bring up the rear. He would make her pay for the insult at some point.

The plan was to wait until all of the warriors were dispatched, and then Altan would let his shabby force blood themselves on an easier target. He had the sense not to wait, and as Chimeg hesitated at the fifth chamber, he went in search of his intended prey. Altan did not know if the Var men would put up a fight like their formidable women, and he worried if his children, many armed with sharpened sticks, were up to completing the task. He needed an edge, and he found it as he searched the storerooms they passed en route. The armory was full of crossbows and bolts, a weapon the Kuruk disdained, but the Sul used to their advantage when they enlisted a vast army of conscripted peasants. He had seen their lethality when he visited the Sul capital, and he would replicate the firepower now.

The Kuruk found the Dandy Great Hall, and the sniveling occupants, who milled around in fear and uncertainty. They made no attempt to seal the entrance to their own great hall, and waited in vain for the Damm Warriors to come and rescue them.

Altan's old men, women, and children streamed into the chamber. The children and old men in front, armed with crossbows, the women behind them, carrying baskets of bolts, and some with fire torches. With a signal from Altan, they fired and the quarrels found targets. The Dandies screamed as the missiles tore through flesh. They huddled together for protection, which offered an easier target, as the Kuruk simply fired into the mass of bodies. The crossbows required too much strength for the younger children to pull back, so they handed them to the tough old women to cock and load, while they took a fresh weapon and unleashed another volley on their helpless victims.

Altan had no stomach for the slaughter of people who displayed no skill or will to fight back. However, it was his father's explicit instructions to kill all of the Var, even babes in the nurseries, and he would not disobey his command if he wanted to be Khagan himself. He was reminded of the *nerge*, the great hunt, when all the clans gathered together and herded the animals in one area, slowly closing the circle. Deer, antelope, marmots, foxes, wolves, lynx, wild asses, wildcats, and the solitary snow tigers, all forgot their differences, and faced the ultimate predator: man.

Altan called a halt to the killing. He knew the Var men had to die, but he did not have to watch their massacre, and he needed the remainder of the crossbow bolts. He ordered his makeshift army to gather up the bedding, bedsteads, tables, chairs, and anything else that would burn. They piled it high around the Var living, dead, and wounded, and when the collective funeral pyre was ready, Altan and some of the Kuruk women put torches to it and walked away as the screams chased after them.

The Konna women met a similar fate to the Dandy men. They did not run aimlessly around or flop to the ground in despair like the brotherhood. They did not fight either, and patiently prepared to meet their fate. Altan knew the usefulness of the Konna and separated out fifty of them before torching their chambers and bolting the doors. There were no cries for mercy.

The battle for the citadel was far from over, and Altan, following the sound of fighting, led his force outside into the main courtyard. He relished the cold night air in contrast to the smoke he had sucked into lungs indoors.

CHAPTER THIRTY ONE

The citadel was an eerie sight. Fires raged in all corners, and plumes of thick black smoke spiraled up, and blocked the starlight. Altan wondered what the people in the town below made of it all.

There was a standoff in the courtyard. The Red Shadows, almost two thousand strong, and now marshaled by a handful of Damm Warriors, were formed up in a long line, five ranks deep. Their halberds were lowered, and they presented a formidable obstacle. To one side of them, there were five Damm Warriors who were causing havoc amongst Chimeg's fighters with volley after volley from their lethal varbows. Some of Chimeg's men were using longbows too, obviously disdaining the unworthy crossbow, but they were having difficulty in mastering it. Despite their skill in nomadic archery, the length and aim of this bow was alien to them, and their arrows were misplaced. Chimeg was having trouble with her own varbow, and her arrows flew high and wild. In a fit of temper, she crashed the bow to the ground, but when it would not break, she flung it in the direction of the enemy.

The battle hung in the balance until Altan seized the initiative. First, he massed his crossbows, and concentrated all of his firing power on the five Damm Warrior archers. The bolts flew across the courtyard, and they went down under the deadly hail. Next, Altan targeted the Damm Warriors commanding the Red Shadows, and picked them off one by one. Bereft of leadership, the Red Shadows simply held their ground and waited.

A volley of crossbow quarrels tore into the Red Shadows, and at that moment, Jargal's fighters under the command of Oktai, streamed into the main square. Many of them had longbows too, and they fired in the direction of the massed Red Shadows. The aim was not true, but at a short distance, all they had to do was shoot in the general direction. After five concentrated volleys from bows and crossbows, the Red Shadow numbers were considerably thinned out.

With a yell from Oktai, his fighters put down their bows, and charged directly towards the halberd line. Chimeg immediately led her force forward too, and the Kuruk army went on the attack. It was too much for the Red Shadows. While the veterans in the front rank tried desperately to hold, the junior soldiers to the rear broke ranks and fled for the main gates. Once they turned their backs in retreat, the Kuruk butchery resumed.

Two large sleighs pulled by snow shovelers came out of a stable, burst into the courtyard, and barreled into the ranks of Red Shadows as they sought to escape through the gateway and over the bridge to safety. Their progress was delayed by the press of soldiers. Altan saw there were eight Damm Warriors in the sleighs, and he could not permit them to escape the confines of the citadel. There were too many Kuruk in the way to fire on them, so Altan led his fastest fighters up on the battlements to bring crossbow quarrels down on them from above. Some of Chimeg's fighters were already there, and they cursed as they struggled to aim the varbows and shoot with any degree of accuracy. Altan pushed them to one side, and his crossbows peppered the fleeing Damm Warriors with greater effect. One sleigh momentarily stalled, and a hail of bolts rained down on them. Then they were moving again, and plowed their way across the bridge to safety.

Jargal was still inside the main building. He had sent Oktai, under protest, with the majority of his force out into the courtyard to support Chimeg in the fight with the Red Shadows, while he took twenty of his best fighters in search of the Dux. The hunt did not take long, and Jargal soon confronted four Damm Warriors who were prepared to fight to the death.

The combat was brutal. Although the Kuruk had the advantage of numbers, the Damm Warriors were fully armored and were expert swordswomen. They fought in unison, which made getting close to them all the more difficult. As one Kuruk fighter lunged forward to engage a blade, another sword crashed down on a head, or skewered through a torso. The Kuruk were lethal killers too, with little regard for their own safety and they prevailed, but not before losing seven of their own.

Jargal was wounded. Nothing too deep, but he bled profusely from his side, and he could feel the muscles tightening up. He moved towards the heavy oak door, and kicked it in with his bare foot and waited, expecting more Damm Warriors on the inside. There were no more Var to fight. Instead there were two dead females, throats slashed, lying at the foot of an oversized bed. There were two other women in the room, dressed in nightgowns. One was a bloated woman, with the frightened face of a child who sat on the bed. The other, who stood beside her, was much older, and held a bloody knife in her hand.

"Don't let the bad men hurt me, Nan," the Dux pleaded, holding tightly to Nan's waist.

"I shan't, dumpling," Nan said, stroking her hair with her free hand. "Time to see your children again in Frotha's Hall. Close your eyes, poppy."

The Var were a warlike people who came out of the west in search of the fabled city of Andalayim. They renamed the city, Varstad, and ruled from the storming of the citadel by Stella the Great, until the final moments of Agitha the Unfortunate. Although they had dominated for generations, their military accouterments only temporarily decorated the walls of another older, richer civilization. They left little of note behind them for the thousand years of rule, and the stamping of their authority on the common folk below. There was no sacred geometry, astronomy, mathematical discoveries, or medical breakthroughs. All they had was selective stolen knowledge, nothing to truly call their own. When future historians wrote about the Var, if any cared to remember, they would record the military prowess of a bellicose people, though they too, like countless conquerors before them, were finally defeated in war. Legends, embellished and distorted over time, would tell of the fearless women who only fought with bows, and who cut off their right breasts to improve their archery skills, and who eventually went down in flames in a final battle against the horse-men. For now, all that remained of a once mighty people was five ships morally adrift in the southern islands, and a smattering of Damm Warriors without a queendom.

Jargal stood on the battlements next to his son and daughter. He was exhausted from all of the killing, but he could not show that weakness to his children. He longed for a slab of horsemeat, and a skin of fermented mare's milk to wash it down and clear the taste of smoke from his mouth.

He stared down at the carnage on the bridge and the town below, which was quickly coming to life. The fleeing soldiers were spreading panic, and the townsfolk would be desperate to know who controlled the citadel and upended their subservient way of life. Utterly destroying the Var had been necessary, though he had lost more than two hundred fine warriors in the conflict, and many more were wounded. They were fighters he would sorely miss. Now, all they could do was sit back and wait.

"What next, father? Do we destroy the town below? Without the Damm Warriors they will have no fighting spirit. Even Altan and his filthy crossbows could clear them out," Chimeg said.

"If you'd done your duty in the first place, there'd be no need for all of this. We'd be riding free on the *Tal Kheer*, not trapped like prey in the *narge*," Altan hissed.

"Easy for you to say. You didn't have to marry a crown prince for the good of the clan!"

"And you didn't have to cut his balls off and roast them in the fire!"

"Silence both of you!" Jargal ordered, and his children had the good sense to stay quiet. "We leave the townsfolk alone. We'll need them for trade, unless you like pickled vegetables, and as a buffer when the Sul Emperor arrives."

The current predicament for the Kuruk truly was of Chimeg's making. Jargal, in a pique of rage, married her off to the Crown Prince of the Sul as his tenth wife after she borrowed his favorite horse and it came up lame. The marriage helped to forge a temporary peace with his overlord, the Sul Emperor, and for a short time, Altan was the happiest Kuruk on the *Tal Kheer*, though it lasted less time than the cycle of the lunar. Chimeg would not go against the wishes of her father, and went through with the marriage ceremony. However, she was not suited for the Sul court life, and a subservient role to an effeminate man. She did not care for his deviant ways in the bedchamber, and severed his manhood as retribution. Chimeg had managed to escape back to her people, and Altan begged his father to send her back in chains. However, Jargal would not give up his daughter to be slowly sliced into a thousand pieces, and so they ran north from the

CHAPTER THIRTY ONE

wrath of the Sul Emperor.

"Will the emperor find us?" Chimeg asked.

"Without doubt. You robbed him of his only son and heir. All he has left is vengeance, and he will chase us to the end of the world. The Sul are truly coming."

About the Author

Originally from North Shields, a fishing town in the North East of England, Malcolm Ishida now resides in Berkeley, California. His focus is on writing, music, and studying languages. **Gastown** is his first venture into writing a grimdark epic fantasy, and world-building.

You can connect with me on:
- https://gastowntimes.com
- https://www.facebook.com/gastowntimes

Printed in Dunstable, United Kingdom